GW01163884

Cyril Cook was born in Easton, Hampshire, but at the age of five was brought to live on a farm in Mottingham, Kent. Educated at Eltham College, he matriculated in 1939, joined The Rifle Brigade in 1940, and was commissioned and transferred to The Parachute Regiment in 1943. He saw considerable service in the 6th Airborne Division in Europe and the Far East where for a period he commanded, at the age of 22, a company of some 220 men of the Malay Regiment.

His working life was spent mainly as the proprietor of an engineering business which he founded, until he retired to start the really serious business of writing the six volumes of The Chandlers.

2 Nov. 07
17. Depenbach Close
Malpas.
Cheshire SY14 - 8AS

THE CHANDLERS

VOLUME 1

THE YOUNG CHANDLERS

Cyril Cook

The Chandlers
Volume 1
The Young Chandlers

For Margaret and Ray with very best wishes from Cyril.

Vanguard Press

VANGUARD PAPERBACK

© Copyright 2005
Cyril Cook

The right of Cyril Cook to be identified as author of
this work has been asserted by him in accordance with the
Copyright, Designs and Patents Act 1988

All Rights Reserved

No reproduction, copy or transmission of this publication
may be made without written permission.
No paragraph of this publication may be reproduced,
copied or transmitted save with the written permission of the
publisher, or in accordance with the provisions
of the Copyright Act 1956 (as amended).

Any person who does any unauthorised act in relation to
this publication may be liable to criminal
prosecution and civil claims for damage.

A CIP catalogue record for this title is
available from the British Library

ISBN 1 84386 199 2

*Vanguard Press is an imprint of
Pegasus Elliot MacKenzie Publishers Ltd.*
www.pegasuspublishers.com

First Published in 2005

**Vanguard Press
Sheraton House Castle Park
Cambridge England**

Printed & Bound in Great Britain

Dedication

This book is dedicated to my mother

LUCY COOK

who had six sons on active service in World War Two, one or another in every major theatre – The Western Desert, Burma, North Africa, Italy, France, Germany and South East Asia. For six long years she was the 'News Exchange' passing information from one brother to the others, wherever in the world they happened to be.

I often wonder how many sleepless nights she endured.

The Young Chandlers

Chapter One

"I'll kick that boy's arse when I come home tonight!" The young David Chandler whose rear end was the subject of these remarks, crept quietly down the bare wooden stairs at the back of the farm kitchen, making sure he missed the one that squeaked so badly, on his way out to collect his barrow and go off on his paper round. The reason for the threatened violence he knew only too well.

It was his job to get the 'morning's wood' in at night. There had to be two piles. The first was used by his father Fred and the older brother Harry to brew up a cup of tea on the kitchen range before they went off to the fields. The second would be used by his mother when she got up, to light the range properly which would then be kept going all day for cooking and generally heating up the big farm kitchen.

There was of course no gas or electricity on the farm. David had to obtain the wood by scavenging the surrounding hedgerows and a nearby copse. Sometimes his father and brother would bring in a bundle and sometimes he was able to scrounge an orange box from the fruiterer in the little village of Mountfield where he lived. Whatever else happened for 365 days of the year he had to provide two bundles of wood to start the day off, and last night the wood had been damp. He had put the first bundle on the range to hopefully dry off during the night from the residual heat, but obviously his plan had not fully succeeded as the men had got a half cold cup of tea, hence the threats being made against his person! He had no fear that his arse would in fact be kicked. He was just eleven years old and his father had never even laid a finger on him, but with the premise that there was always a first time for everything, he slid out as quietly as he could so as not to aggravate the situation. As he was getting his barrow and paper satchels together he knew he was safe, the conversation had changed to other things.

"You were pretty late in last night."
"I was out with Dolly Chalmers."
"You going to marry that girl?"
"Why buy an orchard when you can get your apples free?"
"You'll drop yourself in the cackie one of these days my lad."

They both laughed. David knew his brother, nine years older than he and whom he adored, had a bit of a reputation with the girls, although he didn't really comprehend the full significance of the conversation. As he wheeled his barrow out he heard his father say: "The boy goes for his scholarship today doesn't he?"

"Yes and I reckon he'll get it too – he's a clever little bugger."

"Such a clever little bugger he leaves us damp wood! They both laughed again.

David trundled his barrow up the lane to the main road into the village. It was 6 o'clock on a cold February morning. That year – 1930 – was going to be a bleak year for many people all over the world, but David that morning was hoping that his day might be brightened by getting a peep at the Dolly Chalmers his brother had been with the night before. Her home backed on to the lane and her room was at the rear. The curtains were always undrawn and, on several occasions, David had seen her in just a slip washing at the washstand. She was undoubtedly gorgeous and it gave him a funny feeling he couldn't quite understand as he stood there in the darkness watching her bending over and stretching up and showing most of what she'd got, until he had to tear himself away or he would be late for Mr Roberts at the paper shop, and that would mean another telling off. This morning he was out of luck so he pressed on to the village, collected his papers and did his round. He wanted to get his round done as quickly as possible because, as his father said, he was 'going for his scholarship.' Just outside the village there was a large and prestigious public school called Cantlebury College, housing some six hundred boys from wealthy British and many colonial and foreign countries. The boys in the village used to take pleasure in baiting and snowballing the college day – boys when they went past the village school in their boaters and black blazers, but generally they lived in peace together.

Each year the college gave two scholarships to boys whose parents could not otherwise have afforded to send their sons there, the college providing the tuition fee and the county council providing seven guineas a term to purchase books, clothing, sports gear etc. Since the two places were competed for by boys who had passed the preliminary examination in December from around seventy schools in the surrounding area of the country, it followed that the likelihood of getting in was remote. In fact no one had got in from the village school in living memory. David finished his round and when he got home at about 7.45 his mother was up and getting breakfast for him and his little sister Rose.

"Everything alright dear?"

"Yes thank you Mum. Old Wooldridge's dog came at me again but I shut the gate quick and left his paper jammed in the gate post."

"He ought to keep that animal under better control. Old Crownie will have him for it one of these days."

'Old Crownie' was PC Crown, the village bobby.

"Now, I've done your shoes and pressed your shorts and you can wear your grey pullover Auntie Edie gave you for Christmas. You'll be the smartest one there."

Up until then David felt no qualms about going for the exam. As Harry had said – he was a 'clever bugger' and had walked through all his school exams, but suddenly he realised that this was a different thing altogether. There would be over a hundred boys sitting this exam and only two of them would pass. At this thought he began to have butterflies. His mother, seeing that he was toying with his shredded wheat which he normally woofed into after being out on his round, came over and put her arm round his shoulders.

"Now look, it's only an exam. You may pass – you may not. Just keep your head and don't worry. The fact that you've got this far shows all the credit to you. I've said a little prayer for you this morning and I know that will help, but you can only do your best – no one can expect more."

David wasn't sure whether the little homily had given him any more confidence or not, but he thanked his mother and got stuck into his shredded wheat with his usual gusto. He went up to the cold bedroom in which he shared a big double bed with Harry and changed into the clothes his mother had laid out for him. He moved quickly. The kitchen had already warmed up with the big range going full blast, but every other room in the house was freezing cold. Downstairs again he put on his macintosh and woollen gloves his mother had knitted him and was ready to go.

"Have you got to take anything?"

"No, they provide it all."

"Well you'd better take this in case you have to buy a cup of tea or something."

She slipped a sixpence into his hand.

"I won't need that mum." David knew that sixpences didn't grow on trees.

"You take it. You never know."

He made his way to the college, passing the village school on the way and receiving good-natured but mainly ribald remarks from his mates playing in the playground at the front of the building.

"Where's your bleeding boater David?"

"Who's going to be a college boy then?"

"Blimey, look he's got a clean neck for a change."

They were all convulsed with laughter at this final witticism but David just stuck two fingers up and walked on, grinning. Although the college was only a half-mile away he had never even been in its grounds let alone the building itself. He passed the beautiful chapel, followed the signs 'Examination Candidates' and came to the imposing rows of front steps at the entry to the main building. On passing through the large oak swing doors he found himself in a magnificent domed entrance hall, beautifully panelled and furnished with the stern portraits of headmasters who had reigned here for the past 200 years and more.

A young man behind the desk barked, "Name."

"David Chandler sir."

He looked down the list.

"A village boy I see," he said, looking down his nose. "Over there, Room number 5, see the prefect in charge and he will seat you. – NEXT."

David went over to room 5, on the far side of the entrance hall. The prefect inside the room, who was a much more pleasant individual than the one behind the desk, told him to hang his coat in the adjacent cloakroom and to have a pee because he wouldn't get another chance for an hour. David dutifully did both and when he returned the prefect allocated a desk upon which lay a folder of papers. "Don't touch anything until you are told or you will be disqualified – understood."

"Yes sir."

The room was filling up now and at 9.50 in swept a master. David was completely awe-struck. He read the Magnet and the Gem (and everything else he could get his hands on) and knew that in the schools they portrayed, masters walked around in caps and gowns, but he'd never actually seen this dress in real life. Neither had he seen such an impressive figure as the master who was wearing it. He was tall with broad shoulders, blonde hair worn longer than the short back and sides favoured at the village school and had a handsome open face giving a welcoming smile. The combination of the man and his dress impressed him to such an extent that he found he was saying to himself, "I must pass."

The master announced himself as Mr Scott-Calder and gave them details of what they were to do, starting at 10am. Firstly there was an arithmetic paper with a couple of hundred sums. The object of the exercise was to do as many as possible in forty-five minutes and the marking took into account the number completed, method of working and, importantly, the number correctly answered. The second paper was an English grammar paper and the third paper was an essay, the subject of which would be given later. David sailed through the arithmetic paper and had no difficulty with the English grammar. They then had a fifteen minute break during which time they were all given a cup of tea and a bun, dished out by a genial matronly lady who called everybody 'My dear' and obviously loved the job she was doing. Prior to the break the master had said, "I will now give you the subject of the essay so that you can think about it during the break. It's 'Animals'."

Only a week or so before the boys at the village school had had a lecture from an inspector from the RSPCA, about the care of animals and about what the society did. When the start was given he launched into an account of this lecture in which he included a number of statistics the inspector had given them, which his retentive memory had filed away for no good purpose. He was still writing when the two-minute signal was given and, winding up quickly, felt satisfied he had done a reasonable paper.

Mr Scott-Calder then stood up. "That is all boys, thank you for coming." They all stood up as he swept out and then drifted to the cloakroom to get their coats and make their various ways home.

David walked slowly back through the village, mulling over in his mind the events of the morning. Passing Mr Smith's, the greengrocer, he decided that today he would not nick one of the lovely red apples on display outside the shop because college boys probably didn't do things like that. It was so easy to nick Smith's apples because a hanging blind separated the fruit shop from the haberdashery next door, so all you had to do was to earnestly study something in the wool shop window while you eased your hand through the gap in the blind and lifted the apple. Mr Smith always put the apples right on the end next to the blind so really he was asking for trouble, reasoned David and his mates. Why didn't the silly sod put the spuds up that end – no one in his right mind would go round nicking spuds. The other funny thing was he never seemed to miss the ones that were pinched so the boys felt it was fair game, although of course they kept a weather eye open for Crownie who seemed to pop up from nowhere if you were nicking something, playing knock down ginger or doing something equally as entertaining. He walked on quickening his pace, feeling he could do with his dinner. A cheery voice called out from the front porch of one of the houses.

"How did you get on David?"

Everybody in the village of course knew he was going for the scholarship today and would be almost involved with him in the result. The voice came from a mate of his – Ernie Bolton. Ernie could not walk since both his legs were encased in leg irons as a result of rheumatic fever when he was a young child. All the lads took it in turns to push him around in the strange little wheelchair his father had made for him. David always collected him for choir practice and the two services on Sunday, and all the boys thought the world of him because, despite the fact he couldn't do most of the things they could do, couldn't hike over the fields with them or climb trees, he was at all times cheerful, friendly and being lively and intelligent was good company. There was another thing they took into account. He had a most beautiful sister, a year or so older than him, who most of the lads would have died for and she always thanked them so sweetly when they collected or delivered him that they would have pushed him up to London and back if she had asked them (not that they had much idea how far London was).

"How did you get on David?"

"Well, I think I did alright, but there were so many there and a lot of them looked very posh."

"Just because they looked posh doesn't mean they've got any brains."

"Well they must have some brains or they would not have got through the preliminary."

"Well it doesn't mean they've got more brains than you," said Ernie, his loyalty shining through his emphatic statement.

"Well we'll see – I'm not holding out any hopes."

"When will you know?"

"Not 'til Easter. Anyway I'm going home to get some dinner now – my stomach thinks my throat's cut."

"OK, see you tonight for choir practice then."

David reached the turning to the farm and picked his way down the lane, avoiding the pancakes left by the cows going to the paddock into which they were turned out between morning and afternoon milking. Pancakes were an ever-present hazard on a farm with sixty head of cattle on it. One of the reasons David was so popular in the village was that they had a 'paddock', a level field eminently suitable for cricket, football or bonfire night or whatever. All the other fields around were either under crops or on a slope. So when the lads wanted a kick about, provided the cows weren't out, they used the paddock. But there came the rub. As cows are no respecters of cricket pitches, football pitches or prospective bonfire night sites, inevitably the greatest hazard was the pancake by which genteel name the hazard in question was generally known. In addition to bats, balls and stumps a main piece of the lads' playing equipment was a shovel, but although it was comparatively easy to clear the pancakes on the pitch between the wickets, it was a vastly different kettle of fish to clear the outfield. Cows obviously eat the sweetest grass and crop it short. When they come to a patch of dock or thistle they will eat around it, leaving an oasis of rough in the middle of which, for good measure, one of them would leave a pancake. Many times the lads running backwards to make a catch would hit the rough and go arse over tip into the pancake before they stopped it. They had a local rule for this latter situation. As soon as the ball hit a pancake the batsman completed the run they were on and stopped. This then gave the fielder time to clean the ball in the grass and throw it back in, hopefully not hitting another pancake on the way.

Football was a different matter altogether. The coats were put down for goal posts in clear patches, but there was no way they could avoid the pancakes when they were playing. Furthermore, volunteers to play as goalkeepers were few and far between for obvious reasons. In football again they had a local rule. If the ball went 'plop in', the game stopped, the ball was cleaned and the game restarted with a dropped ball one yard from the pancake. As one of the lads once observed, "they don't have to do this at Wembley."

Bonfire night was even more adventurous. At least in the daylight the pancakes could be seen, but in the dim light of bonfire night they were more or less camouflaged. Furthermore GIRLS came to bonfire night and they, for some unknown reason, couldn't accept that if you put your foot in a pancake you just rubbed your shoe on the grass and carried on. It could never be positively discerned whether the girls were squealing because of the noise of the fireworks, encountering a pancake or the usual reason for squealing when they were with the lads of the village in the half dark. One never to be forgotten incident featured Ernie Bolton. The lads collected Ernie one morning during the school holidays and it was suggested that he brought his crutches with which he moved himself about indoors, the idea being he could sit in his chair in the goalmouth and be goalkeeper, stopping the balls with these crutches. During the course of the game someone booted a shot which bounced on the edge of a pancake collecting a fair dollop on its way, glanced off Ernie's outstretched crutch, hit him with enough force to topple him backwards, chair and all, and plastered his jersey then his face and hair, with what seemed impossible quantities of rich brown pancake. The lads ran over to see if he was hurt, only to find him laughing his head off and, seeing him covered in pancake, they gradually subsided into total hysteria.

"Look at his bleeding face."

"No one will come near you for a month Ernie."

More hysteria.

David grabbed a handful of wet grass in an endeavour to wipe his face clean but it only made matters worse as it smeared it over his neck and ears. At this there was even further hysteria.

"We'd better get him home," said David.

They trundled him back. David and another lad walked up the short garden path to the front door and rang the bell whilst the others stood giggling at the gate.

"What on earth have you been up to?" exclaimed Mrs Bolton.

"He got hit by a ball that had been in a pancake," said David.

At this uncontrollable laughter started all over again. Ernie was crying with laughter, rivulets of tears streaming down his face. David was doubled up and gradually Mrs Bolton's face changed from a state of shock and horror until she too was bursting at her sides.

"Come on in then and let me clean you up." She at last said. "And thank you boys for bringing him back."

She loved the boys dearly because they all did so much to give Ernie as normal a life as possible, and especially David who was always so kind and went out of his way to see he was included in everything that was going on. There was no way she could be cross with them. Remembering this incident and grinning to himself at the recollection, at last David reached home and, as soon as he got in his mother said, "How did you get on then, tell me all about it." He went into every detail about the college and Mr Scott-Calder and the prefects and finally his mother said, "But how did the exams go?"

"Oh I think I did alright, but I'm going to put it out of my mind until Easter."

He didn't of course. He kept thinking about it. He now so wanted to go to the college that he forced himself to think of other things in case it was bad luck to want something so much. He was casual about it to his mates, but he didn't fool his mother who realised what this glimpse of another world had done to him. She somehow never believed he wouldn't pass, despite the odds against him, but it concerned her as to what effect it would have on him if he did pass and then mixed with people above his station in life. The next minute she would be saying to herself 'That's nonsense, he's as good as anyone else'. Talking to his father about it later she expressed her fears but he pooh-poohed them and said, "the boy's got a sensible head on his shoulders and, anyway I can't see the point of worrying, he hasn't passed yet. Sufficient unto the day is the evil thereof mother."

And that's how it was left.

Chapter Two

The six weeks between the exam and Easter passed in its usual uneventful way as far as David was concerned. A daily routine of paper round, school, getting the morning's wood, going to choir practice, the occasional kick about on Saturday, church on Sunday

One or two special events took place however. On one Saturday it was David's birthday. His mother said he was too old for parties, what would he like to do. To which he replied he would like to go to the pictures in the small nearby town of Sandbury, some five miles away. You could get there on the local steam train.

The whole outing was one great adventure. Going to the station and buying a ticket all on your own, sixpence return, another sixpence to get in the pictures, two penn'orth of sweets to chew and a tuppenny ice cream during the interval. At the end of the afternoon you had eight pence left of your two shillings birthday money. You could get a Cadbury's bar out of the slot machine to eat on the way home and still have money left over for another day.

And then the films. Always a good cowboy to start with, and then whatever was going for the second feature. What a marvellous day out it all was and what a pity birthdays didn't come round every week

The second thing that happened, which indirectly changed David's life, was Harry bought a wireless. There was great excitement when he brought all the pieces home and connected the accumulator and the outside aerial. The aerial was, after much swearing with moving the heavy rick ladder, strung from the apex of the house for about forty yards across to the roof of a nearby barn. All these preparations being completed, he plugged in a big horn-shaped attachment to the top of the small cabinet and all waited excitedly whilst he commenced switching the knob and turning the dial. Nothing happened and then there was a dead silence.

"Right," he said, "I'll have to go over it again."

He read the instruction leaflet over once more and said, "I think I've got the polarity on the accumulator wrong."

Nobody understood a word he was talking about.

"If you were to speak plain bloody English we'd all be the wiser," said Chandler senior.

"Well, you've got these little spade attachments," said Harry, "and they only work one way."

He reached into the cabinet and lifted out the accumulator from its recess at the back, changed the leads over, and replaced it. Once again there was complete silence while they waited for him switch on. He must have been more or less on the station because out of the horn came the sounds of a military style band. Everybody clapped excitedly, little Rose went skipping around in time to the music and, after a little bit of tuning resulting in peculiar squeaks and whistles, they settled on the station and sat back to listen. It was fabulous. The band turned out to be the Salvation Army band which must have surprised the father who, being an ex regular soldier himself, much disdained any music other than that of the Hampshires. "I don't think it's quite as good as the gramophone," he said, "but I expect they will improve as they go along."

In the following days they listened to the various programmes until they got fainter and fainter and David was delegated to take the accumulator down to the little garage in the village to get it charged. It seemed very odd, even though they'd only had it a few days, how much they missed the friendly voices and tuneful music coming over the airwaves. Harry decided that as soon as he was flush again he would buy another accumulator so they could switch them over when one was running out.

It was during the course of the second week that David switched on during one evening and heard what he thought was most beautiful music, of a type he had never heard before. He revelled in the organ music he heard at Church, in fact he used to go and pump the organ quite voluntarily every now and then when the organist, a middle-aged lady named Miss Parnell, wished to practise music she was due to play for a special occasion. He got to know Bach, Handel, Stainer and others and was sublimely happy sitting in the organ loft listening to Miss Parnell thumping out the chords. She was a superb musician, far too accomplished to be playing in a little parish church, but she lived in the parish and was known to be 'well off', keeping a maid, cook and gardener, who doubled as her chauffeur in the Wolseley she ran around in. One evening David was so transported by the music he lost sight of the plumb line, which indicated when the bellows were full or empty. Miss Parnell was in the middle of a particularly complicated fugue when suddenly the huge organ ran out of wind. It was like a thousand bagpipes all being let down a once. David leapt to the handle and started pumping like mad but it was too late. Round the corner into the loft appeared Miss Parnell.

"David, you've never done that before – what happened?"

"I was so enjoying the music miss – it had knotted all my stomach up and I completely forgot to pump."

She looked at him in a kindly manner – she was very fond of David.

"David why don't you come and learn to play the piano, and then go on to the organ later if you love it so much?"

"Well Miss, my mother wouldn't be able to afford the lessons, let alone buy a piano to practise on."

"Well, have a word with your mother. You've got a wonderful ear for music as I can tell when you're doing solo pieces in the choir – I'm sure you would do well. And as for the lessons, I wouldn't ask you to pay, after all you've pumped the organ for me so many times and you don't charge me!!"

"Well that's because I love to hear you playing," said David.

"Well you ask her."

The music David heard coming through on the wireless was an entirely different kettle of fish. Each note was crystal clear unlike the sonorous tones of the organ. Part of the music consisted of just piano playing, sometimes slowly, sometimes at scintillating speeds, being joined by the orchestra and then left to play by itself. It was captivating. At the end he learned it was a piano concerto by a chap called Mozart. They did of course have a gramophone which, when it was wound up, played a couple of dozen records comprising music hall songs, dance music and a few military marches of Mr Chandler's, which were kept in the cardboard box at its side, but they certainly had no Mozart.

Mrs Chandler was sitting with David listening. "What was that dear?" she said.

"They said it was a piano concerto by someone called Mozart"

"I wonder why they didn't tell you what his christian name was?" said his mother, "it seems very rude to me to go around calling people just by their surname, not even calling him Mr."

David pondered on this latter point. "Yes, it does doesn't it," he said, "but wasn't the music beautiful," he continued and then carried straight on with, "Miss Parnell wants me to go and learn the piano and she won't charge anything, but the only thing is I would have to have a piano here to practise on."

Mrs Chandler put down her sewing and looked at the flushed face of her son. "Well dear, you know how things are, we couldn't possibly afford a piano and, if Harry leaves home soon and I don't have his money coming in, and if you go to the college and we've got to struggle to keep you there until you're sixteen, things are going to be really difficult."

David felt a mixture of emotions. Disappointment at not having the lessons made him feel worse than he would have believed possible and anger at himself at having to put his mother in a position to have to say no, when he knew that she would give him the top brick off the chimney if he wanted it and if it were possible for her to climb up and get it, and finally the realisation that if he did go to college he was going to make things even more difficult for her than they were already. "Well perhaps I wouldn't have been any good anyway," he said.

"Well dear, if you listened like you did tonight and you appreciate it like you did tonight, you'll still get lots of pleasure out of it without being able to play. After all, Ernie Bolton can't play cricket but he loves watching you lot play."

"Yes I suppose so," he said, but thinking, 'Poor old Ernie would give his right arm to be out there on the field himself.' Then he had another thought, 'then the silly sod still wouldn't be any good – how would he bowl or hold the bat.'

The days passed and at last it came to Easter Week. Tuesday, Wednesday, Thursday, no post on Good Friday and then on Saturday Snowy White the postman rat-tatted on the door. In his hand he had an official looking brown paper envelope.

"Looks like your letter from the scholarship people," he said.

Snowy was an old soldier, like most postmen. There were four deliveries a day, the last at ten at night except Saturdays, and many times Snowy had walked down the dark lane late on a rainy night to deliver just a postcard that could easily have waited until the morning, but his professional pride wouldn't allow him to do that. On the other hand, because a lot of people write on postcards with a penny stamp, thereby saving a half penny on a sealed letter, Snowy knew everybody's business and would openly ask 'how's that cousin of yours in Wales now who was poorly'? details of which of course he had gleaned from the postcard. No one took exception to this as he didn't tittle-tattle to others about it, but he had no hesitation in talking to the original recipient as if he was one of the family, which he very nearly was.

"Looks like your letter from the scholarship people."

Mrs Chandler asked him in and opened the letter while David hearing the commotion came running in from the scullery at the back.

"Well David," she said. "It looks as though you're a college boy."

With great excitement from Snowy he took the letter and read it, almost jumping up and down on the spot.

"Well done David," said Snowy clapping him on the back. "We all thought you'd do it too. I suppose it will be tuppence to speak to you now. When do you start?"

"Nineteenth September," said David.

With Snowy in possession of the knowledge that David had passed, it flashed around the village and it seemed that in a matter of minutes almost, a procession of lads came to the farm to congratulate him. When his father and brother came home at lunchtime they were delighted, Harry saying, "I told you he was a clever little bugger didn't I," to which his father replied, "do you think they will teach him how to give us dry wood?" They all laughed at this.

That night when Mr Chandler came home from his Saturday-night drink at the Prince of Orange in the village, in addition to the 'War-Cry' and the 'Young Soldier,' he always brought home to David from the Salvation Army girl who went round the pubs, he brought home a bottle of lemonade and a packet of Smiths crisps in honour of the occasion. Giving them to David he said, "don't win too many scholarships or you'll make me broke."

The weeks crept by through the summer. The grant money came so that David's mother was able to take him to the school outfitters, conveniently located next door to the haberdashery shop in the village, the uniform and boater being stowed away in the chest of drawers, suitably protected by camphor balls to keep the moths out. On his last day at the village school he was presented with two presents by the headmaster. One from the halfpennies collected in great secrecy from the children in his class and others who wanted to chip in. This provided him with a pencil box and set of geometry instruments. The second came from the four teachers who had clubbed together to buy him a satchel. In presenting it to him the head teacher said, "you've bought honour to the village school in being the first boy since well before the war, (all time in the village was measured by before the war or after the war, the Great War of 1914 - 1918 being such a catastrophic event in the lives of the people of the village), to get the scholarship to Cantlebury and we wish you well." He then shook hands with David.

David wasn't used to shaking hands and was a bit embarrassed but managed to stammer out, "thank you very much sir, I'll do my best," before escaping back to the anonymity of his crowd of mates.

So one phase of his life ended.

Chapter Three

David soon settled in at the college, although he felt very ill at ease at first among the upper-middle class accents. It was not that he was badly spoken, but it was obvious even to him that they were different. He therefore tried to cut out the village accent and casual slang he'd been brought up with, but the difficulty was in the process not to sound affected to his family and the lads he met in the village every day. He therefore developed a two-track voice, improving on his college speaking day by day but reverting to village speaking when he was at home. In the event he reached some sort of compromise at home so that he spoke nicely and grammatically without putting it on, and his family soon accepted it as normal.

He was put in the A form, the B form being for those well-off lads, sons of former pupils etc, who weren't very bright. He found the new subjects he was studying, chemistry, physics and French to be absorbing and interesting, but he couldn't get on with the Latin at all! So much so that at the end of the first year his Latin master told him, 'you're not cut out for the classics Chandler, go and learn German'. Which he did and made a good job of it.

One thing he found a bit odd at first was their habit of calling everybody, even prefects by their surname only. The second thing was that when you passed a prefect, if you were wearing your boater, and this applied particularly out of school, you raised it. If you didn't you were reported to the head boy and you got a tanning, four of the best for first and second years, six for the remainder.

He was seated in alphabetical order next to a boy called Cartwright, with whom he struck up a firm friendship. Cartwright's father was a stockbroker, and their home was down in Hampshire. They had to go to school on Saturday mornings but they had Wednesday afternoons off, unless they were picked for one of the school rugby or cricket teams which obviously didn't apply to them in the early stages.

After a few weeks, David asked Cartwright if he would like to come home and have tea with them. He jumped at the chance of getting out of school. David was a little apprehensive that the farmhouse was not very posh, but when he expressed this fear to Cartwright, he was told not to be a chump. He made the introduction to his mother.

"Mum, this is Cartwright"

"Cartwright? Doesn't he have a christian name?"

"Well yes, but we never use christian names at school"

"You do here. Now Mr Cartwright, what is your christian name?"

"It's Jeremy, Ma'am"

"Right then," she said to David, "you can call him what you like at school, but here he's Jeremy."

They had a super tea of toast, jam and scones and cream straight out of the dairy. Rose sat shyly looking at Jeremy, she was only eight, but she was obviously smitten with this nice-looking eleven-year-old. When it was time to go, he had to be in by 6 o clock, Jeremy politely thanked Mrs Chandler for a wonderful time and reached out and solemnly shook hands, and then shook hands with Rose. David said, "I'd better walk down through the village with you. No one will rib you if you're with me."

They repeated this two or three times during the winter.

One day in December, David's father came home before Jeremy left and was introduced.

"So you're a boarder – what's it like being a boarder?"

"Well sir, my father says it's a bit like being in the army only worse."

"So your father was a soldier eh? Which regiment was he in?"

"The Hampshires sir, he was in the Boar War and then in the Great War until he was wounded."

"And what's you're name, Jeremy?"

"Cartwright, sir."

"I was in the Hampshires in the Boar War and the beginning of the Great War until I was invalided out, and at one time my company commander was chap called Buffy Cartwright – would that have been him?"

"Yes sir it was, that was his family nickname from the days when he was at school and always said he wanted to go into the Buffs."

"Well it's a small world. Next time you see him you give him the kindest regards and best wishes from Sergeant Chandler who was with him in South Africa and France."

"I will do that sir, perhaps when we have a parents day you will be able to meet him again."

"Ah well, we'll have to see about that."

As Mr Chandler said to David's mother later that evening, "I can't see one of the officers wanting to go around being chummy with one of his old sergeants, Mother, even if their boys do go to the same school."

"Well, if he's as nice a man as his son that won't make a scrap of difference."

"I'm afraid you don't know the way it works Mother, it's bred in them being officer class. All they understand is station in life and money, if you've got both you can get away with anything and if you've got just one or the other you can get away with most things. But officers are officers and sergeants are sergeants and the twain don't mix."

"What about when you were in the trenches?"

"In the trenches I grant you it was a bit different, but it wasn't in South Africa. In the trenches we did begin to get more comradely than ever before, mainly because I suppose we were all living together in filth, and captains stood as much a chance of being blown to bits as corporals. It's a great leveller when you know that in ten minutes time you might both have departed this world, rank and social standing didn't mean much. Mind you having said that when you went back out of the line the old system soon started up again."

Mr Chandler rarely spoke about war. He had been a regular soldier, and in the Great War his battalion was one of the first in. In six months they were decimated. Of the eight hundred odd men that he had served with, some of them for sixteen years, there were not more than a couple of score left intact, plus another score or so left crippled, limbless or blinded. He used to get cross at hearing men in the pub, sometimes with too much inside them, saying what a great time they had in France. 'Base Wallahs' he used to say.

"If they'd had to carry a bayonet over four hundred yards of no-man's-land and stick it in a Jerry's guts they wouldn't say they had a great time."

He'd won the Military Medal for leading an attack on a machine gun emplacement, and the following day was wounded by a 'Whizz-bang', which effectively ended his military career. He got a small pension, but as he hadn't done his twenty-one years he didn't get a long service pension. All the same he was a steady sort of bloke, and usually had a shilling in his pocket even though he was poorly paid on the farm.

Although he didn't say much, mother knew he was very proud of David, but coincidental with that she knew he was concerned that David was moving out of his class and that this might cause the lad unhappiness in some way. It never crossed his mind for one moment that David might grow up to look down on them, he just had this nagging feeling he couldn't quite define. They wouldn't be able go to the parents day, both he and Mrs Chandler knew this – although David was part of the scene, they certainly weren't.

"Oh well it will sort itself out I expect," he had said to himself, and then to mother later on.

Spring came and just before they broke up for the Easter holidays David came home at lunchtime on a Wednesday, it being the usual half-day. For some reason instead of coming straight down the lane he detoured through the farmyard. As he was walking through the yard he heard someone suddenly scream in agony and realised it was coming from the bullpen.

The bull was a massive animal and was generally docile, but as with all bulls you had to treat them with great respect indeed. There were two cowmen on the farm, Charlie Robbins and George Tanner, and it was a strict rule that no one went into the pen to clean it out without the other attached the five-foot pole to the bull's nose ring to keep it steady. On this particular day Charlie Robbins had badly cut his hand and had gone down to the district nurse in the village to get it stitched up and have a dressing put on it. Despite his years of experience, George decided to give the bull his feed of grains and mangolds on his own. Instead of going round the back of the pen and dumping the feed in the manger, which in itself was risky as the bull had been known to mount the manger before today and try to pin the unfortunate cowman against the wall. Reasoning the bull was quiet, George went into the pen with the bull and proceeded to empty the heavy bin food into the manger. At this the bull had moved like lightning despite its bulk and had plunged one of its horns into George's side just under the armpit, and it was this sight that greeted the horrified David as he ran in. The bull's head was going side to side with George impaled on it. There were two five-foot poles on the rack on the wall, David grabbed one and started to prod the bull on the side of its head. The bull put its head down to meet the new challenge and as a result George slid off the horn onto the floor bleeding copiously.

The bull could not turn round to attack David as it was fastened to the wall by a fairly long chain which had only just enabled it to attack George. As George was near the manger the only thing that David could do was to grab his ankles and try to drag him out of the danger area hoping that the bull would not gore George again. He ran into the pen and grabbed George's feet. The bull tried to turn to attack him but the cunning beast, realising that it couldn't get David with its horns, swung its rear end round, and half a ton of solid beef lashed out at David. Though he managed to dodge the full force of the blow he was knocked sideways against the staging of the pen, giving his head an almighty bang in the process.

David sat up, he was out of reach of the bull, but he saw the animal's malevolent little eyes looking at him as if he was trying to work out a new plan of attack. David rolled along the floor, stood up and once again grabbed George's ankles and while the bull was gearing itself to swing its rear end round again, pulled the now unconscious cowman out of the pen, and banged the door shut.

He now steeled himself to look at the wound. He had heard men talking about the wounded during the war, and one thing that stuck in his mind was 'stop the bleeding'. It was a dreadful hole in George's side, so the only thing he could think of to do was to take his own shirt off and ram it into the wound and then tie it round with binding string, of which there was a plentiful supply lying around where they had cut the straw bales open. This done he put his jacket back on and ran to the farmhouse.

"Mum, George has been gored by the bull."

"Oh my God!" she said. "David run up to the pub and get them to phone for an ambulance."

Little did she realise that at that time David too was hurt. Neither did she notice he had no shirt on under his blazer. His mother got a blanket from the airing cupboard and ran down to the yard and in the meantime David ran up the lane to the pub and burst into the public bar.

"Will you pleased phone for an ambulance – George has been gored by the bull."

"Righto boy – now you sit down, you look in a right mess yourself."

The landlord quickly got on the phone to the village exchange. "Can you get an ambulance out to Home Farm, a chaps been gored. Tell them it's down the lane by the Prince of Orange.

A voice from the saloon bar called out, "Lovell, when are we going to get a drink round here."

"Oh Doctor, I'm glad you've come in – there's been an accident down on Home Farm, George has been gored."

"Right I'll go straight down, have you sent for the ambulance?"

"It's on its way."

Dr Towers jumped into his Armstrong Siddeley and roared off down the lane. He was regarded with a mixture of dislike and admiration in the village. Dislike of his abrupt manner and the fact that he always walked into your home without wiping his boots, and admiration because whenever you needed him, at whatever hour or in whatever weather, he would turn out without a murmur. He had delivered half the babies in the village over the past twenty years, but was a widower himself and had no children of his own. Rumour had it that the district nurse, who was a widow, her husband having been killed in the war, had a definite fancy for him and intended to be Mrs Towers one day.

"You'd better get home young-un."

"I'll wait for the ambulance and flag it down," said David.

He wandered outside and in about ten minutes the ambulance appeared, clanging its bell like mad although there was nothing else on the road for miles. He flagged it down and jumped on the running board.

"He's down here," David said.

They arrived in the yard; the doctor had not moved George other than to make him more comfortable.

"Who plugged this wound?" he said.

"I did," said David, hoping he'd done the right thing.

"You saved his life," he said. "Did you drag him out?"

Before he could answer David felt himself going faint. The excitement, the reaction from the danger, running to the pub and the blows to his body and head all now flooded in on him and his legs would no longer support him. He crumpled into the doctor's arms.

"Take him as well," said Dr Towers, "and I'll come with you. You stay at home Mrs Chandler and I'll let you know what the position is when I come back. The lad's alright, it's just that it's all been a bit much for him."

The ambulance went off to Cottage Hospital about four miles away, followed by the doctor in his Armstrong. He had uttered the reassuring words to Mrs Chandler, but in his own mind he was not entirely happy with the blow on the head. It had bled quite a lot and from the cursory examination he had been able to give the lad as they were loading him in, he could see it was very swollen.

As the ambulance man was putting a bandage on around his head David came to. He sat up with a jerk. "I can hardly see," he said, "is it dark in here?"

"You're alright son, you've had a bang on the head and that often makes your vision funny for a little while."

David lay back on the stretcher. "I'm frightened," he said softly.

"You're bound to be old son," said the kindly ambulance man, "but don't worry, you'll be as right as ninepence in a couple of days, and then I rekon you'll be a right bloody hero, if what they tell me is true."

What happened after that remains a confusion in David's mind. He remembered being lifted out of the ambulance after they'd rushed George away. He remembered their cutting his clothes off him and the sisters saying to him, good humouredly, 'I've never met a smellier boy'. Then he realised he had got cuts and abrasions all down his back and it hurt like mad when they eased the clothing off his dried wounds. They washed him gently and cut his hair all around the head wound, and when they had got him clean from all the manure that he had been rolled in and had collected from George when he dragged him out, they covered him with a soft warm blanket telling him the doctor would be with him in a few minutes. When the doctor arrived he had Dr Towers with him.

"How do you feel?" he was asked.

"I don't feel very well sir, and I can't see properly."

"Right, let's have a look at you." He then gave David a very thorough examination making sure no bones were broken, and at last came to the head wound.

"Well it looks as though that bang on the head has given you concussion. How did you get it?"

"The bull kicked me"

"What, in the head?"

"No sir, he kicked my side and back and that sent me flying into the side of the pen."

Dr Towers, sensing that David was emotionally very upset at the remembrance of all that had happened, spoke up.

"I'll tell you the whole story later Doctor," the tone of his voice indicating to the houseman not to question the boy further.

Right, now we'll get you to a ward and then the consultant will come and see you."

The houseman left.

"Now David," said Dr Towers, "they'll be keeping you in for a few days under observation. I shall go straight back and tell your mother what has happened, but you have nothing to worry about, just lie back and get some rest."

"But Dr Towers – how is George and what about my clothes?"

"Well firstly, George is badly hurt and lost a lot of blood, but provided he doesn't get a bad infection he'll be alright. What's all this about your clothes?"

"I had my school uniform on, now it's ruined and we don't get another grant until September term. I can't go to school without clothes."

"David – don't worry about school and don't worry about clothes. Somehow or other we'll sort that one out. I'm going off now, but I'll pop over tomorrow afternoon and bring your mother to visit you, so you just get to sleep and get better."

But David didn't sleep. His blazer and shorts had been cut off him and dropped in the bin beside the bed he was on. His shirt was probably in another bin wherever George was, where his tie and boater were he hadn't the faintest idea, probably still in the bull's pen. The only things he had left were his shoes and stockings, they wouldn't have thrown those away would they, he thought.

After a while two young men came and lifted him on to a trolley and he found himself being wheeled through corridors until they came to a ward. He heard an authorative voice say, "put him in the side ward and pull the curtains."

This same voice followed them in and when he was neatly tucked up she said, "Can you see me David?"

"Not properly miss."

"You call me sister."

"Sorry sister."

"Well I'm going to leave you here for a while. Dr Roberts will come and give you some tests and then you can rest."

"Sister."

"Yes?"

"I'm hungry."

"Boys are always hungry. When the doctor's been I'll get Nurse Lloyd to bring you some tea."

When the doctor had been and repeated the houseman's examination, plus flashing lights into his eyes, and taking his pulse and blood pressure, all of which were new experiences for David, the sister did in fact bring him some tea which he strangely enough only half ate before he slipped off into a sleep of total exhaustion. But it was more than a couple of days before he left the Cottage Hospital.

Chapter Four

If you throw a stone into a pond, as everyone knows, you get many ripples resulting from that one action. So it was with the incident in the bullpen.

The first ripple concerned George. George was a bachelor. He was about forty years of age and had been in the war in the Royal Artillery. He was a very thoughtful type of chap who loved the animals in his care, and as he once confided to David's father, although he was sickened by the carnage of men being blown to bits in France, he was so ashamed of what they did to the poor horses. Many times the guns of his battery had been un-limbered and they had taken the horses back some distance to be tethered. The guns would then open up on their targets. In a short while the Germans would open up on counter-battery firing and so often the shells would land in the horse-lines. Having to put badly injured horses out of their misery was an appalling task, the horror of which would never leave him.

George's father had worked on the farm before him, but now both his mother and father were dead and he lived with his thirty-five year old sister Tess in the cottage in which they were born, next door to the Chandlers. George's sister was a mongol. She was quite the ugliest person one could imagine, and she was grossly overweight. She sat in her winged armchair all day, while George popped in from time to time to see that she was alright, to take her to the toilet and give her food. Despite the fact that she was ugly, she always had a beautiful smile on her face and when she looked at you she had pale blue eyes that were really quite nice and seemed to have such depth to them that you wondered whether she did comprehend anything, or did she just not know anything that was going on, as everyone said.

If you were near her she had an enigmatic way of gently holding out her hand and sitting you on the footstool beside her. At first people who approached her were put off, almost repelled, by this poor unfortunate woman with a baby's mind, but just as a baby holds your hand, so did she and she got much pleasure from doing so. It was not a hard grip that you might have expected from someone so handicapped, neither was the hand flabby or moist, it was a pleasant hand, and after the first contact visitors would automatically take the hand and sit down while she smiled her slow gentle smile.

As soon as George had been taken away in the ambulance, Mrs Chandler went in to see Tess. "Tess, I don't know if you understand me or not, but George has been taken away and I shall be looking after you."

Tess just held her hand and smiled, and then stood up which meant she wanted to go to the lavatory. Mrs Chandler looked after her, as she would have done a child, brought her back to her chair, and then went to make her an omelette and cook some potatoes for her dinner. She spoon-fed her, and then left her for the afternoon, looking in now and then as George would have done. At about seven o'clock she went back in to take Tess some pie and cocoa for her supper and to get her to bed. Tess was clearly puzzled as to why she had not seen George, but Mrs Chandler fed her and she ate most of the food. She then held Tess's hand to take her to bed, but Tess became increasingly disturbed because only George had put her to bed since her mother died many years before. Mrs Chandler eventually got her undressed and into bed, reasoning that once she was there she would sleep until morning as she always did. In any event she'd look in later to make sure she was alright. When she looked in Tess was sound asleep. George normally would start milking at 4.30 in the morning and would come in for his breakfast at 7.30, at which time he would wake and dress Tess, and seat her downstairs. Mrs Chandler came in at 7.30 and found Tess already awake and clearly agitated not to see George. She dressed her and took her downstairs to her chair and fed her breakfast, but all the time poor Tess was looking around not understanding why George wasn't there.

During the day her agitation increased, and Mrs Chandler was not sorry when it was time to put her to bed again. Although it was early April, there was a heavy frost that night, with temperatures well below freezing point. Looking out of the window when she awoke, Mrs Chandler said to Rose, "I don't know what the weather's coming to these days, frosts like this and it's nearly Easter."

She dressed and went downstairs and let herself in next door to wake Tess. Doors in this close community were never locked, so she walked straight up to Tess's bedroom. To her surprise and alarm the bed was empty. She looked in the other rooms and then downstairs in the outhouse but there was no sign of Tess anywhere. She went back to the bedroom and found that the girl's clothes were still in a neat pile, in which they had been left the night before, and seeing this she became very concerned indeed. She ran down and across the lane to Charlie Robbin's wife.

"Have you seen anything of Tess?"

"No, what's wrong?"

"I put her to bed last night and she's disappeared."

"I'll go and get Charlie."

She ran down to the yard and brought Charlie and Harry back with her, Harry was standing in for George while he was away in hospital.

"She's not down the farm," said Charlie. "I've been in all the buildings this morning for one reason or another."

"We'd better have a look around the fields," said Harry, "and if we don't find her we'd better get Crownie."

The two men set off across the paddock, heading for the far gate into the other fields. In this corner of the paddock there was a large pond surrounded in the main with tall reeds, apart from the beaten down section where the cattle walked in to drink.

"Better look here first," said Harry, and then almost immediately, "there she is."

The poor girl, barefoot and wearing only a flannelette nightgown was lying face down in the reeds, her body covered in frost. She was obviously dead.

"Better not touch her – better get Crownie," said Charlie.

Harry jogged off down to the village while Charlie went and broke the dreadful news to the two women and got a small tarpaulin to take back and lay over her. In a few minutes PC Crown arrived on his bike and walked across the paddock to the pond.

"I'll get the ambulance," he said, "nothing much else we can do."

It was several days before they could tell George. When he was told, he accepted it with the stoicism of a man who had seen so much death that it did not come as a blinding shock to him. What he felt in the depths of his heart no one would ever know. All he said was, "poor soul, poor soul," and later to Mrs Chandler, "will you organise the funeral and ask Frank Lovell to give you the money out of my club money." A fair proportion of the village population belonged to the Prince of Orange loan club into which they paid money each week and could draw money during the year in case of emergency. Mr Chandler was a steward of the club, so he would organise it for him.

The inquest, which Mrs Chandler and the others concerned had to attend, was duly held and a 'death by misadventure' verdict returned. The Chandlers organised the funeral with only one car following. A large number from the village attended the church and she was laid to rest in the village churchyard next to her mother and father.

The second ripple concerned David.

One of the administrators in the Cottage Hospital used to earn a few shillings from time to time by phoning a friend of his on the local paper to let him know of any unusual admissions, road accidents, suicides and the like, which he could build into a story. When George was admitted he contacted his friend, as a result of which the reporter went post-haste to the farm to get all the details. He found not only a bloodthirsty story of someone being gored almost to death, but also of a young lad saving the victim at the risk of his own life.

He went then to the hospital to secure interviews from the two luckless people involved only to be shown the door in no uncertain manner by the sister in charge.

However, he pieced the story together and decided that there was a chance that he could earn some money by passing it on to a friend of his on one of the nationals. His friend on the London Graphic said it might be a goer, in view of the fact that the young lad had been involved. (A simple goring wouldn't get in the nationals, that was strictly local stuff). For sob stuff he included the fact that David had lost his clothes in the course of his bravery etc, etc.

The next morning the story appeared on an inside page, along with a photograph of David, borrowed from Mrs Chandler, which had been taken at school the previous summer. The day after that the hospital received a avalanche of mail for David, many of the letters enclosing postal orders and some even a ten shilling note, all from people who had been touched by the story. A few more letters appeared the next day and when a final count was made he had been given a total of just over twenty pounds, an absolute fortune. This total was added to by a whip-round designed to replace his clothes, organised by Frank Lovell at the request of Dr Towers who had put the first ten shillings in. This was matched by Frank himself and with the sixpences and shillings put in by the regulars, the total soon exceeded a fiver.

David was quite overwhelmed by all that was happening. He was still in his dark room. Sister had told him he would have to answer all the letters, but not to rush at it the minute he was out and about again. She was basking a little in his reflected glory, particularly with regard to his visitors. In addition to Dr Towers and the Reverend Pearce, the vicar of his church, he had a visit from his headmaster at the village school, Mr Marshall, his father's landlord and the biggest landowner for miles around Sir Oliver Routledge. Finally the local MP, seeing the write-up in the Graphic decided it wouldn't do his popularity any harm to be seen visiting the boy, organising a photographer from the local paper to be around to take his picture on leaving the hospital for good measure.

The third ripple concerned Harry.

Harry biked over to visit him every evening, mother coming most afternoons on the three times a day local bus, which gave her only half an hour to be with him before she had to catch it again on its return trip. His father could only come at the weekend.

On Harry's second visit Nurse Lloyd came in to see if David was OK, and immediately Harry was sunk, hook line and bloody sinker, as he described it afterwards. He was fancy free at the moment; Dolly having taken up with a commercial traveller in greetings cards who, a newcomer to the village, lived with his mother in a flat above the shops. The attraction was he had a car, which was a rarity for people of the village, and riding in which made Dolly feel superior. David introduced his brother to Nurse Lloyd, and for the first time in his life Harry felt totally tongue-tied, other than the inane "pleased to meet you." He kept saying to himself, 'think of something to say you gormless prat,' but nothing would come out, and after a minute or two Nurse Lloyd carried on her duties elsewhere.

"Is she on every night?" said Harry.

"She is all this week," said David.

There was a long silence.

"You gone all soppy on her?"

"Well you've got to admit she's a bit special, try and find out if she's courting or anything."

"How do I do that?"

"Just ask her, you'll think of something, you go to bloody college don't you?"

David gave a little chuckle.

"What are you laughing at twit?"

"I reckon you're stuck on her, and you've only seen her a couple of minutes."

"It's a good job you're in a bed or I'd thump you. Anyway see what you can find out."

The next afternoon when Nurse Lloyd came on duty David said to her, "Nurse, you know my brother who was in here last night?"

"Yes, he's rather good looking isn't he?"

"What would you say if I told you he's got a crush on you and wants to take you to the pictures?"

"I would say he's got a cheek, and that he ought to ask himself and not leave you to do all his dirty work!"

She walked out, but smiling all the same. David reckoned he'd done a good job. When Harry came in that evening he said, "Well, what have you found out?"

"I told her you wanted to take her to the pictures and she said you've got to ask her yourself."

And that's how Harry's great romance began. He asked, she accepted, arrangements were made for the weekend, and then became regular occurrences, much to David's amusement and the satisfaction of Mr and Mrs Chandler who came to like the girl enormously – "A better class of girl altogether than that Dolly," was their general observation. There was however inevitably a certain amount of leg pulling in the Prince of Orange.

"Don't forget she'll be comparing yours with all the others she's seen," said one wit, Jimmy Case.

"Good job she won't be looking at yours Jimmy," said another.

"She'd need a magnifying glass."

"You don't have to worry about me," said Jimmy.

"I found what my old Dad said was true. He was a cavalry man and he always said, 'it's not the size of the whip that matters, it's the way it's cracked', and I've never had any complaints on that score."

There was general laughter and the conversation moved to other subjects.

Chapter Five

David was in hospital for two weeks, and was released on the Thursday of Easter weekend, being told that he was not to rush around for another couple of weeks, and to see Dr Towers before he started his paper round again. He went in to say goodbye to George, who would be there for another two weeks himself and was then to be sent to a convalescent home for two weeks. George held his hand in both of his and said, "That's one I owe you David."

David couldn't find any words to answer, so he gave a little grin, and then, remembering Tess, was serious again.

"George I'm so sad about Tess," he said.

"Well," said George, "it is so sad. No one could tell what went on in her mind. She was obviously looking for me. Knowing that when I pass the house I go down to the paddock for the cows, then she sees me bring them back, I suppose she associated the paddock with me being missing. We shall never know. Anyway take care of yourself old son."

Having said his goodbyes to sister and the nurses, off went David with his mother who had come on the bus to collect him. It felt good to be out in the open air again and to see the countryside going by.

The Easter holidays were soon over and David was back in the old routine of paper round, school and homework. Harry brought Megan Lloyd home to Sunday tea, which indicated they were going steady. Megan was a lovely, lively girl from a farming family in Carmarthenshire. She had a lilt to her voice, which was not only music to Harry's ears, but was a source of pleasure to all the Chandlers, particularly Rose with whom she became great friends.

The summer end of year exams were imminent, and David was a little apprehensive. He told himself he had no need to get the wind up. His first term report had been concluded by Dr Carew writing, 'A good start', the second term, 'Has made good progress', and his general standing on term work was in the top five in the form, except of course for Latin where he was in the bottom five. In the event he didn't do quite as well as he had hoped, prompting Dr Carew to write, 'His accident has set him back a little'.

"Poppycock," thought David, "I just didn't get the right questions."

The college was heading for its long vacation, nearly nine weeks, much longer than he had experienced in the village school. He said to his mother, "perhaps I can get an errand boys job in Sandbury for part of the term."

She thought for a moment and said, "you're sure you want to do it?"

"Of course," said David.

"But suppose some of the college boys see you on an errand boy's bike, won't you be ashamed?"

"I doubt if I shall see any in Sandbury, most of them are boarders and will all be at home. Anyway, even if I do what does it matter – there's no disgrace in earning a few shillings."

"Alright. I'll get your father to ask Frank Lovell if he knows anybody – he came from Sandbury so he might well know."

By a stroke of luck Frank's brother Tom, who was a family butcher, needed a relief for four hours a day for five to six weeks to assist in covering other staff on holiday. It meant that David did his paper round, was home by eight o'clock, had breakfast, cycled the five miles to Sandbury to be there at nine o'clock, left at one o'clock and was home by about half past. The paper round paid six shillings a week and the errand boy got paid fifteen shillings, and of course, he gave all the money to his mother, just as his father did. She then gave him back half a crown spending money, telling him to save at least sixpence of it. He enjoyed the ride to and from Sandbury. Instead of the old 'Bitsa' bike that Harry had put together for him, he now had a brand new Raleigh complete with dynamo and Sturmey Archer three speed, bought from his hospital money. This put him in the Rolls Royce class in the village as regards bikes. One or two of the lads had Hercules, but most of them had to make do with 'Bitsa's' as he used to. It had cost him altogether the enormous sum of five pounds five shillings, which still left him over twenty pounds in the Post Office, although this included his new grant money which he hadn't used yet.

Sailing along, he noticed after a few days that he passed a young girl riding a Sunbeam in the opposite direction. She had jodhpurs on and was quite pretty, blonde and about his age. Each day they met about a mile outside the town and on the fourth or fifth day he smiled at her, and the next day stopped when he saw her coming towards him.

"Hello," he said, "my name's David – what's yours?"

"I'm Pat," she said.

"Do you go riding every day?"

"No, I'm doing a holiday job in the stables just along the road."

"I'm doing a holiday job too in Sandbury," he didn't say what, suddenly embarrassed.

"Well, see you tomorrow then."

They rode off.

She was a well spoken, open-faced girl, obviously from a well off family if she had her own Sunbeam. He found himself thinking about her a lot during his rounds. His first job on arrival at work was to get out the heavy old delivery bike with its big frame on the front housing the cane basket. He then cycled around the regulars' houses and took their orders for lunch and dinnertime meat. It was a good class trade was Lovell's. He then went back to the shop and handed his book over to the two cutters who made up the orders and loaded them into his basket in the reverse order to which they would be delivered. While they were cutting and chopping he would make himself a big cup of cocoa and watch them work. He found himself constantly amazed at the dexterity with which they wielded those enormous choppers, holding the meat with one hand and missing their fingers by what appeared to be only a hair's breadth. He wore a white coat with a blue and white-striped apron, which because he had to ride the bike was gathered up from one corner into a triangle. Once they had loaded the basket the hard work began. The district was rather hilly, and pushing sometimes well over half a hundredweight of meat was no light work. In particular, three of the roads were not made up and were covered in pebbles, which was lovely when the bike was empty and you were going down hill – you could do some glorious broadsides – but pushing it up hill with a load was far from a joke.

Anyway, when the round was finished he was back to the shop, scrubbed his basket clean and was finished. Because he was such a keen and willing lad, Mr Lovell thought highly of him and often said, 'Take your mother a few sausages David', or sometimes he would wrap up some steak and kidney and give it to him as he left.

The cutters liked him too, because he was keenly interested in how they received, for example, a hind quarter of beef and then, in what seemed a short space of time but with considerable effort and expertise, made it up into joints, trays of stewing beef and the shaven bones put to one side, to buy for making soup, small ones for their dogs and the bulk to go to the glue man when he came round once or twice a week. He learnt to make sausages, pluck chickens and geese, but they wouldn't let him loose on partridges and pheasants yet – there was an art in de-feathering small birds, their skins being so soft they were easily damaged.

Although still only twelve, he found it a bit heavy going at times but he quite enjoyed the work, and so far he had had good weather. Along with the bike, his parents had bought a yellow cape, sou'wester and leggings, which were rolled up in the saddlebag at the back. He was longing to try them out and one morning he got his wish. It poured down after he came in from his paper round, so on went his waterproofs to ride to Sandbury. He had the wind against him and found it hard going, but he put his head down and eventually arrived at the shop with only a minute to spare.

"We thought you were going to blot your copybook today David," said Mr Lovell.

"I had the wind against me and the cape seemed to hold me back," said David

One of the cutters chimed in. "If anyone calls you old French letter back when you're wearing that yellow cape, you come and tell us and we'll sort them out."

There were hoots of laughter at this but David was a bit puzzled – he didn't really know what a French letter was – I'll have to ask Harry he thought, he's bound to know. So as not to appear ignorant he did a little grin and went out to the back to get his delivery bike. He didn't see Pat that day, nor the next, nor the next, and was getting a bit worried. It was Friday morning when he saw her coming towards him. They both stopped.

"Where have you been?" said David.

"Don't tell me you missed me," Pat said cheekily.

"I did miss you, wondered if you were alright."

"Yes, they asked me to go in the afternoons for a couple of days."

"Look I finish early on Mondays, could I come in and see the horses on my way home?"

"I don't see why not, I'll ask Mr Mascall but I'm sure he'll say yes. I'll tell you when we pass on Monday."

"Jolly good. I must dash now or I'll be late."

The weekend dragged past. On Saturday he got Harry on his owns and said, "Harry, what is a French letter?"

Harry couldn't have been more flabbergasted if David had told him he was the father of twins.

"What does a whippersnapper like you want to know about French letters for?"

"The cutter at the shop said that when I wear my cape I might get called an old French letter back, and I was to tell him if somebody did."

Harry laughed until his sides ached, and then he had a sobering thought. How the hell do I tell him about French letters without going through the whole rigmarole of what they're used for, women, babies, the lot.

"Look," he said, "it's just a silly joke. I'll have a word with your Dad, perhaps he knows."

"I think you're having me on," said David, "but I'll find out, don't you worry."

That evening Harry had a few words with his father and told him he didn't want to go into all the detail to David, that was his job. His father agreed, but said he wasn't much looking forward to it. He'd have some thoughts and broach the subject when a suitable moment arose. "Anyway," he said, "I don't remember telling you anything and from what I hear you've never been backward."

"Well, I suppose David is a bit innocent because he takes after his mother, whereas I take after you and I bet you were a randy goat when you were young."

"Young!! I'm still bloody young and don't you forget it."

And so the matter was left for the time being.

Monday morning came. David had had another brush with Wooldridge's dog, but had beaten him by a short head to the front gate. As he stood outside the gate panting he looked at the ugly beast straight in the eyes, and after a short while the dog stopped growling, looked to one side and then to the other, and then unmistakably moved its tail a fraction of an inch either side.

"Do you know, I reckon you're all mouth and trousers?" he said, using a phrase he'd heard the grown ups use. What prompted him to open the gate again he didn't know, but he did and stepped slowly inside.

"Now what's the matter with you?" he said. "Sit down and behave yourself." To his total and complete astonishment the dog did exactly that. David slowly stretched out his hand and, seeing no antagonism from the dog, slowly stroked his head.

"I reckon just because you're ugly you just act tough," he said. The dog didn't move. "Well I must go now," he said moving slowly back through the gate, and when he had closed it the dog stood up on its hind quarters for David to stroke it again.

When David got home he told his mother and Rose about it, saying, "for nearly two years he's been chasing me up that path and today he suddenly decides he wants to be friends."

"You'll find a lot of people like that, not just animals," said his mother.

On his journey to work that morning as usual he met Pat and they stopped for a minute or two. "Mr Mascall says it's alright for you to call in," she said.

"Right, I'll be there about one o'clock."

He had told his mother he would be an hour or so late today and she had said, "Well don't make it any more or I shall worry and not only that, you must have your nap."

Because David was up and about at 6.30, walked probably three miles on his paper round, did a ten mile round trip on his bike and then three to four hours work on the heavy delivery bike, she insisted he went to bed for an hour when he got home before he went off to play cricket or football with the lads of the village. He never really wanted to go to bed, but always dozed off soundly as soon as he got there until his mother woke him with a cup of tea.

There wasn't much doing at all that Monday so Mr Lovell let him off as soon as he was finished and he was at the stables well before one o'clock. He spotted Pat and waved and she came running over. "Come and meet Mr Mascall," she said. David was taken over to the office and introduced to a tall very good looking man of about thirty-five dressed in cavalry twill trousers and a yellow polo necked pullover.

"Oh you're the young man who's at Cantlebury aren't you?"

"Yes sir."

"Wait a minute, wait a minute, I've seen your face before. In the paper, that's right. You're the boy who rescued a man being gored to death by a mad bull aren't you?"

"Well sir, it wasn't quite like that."

"Oh yes it was, I read all about it. Well now, look here, I admire guts like that so if you want to ride in the paddock anytime with Pat she'll find you a mount and it won't cost you a penny – alright?"

"Thank you very much sir, but I can't ride."

"What? You live on a farm and can't ride?"

"Well, I've ridden the Shires all my life, but I've never been in a saddle."

"Right then, Pat will give you lessons. In your own time though Pat, not in working hours."

"Thank you very much indeed sir."

David couldn't believe his good fortune, but Pat was looking at him sternly.

"What's all this about the bull?"

"Oh. It was nothing really, I'll tell you all about it another time," and they went out to look at the horses.

It was a big stable with a main block and two wings. It housed a number of hacks, a wide variety of ponies and horses in livery, and half a dozen hunters. All the livery and hunters had to be exercised in the big paddock every day when they were not being used, although Pat of course was restricted to the smaller horses and ponies. David was fascinated by the regimentation of it all, loose boxes and tack rooms immaculately clean and whitewashed, tack all hanging or positioned in neat rows ready to hand. On the farm there was a place for everything and everything more or less in its place, but because the harness sets were so different and cumbersome there was always the impression of organised chaos rather than military precision. "Was Mr Mascall a cavalryman?" said David.

"Yes, he was in the Lancers."

"That explains why it is all so neat and tidy I suppose," said David.

"Well it's not only that. People pay a lot of money to make sure their valuable horses are being well cared for, and first impressions count a lot."

David grinned. "What are you grinning for?" said Pat.

"I was going to say, good job they don't look at you first but I thought better of it."

"Cheeky devil," she said and playfully punched him. They were pals already.

The hour fled past and David, looking at the big clock on the main block said he'd have to go.

"When will you have your first ride?" said Pat.

"Would tomorrow be alright?"

"Yes, that will be fine."

"Well, see you tomorrow then, and Pat – thank you so very much it really has been lovely."

With that he mounted his bike and whistling cheerily rode home. When he got indoors his mother said, "You look like the cat that ate the cream, what's the big secret – come on, out with it."

So he told her excitedly about the day's happenings and in the course of his discourse the name Pat seemed to come in at about every third word.

"I take it this Pat is a girl," said his mother.

"Oh yes – didn't I tell you?" he said in all innocence.

"Well you've obviously been so bitten it could hardly be a boy," she said laughingly. "Come on now, eat your lunch and off to bed with you."

"I'm having my first lesson tomorrow Mum, so I shall be a bit late again."

"Alright, one hour, no more. We're not having you worn out when you go back to school."

During one of the lessons, Pat said she'd love to come and see the shires one day. David said the only time to see them was on Saturday afternoon, otherwise they were out working. It was arranged therefore that after his rounds on the next Saturday he would meet her outside the Sandbury General Post Office and she would cycle with him to Mountfield, stay for tea, and then go back on her own. David protested he would go back with her but she insisted on this arrangement as being the most sensible, it was silly for David to see her home then ride all the way back again. And so it was agreed. They duly met and rode to Home Farm. Pat wasn't quite her usual chatty self as they rode along but David had enough to say for both of them so it wasn't particularly noticeable. Mrs Chandler took to Pat straight away and told them to go off and see the horses and then come back and they'd all have a nice cream tea together.

The biggest of the shires was Swainey. He was enormous, nearly eighteen hands and with a back like a barn door. Even Pat who was used to horses was a little apprehensive at being boxed in with him. Yet he was as gentle as a lamb. His huge head and big brown eyes and muzzle as soft as velvet so affected Pat that she impulsively put her arms around his nose in pure joy. The horse didn't move an inch as she gently stroked him and talked to him – she would have stroked his ears but she couldn't reach them.

"Do you want to sit on him?"

"Oh yes please," she said.

"Right, hold his mane and I'll give you a leg up."

This he did. She sat there with her legs sticking out, no way could she have got them round him. At last it was time to go home for tea, and as she slid down she gave a little cry and held her stomach. David was most concerned.

"Are you alright? What's the matter?"

"I've got bad stomach cramps or something."

"We'll go and see Mum, she'll have some Dr Collis Browne's or something."

When they walked in the big kitchen David said, "Pat's got a pain Mum."

Mrs Chandler looked at the girl's pinched white face and knew straight away what the problem was.

"Come in the front room my dear. Rose pop up to my bedside cabinet and bring the pink sachet that's in there."

She followed Pat into the front room, normally only used for Sunday tea, telling her to lie on the sofa.

"Have you had this before?" she said.

"No, not like this," said Pat. "What is it, I feel funny here," she continued, pointing to the base of her stomach. "Hasn't your mother told you this might happen?"

"I haven't a mother. Leastways I have one but I haven't seen her since I was six. She went away and left Daddy and me and went to live in Malaya."

At that moment Rose came in.

"Now be a good girl and go and put the kettle on and lay the table," said her mother, at the same time shooing David away who was anxious to know whether Pat was alright or not, "and you help her David."

By this time Pat was in tears, firstly with the unaccustomed pain and secondly with the feeling of fear of what might be happening to her. Mrs Chandler attended to her from her pink sachet.

"There, there my dear, everything's alright," and she went on to gently explain to the poor bewildered girl exactly what was going on.

"It's a curse you've got to live with."

Pat laid against Mrs Chandler and whether it was the fact that she'd never really had a mother to be soft and gentle to her, or whether it was the relief of knowing she wasn't seriously ill, whatever it was tears of pent up emotion burst from inside her and she sobbed and sobbed while Mrs Chandler stroked her hair and soothed her. After a while she stopped and Mrs Chandler said; "Now you're going to rest here for a while. I'll get David to go and telephone your father and he can come and pick you up. By the way, we don't know your surname."

"It's Hooper, and Daddy's telephone number is Sandbury 300."

Mrs Chandler packed David off to the grocer shop in the village, outside which was the sign, 'You may telephone from here'. (But only when they're blooming well open thought David).

He got on to Millie and asked her to get Sandbury 300 and a deep pleasant voice answered.

"Hooper speaking."

"Mr Hooper, it's David Chandler. Pat's at our house but she's not feeling well. Mum says can you please come and collect her," as an after thought he said, "she's got her bike of course."

"Right," said Mr Hooper. "I'll borrow a van from my garage friend down the road and come and pick her up and put the bike in the back."

"Mum said to be sure and give you good directions," which he was doing until Millie butted in, "You're tuppence is up David."

"Don't worry," said Mr Hooper, "I know where it is now, see you later David."

Sure enough in about half an hour a rather decrepit looking Ford bumped its way down the lane and stopped outside the Chandlers when David ran out. Mr Hooper climbed out saying, "I wouldn't like to drive that to Brighton."

He was a big genial man; David's hand was lost in his as he shook hands with him. He walked into the kitchen and shook hands with Mrs Chandler, giving Rose a warm friendly smile on the way.

"Come in the front room," said Mrs Chandler, leaving David and Rose in the kitchen.

"Hello my love, not feeling very well?" he said, stating the obvious because he couldn't think of what else to say.

Mrs Chandler said, "I'm afraid it's just that her age has caught up with her. I've explained it to her thoroughly and told her what to do. I've told her it's quite natural and that she's not to feel embarrassed in any way about your knowing about it, and to talk to you openly about it."

"Mrs Chandler you're an angel. I've been worrying my insides out about this happening, with her having no mother to lean on. What an enormous good fortune she was here with you," and after a second or so pause he said, "my wife left me you know, six years ago."

Mrs Chandler looked at him with complete candour and said, "She must have been mad."

He smiled. "You know that's the kindest thing anyone's said to me in years. Now my dear how do you feel."

"I feel a lot better now thank you Daddy."

"Right," said Mrs Chandler, "let's all go out and have some tea."

They were all sitting around the huge deal table in the kitchen, gradually the talk began to flow and Pat's colour started to come back into her face. Then they heard the back door open and close and a minute later Fred Chandler appeared in his stockinged feet – he wouldn't dare walk into the kitchen in his working boots – saying, "Oh, so I've caught you being unfaithful to me in my kitchen have I?"

Mr Hooper stood up laughing and shook hands with Mr Chandler.

"Jack Hooper," he said.

Quickly Mrs Chandler spoke up. "This is Pat, and this is Pat's father who's come to collect her as she was taken poorly."

Mr Chandler gently ruffled Pat's hair and said, "Alright now are we? That's the idea. Well it's very nice to see you after we've heard so much about you. But I'm looking for the lumps on your shoulder blades."

Pat looked at him mystified.

"Well, according to David you're a real little angel, but I can't see any sign of the wings."

They all laughed.

"Get your Dad's slippers Rose," said Mrs Chandler, which Rose dutifully did, slipped them on whilst he sat down and was rewarded with a hug and kiss for her labours. They all then carried on with the tea, ham and salad, lots of bread and butter, banana jelly, farmhouse cake made the day before just melting in their mouths, and then scones, strawberry jam and lashings of fresh cream.

"That was tea fit for a king!" said Mr Hooper. "In fact you know we sat down at five o'clock and now it's seven – what a tea. Now, who does the washing up?"

Mr Chandler looked at him in total astonishment. "Why mother and the kids of course." He had never held a dishcloth in his life, nor a tea towel for that matter.

"Well I've got used to it over the years so I bags the washing up and the kids can wipe and Mrs Chandler can put her feet up and watch us."

"Well, I don't mind," said Mr Chandler, "as long as she doesn't think it's going to catch on!"

They all laughed. David got the small galvanised bath out of the washhouse and put it on the table. Mr Hooper lifted the big kettle off the range and poured the hot water in. Rose sprinkled in the soap flakes and in the meantime David had got an enamel jug of cold water to add to the hot. Pat was told to remain seated and given a tea towel, as was Rose. "Don't break anything," Mr Hooper said, "or they'll make you pay for it,"– they all laughed again.

When it was all done, the big deal table washed down and David and Mr Hooper having carried the bath of water out to the drain, they came back in.

Mr Chandler having thought over the fact of Mr Hooper doing the washing up for years said, "I take it you lost your wife then Mr Hooper."

"Please do call me Jack," he said.

"Well I'm Fred," said Mr Chandler.

"It wasn't so much I lost her, she rather got mislaid, in fact she went off with someone else."

"She must have been mad," said Mr Chandler.

"That's the second time today those exact words have been said to me. This is certainly a red letter day for me."

"Would you like to come down and have a look at the shires sir?" said David.

"Yes I would really love it."

"Yes do go daddy they are really so beautiful, and I sat on Swainy, he's gorgeous."

Mr Chandler wandered down with them, and as they ambled along, Mr Hooper said, "David, what's this I hear about you and a mad bull?"

"It wasn't a mad bull sir, he was just being his normal self," said David.

This remark so amused the two men that they stood roaring with laughter

"Can I see him?"

"Yes of course," said Mr Chandler and led him over to the bullpen.

"By God, what a mean looking piece of meat that is," said Mr Hooper as the bull fixed him with vicious little eyes. "I wouldn't like to meet him in a field."

"Yes, you certainly can't take any chances with one like him," said Mr Chandler.

"What actually happened?"

David's father then related the story, along with one or two little embellishments that David let pass without comment.

"It must have been very frightening," said Mr Hooper, "seeing a man wounded as badly as that for the first time, to say nothing of being knocked about yourself."

"It did give me the wind up," said David.

They went on to see the shires, and the four cobs, which were kept for the lighter work, all of which Mr Hooper found most interesting.

"I suppose one day these will be a thing of the past," he said," everything will be taken over by tractors."

"Well we've got one on one of the other farms and when it's going it doesn't half cover the ground. Just think if you could do your haymaking twice as quick you would only run half the risk of it being spoilt by rain."

"Yes, but conversely you would only need half the men to do it."

"That's progress I suppose. After all it wasn't long ago they cut hay with scythes, now we do it with horse mowers. I suppose it follows it will be done with mechanical mowers in the not so distant future."

And so the two men talked on, with David avidly listening. It didn't occur to either of them that, despite their gap in the social scale readily obvious from their clothes and accent, one was inferior to the other. They had hit a rapport, were talking as equals, were interested in each other's points of view and enjoying each other's company. Although Fred couldn't possibly know it, the sort of wealthy people Jack spent most of his time with in the city during the day were self-centred, mainly avaricious and frequently plainly boring with one or two exceptions for whom he had a high regard. Fred was too polite to ask him what he did for a living knowing that when Jack wanted to tell him, he would.

When they got back to the house they found Megan and Harry there. Pat had perked up quite a lot and was playing snakes and ladders with Rose.

"Are you up for a drink tonight father?" said Mrs Chandler.

"Now that's a good idea," Jack chimed in – "Do you mind if I join you. I won't be able to stay too long. I've got to get this lump of trouble home at a reasonable hour."

"I'll come for a quick one as well," said Harry, knowing that Megan enjoyed talking to his mother, since she saw so little of her own. "But I've got to get Megan back by eleven to the hospital."

"It won't take two hours to get Megan back to Sandbury," said Fred mischievously.

"It will the way we go," said Harry laughing, and with Megan blushing, the three men went out to the Prince of Orange.

The class difference did arise momentarily as they approached the pub.

"I'd suppose you'd prefer to go to the saloon," said Fred.

"If you always go in the public, I go in the public," said Jack, "the beer's the same and I'm sure the company will be as good if not better."

And so it was. After the initial quiet reception by the regulars, the banter soon started to fly.

How's that nurse of yours Harry – has she got her tape measure out yet?"

"Harry's behaving himself with this one – pretending he hasn't got one." Then there were roars of laughter.

Jack let Fred buy the first round, after all it was his pub. Then he bought a round of mild and bitter and while he was in the process of so doing in came PC Crown, off duty that weekend.

Crownie looked at him, touched his cap and said, "Good evening sir."

"Oh, it's Mr Crown isn't it? Good evening to you, how are you?"

It was known that Crownie only called the squire, the doctor and the vicar 'sir' but neither he nor Jack said anything about how they knew each other and Fred was too polite to ask. They were both looking at the clock – "I think we should be getting back," said Fred, "or we shall be given a good hiding for keeping you here."

With good nights to everybody they left and walked down the lane and into the house to find the girls had laid the table again and on it there was a nice pork pie and other goodies for supper.

The conversation bounded around the table and at ten o'clock Jack said, "Well, I haven't had a more enjoyable day in years and years and I do thank you all for looking after Pat so kindly and for very great hospitality." Shaking hands with everyone and with the bicycle in the back, he and Pat climbed into the old van and started off.

"I hope it manages to get up the lane," he roared as they drove away.

"There goes a proper gentleman," said Fred.

Chapter Six

The holidays slipped past and at the beginning of September, the weather was set fine. On the first Monday a letter arrived from Jack Hooper. "Letter from Sandbury," called Snowy as he left it on the kitchen table. Inside there was a short note –

Dear Mr and Mrs Chandler,
If you're not otherwise engaged on Sunday, will you all come on a picnic with Pat and me to the sea? I will provide food and drink and will collect you at 8.30. I suggest we go to Eastbourne and lunch on Beachy Head and then get a bathing hut and go for a swim. This includes Harry and Megan of course, if Megan is not on duty.

Little time was lost in excitedly agreeing with the proposal, so Mrs Chandler wrote a postcard in her best copperplate, thanking him for the invitation and saying that they could all come. David then went down to the village and got a penny stamp out of the machine on the post box and it went out with the ten o'clock collection to be delivered first post the next morning at Sandbury.

"I hope he's not going to put us in that van," said Fred, "what sort of a car has he got David?"

David didn't know, he'd never thought to ask Pat about whether they even had a car.

"It's no good asking him," said Harry, "he's always got luvvy-duvvy things to talk about when he's with Pat."

David lunged at him and there was a certain amount of horseplay until Mrs Chandler said, "That's enough you two. Now there's one thing you haven't thought of Fred, we two haven't got bathing suits."

"Well I've got a few bob from my overtime money, ask Marshall to bring us one each on Wednesday when he comes."

Marshall was the tallyman who came round each week and collected half a crown from which Mrs Chandler would, during the course of the year, buy all the basic clothes for the family. She would send a postcard in the morning asking for bathing suits and he would then put a selection in his van from which she could choose. She bought two woollen costumes, each costing seven shillings and elevenpence, and without telling the others bought a very fetching straw hat in the village for five shillings.

The week dragged by until Sunday eventually came.

"How is he going to get us all in his car?" said Harry, "There's seven of us."

"Perhaps he's hired a char-a-banc," said Mrs Chandler, not normally given to facetious remarks.

As they spoke they heard the noise of a car coming down the lane.

"Here it comes," squeaked Rose excitedly.

When the car appeared it was obvious how the seven would be accommodated. It was a Daimler limousine, its corrugated radiator glistening in the morning sun, and its paintwork shining like a guardsman's toecaps. At the back was a luggage rack strapped to which was an enormous hamper and on the running board a black painted spare can of petrol. Jack jumped down and said, "Right, all aboard, you come up the front with me Fred, Rose can go on your lap, Pat and David on the occasionals and the three grown-ups on the rear seat."

Storing their bags with the costumes and towels around their feet they all got settled, and turning round in the yard, off they went.

They headed for Tonbridge, and then Tunbridge Wells and then on to Mayfield and Polegate to Eastbourne. The countryside was unbelievably beautiful and they all from time to time noticed the admiring glances of pedestrians and other road users at their beautiful car.

Reaching the outskirts of Eastbourne Jack said, "I'll fill her up with petrol, then we shan't have to bother on the way home," and proceeded to pull into a roadside garage with a National Benzole sign, which brand Jack apparently favoured. Whilst the garage man was winding the pump handle around and then reversing it twelve times to provide the necessary twelve gallons, all the others dismounted and went to the lavatory. They'd all been wanting to go for some time but each had been too shy to mention it.

The general opinion of that particular facility was of a very low level indeed but as Fred said, "Needs must when the devil drives." They soon reached the front at Eastbourne and turned towards Beachy Head. After the long pull up the narrow road to the top, which the Daimler effortlessly accomplished, despite its load, they stopped and looked in sheer delight at the beautiful blue sea stretched before them.

"Make sure the brakes are all on, we don't want the lunch to disappear over the cliff," said Fred.

"How about a nice walk across the headland and then back for an early lunch before we go down to the beach," said Jack. Mrs Chandler slipped on her new hat that she had carried concealed in a carrier bag.

"What have we here," said Fred. "I do believe Lady Mountfield has joined the party."

"It's a lovely hat Mrs Chandler," said Megan, "don't take any notice of them."

"I agree entirely," said Jack. "It's very fetching."

They walked for half an hour and on returning to the car Jack told them, almost as an apology, that he hadn't prepared the hamper himself but had got Mace's, the large general grocers in Sandbury to make it up. He said he had told Mr Mace that his guests provided such a superb table themselves that he would have to be very particular as to what he included. He was also to include some quarts of Whitbread Light Ale for the men, a bottle of white sparkling wine for the ladies and ginger beer for the children. They unstrapped the hamper. On the top was an oilcloth ground sheet, under that a large starched linen tablecloth, and then food and drink in abundance. Everything unpacked Jack said, "Right Mrs Chandler, you're in charge from now on."

They had a royal feast of cold chicken, ham, pork pie and all the salads, pickles and cold vegetables that go with them. Gooseberry tart and cream ('not as good as yours Mrs Chandler') followed by cheddar and stilton, all washed down with drinks Mr Mace had included.

"I don't know about swimming," Fred exclaimed, "I'll sink like a stone."

They cleared up the lunch and after a few minutes rest got back into the Daimler to go down to the beach. On arrival Jack hired two beach huts where they took it in turns to get changed and where they left their clothes. Everyone went into the sea although neither Mrs Chandler nor Megan could swim, but it was a nice calm day and they were able to wade out to join in the fun the others were having. After a while the two men and Mrs Chandler came out, leaving the others sporting with some other children and young people they had met.

As they lay back in the sun Jack said, "Don't think I'm being nosey Fred, but how did you come to get on the land?"

Fred then told him briefly his story. His father worked on the land in a village in Hampshire. Chandler senior had been a regular soldier until his twenty-one years were up and then married his mother and settled down. Fred himself had always wanted to go in the army, either the Hampshires or the Rifle Brigade, both of whom were at the Winchester Depot, nearby. In the event he joined the Hampshires when he was eighteen in 1898. After recruit training and a few months in Ireland he was sent to South Africa joining a Hampshire battalion newly arrived from India. He saw considerable service, and then in 1903 came back to England, had another spell in Ireland, and then back to England again. In 1914 they went to France, by which time he was a sergeant and married with a little boy, was badly wounded and invalided out. Discharged from the Herbert Hospital at Woolwich he got a job in the nearby Woolwich Arsenal, a house in one of the hutments being built for the munition workers on the slopes of nearby Shooters Hill, and his wife and young Harry joined him from Winchester married quarters.

Although unskilled, he took to engineering and in the following three years became a foreman, learnt a lot about production methods and the use of tools and machines, and in the process was able to put away a little money.

When the war ended and the arsenal shed tens of thousands of jobs, he found himself out of work, and the only places that still needed men were the farms, starved of men by the war years and now losing their female labour. He applied for the job at Home Farm and got it. With his bit of pension and a tied cottage that went with the job, they managed quite well.

"What would you rather be doing Fred, the engineering side or the farm work?"

"They've both got their advantages and disadvantages. The engineering people work shorter hours than we do on the land, and they get more money. Not only that, depending on the job you're doing, you've got the chance to use your brains to improve production methods, although when you come to think of it there are a lot of improvements, particularly to equipment, I can think of that need doing on the farm. On the other hand on the land you're out in the open all day, and mostly you're your own boss. On balance though I think I'd get more satisfaction from engineering, though at fifty-one I wouldn't be able to get another job anyway."

Jack didn't pursue the subject.

Gradually the others came in from the sea and at about five o'clock Fred suggested they all adjourn to the nearby tea shop for a cup of 'Lyons' best, and having come to the conclusion that it definitely wasn't 'Lyons' best but would have to do, they then moved back to the car to join the general exodus home. The movement of the car and the general excitement of the day was too much for Rose, she went fast asleep on Fred's lap. Pat too dozed off with her head on David's shoulder, much to his embarrassment at first, since he was expecting rude remarks from Harry sitting behind him, but then he got such great pleasure at her hair brushing his face he put Harry out of his thoughts completely.

Halfway home they stopped at a country pub and the men had a couple of drinks, bringing sherry out to the ladies and ginger pop to the children. Back in the car again and it seemed in no time they were back at the farm. When they had waited a short while for Harry and Megan to say their goodnights at the back of the car – Jack was going to drop Megan off at the hospital – Fred shook hands warmly with Jack thanking him for a lovely day out, Harry and David shook hands. Rose held her arms out to him and he picked her up and gave her a big kiss, and finally Mrs Chandler approached him and gave him a little peck on the side of his cheek.

"You've given us a wonderful day," she said. "Thank you very much."

"It was wonderful for me to be part of a family again," he said, "so the thanks are all on my side."

And with that the Daimler moved silently up the lane leaving them all tired and happy.

Chapter Seven

Back at school David found himself in the second form, and his form master was none other than Mr Scott-Calder, who had impressed him so greatly at the original scholarship exam. The master did not actually take them for any of their subjects, they moved around to other rooms for their various lessons but he did check them in every morning, and generally if they had any problems they could go to him with them.

David worshipped him from afar.

Jeremy had been abroad for most of the holidays. He came to the farm at the first opportunity and told Mrs Chandler and Rose all about his stay in Provence, and they got an atlas out to see where Provence was. Rose of course hung on his every word much to Mrs Chandler's inner amusement.

"David's got a girlfriend," said Rose.

"Oh don't be daft, she's just a girl I happened to meet," he protested.

"She's his girlfriend, isn't she Mummy?"

"Well, I suppose since she's a girl, and she's definitely his friend, it's probable she's his girlfriend."

"You two are rotten," said David, "look Jeremy you say a word of this at school and I'll thump you black and blue."

"Oh don't worry, trust your Uncle Jeremy, I won't let on. Now tell me all about this lovely lady you haven't mentioned before you rotter."

So David told him about the riding lessons and how she came to the farm.

"And we went to Eastbourne in this Daimler," said Rose excitedly.

"Well well," said Jeremy, "I think I shall have to meet this young lady."

"Not if I can help it," said David.

The first term flew past. David missed seeing Pat, although they did arrange fortnightly lessons on Saturday afternoons. Now that he was in the second form he had games on alternate Saturday afternoons. They finished school at 12.30 and then had rugby lessons at 2 o'clock. Wednesday afternoons were still free, but Pat was at school on Wednesdays, and went to the stables on Saturday mornings.

As Christmas approached, David one day asked Pat what they were doing for Christmas.

"Same as usual I expect," said Pat, "we have no relations, so nobody comes. We've been away to a hotel a couple of times but we don't like it very much."

David repeated this to his mother, who later that evening

mentioned it to Fred.

"Do you think they'd like to come here?" said Fred. "What's Megan doing?"

"She's off on Christmas day but on duty on Boxing Day, then going home for New Year."

"We'll drop him a line and ask if they've nothing else arranged whether they'd like to join us, but don't forget if they do come that will be an extra couple of presents to buy."

"Oh, we'll manage."

And so it was arranged. Furthermore Jack said that on Boxing Day, if they were in agreement, they would all be his guests at a theatre in London, travelling in the Daimler, and having a supper afterwards.

"Rose will have to go to bed in the afternoon because she'll be up late," said Mrs Chandler.

During the Christmas rush David had helped out at Mr Lovell's butcher's shop, working quite late for several days before Christmas.

"Ask your mother," said Mr Lovell, "whether she would like a goose or a turkey."

David was a little apprehensive. They had fattened a cockerel at home for the Christmas dinner, but Mrs Chandler had expressed doubts that with the extra company they were expecting they would find it enough.

"Can you tell me how much it would cost?" asked David.

"It won't cost you anything you chump," said Mr Lovell, "everybody here gets a bird at Christmas and you're one of us now."

David excitedly broke the news to his mother when he got home. She said, "You thank Mr Lovell very much indeed from me and say we would love to have a goose."

They had a great time on Christmas Day. Jack got a tasteful tie from the Chandlers and Pat got a pair of riding gloves. Coincidentally Jack bought Fred his regimental tie with which he was very pleased, Mrs Chandler a silk scarf and David received a set of records of a Mozart Piano Concerto. These were the first records he had ever owned and he was greatly thrilled.

As a result of Mr Lovell's generosity they had both chicken and goose on the table for Christmas dinner, and enough over to help out the ham and tongue for supper. Jack insisted on doing the washing up again to a lot of leg pulling from Fred and Harry, which he not only took in good part, but seemed to thoroughly enjoy to the extent that he started to give as good as he got, which is always a sign of companionship and true friendliness.

On Boxing Day they went to a musical in the West End, had supper in a Lyons corner house and in no time Christmas was over. For

David it was back to the routine of morning's wood, paper round, school and homework, which by now was beginning to get rather demanding.

Spring came and then summer and once again David and Pat got their respective summer jobs and began to see more of each other again. Their relationship was now a year old. It gave them great pleasure to be together, but when they were apart for two or three weeks without seeing each other, neither suffered any degree of heartache. Having said that, when they did meet they both showed the other how pleased they were to be together by the way they looked at one another and the gentle way they talked to each other. They were very, very dear friends.

One day Pat had ridden a larger horse than she normally did. David had given her a leg-up to mount it, and when they returned David dismounted first, and then went round to see that Pat got off safely. He found her sliding down the side of the horse and caught her just as she would have overbalanced. His arms went round her waist and held her secure and for a moment or two she did not move. Then slowly she turned in his arms and she looked up at him, and he bent and kissed her. She put her arms round his neck and they kissed again. David held her very tightly for a few moments more and then released her, turned and walked back to see his horse.

They both busied themselves with the chores of hanging the harnesses, rubbing the horses down and seeing to their drinking water, and about twenty minutes later emerged from their respective stables ready to cycle to their homes. Neither said a word. Pat walked up to a somewhat self-conscious David, and took his hand and led him across the yard to their bicycles.

"Goodbye David," she said, "see you again on Monday," and with that she again put her arms lightly around his neck and kissed him firmly and sweetly in all true innocence. From that time they always held hands when they were together, and always kissed when they met or parted, even in front of the family. Harry, who under normal circumstances would have made great capital out of this situation, was threatened by Megan with his very life if he uttered a word.

They were an extraordinarily handsome young couple. Pat was tall and slender with a thirteen-year-old figure just beginning to blossom. She had very fair hair and deep blue eyes. Whether she was riding her horse, walking or riding her bicycle she had a grace of movement, which immediately caught the eye.

"She's going to be a real beauty when she gets older," said Fred Chandler to his wife.

"And that won't be very long," said Mrs Chandler, "I only hope that she doesn't outgrow David and look for someone older in a year or two's time. Girls mature a lot quicker than boys."

"Oh I don't think we can expect them to stay together for the rest of their lives – they'll probably each have half a dozen other loves before they settle," Fred replied. "Anyway there's nothing we can do about it, we should be more than happy that they go well together now."

David was filling out rapidly. Above average height and build with a clear complexion, brown curly hair and hazel coloured eyes, he was a very good looking boy, and although he was big he moved quickly with shoulders well back giving him a good manly carriage beyond his years. He had the natural habit of being unfailingly polite to everyone, particularly older people. He had got another good report at the end of the 1932 year, being in the top five at most things, and right at the top in German in which he had made such strides he was already half way through the third form syllabus, giving his German master all sorts of headaches.

The summer holidays finished and Pat and David reconciled themselves to not seeing each other so frequently, in fact it was decidedly infrequently as David found himself picked for the school under XV rugby team, which meant he had to play three Saturdays out of four each month. However, just before half-term came, during the last weekend in October, a letter arrived at the farm along with the customary yell from Snowy, "Letter from Sandbury – looks like a girl's writing."

And a girl's writing it was, from Pat, but addressed to Mr and Mrs Chandler not David. In it they, Mr and Mrs Chandler, were asked if they could go over and see her father as early as possible on the half-term Saturday afternoon. David and Pat would then join them for tea and her father would take them all to dinner at the Angel Inn in Sandbury that evening, bringing them home in the Daimler. None of them, not even David, had as yet visited the Hooper household. The letter told them that if they took the bus to the Three Tuns, half a mile before you got into Sandbury, the house named 'The Hollies' lay back off the road a hundred yards or so further on. Mrs Chandler, as the family's letter writer immediately replied saying how much they were looking forward to seeing them again and that they would be there about 2 o'clock.

"I wonder why he's asked us to his house?" Fred asked his wife.

"Well he has been here several times I suppose he wants to pay us back. On the other hand he has taken us out before without our going to the house. Anyway I shall look forward to seeing the place very much. The trouble is we can't ask David to ask Pat what's in his mind because he won't see Pat until Saturday. I expect he wants some company; he must get very lonely there with only the old housekeeper Mrs Westcott to talk to. By what he's said in the past she doesn't exactly say a lot, and her cooking leaves a lot to be desired." Then as an afterthought – "Perhaps he wants to arrange Christmas."

So they each wondered in their own minds the purpose of their forthcoming visit, but not in their wildest dreams could they have known the changes to all their lives the forthcoming visit would bring.

Chapter Eight

Saturday arrived and when he had finished the morning's work promptly at noon, Fred went home, had a wash and a shave and, having eaten a hasty meal, got himself ready to join his wife and Rose, both in their Sunday best, to catch the 1.30 bus at the end of the lane. Arriving at the Three Tuns they alighted as directed and quickly reached The Hollies, which they found to be a large Victorian house set in well over an acre of grounds. The grounds were well maintained, contained a number of quite unusual trees, and in the far corner there was an enclosed tennis court.

They were met at the door by Jack himself, who had obviously been looking out for them. He swept Rose up into his arms and shook hands cordially with Fred and Mrs Chandler.

"What a beautiful house," she said, looking at the ivy covered walls and the tall elegant chimneys.

"Well," replied Jack, "I have a gardener/handyman who looks after the grounds and then does a 'Forth Bridge' job on the external paintwork which keeps at least the outside looking reasonable. Now come on in, Mrs Westcott is away this weekend so I shall be looking after you."

They walked into the large hall and were faced by a large wide mahogany staircase going up to a landing at the rear of the building, from which two other landings ran back again to the front of the house, with doorways opening off each, presumably to bedrooms on either side of the house. Turning left out of the panelled hall, they found themselves in a comfortably furnished sitting room. Although all the furniture, curtains and covers were obviously of fine quality, they had the air about them of not being properly looked after. Mrs Chandler mentally noted, he needs a woman's touch in here – the whole lot could do with a thorough spring clean – whoever does the cleaning needs a toe behind them. She looked to her front again and saw Jack smiling quizzically at her. "Mrs Chandler, having seen your home I know exactly what you are thinking," he said. Mrs Chandler blushed at his astuteness; Fred looked at both of them in complete perplexity and wondered what the devil Jack was talking about.

"Come and sit down," he said, "and I'll tell you why I've asked you to come over, though the Lord knows I've owed you a visit for long enough. Now if Rose wants to stay she is most welcome. There are some books and pictures over there," pointing to a low table in the corner, "which belonged to Pat, and if you want to go out into the garden there is a swing and a slide over by the tennis court."

"Oh she'll amuse herself alright," said Mrs Chandler.

"Right then, away we go. First of all Fred I would like your permission to call your wife by her christian name, and for her to address me in the same manner. The only problem is, I don't know what it is, in fact I've only ever heard anyone address you," looking at Mrs Chandler, "as either mother or Mrs Chandler."

"Well, it's Ruth," said Mrs Chandler, blushing for the second time that day, "and I don't mind at all," but at the same time looking at Fred who was nodding vigorously at his assent.

"I'll tell you what this is all about. First I'll tell you about me. I've noticed how courteous you and all your family are Fred, no one has ever asked me what I do for a living, I could have been a professional cracksman for all you knew." They all laughed. "However, I am a commodity broker. My father built up the business over many years, surrounding himself with first class staff. I was twenty-two when war broke out, having just left university, so I went straight into the Royal Artillery and spent most of the war in the Middle East, which apart from the Dardanelles was a great deal less hazardous than your lot Fred. I married the daughter of our ambassador in Cairo in 1917. After the war I went into business with father who died in 1925, seven years ago, my mother having died during the war. They had no relatives; I am an only son, so all I have in my life is Pat. I have to tell you my work is totally unsatisfying in the sense that as a result of the highly experienced staff we have the business runs itself, leaving me very little to do except make the odd decision regarding policy, attend monthly board meetings and deal with one or two special clients who previously dealt with my father and now expect to deal direct with me. In a word I am bored. I have therefore been looking around for another interest and I've come to the conclusion that agriculture is rapidly going to become more and more mechanised. The day of the horse and cart, very sadly, is over, or will be in the not so distant future. It breaks my heart to say that when I look at those beautiful shires at Home Farm, but we can't escape progress.

"We are in an interesting farming area here. There are sheep on the downs, dairy farms lower down and in the Weald, and a fair amount of arable land all around and, of course, fruit galore. My idea is briefly as follows. There are premises about half a mile from here, which comprise about 4000 square feet of workshop and offices, and at least an acre of hard standing. Now, bearing in mind the nearest agriculture equipment firm is over twenty miles to the south east, to the north there is nothing between here and London and to the west the only one of any size is at Guildford. I think this would make a first class sales base. However, if you're going to see this equipment you've got to be able to service and repair it, hence the workshops.

"Now this is where you come in. My idea is that we form a limited company, I will look after the commercial side and you would be responsible for running the sales and workshop side. I can quite see what your first thoughts might be on this. Up until now we have had a good friendship all due to two youngsters meeting as they did, and there is absolutely no question whatever of that altering. I do not intend that you should work for me; my honest intention would be for us to be equal in this venture and to work together. Well I don't think I've made such a long speech in years – any questions so far?"

There was a silence as Fred and Ruth looked at each other. Then Fred said, "there are two things that come to mind immediately as far as my involvement goes. Firstly, I've had no experience of running a factory like this, and secondly I've no money to put into it worth mentioning."

"Right, lets answer those two first. As regards experience, you had experience in the arsenal of general factory work and I have the highest opinion of your ability in absorbing other skills, as they are required, so that side we will get over. Secondly, as regards money, we will have a small share capital, equally split. I will lend sufficient money at the same interest as I would get anywhere else to provide start up and immediate working capital and to buy stock, and then we would use the bank for day to day requirements."

Ruth then spoke, "What about our house? We have a tied cottage which would mean that we have to move and then pay rent."

"I don't think that would be a problem unless you are very attached to your present house."

"Oh no, I would like to move somewhere with electricity instead of oil lamps, and a gas stove would be heaven."

"Well in that case there are several nice houses going around Sandbury that you might think of buying on a mortgage. After all, we haven't discussed salaries yet, but obviously you would be getting a great deal more than you would get on the farm. You see, this isn't something that I'm doing just for your benefit. I want to do it myself, but I know I can't do it on my own. I want someone with practical skills and knowledge of farmers and farming to make it a success. And I must have someone I know and like."

Ruth spoke again, "Now what about Harry, he would still be working at Home Farm."

"I've got an idea I wanted to discuss with you about Harry, if you're generally in favour of at least considering what I've said so far, and that is, Harry is a practical, likeable young man. This agricultural equipment is going to need to be sold by someone who not only knows how to use it, which he can learn, but also knows the problems and difficulties farmers have with existing equipment, someone who can actually demonstrate the benefits of the machines to the farmer. That's where Harry comes in. At the same time Harry can understudy you Fred. You've got fifteen good years ahead of you at least, and it would be good to know that someone could step into your shoes when the time comes."

They all sat back thinking things over until Jack said, "Now what say we climb into the car and go and see the premises just to give you an idea of what I've been talking about, then we can have some tea and leave the whole subject until you've had an opportunity to discuss it fully over the weekend."

Having called Rose in they got into the Daimler and went off to the factory, which comprised a main square workshop building with four offices in the front, the whole laying well back off the road and fronted by the concreted hard standing, which as Fred could readily envisage would be ideal for siting the equipment. The buildings were in first class condition and the site was well fenced. The offices were clean, light and airy and fitted with radiators powered by a hot water boiler located presumably inside the factory. They were both most impressed.

"Right, lets get back, the kids will be home any minute."

When they got back Pat and David were already there and Pat had started getting things ready for tea. "Now don't scoff too much cake youngsters," said Jack. "We're going to the Angel tonight, so leave plenty of room." Pat had been looking quizzically at Jack during tea to try and gauge whether Mr and Mrs Chandler had taken to the proposals or not. She hadn't said anything to David, and he in turn was keenly interested in finding out what it was that Mr Hooper wanted to talk to his parents about. All sorts of things were going through his mind, including the thought that Mr Hooper might be objecting to his seeing so much of Pat. Perhaps he wanted her to have other boyfriends so that she didn't get too keen on him. Perhaps he really wasn't good enough for her except as a pal to go riding with. Perhaps…

"David, you dreaming or something?"

"Oh no Dad, that is, yes I was miles away."

"I was going to say, how would it be, as far as you were concerned, if we came to live in Sandbury?"

Immediately Jack looked at Ruth, Ruth looked at Fred, Rose clapped her hands, Pat displayed her widest of smiles and David was speechless. Finally he said, "Do you mean leave the farm, no more morning's wood?"

"No more morning's wood."

"I'd love it," although there was no doubt in anybody's mind present that his enthusiasm was not mostly if not wholly due not to his not having to get the morning's wood but to the fact he would be nearer Pat.

"Well your mother and I may very well move here, although it's not finally decided yet. And by the way not a word to Harry if you're awake when he comes in tonight, I need to talk to him first."

"With Harry on the hospital doorstep you won't have any arguments there," said David, and they all laughed. David knew his brother very well indeed.

They had a marvellous meal at the Angel, being treated as preferential customers by the manager and, a very rare event indeed, the chef came out to Mr Hooper to ask if everything had been satisfactory. After the meal, Jack took them home in the Daimler, and on leaving them at the farm said, "Well, talk it over, and I'll pop over again next Saturday afternoon for an hour, and we can plan accordingly. But don't forget, if you decide to stay here I shall fully understand and it will make no difference to our friendship whatsoever."

Harry was told the next morning, and they talked it back and forth all day long, mainly trying to find objections to it, but after going over the same ground time and again they all came to the conclusion it was an opportunity that would come only once in a lifetime, and anyway if they fell flat on their faces they could always go back to farming.

"I don't think I'll keep him hanging around all week," said Fred, "I'll go and phone him."

Fred went down to the new call box that had recently been installed outside the Fox and Hounds in the village and asked Millie to put him through to Sandbury 300.

"That plan you were talking about Jack, we've decided to go for it."

Jack realised that Fred was being cagey because if other calls were not going through the exchange Millie wasn't averse to having a listen in.

"Right Fred. I'll pop over tomorrow evening if you're not doing anything and have a further chat."

The following evening the three men and Ruth sat around the table and it was finally decided they would aim to move on the March quarter day, spending as much time as was necessary at the factory at weekends before that to get it ready. With getting the stock and machinery in they should be able to start trading by mid-summer.

"We may miss the hay making season but I suppose whenever we start we'll miss something," said Fred.

So it got underway. Jack organised the company formation and

Sandbury Engineering Limited was born. He organised the stationery, consulting Fred all the way, and after their evening sessions on these and relevant matters such as purchase of tools and equipment, what initial stock to buy, and other things, they could repair to the Prince of Orange. Here, Jack, despite his posh accent and the fact they all knew he had a Daimler, was soon accepted by the regulars and after a comparatively short while was able to make jokes against them as they did against each other. Humour in the pub was fairly basic, as indeed it is in most places where men congregate, but it was mostly spontaneously funny and never hurtful.

Lenny Tupman drove the horse and big high sided tip cart which collected the rubbish in the village and took it to a dump about three quarters of a mile away in an old quarry. He was accident-prone. One lady had put a carpet out near the bin, intending to beat it later. She went off to the village shop and in the meantime Lenny called, slung the carpet on the cart and was on his way up the road to the dump when the good lady returned. The village turned out to see a portly, black skirted, red faced lady running up the main street waving a rolled up umbrella and screaming, "bring my carpet back you rogue." For weeks after that the usual salutation when Lenny walked in the four ale bar was; "Nicked any carpets lately, Lenny?"

On another occasion when the cart was well laden, he turned it round in the narrow street running down beside the Fox and Hounds. There was a steep camber on the road and on the reverse part of his turn the horse's slippery shoes couldn't get a purchase on the tarmac, horse and cart slid back before he could do anything and the corner of the high cart went right through the pub window, taking the frame with it. The landlord came running out and was reported as saying, "Bloody hell Lenny you may be dying for a drink, but can't you use the door like everybody else."

Other stories about ferrets in trouser pockets, courting couples on haystacks – lurid stories about these goings-on were commonplace, apparently half the unmarried population (and probably some of the married too, if not to each other) of Sandbury and regions adjacent ended up on or under Mountfield's haystacks. As one of the farmhands once said, 'we don't mind them having a tumble, but they always have a fag afterwards and if they're not careful set the blooming rick alight'.

All this type of conversation, although basic, was music in Jack's ears after the pseudo-sophisticated talk he normally had to listen to at the club and in his city pub. He liked these people and he felt they liked him too. He enjoyed his visits to Home Farm, being with the Chandler family, and after the misery of his wife leaving him which had dragged on year after year and which he had not been able to shake off, he was now beginning to feel happy again. He was still not divorced from his wife but he found himself seriously thinking about it without it causing him too much turmoil in his mind and stomach. "I'll go and see the solicitor," he said to himself as he drove home one evening.

Christmas came and they made the same arrangement as the previous year. Leaflets had been coming in from the two estate agents in Sandbury and they had seen several houses, none of which really suited Ruth. "I must have a big kitchen," she said, "most of these houses have such small kitchens, I don't know how they work in them."

Just before Christmas some leaflets had arrived from Hemworthy's Estate Agents, and one of these described a property that Ruth immediately fell in love with and which by sheer coincidence was called Chandlers Lodge. It was a detached Edwardian house in a garden of manageable size with a reasonably sized vegetable patch. It had a large stone flagged kitchen and a separate dinning room, drawing room and four bedrooms. There was a big snag. It was expensive. The lady who lived in it had died and her family wanted £820 for it. They consulted Jack about it. "Let's go and have a look at it over Christmas time," he said. "Hemworthy will lend me the keys."

And so they did. Surprisingly it was in very good condition. Ruth had thought that with one old lady living there it could well be shabby at least, but obviously the lady had had help and it really needed very little doing to it before they moved in – "If of course we decide to have it," said Ruth hurriedly, while the two men raised eyebrows at each other.

"I know one of the general managers at the Woolwich Equitable Building Society," said Jack, "They are first class people. If you like I'll have a word with him and see what it is going to cost. But first let's see if we can knock the price down a bit."

Fred got on to Hemworthy and said they were very interested but he didn't want to go above £750. Hemworthy consulted the owners. "They say £800," he said.

"Make it £780," said Fred "and it's a deal, subject to the mortgage being agreed."

Hemworthy came back, "£780 it is."

Fred was as pleased as punch at the success of his first taste of financial haggling; little did he know that it would certainly not be his last. However, having got the price settled, a young man from the Woolwich Equitable duly called and set out the costs. "You'll need £80 deposit," he said, "and we can arrange for a twenty year mortgage on the remainder at 6¼% interest, which means you will pay a little under £5 per month." Fred's starting salary had already been agreed at £34 per month to increase each six months according to the progress of the business until it was £50 per month, so they could comfortably afford the payments. "Finally," said the young man from the Equitable, "we shall need two references." Fred gave him Mr J Hooper and Sir Oliver Routledge his present employer to whom he had confided his plans when he gave his notice to leave. Sir Oliver had wished him the very best of luck and promised to be his first customer. The obviously impressed young man looked at these two names and said, "With names like that you will have no problem whatsoever."

And so it was arranged.

They took possession on the March quarter day and moved in the following weekend.

Chapter Nine

The excitement of the move was tinged with sadness as far as David was concerned at leaving his mates at Mountfield who he had known all his life. He was an intelligent lad and realised that apart from casually bumping in to them on odd occasions, they would no longer be part of his life. In particular he was sad about Ernie Bolton who he had looked after so much, and when they moved Ernie was sitting outside his home although it was a cold March day, and waved to them as they drove past in the removal van. Apart from that he was excited at the fact he no longer had to do the morning's wood, he no longer had to do his paper round and he would be able to see Pat more often than he normally could on term time, though he found to his dismay that plans were being made for Pat to go to a 'Young ladies college' in September, the first two years in the west of England and the final year in Switzerland.

Academically she was bright but not brilliant and Jack thought these schools would be able to cram her a little to get some sort of qualifications for a job in life.

"She's not going to live on my money," he said to Ruth and Fred. "She's going to earn her living the same as the rest of us – I've no time for people who don't work."

Shortly after moving in Harry came in one evening and asked his mother if 'The boss' was at home. Fred came into the kitchen where they were and said, "You looking for me?"

"Dad, I want to join the Terriers. There's a RASC company at the Drill Hall here and they teach you to drive which will be useful to us. They want more recruits."

"How will it affect your work?"

"Not in any way. You have to do so many drills a year on Saturday nights and two weeks camp in the summer."

"What does Megan think about it?"

"She's agreeable to my doing it. I think she likes the idea of my being a soldier, even if it is only a Saturday night soldier."

"Well you can't call Service Corps people real soldiers, like the Hampshires. Anyway I'm agreeable but I must have words with Mr Hooper, we don't want to go rushing off in all directions the minute we've started." When talking of Jack either to David or Harry he was always referred to as Mr Hooper.

Jack readily agreed, so Harry duly presented himself at the Drill Hall on the next Saturday evening and was sworn in and issued with his kit. He was a keen muscular young man and, once his mother had taken the tunic in a little at the waist, and shortened his trousers by half an inch, he really looked quite smart in the high-necked, brass buttoned, belted serge uniform. On the farm he had always worn boots so unlike some of the chaps who had joined with him and had only ever worn shoes, he didn't find the army boots clumsy or uncomfortable. It took some of them quite a while to get used to them.

"You turn and your boots will follow you, you idle lot," shouted the regular army drill sergeant under whose tender care they were first put. "The first thing you learn is that when you talk to me you stand to attention and you call me Sergeant – do you understand – not sarge – Sergeant." He bellowed. "Secondly, when you talk to the Sergeant Major or to an officer you call them sir."

Then he taught them the first drill a recruit learns, which is probably the same in all armies – how to salute.

"And you remember you horrible lot, you only salute if you've got your cap on, otherwise you just stand to attention or eyes right or left as I will show you." So by the end of the first evening's drill they knew how to stand to attention, and how to salute in case they met a general on their way home.

As it transpired they didn't so much plan the work in the factory from April onwards, it planned them. Farmers are notorious for leaving equipment lying around in the corners of fields or in old barns until they need to use it again, by which time it had rusted up or needed a new part, which should have been put on when it was last used. As a result farm carts, grain lorries and other vehicles started to arrive with equipment on them needing repair and overhaul for use in the forthcoming haymaking. It was all hands to the pumps. Fred speedily engaged a blacksmith and mate and a fitter and mate and he and Harry got their hands dirty as well, so they kept the jobs going out. They had both gradually got used to using the telephone although of course most of the smaller farmers and smallholders had no phones, they either used to just arrive or send a postcard. Jack had engaged a middle-aged spinster lady, Miss Gladys Russell, with engineering office experience to deal with the paperwork and wages and she turned out to be a gem. Her main problem was she couldn't make up her mind who she fancied more, the big bluff younger man Mr Hooper or the tall wiry, handsome Mr Chandler who was a bit older than her. Young Harry was nice, he pulled her leg mercilessly and she thoroughly enjoyed it.

So by dint of late hours and hard work they got a reputation during the summer of turning out good work on time. Jack came in from time to time and even got his hands dirty on a number of occasions. Every Friday afternoon they had a management meeting and every month a board meeting, which their accountant Reg Church was invited to attend. Towards the end of the summer Fred said, "From a sales point of view do you think we ought to plan our next year's strategy both as regards the range of products we should sell, and agencies we should apply for?"

The accountant, being an accountant, immediately said, "As you'll have to borrow to finance any major stock items don't forget to take the interest into account on your final selling price, and where you've got to sell at a set advertised price that's got to come off your gross profit."

By now Fred was getting used to all this jargon, usually staying quiet in the background while Jack and Reg settled everything to do with money.

"Perhaps we can get some extended credit terms from the manufacturers?" said Fred.

"That's a point," said Jack.

"The thing to do is get sixty days and sell it in thirty days," said Reg.

"Knowing farmers that's wishful thinking," said Fred, "But you're right, we can always try. Anyway the first thing is to establish what we're going to sell, we've proved our repair work can make money, now we've got to establish which machines will sell and make money, and wherever possible become a sole distributor."

After a long discussion, lasting well into the evening, they decided their main objective must be to establish a tractor agency, and Jack elected to initiate enquiries in the next week or so and report back at the next meeting, hopefully with sufficient information to be able to conclude a deal.

"What about visiting the County Show?" said Fred. "Not only to see what's around but, also with a view to exhibiting next year. The next one is early September."

"Let's go to that, and to the Royal, we're at the learning stage and the more we see the better it will be. Can you come as well Reg? Do you good to get out in the fresh air."

Reg readily agreed so it was left to Fred to get the tickets and to arrange their overnight stay at Warwick for the Royal.

When Fred got home to a late dinner kept warm for him, he told Ruth he was leaving her.

"Leaving me?" she said in astonishment.

"Yes, now I'm a businessman I'm leaving you."

"Fred Chandler, if you don't stop your games I'll tip your dinner in the bin."

"It's no game. I'll be leaving you. Only one night, but I don't want you to get up to anything while I'm gone."

She started playfully pummelling him, "Oh you fool, I wondered what you were on about."

He had by now put his arms around her in a most unusual demonstration of affection for him, and was cuddling her up. "I think I'd better make sure before I go that you won't want to get up to anything while I'm gone. I know it's a month or more away but perhaps I'd better make a start now," stroking her bottom with one hand and holding her tight with the other.

"Fred, what on earth's got into you?" she said, laughing and thoroughly enjoying this unusual behaviour. At that moment the kitchen door opened and in walked Megan and Harry.

"Hallo, hallo," said Harry, "what's all this going on in the kitchen of all places?"

Ruth pulled away. "Your father's going off his head."

"Well it didn't look like that to us," said Harry. "I reckon you've been leading him on again and he suddenly got wild with passion. It's always the women that leads the men on isn't it Dad?"

"Oh come in and sit down and shut up," said Ruth, still flushed but laughing with them.

"Well, we've got a bit of news," said Harry.

Both Fred and Ruth looked at both of them intently.

"Megan and I are going to get married."

Everybody started talking at once and after handshakes and kisses peace resumed.

"We couldn't wish for Harry to have a better, or for that matter prettier wife than you Megan and we wish you all the happiness in the world," said Fred.

"I'm going down with Megan to Carmarthen at the weekend," said Harry, "to formally ask her parents' permission. I've been excused drill. Can I have Friday afternoon and Saturday morning off? I shall come back on Sunday night ready for work Monday, although Megan is staying on for a few days holiday."

"Yes, of course you can have the time off, you've earned it with all the extra time you've put in over these last three or four months."

Ruth stood up. "I'm going to call the children," she said, "they'll be thrilled."

And thrilled they were. Rose learnt she was to be a bridesmaid, and the wedding would be in Carmarthen the following Easter.

"This calls for a drink," said Fred. "David, pop round to Mr Hooper on your bike and ask him if he and Pat can come over to see us – don't tell them what it is about."

A few minutes later the Daimler arrived in the driveway closely followed by David on his bike.

"What's the matter Fred? – Anything wrong?" said Jack almost running into the room with Pat and David on his heels.

"Quite the reverse, you are part of the family and we wanted you to be present to hear that Megan and Harry are going to be married."

"Hurray," boomed Jack, hugging Megan and pumping Harry's hand. "Now when and where?"

He having been given all the details Megan then said, "Pat, would you like to be a bridesmaid?" Pat was as thrilled as Rose had been at this news.

"I've never been a bridesmaid," she said, "I shall love it."

The only drink they had was some Harvey's sherry and the usual quarts of Whitbread's Light Ale of which there was always a supply in the cupboard under the stairs. Toasts were drunk in good measure and then Fred said, "I'm hungry, I've had no dinner yet."

"Neither have I," said Jack.

"Well, there's enough here for both of you so you sit yourselves down while I shoo the others out into the drawing room," said Ruth, swiftly and expertly dishing up a casserole and vegetables which had been on the warming plate.

The men tucked into the food voraciously, every now and then sampling the Whitbread's.

"How can you drink beer with stew?" said Ruth.

"Whitbread's goes with everything," said Jack, "better than any of your continental wines I can tell you." After a pause he went on. "While we're here on our own I have something to tell you. I saw my solicitor yesterday and I'm suing for divorce. I haven't had either the heart or the guts to do it up until now, but I think it's time for me to rearrange my life and get things sorted out. After all Pat won't be with me a lot longer and if I leave it until she does go it will be too late for me to do anything."

"I'm sure Ruth and I feel you're doing exactly the right thing," said Fred, "but when you say it would be too late for you to do anything, what had you in mind? Do you think you might marry again?"

"Well I tell you both it was such a shock to my system when my wife went off, such a blow to my pride and self esteem as well for that matter, that I never thought I could ever have a relationship of that nature again, either physically or emotionally. Since I've got to know you people I've begun to realise that there is reality and normality to life and, yes, if I found the right person I would marry again."

"There's always Miss Russell at the factory," said Fred cheekily.

"Oh don't be so unkind," said Ruth.

They all laughed. "You were good enough to give me a reference for the building society," said Fred, "perhaps I can do the same for you on the marriage stakes." They laughed again.

"Let's join the others," said Ruth, slipping their almost spotless plates into the bowl in the sink, "unless you'd like some cold tart with cream, or cheese.

"Not me," said Jack, "I'm full to bursting."

"Me too," said Fred, and they wandered into the dining room.

Pat and David were seated on the settee, lightly holding hands. Rose was sitting on the floor by Megan's armchair, the three girls talking about the colour of the bridesmaids' dresses and what headdresses they would have, whilst David and Harry just listened to their excited talk. Seeing Pat and David together Jack thought, they never seemed to get out of sorts with each other, as I'm sure I used to with girls when I was their age. My crushes never lasted more than two or three weeks, but they don't seem to have a crush on each other and yet there didn't seem to be passion either that you would expect from older teenagers. Then he realised they were only fourteen, perhaps they were in that marvellous situation of being in love with each other without actually knowing anything of what love was all about, in fact possibly not knowing they were even in love but thought of themselves as being very dear friends. Whatever it was it was not providing any problems either for them or their parents. He had discussed the situation briefly with Fred on one or two occasions, but Fred had reasoned as he did that 'they were two lovely kids who liked being together and there was nothing for anybody at least for the present to be concerned about'.

At last Megan said, "I'm afraid it's time for me to be back at the nurses' quarters or I'll be shot at dawn."

They all stood up and Jack said, "It's been a long day today for all of us I fancy, but I will say this, as far as Pat and I are concerned it's one of the happiest days we've had in a long time."

"And so say all of us," Fred concurred.

They all went off in their various directions and Rose and David went to bed leaving Fred and Ruth in the drawing room.

"Cup of cocoa before we go up?"

"That's not a bad idea."

They sat drinking their cocoa until Fred said, "What are you thinking about?" naturally assuming Ruth had got the prospects of a wedding and even eventually being a granny on her mind.

"I was just thinking whether we could afford a telephone."

"You never fail to surprise me, what do you want a telephone for, there's always the post and telegrams if you are in a hurry."

"If I had a telephone I could call you at the factory, you could call me if you were going to be late, you could telephone me when you go to the Royal."

"And if a fella answers what do I do then?" he said laughingly.

"No I do think we should have one, then the family can always get in touch with us no matter where they are."

"Organise it on Monday," said Fred, "and now what about this fella who's going to visit you and find he's not needed anymore?" and he led her up to bed.

Chapter Ten

When David went back to school for the September term it was with a sad heart. He had got used to seeing Pat almost daily, but at the weekend he had had to wave goodbye to her with all the rest of the family when Jack drove her away to Gloucester in the Daimler. It would be Christmas before he saw her again and Christmas seemed such a long way off. Once he got to school, where every hour of every day was mapped out, and back home in the evening where homework had become even more demanding, he had little time to think of anything or anybody, only the job in hand.

He had done well in the previous year, up in the top five as usual, but his aptitude for German was so pronounced that Dr Carew had called him in and told him he was going to put him up a form for this subject. In other words instead of being in the fourth form he would join the fifth form for German. He found he'd been made captain of the under XV rugby team and was in the house 1st, so both Wednesday and Saturday afternoons were taken up with sport.

In the meantime Harry was making good progress in the Terriers. Having finished basic drill he had started to learn to drive three tonners, and during the August camp, at which he had missed Megan so much he had proposed a few days after his return, he had been on a basic engine maintenance and repair course which he not only found interesting but also would find very useful at Sandbury Engineering. Very soon now they would get a decision on their tractor distributorship, and other equipment and he was looking forward to getting his overalls off and getting out on the road. The summer had shown they could almost cover their costs with repairs and servicing alone, but of course that would drop off somewhat during the winter, and that's where the equipment sales would come into their own. He and Megan had started house hunting and just before Christmas they came upon a nice end of terrace cottage, a little larger than usual, two-up-two-down with a small extra bedroom, which Harry said he could make into a bathroom.

"I'm not going back to the tin bath like we used to have in the wash house at Home Farm," he said. A feature of the cottage was it had a nice lawned garden running along down to the river which ran on through Sandbury, and was not overlooked in any way, except of course on one side by the next door neighbours. The asking price was £460 and though they haggled they couldn't knock the owner down. They got in touch with the nice young man from the Woolwich Equitable with whom Fred had dealt, and with £60 down and the balance on a twenty-five year mortgage in their case, it was all settled for them to take possession on March quarter day, and to move in after their honeymoon the week after Easter.

Pat came home at Christmas and David and she were as inseparable as always. However, one little cloud did appear on the horizon, when Pat said they had had a number of social occasions when senior boys from a well-known public school nearby were invited to tea dances at the Young Ladies College. She had happened to mention, 'Gerald said this, Gerald said that', on a couple of occasions and with a little pang of jealousy inside him very carefully concealed he asked almost too casually, "Who is this Gerald then?"

"Oh, he's the son of Lord Coleford and when we have these tea dances, which presumably are designed for us to practise our social graces, he always seeks me out because he's tall and likes to dance with me."

"How old is he?"

"Seventeen or eighteen, I should think."

"You tell him to watch it, and what's more tell him that I've got the best left uppercut in the southern counties."

She smiled and squeezed his arm.

They spent all Christmas together at Chandlers Lodge, Jack taking them all out again on Boxing Day evening. On Boxing Day afternoon after a very filling cold lunch the grownups were sitting in the drawing room when Jack said, "What do you think of this Hitler fellow in Germany Fred?"

"There's no doubt in my mind the blighter means war," said Fred. "He's been in power now for nine months and from what I read and hear on the wireless he is carrying out a campaign of working up the German people with constant warnings of threat to them by the Bolsheviks, by which he means not only the Russians but also the four million communists who voted against him in the March election this year. The gaols are so full of communists and left wing sympathisers I hear they're building special camps for them, like we did for the Boers in South Africa. As for the Jews, they have become the scapegoats for everything that Germany has suffered from the year dot as far as I can see."

"Yes," said Jack. "I know several important Jewish people in the city, and they are very worried about the state of affairs in what has always been considered a cultured country. When Goebbels came to power in March he issued orders that German firms were immediately to dismiss all Jewish employees, Jewish firms employing non-Jewish staff were to dismiss them with two months pay. All Jewish newspapers were to be boycotted, judges sacked and Jewish doctors had to have their surgery doors painted one colour, yellow I believe, and non-Jewish doctors had to paint their doors a different colour. But the thing that frightens them most is the speech by Streicher, one of the top Nazi bosses, who said in front of a rally of eighty thousand people in Berlin – 'The day is at hand when humanity will at last be freed from the eternal Jew' – or words to that effect. The top Jews here are in no doubt that the ferocity with which their German counterparts have been dealt with right at the beginning of the Nazi regime leaves no doubt in their minds as to what their final intentions are – liquidation of the lot."

"Oh come now," said Fred, "you and I know the Germans, they wouldn't sink to that level."

"Well I wouldn't have thought so. All I can tell you is that these people think they will."

After a pause for thought, "And another thing, this racial theory of Aryan superiority, this master race concept they go on about, the bottom of the pile as they see it are the Jews and Niggers, as they put it. During the war in East Africa from 1914 onwards von Bulow commanded a German army consisting almost entirely of black Askaris and they fought like demons for three and a half years against British and South African troops pinning down tens of thousands of soldiers who otherwise would have been on the Western Front. I think Mr Hitler must have a short memory about Niggers, or perhaps he doesn't know where Africa is."

"But what makes you think he will want to start another war?" said Ruth.

"I think there are several basic reasons. The first is that the German Army never believed it was beaten in 1918; they always maintained the German civilians were starved into submission. Secondly they openly declare they need more living space and they want all German peoples to be united. That means the Saar, Austria and bits of Czechoslovakia and Poland partitioned off by the Treaty of Versailles will all come under German control. We have a treaty with Poland, if Germany moves in and we uphold the treaty we're at war again."

"Well let's have no more about war, its Christmas remember," said Ruth.

"All I hope is there isn't a war for a very long time. The state we're in at the moment we couldn't punch the air out of a paper bag let alone clout the German army," said Fred.

"I agree with you there," said Jack.

Changing the subject he continued, "By the way have you read about that 'Home Television' machine that chap Baird has invented?" Fred said he had read a bit about it in the paper. Baird apparently had demonstrated an improved version of his original invention of the previous year, and had broadcast a picture nine inches by four inches. The unit was used in conjunction with a wireless set which carried the sound. This new development ran off the electric mains instead of batteries.

"Just think," said Fred, "you won't have to go to the pictures anymore to see the newsreels, you'll be having the pictures in your own house."

"I'll believe it when I see it," said Ruth. The day did come when she did see it, but a very great deal had to happen to her and her family before that day eventually arrived.

At the factory things were beginning to move. In the three months after the Royal, Jack and Fred had visited the Ford Motor Company at their head office in Regent Street, and then went to Dagenham to see tractors being made. As a result of these visits and after a visit by a Ford representative to Sandbury they were appointed distributors for the Fordson tractor in the area. They decided to order six in the first instance for delivery February 1st. The new models sold at £156 each, and they had to be able to provide a good level of service for prospective buyers. They sold the first six in the first three weeks. In the meantime they had negotiated a similar deal with other suppliers of ploughs, harrows, seed drills and other equipment for arable land as well as tedders, rakes and elevators for haymaking.

Next to the factory there was a field, unused except for haymaking. It was about four acres.

"It wouldn't be a bad idea to buy that to demonstrate the equipment," said Fred, "if funds will run to it."

As it happened it was a divorced bit of land as far as the owner was concerned, the main part of his property being some half a mile away, so when approached he asked a reasonable price and Reg Church raised the funds and they bought it. This purchase was to be very significant in later years.

Easter approached and with it the excitement over the wedding. The wedding was on Easter Saturday, Megan was travelling down on the Wednesday and the remainder were to go down in the Daimler on Good Friday. "Better get some extra cans of petrol in," said Fred, "I don't suppose there will be any garages open on Good Friday."

Harry had his stag night on the Wednesday night and elected to have it at the Prince of Orange back in Mountfield. In addition to all his old pals in the village and Jack and Fred, a number of his Territorial Army friends were invited, including the sergeant who once they got to know him turned out to be not nearly as fearsome as he had first made himself out to be. Crownie had been tipped the wink and had told Frank

Lovell the landlord that he wouldn't be around that way until after midnight anyway. It was a riotous evening. Frank had laid on snacks of pork pies, pickles, sandwiches, and the beer flowed like Niagara Falls!

Halfway through the evening Jack had said, "One of us has got to keep a clear head so it had better be me."

To which Harry had replied, already well away, "we can always walk home."

"Is that what they do in the Service Corps?" said Fred – "Walk!!! In the Hampshires they bloody well march!!!"

"So they do in our lot," said the sergeant. "Fall in you lot," and he got them 'fell in', into two files at one end of the bar. "By the left quick march," reaching the other end, "about turn," all the time the Terriers were singing their regimental march, or at least singing a tune, the words were rather less than regimental.

"Wait for the wagon the donkey wants a..."
Wait for the wagon we'll all have a ride.
Wait for the wagon wait for the wagon
Wait for the wagon we'll all have a ride."

The locals with Jack, Fred and Frank Lovell looked on in hysterics and when the sergeant halted them a tremendous burst of applause arose that they swore could be heard in the Fox and Hounds half a mile away.

They took Harry home at about midnight and poured him into bed. Fred wasn't much better, Jack was noticeably three sheets in the wind and Ruth, who had waited up for them, said, "Goodness what a sorry looking lot you are, I wouldn't like to have any one of your heads tomorrow morning."

And right she was. Fred crawled down at 8 o'clock, Harry didn't surface till nearly ten but by lunchtime and after a livener apiece they agreed it had been a memorable party. They set off very early on Good Friday morning making their way to London and then Northwest to the A40, to Oxford, Gloucester, Monmouth and past the smoky valleys of South Wales to arrive at their hotel in Carmarthen at teatime. The Daimler laden though it was covered two hundred and fifty odd miles without a murmur. They stopped at lunchtime to eat sandwiches and coffee they had brought with them knowing the likelihood of getting food on the way on Good Friday was remote, and from time to time they stopped 'to water the horses' as Jack succinctly put it. The weather was fine and to all of them except Jack, who had all the driving to do, it was a most enjoyable and interesting experience.

That evening it had been arranged that Megan's parents would come to the hotel after dinner to meet Fred and Ruth and the others. Megan's father Trefor was a hefty six-footer with a deep bass voice, an ex-Welsh Guardsman who had been 'knocked about a bit' as he put it, during the war. He had been wounded no fewer than on four separate occasions, in fact as he said, "they used to have a bed reserved for me," accompanied by a deep resounding, most infectious laugh, that could be heard throughout the hotel. Megan's mother Elizabeth on the other hand was quite the opposite – small and dainty, dressed like a bandbox, and with a beautiful lilting voice in which you could hear Megan all the time, she captivated them all.

"Well I can see where Megan gets her beauty from," said Fred gallantly when they were all seated. This surprised Ruth; Fred wasn't the type to go around passing compliments, particularly when he had only newly met someone.

"Our Megan got her good looks and poise from me I'll have you know," joked Trefor.

"You're too big for me to argue with," said Fred, "so lets say I'll just reserve my judgement."

It was obvious that they were all going to get on like a house on fire. They told the Chandlers how they had instantly taken to Harry when he first visited them. "Nervous as a kitten he was mind," said Trefor "but he soon got used to us." The Lloyds farmed about two hundred and fifty acres a few miles out of the city towards St Clears, so were reasonably comfortably off.

"When are you going back?" said Trefor.

"That brings back memories," said Jack. "Do you remember when you came on leave in the army, the first question you were asked when you walked in the house was – when are you going back?"

They all laughed at this, although it is very true as any old soldier can testify.

"We're going back on Monday," said Jack.

"Right, since we'll all be busy tomorrow and won't have much time to talk let's arrange Sunday. How about if you come out to us at say 10 o'clock for a big farmhouse breakfast. The drive to the farm will clear the wedding cobwebs out of your heads. Then after breakfast we can go down to Tenby, provided the weather's alright mind – it's less than an hour's run. It's a lovely place is Tenby when the weather's nice."

So it was arranged, and with the evening getting on they decided they'd break up and look forward to seeing each other the next day at the church. "If you've forgotten any collar studs or anything get on the telephone and we'll bring them in with us," joked Trefor, his booming laugh echoing through the foyer.

The Saturday of the wedding was a glorious mild day. They all ate a leisurely breakfast and then went out for a stroll around the centre of the city. The wedding was set for two o'clock, so at 11.30 Ruth and the two bridesmaids went to their rooms to start to get ready for the big occasion. After a drink at the bar the two men went up and after a certain amount of suppressed bad language managed to get into their morning suits hired from the Moss Bros agent in Sandbury. Jack went along and knocked on Ruth and Fred's door and, on being told to come in, said to Ruth, "Where's Fred?" who of course was standing there looking at him. Ruth pointed in Fred's direction smiling hugely. "That's never Fred is it?" said Jack walking round and round the man in question. "My word, you wait till I show his picture back at the Prince of Orange – he'll never live it down."

"Well I must say," said Ruth, "you must be the two handsomest men in South Wales today."

"What about North Wales?" said Fred.

"May I say Mrs Chandler," said Jack in his most gallant voice, "you look so utterly charming that if you weren't already spoken for I'd take you away from all this myself."

"Oh get away with you. Now I'm off to see that the girls are alright and we'll meet you downstairs in the foyer. In the meantime you'd better check on Harry – and that doesn't mean liquid support either. The car is coming for us at 1.20 so don't get lost anywhere."

Ruth found the two girls bubbling with excitement and looking very pretty. She made each one sit down in turn and arranged their hair and then went through with them again the procedure of the wedding, what they were to do and what to be careful not to do. Jack and Fred in the meantime had knocked on Harry's door and found him sitting on his bed and obviously in some degree of agitation.

"I know what you need," said Fred, and they took him downstairs to the bar.

"I mustn't breathe all over the parson," said Harry.

"One quick one won't be noticed, and anyway you can always breathe out of the corner of your mouth."

"That means he'll either be breathing whisky over Megan or over me," Jack pointed out.

Harry had pondered long over who to ask to be his Best man. He wanted Jack to be the one but he had somehow thought that Jack might think he was being presumptuous. In the event he asked Jack and Jack was utterly delighted to accept. "You could breathe upwards," said Fred, "like this," and he proceeded to stick his lower lip out and breathe upwards over his nose. The barman was listening to all this with amusement and when Fred started the demonstration he roared with laughter, several other people at the bar turned to join in the amusement and the barman had to tell them why Fred was pulling such an unusual face. One of the bystanders suggested that conversely he could breathe downwards, he would still look a bit peculiar but not as bad as blowing upwards, and in next to no time they were all trying out the best way to breathe.

At last one of the participants said, "Is the Reverend Griffiths conducting the service?" and on being told that he was, he said, "You've got no need to worry because he will be in the Feathers this very minute having a few so he wouldn't even notice if you've drunk a bottle full."

Harry shook the gentleman by the hand, "Sir, I don't know your name but you have saved my life. Dad, I'll have a double."

"And only one my lad," said Fred ordering it up, and including one for the lifesaver.

"There's an extraordinarily pretty lady trying to catch your eye from the door sir," said the lifesaver pulling Fred's sleeve. It was Ruth miming him that the car had arrived. The men drank up, said their goodbyes to their new friends and went out into the foyer.

"My word, don't you all look beautiful," said Harry to his mother and two girls, and they really did look an absolute picture, creating no small amount of interest from people coming in and out of the hotel. They went out and down the steps and there waiting for them was a gleaming Rolls Royce, fitted with wide white silk ribbons and having a liveried chauffeur holding the door open for them.

"Crikey, Trefor Lloyd's pushed the boat out," said Fred, "Rolls Royces!!"

"If he's got that sort of money perhaps we can sell him a couple of tractors while we're here," said Harry as the men stood waiting for the ladies to be carefully seated so that they did not crease their dresses. With the two men sitting on the occasionals, David squeezed in between and with Harry up front with the chauffeur, they moved noiselessly away to the church where a number of the guests had already arrived, including Megan's mother who began to make introductions which they all immediately forgot, but which in one or two cases were to be very much remembered later.

On the short journey to the church David was feeling just a little bit out of it all. Whilst walking in the town he was with Pat, but Rose was occupying her time to a large extent. The two men included him from time to time in their conversation and so did his mother, but nevertheless he had the slightly off-putting feeling that he was the odd one out. He was wearing his best school uniform for the wedding and rather wished that he too could have a morning suit, at fifteen years of age he rather wanted to be a man rather than an over grown schoolboy. Little did he know that as he sat between the two men and thinking along these lines, his mother seated behind was thinking the same thing. "We should have got David a morning suit. He's such a fine built boy it would have suited him down to the ground. Oh well, it's too late now, but it's a pity all the same."

Elizabeth Lloyd started to usher people into the church. There were four bridesmaids altogether, two of Megan's cousins who were each about eight years old, and Pat and Rose who would be bringing up the rear. They waited in the porch. As David walked into the church he thought of all those weddings at which he'd sung at Mountfield and the wonderful music that Miss Parnell used to play. He whispered to his mother, "I must go and see Miss Parnell soon."

His mother intuitively knew what was going on in his mind and squeezed his arm, "Yes dear you really must."

The choir filed in and David was surprised to see some twenty-four boys and an equal number of men – his choir at Mountfield would have been lucky to get half that number. The organist had stopped playing and was looking in his rear view mirror for the signal from the usher to start the music for the bride's entry. He was an old hand at this game and wasn't at all flustered when the signal was slow in coming. Harry however had to force himself not to look around, as every second's silence seemed like a minute.

Whisper, "Have you got the ring?"

Whisper, "No, I've pawned it."

Startlingly the first chord thundered out and the procession made it's way down the aisle. Trefor Lloyd was the proudest man in Wales that day, until at least after the ceremony when the claim could justifiably be made by Harry, his new son-in-law. The congregation eager to know what the bride and bridesmaids were wearing, but trying not to make it too obvious, gave gasps of admiration at the picture they made as they walked slowly down the chancel steps. Megan was radiant in a dress of white slipper satin. It had a boat shaped neck and fitted bodice, which showed her figure to perfection. The back of the dress had an inverted pleat from just below the waist, making a fishtail which fell into a small train, the smaller of the bridesmaids walking at the sides and the older girls coming up at the rear. On her head the bride wore a simple wreath of orange blossom with a veil attached worn over her face and which would be thrown back when she left the church. She had a most tastefully assembled bouquet of white stephinosis, lilies of the valley, white carnations and soft yellow and white freesias. The two smaller bridesmaids wore dresses in soft butter yellow and they had garlands of yellow and white daisies on their heads. These were matched with posies of the same flowers, with two matching ribbon streamers. The older girls wore the same soft butter yellow dresses, gathered slightly at the waist, around which was fitted a matching ribbon. Again they had yellow and white daisies in garlands in their hair but they wore long white gloves whereas the younger girls wore short white gloves.

The whole picture was one of beauty and taste, which brought tears to many eyes not least to Ruth and Elizabeth. The ceremony went without a hitch. The photos afterwards were taken in the usual atmosphere of organised chaos, and eventually the bride and groom were whisked away through a virtual storm of confetti.

For the reception the guests all moved back to the ballroom at the hotel where Ruth and the family were staying. As Best man Jack made an excellent MC, Trefor Lloyd made a witty booming speech thanking everyone for helping to make this a great day. Harry was loudly cheered when he stood up to speak and said, "My wife and I," and cheered again when he gave each of the bridesmaids chased silver bracelets as a memento of the occasion.

When the guests first arrived back from the church and were sipping a glass of champagne, before being seated Elizabeth Lloyd had called to Jack and said, "Oh Jack, I'd like you to meet my sister Moira. Particularly as she will be seated next to you on the top table."

"Well I couldn't wish for more charming company," said Jack gallantly. Moira was taller and a little fuller in the figure than Elizabeth and Jack estimated probably a couple of years younger. She did however have the same classic good looks as Megan and Elizabeth and the same beautiful lilting voice possessed by the other two. Jack noticed she wore a wedding ring and assumed her husband was among the other guests. After a few pleasantries they were asked to be seated. At the table the gentlemen on the other side of Moira, who was quite a bit older than her, seemed to direct very little conversation in her direction, talking mainly to a matronly lady on his right. Jack opened the conversation with "Do you and your husband live in Carmarthen?" nodding towards the man on her right.

She gave a pealing little laugh. "Oh, he isn't my husband, this is Uncle Freddy," at which Uncle Freddy turned towards Jack and they shook hands across Moira.

"I do apologise I got it all wrong. I should have realised," said Jack in some embarrassment.

Moira smiled at him and said, "I should have told you my husband was killed in the last days of the war. He was nineteen and I was eighteen when we married, and all we had were two weeks together at the beginning of 1918."

"Oh how awful," said Jack, finding he had quite involuntarily put his hand on hers on the table, "I really am sorry, I shouldn't have asked, on today of all days."

She looked down at his hand and then at him, and he realising his action swiftly withdrew it and looked around to se if anyone else had noticed. They apparently hadn't.

"It's a long time ago now, so don't apologise, in any event I told you, you didn't ask me."

The proceedings interrupted their conversation so that when eventually it resumed there was no strangeness between them. After the wedding breakfast and speeches there was a break before the dancing and cutting the cake during which Elizabeth said, "How did you get on with Moira?" with a little smile on her lips.

"Marvellously," said Jack and then asked, "She told me about her husband being killed – how dreadful," and then almost too casually, "is she attached at all now?"

Elizabeth teased him on, "Attached – in which way do you mean Jack?"

Jack was getting a little flustered, "Well I mean has she a gentlemen friend or anything like that?"

"Oh we don't do that sort of thing in Wales Jack," she said.

"You're teasing me," he said looking down into her eyes. "Is it as obvious as that?"

She put her hands on his forearm. "Only to me Jack. To answer your question, no she hasn't a gentleman friend to my knowledge, tho' Lord knows why, she really is very attractive."

Jack looked across the room to where Moira was talking to David. "Yes she is, she's devilishly attractive."

"Well you'll get to know her better tomorrow. She's staying with us and coming with us to Tenby."

At this bit of information Jacks heart raced, and he found he was saying to himself, 'Act your age you lunatic, you're not a seventeen-year-old', but all he said to Elizabeth was, "I shall look forward to that."

In the meantime David had sought Pat out and told her how beautiful she looked and how well she marshalled the bridesmaids. When Pat said, "Shall we dance?" David suddenly had a moment's panic. He had never had dancing lessons; in fact he'd never been on a dance floor in his life. When he told Pat this she said, "Now, don't worry, one of the things we are taught at college is how to dance with people that can't dance, and the thing to do is not to try to keep in time with the music and do the fancy steps that the know-alls do, but just move together like this," and she showed him the simple way of just getting around the floor. To himself he decided that he would find out about dancing lessons when he got back to Sandbury – he had no intention of bloody Gerald upstaging him.

The evening sped past and at nine o'clock the bride and groom disappeared to change into their going away clothes. They planned to stay at the Grand in Swansea overnight and then go on for the remainder of their week's honeymoon in London. To the clatter of tin cans tied to the rear bumper of the car and to the cheers of the guests, they drove away. Everyone waved furiously whilst Mr and Mrs Harry Chandler waved back out of the small rear window of the Rolls Royce, which was to take them to their hotel. Gradually the party thinned out. "Don't forget ten o'clock breakfast," boomed Trefor.

Jack solemnly shook hands with Moira with, "Look forward very much to seeing you tomorrow," and thinking to himself, 'couldn't you have found something a bit more intelligent to say?' She smiled sweetly. She had a firm friendly hand, which he held perhaps a fraction longer than he should have done.

Going up to their rooms up the broad staircase, the leg pulling started. "That Moira seems a very pleasant young woman," said Fred, "you got your eye on her Jack?"

At this Pat spun round, "What's all this Dad? I didn't notice anything."

Ruth said solemnly in reply to Pat's question, "What it was Pat, this Moira was on her own, and being lonely and vulnerable among all we rough people your father had to look after her. The fact that she's very pretty and a widow to boot had nothing whatsoever to do with it. That's why he had to stay close to her all the evening."

They were now all grinning. Fred chimed in. "And I understand tomorrow she's been given the front seat in the Daimler when we go to Tenby so that she can show Jack the way."

"Oh has she dear?" said Ruth; "I do hope Jack can keep his eyes on the road. Do you think we should all go in the other car for safety's sake?"

"I'm sure Jack wouldn't mind," said Fred.

All of this later conversation had been going on as if Jack wasn't there, he by now also grinning widely. "Well," he said, "I confess to you all that I found Mrs Evans very pleasant to be with. I shall enjoy her company tomorrow, as I will enjoy the company of all of you, but since she lives in Cardiff and I live in Kent I don't somehow think our paths would cross that often."

They had a glorious afternoon at Tenby where, having taken a couple of hours over their breakfast, and the journey taking just under an hour, they arrived at one o'clock. The weather was fine and sunny but still a little chilly. They had a lovely walk along the sands and then tea in one of the few cafés open at that time of year. They drove back to Trefor Lloyd's farmhouse, a low rambling stone built group of buildings set into the side of a hill. Elizabeth had a kitchen help who had come in especially on the Sunday for their guests and had prepared a buffet supper for them.

"We can't have them going back home hungry can we?" she had said to her family.

"I'm sure I've put on a stone since Friday afternoon," said Ruth.

"Nonsense," said Trefor. "You've a lovely trim figure any woman would be proud of."

"I'm inclined to agree with Ruth," said Fred. "I had to let my belt out a notch after that breakfast this morning, so Lord knows what it will be like after this,"– waving his hand at a table groaning with the food being piled on to it.

All day Jack had been increasing his friendship with Moira. He had established that she was a senior civil servant in, of all places, the War Department. Having asked her what she did she said that she didn't want to appear secretive or silly, but a number of things she did involved matters of national security, whereas other parts of her work didn't. However, she had always made it a rule that she didn't talk about details of her work at all, in that way she wouldn't inadvertently say something that was forbidden. Jack said he quite understood. During the course of the evening she mentioned that her work necessitated coming to London for two or three days each month. At this Jacks eye's sparkled like a Catherine wheel on bonfire night, and without a moment's hesitation he jumped in with, "On your next visit will you meet me so that we can have dinner together, or go to a theatre or whatever?" and then, a little embarrassed at his impetuosity he added, "that's if you're not already engaged of course."

She was not already engaged, she would be delighted and would telephone him a day or so before her next visit in about three weeks time. Jack had not felt this pleased with himself in years.

It was a lovely supper party during which David had said to Trefor, "Sir, wasn't that choir marvellous yesterday."

Trefor boomed, "Choir! I tell you my boy they're third division compared to some of the choirs around here. To give them credit they're very good compared to a lot of church choirs, but if you love choirs you must come down and stay with us for a while and I will take you to hear choirs that will make your blood tingle in your veins one minute, make you cry your eyes out the next and then make you want to fight the whole German army on your own after that. We've got choirs down here that could raise the dome of St Paul's, and yet I've heard a thousand voices singing so quietly you could hardly hear them and still you could understand each word – a thousand of them and you could hear every word!" he repeated.

"Now you've got Mr Lloyd on his hobby horse," said Elizabeth to David, "Do you like music – who's your favourite?"

"Well I was brought up on church music, but when we got the

wireless I started listening to Mozart, Beethoven and the others. I think most of all I like Mozart, but listening to Bach at full blast on the church organ sends shivers all down my spine."

And so the conversation continued until eventually Ruth said, "You know it's nearly midnight and we've got an early start tomorrow."

"What time are you leaving?"

"We plan to leave after breakfast at nine o'clock."

"Nine o'clock it is then, we shall come and wave you goodbye."

The next morning, Easter Monday, the Lloyds duly arrived at a quarter to nine bearing two huge bunches of daffodils. "Picked this morning – real Welsh ones they are – best in the world." Just after nine o'clock they climbed into the Daimler after much handshaking, hugging and kissing and with a long deep look from Jack into the eyes of Moira, they drove out of the coaching yard on to the road to London.

"What a wonderful weekend," said Ruth.

"Yes," said Jack, "What a wonderful weekend."

Chapter Eleven

On his first week back at school after the holidays, David was told he had to go and see the Headmaster. His first thoughts were, 'What have I done?' but he could think of no sin of either commission or omission. On being called in the Head told him to sit down, that in it self was unusual. Usually boys had to stand in front of the desk.

"Chandler, your German is coming on in leaps and bounds, you really are two forms ahead of the norm. This summer we have an opportunity of sending a boy to Ulm in Southern Germany to live for one month with a family, the father of which is the Headmaster of a similar school to Cantlebury. This will be an exchange arrangement whereby you will then invite the son of the Headmaster back to England for one month. I think you will gain enormously by going, but first of all we would like you to discuss it with your parents, particularly the question of having the other boy back. From a financial point of view your rail fare will be paid from a school fund raised specially for these types of exchanges, and secondly your lodgings will be free as you will ultimately accommodate the other boy. All you will have to find is a small amount of pocket money. I shall add that when you are in Germany you will not be aloud to speak any English; similarly the other boy will not speak German when he comes here. Do you understand all of that?"

[margin note: allowed]

"Yes sir."

"Very well then. Discuss it with your parents and come and see me straight after chapel the day after tomorrow."

David went home in some excitement and eagerly explained the details of the proposed exchange. Fred never hurried a decision so he said to David, "It sounds very interesting – your mother and I will talk about it this evening and let you know tomorrow."

They did discuss it that evening. As it happened Jack popped in to tell them how his divorce proceedings were going through. A date for the hearing had been set in the High Court for mid-May and both his solicitor and barrister had assured him there would be no hitches and that by the beginning of 1935 he would be a free man. Almost too casually he added, "Oh by the way Moira is in London next week and we are having dinner together."

"I don't know much about these things," replied Fred, "but I do know you have to be very careful whilst these proceedings are going on. I'm not making insinuations I hasten to add, but you do have to be very careful indeed."

"Point taken Fred. To be fair I haven't even had the opportunity to talk about the divorce to Moira. She knows my wife left me, but that's all she knows as far as I am aware. I propose telling her the full story when we meet next week. Now, what about David? What are you going to do?"

"Well Ruth and I think it would be a great opportunity for him, though to be honest I don't know what use knowing German inside out is going to be to him."

Little did Fred know that one day it would in fact save David's life, and the lives of several others.

Fred continued, "It's not as though it's going to cost much and it will be interesting having the German boy back here, we might find out a bit of what is really going on in the Third Reich at the moment. With all the propaganda flying about on both sides you don't know what to believe."

"So you'll let him go?"

"I think so, don't you Ruth?" She nodded assent thinking he often calls her Ruth these days, on the farm it was always mother.

"Well in that case I'd like to chip in ten quid towards his spending money – I owe him a hell of a lot more than that."

"You owe him? What do you owe him for?"

"If he hadn't had the guts to stop and talk to Pat I wouldn't have met you all. If he hadn't tackled the bull he wouldn't have gone into hospital and Harry wouldn't have met Megan. If Harry hadn't met Megan I wouldn't have met Moira – so he started it all didn't he?"

Fred and Ruth both thought there must be a flaw in that logic somewhere but they couldn't spot it so they laughingly agreed that Jack could chip in his tenner.

"That's settled then, and in addition he can borrow my camera and field glasses, they're quite good ones and he can come back and show us all the pictures."

"Oh Jack you are kind," said Ruth.

The next morning they gave David the go ahead and told him of Jack's kind offer, and on the following day David presented himself at the Headmaster's study to pass on his parents assent. Dr Carew said, "Well now, for the rest of this term I will have a German newspaper placed in the school library and will give instructions that at the end of each day you may take it home with you. I realise that with the amount of prep you have to do and with end of year exams coming up your reading time may be restricted, but if you can find the time it will prepare you for your visit, particularly with regards to knowing the names of the National Socialist Party leaders, the general situation in Germany at the moment and their attitudes to other countries beyond their borders."

David thanked Dr Carew very much and began to get excited at the thought of this new adventure. During the summer he took to reading the newspaper each night for a minimum of thirty minutes and found that more and more he was reading German without consciously changing it to English. His father had warned him to keep an open mind on what he read, since the press in Germany by now was strictly controlled. One thing for certain that he came to expect was that there would be at least one and usually two pictures of Herr Hitler in each copy, and an attack on either the Jews or the communists, either direct or indirect, on virtually every page – even the sports pages.

Jack had his first meeting with Moira in London and this was repeated during the summer. He got his decree without difficulty after a sworn affidavit was presented from an agent in Muar, Malaya stating that his wife was living as man and wife with a planter in that area. This meant that the decree absolute would be made sometime in January 1935. Ruth remarked on the change in Jack since he had met Moira, the sadness had left his eyes, and as far as they could tell from the two occasions he had brought her to see them, she too was very happy with the situation and much enjoyed being with Jack.

Harry and Megan had settled in at their cottage by the river. With the money they had saved before the wedding and the generous presents they had been given by both families, and by Jack and the others, they had furnished it tastefully. However there were several things they still had to buy, such as a wireless, electrical washtub and a settee and armchairs. They decided therefore to get these on hire purchase and Jack suggested two stores that he knew well. One was Chiesman's at Lewisham and the other Cuff's at Woolwich, both towns being within reasonable travelling distance from Sandbury and only a bus ride from each other. The following Saturday Megan was off duty, Harry asked for the morning off and off they went to Lewisham. Having seen what was available at Chiesman's they got the bus to Woolwich, and finally found themselves in Cuff's talking to a very knowledgeable young man named Mr Salmon for whom Jack had told them to ask. Jack had advised this gentleman that two newly married young friends of his were intending to visit the store, and he would be grateful for any help he could give them. Even so Harry thought for a young executive to devote time personally to them must be somewhat unusual, so during the course of their visiting the different departments Harry said, "I take it you know Mr Hooper quite well?" to which Mr Salmon replied, "His family and my family have been friends now for three generations. They have served together in the same ward in the city, they belong to the premier Livery Company, the Mercers, and are patrons of a number of charitable ventures in both the city and the East End of London. Mr

Hooper is of course a very wealthy man indeed, yet never flaunts his wealth in any way. He incidentally spoke very highly of both of you so you must know him quite well."

"He and my father own an engineering business," said Harry, "and I work for them."

"Well now, it's gone twelve o'clock, you must be starving if you've had nothing since you left Sandbury this morning. Excuse me a moment."

He beckoned to a floor manager, "Telephone Mr Scott at the Star and Garter and ask him to set a table for three in a quarter of an hour will you Mr Talbot – thank you." Turning to Megan and Harry again he said, "By the time we get there all should be ready."

They walked down through the store again and out into the bustling crowds in Powis Street. All manner of people thronged the street. Lascars, Chinese, Scandinavians, all sorts of men from the ships in the docks across the river.

"Certainly makes Sandbury look a bit slow doesn't it?" Harry said to Megan.

"I understand you are a nurse," said Mr Salmon. He's well informed Harry thought.

"Yes, it's only a small hospital and all our really serious cases are moved on to Maidstone or up to London."

"That's where we met," said Harry.

"You were in hospital?"

"No my younger brother was and I visited him, I saw Megan and that was that."

"Why was your brother there?"

By this time they had reached the Star and Garter and went through the saloon bar into the dining room, which was absolutely full except for a newly set table for three on the far side of the room. Mr Salmon acknowledged salutations from a number of people on his way to his table. It was obvious that although he was quite young he was well-known and respected. They were seated and had their order taken when Mr Salmon repeated his question, "Why was your brother there?"

David and the bull and Cantlebury then became the main topic of conversation during the excellent lunch provided by the Star and Garter, in the course of which the landlord Mr Scott, a huge man with equally huge white mutton chop whiskers, came over to see all was well. Mr Salmon, having introduced Megan and Harry as newlywed friends of his from out of town, thanked him profusely for his kindness in fitting them in on such a busy day, and Mr Scott withdrew only to reappear a moment or two later with a box containing a bottle of Courvoisier which he gave to Megan saying, "a belated wedding present – save a drop for the christening!" and with a bellow of laughter went back to his inner sanctum.

When they had been served coffee Harry called for the bill but Mr Salmon said that had already been taken care of, and that it was a privilege to entertain such nice people. Afterwards Harry said, "I think he fancied you."

"Oh don't be daft," said Megan, "he was just a very nice man."

They went back to the store and added up their proposed purchases to make sure they could afford the repayments. One of Mr Salmon's stalwarts was called to work it all out and eventually their purchases of a wireless, electrical tub, and various other small items came to £64.11.6.

"That will be a little over £3 per month so that's alright." He was assured they could manage that. Mr Salmon then beckoned the floor manager again and spoke to him quietly on one side. Returning again to Megan and Harry he said, "Now we deliver in Sandbury on a Wednesday, will next Wednesday be satisfactory?"

Upon being assured that it would be, Megan was on night duty next week – and upon the return of the floor manager with two parcels in his hands, he said, "now here is a small present from us as a wedding gift," and unwrapping one of the parcels presented them with a beautiful cut glass bowl.

"How gorgeous," exclaimed Megan. "You really have been so kind to us today, I just don't know what to say," and with that she took his hands and kissed him on the cheek, much to his embarrassment and the carefully concealed amusement of the floor manager.

Mr Salmon recovered his composure then said, "And here's a small present for your brother. He is obviously a very hard-working brave sort of chap and I hope this will be useful to him when he goes to Germany." He gave them a green linen knapsack with all sorts of pockets on the outside.

"David will be thrilled to bits with that," said Harry, taking Mr Salmon warmly by the hand.

"I do hope we see you again soon and do give my regards to Mr Hooper," said Mr Salmon as he walked them through the store back into Powis Street. "Goodbye, safe journey."

David was indeed thrilled with the knapsack as were the others at the account of their day at Woolwich when they all, including Jack, met for Sunday lunch at Chandlers Lodge next day.

"When are you off?" said Jack to David.

"On July 14th, all my tickets are arranged and Thomas Cook have given me an itinerary which sounds pretty foolproof."

"It would have to be if you're going to follow it," said Harry.

David lunged at his brother. Harry started sparring and before you could say Jack Robinson there was a mini free-for-all going on.

"Now stop it you two," said Ruth, and aside to Megan, "they never really grow up you know, you'll find that out."

"I think I already have," said Megan laughing.

Peace reigned and David was asked how he would get to Ulm.

"I have to get to Harwich from Liverpool Street and then on the night ferry to the Hook of Holland. From there by train to Cologne where I change for another train to Mannheim and then Ulm."

"How long does it take?" asked Megan.

"Well I leave here at 4 o'clock in the afternoon and I arrive in Ulm at about 7 o'clock the next evening."

"I hope it's a corridor train in that case," joked Harry.

"There is of course some waiting around at the change points," said David, "but I shall get some sleep on the boat. Mum is going to pack me lots of food and my seat is reserved all the way so I shouldn't run into any problems."

"Don't forget to send us all some postcards," said Megan, "we shall feel very important having foreign correspondence arriving."

"This would have given Snowy a field day Ruth wouldn't it?" Fred was referring to the Mountfield postman, but Jack wasn't in on this, so in answer to the question on his face Fred told him how Snowy would walk in and say, 'Letter from aunt in Winchester, how is she these days?'

The post in Sandbury was delivered by a man whose name they didn't even know and who had far too many postcards in his delivery to be able to stop and read them, "Unless they're rude ones from the seaside and then I bet he does," said Harry.

Chapter Twelve

July 14th arrived. Ruth, Fred and Rose went with David on the first leg to Liverpool Street and saw him off on the boat train. David had telephoned Pat the night before and she had warned him to beware of the blonde German mädchens, and to tell him she was going to miss him until he came back in the middle of August, then they could go riding again. Fred said afterwards to Ruth, "It's a good job he doesn't have to pay his own telephone bills, he'd have no money left for spending in Germany."

He found everything about the journey interesting. Everything was a new experience, the docks, being on what to him was a big ship and feeling the unaccustomed movement of the vessel as he lay in his bunk. Fortunately there was only a slight swell so, before he climbed back into his bunk, he ate some of the food which had been packed into his knapsack and which had all been carefully rationed out into different packages for the different times of the day. He bought a bottle of pop in the refreshment bar to wash it down and turned in as the boat was under way and moved out into the North Sea. He woke up to the noise of engines reversing, men shouting, hooting from other ships and there they were docking at the Hook. One of the pursers directed him to the Cologne train and he soon found his seat and sat back for the second part of this great adventure. He had bought a map upon which he had intended to follow his journey.

As they sped across Holland he saw the dykes and the huge canals he had read about and was struck by the flatness of the country compared to the rolling countryside of Kent. Soon they were at the frontier with Germany and here he had his first sight of the swastika armband, which became so commonplace over the next month. This was worn by a grim unsmiling immigration official who looked searchingly at the fifteen-year-old David. The customs official who followed him was more pleasant but still wore the inevitable armband.

Another English man in the carriage was heard to say, "The armband manufacturers must be making a fortune in Germany I should think,"only quickly to be hushed by his wife in case presumably he got himself locked up for saying things against the Third Reich. Then onto Cologne and a forty-five minute wait to change on to the train for Ulm via Mannheim.

David had had little chance to practise his German yet, since the people he had travelled with so far had been either Dutch or English. At Cologne however his new travelling companions were all German who treated him in a very friendly manner, asking where he was going, had he been to Germany before, remarking how good his German was and the usual sort of conversation that train travellers the world over indulge in. At points along the way his companions left him, and eventually he arrived at Ulm dead on time.

He clambered down from the train carrying his suitcase and wearing his knapsack and looking along the platform saw a group of people who instantly concluded he was the person they were looking for and moved towards him.

"Herr Chandler?" said the leader, a middle-aged scholarly looking man with pince-nez glasses.

"Ja Herr Doktor," said David and they shook hands warmly.

"This is my wife, this is Dieter my son and Inge my daughter." David shook hands with all three. He was to get used to shaking hands over the next month. It seemed to him the Germans were always shaking hands, whenever they came into a room or left a room they shook hands with everybody.

Dieter was a well-built boy, the same age, but not quite as tall as David. He was very fair and had a very nice open smiling face that made David feel sure they were going to get on well together. His sister Inge was a tall slender girl, probably about eighteen years old, again very fair, not strikingly beautiful, but with classical good looks and very blue eyes. Both obviously inherited their good looks from their mother who appeared somewhat younger than her husband. They moved off down the platform, Dieter carrying the suitcase, and out into the station yard where a large open-topped Mercedes was standing. The luggage stowed they drove off out of the city, dwarfed by the magnificent spire of the cathedral. "The tallest spire in the world," said Dieter proudly seeing David admiring it.

"Now you must not speak too quickly to David at first," said the doktor. "He must only speak German while he is here, but it is bound to be difficult until he gets a little more used to it. Not only that, he has learnt Schul Deutsch so our accent will be a little strange to him at first. By the time he goes home we'll have him talking like a native, South German accent included."

They drove about ten kilometres out of town and eventually arrived at the small village of Neudorf on the edge of which was the von Hassellbek house, lying back off the road behind a line of trees. It was a typical steeply roofed largish house along the front of which, the south side, ran a veranda on the first floor. Above this were three small sets of windows to smaller rooms contained in the roof, which were obviously extra bedrooms. The horizontal beams on the face of the building and the inverted V's over the upper windows were all beautifully decorated in red and green, giving the house a warm and welcoming look.

"What a magnificent house Herr Doktor," said David.

"It has been in my family for over two hundred years" said the doktor, "and I hope, will stay that way for another two hundred."

Having driven up to the front steps of the house David saw that standing to welcome them was an elderly couple, the lady in a spotless white starched apron. "This is Susanne and Hans," said Doktor van Hassellbek, "who will be helping to look after you while you are here." Susanne bobbed a little curtsey and Hans clicked his heels and gave a little bow.

"I am very pleased to meet you," said David, wondering whether to shake hands or not – does one shake hands with servants he thought. Fortunately the predicament was solved as Susanne bobbed another curtsey and almost ran back into the house while Hans bustled round to the luggage grid on the car and started unstrapping David's suitcase. They moved into the panelled entrance hall and the doktor and his wife sat down on a choir stall type of seat indicating to David to sit on a similar one opposite to them, where he was immediately joined by Inge and Dieter.

"Now," said the doktor, "you have had a long journey and must be very tired, so first of all we must book a telephone call to your parents to let them know you have arrived safely. When I phone Dr Carew it is normally at this time in the evening and it takes about half an hour to get through. Whilst the phone call is coming through you can wash in your room, Dieter will look after you, and then come down and we will have supper together. Tomorrow morning we shall have breakfast a little later than usual at nine o'clock instead of eight o'clock. After breakfast I will talk to you for about half an hour and then Dieter will look after you. We have borrowed a bicycle for you from some friends of ours who are on holiday so you will be able to explore the countryside. We have few rules in our house except that meals are always on time otherwise it is most unfair to the servants."

David was to discover that in addition to the two staff he had already met, there were two other maids and a gardener on the establishment.

"Right then, Dieter will show you to your room and I will organise the telephone call."

David was most impressed by the calm efficient organisation outlined by the doktor and expressed his thanks most gratefully for all they were doing for him and for making him so welcome. He had to struggle to get the words into the right places and not to try and say things he wouldn't have a hope of translating into German, but he did quite well as they all listened with studied courtesy. Dieter took him to his room, which faced on to the balcony on the first floor. It was a large airy room with a washbasin in the corner. Frau von Hasselbek had put a large bunch of flowers on a small table in the middle of the room, and David found to his surprise that his suitcase had been unstrapped and unpacked by Hans and his clothes put in the large mahogany wardrobe and chest of drawers, and his toilet bag emptied on the washstand.

He quickly washed and put on a clean shirt and tie, but Dieter said there was no need to wear a tie unless they were having guests, so he took it off again. He was finding it a little difficult to make conversation with Dieter. Although the German youth was obviously a friendly sort of chap the casual chat that goes on between young fellows was stunted by David having to think of what to say in English, translate it in his mind and then speak it in German, which slowed up the conversation somewhat. The fact that he was beginning to feel his tiredness didn't help, but he consoled himself with the thought that he would improve as the days went on.

As they were going downstairs to rejoin the rest of the family there was a shrill ringing of the telephone, which was immediately answered by doktor. "David, it is your mother."

David quickly told his mother that he had arrived safely, that everyone was most kind to him, that the house was beautiful, that he could write a long letter describing his journey and that they were just going to have supper. A quick hello to Rose and his father and his first international phone call was over.

He turned to the family and said in English, "My family all send their best wishes."

In what was obviously a carefully rehearsed reply they all looked at each other and said, "We don't understand this language, I wonder which language he is talking?"

David smiled and then repeated the sentence in German. They sat down to a hearty supper towards the end of which David had great difficulty stifling yawn after yawn, until eventually the doktor said, "Right young man, off to bed. Dieter will call you at 8 o'clock, breakfast at nine."

David fell into bed and was asleep as soon as his head hit the pillow. It was a large comfortable bed having a feather quilt instead of the blankets he was used to. At 8am prompt in came Dieter and woke him up and told him he would see him downstairs when he was ready. After breakfast the doktor told the two youths to come into his study and proceeded to give David some background knowledge of the Germany he had come to visit. "We are experiencing a great deal of change here David and we are all having to adapt to the new way of things. There are one or two things that you need to know. Many of the youth people you will meet are fanatical National Socialists, in fact Inge is very supportive of the movement." David took it from that that neither the doktor nor Dieter were supportive of it. The doktor continued. "Some people will openly greet you with the salute and 'Heil Hitler', it is becoming very common. They do this to gauge the degree of enthusiasm with which the person greeted responds and by this means calculate the party allegiance of this person. It is best if you answer such a greeting by just saying 'Good morning' or whatever, and they will know then you are a foreigner and will almost certainly be pleasant to you as they wish to impress the outside world. Now with regard to the Jews, it would be best if you made no mention of any Jewish friends you may have, not that it will cause you personally any inconvenience but it could reflect on me and my family. I have had to discharge the few Jewish teachers I employed, I had no option whatsoever. Remember, don't get involved in political discussion of any sort and particularly don't make favourable remarks about communism or unfavourable remarks about National Socialism. I am very sorry to start your stay with us with remarks of this nature, I'm afraid it is a sign of the times we are living in. Well now, how did you sleep? I hope Dieter will now take you out for a ride on the bicycles and we shall see you back for lunch. I believe you are going swimming this afternoon." And with that he shook hands and the two youths went off to one of the outhouses to collect the cycles.

Like all people travelling the continent for the first time, it took David a little while to get used to riding on the right-hand side of the road. There was little traffic about as they cut through the country lanes and eventually reached the banks of the Danube. They had a beautiful ride along the pathway running alongside the river finally reaching a café where they stopped for refreshment.

"The river doesn't look very blue," said David.

"Everyone says that," laughed Dieter, "I think Mr Strauss has a lot to answer for misinterpreting it so."

"Did your sister not want to come with us today?"

"No, she is busy packing, she goes on holiday in three days time to stay with my uncle in Belgrade. He is a senior diplomat there and she will be there in Belgrade and then on to the coast, and will be away for one month. However she is coming swimming with us this afternoon. Do you have a girlfriend?"

The sudden switch in conversation took David off guard. He suddenly realised he hadn't thought of Pat all morning.

"Yes, she's very lovely, her name is Pat. I will show you a photo when we get back to the house. What about you, do you have one?"

"No, not steady. A crowd of us go swimming together and there are one or two I like."

"I imagine Inge has lots of boyfriends, she is very attractive."

"Oh yes she has a whole string of them, most of them have a uniform of one sort or another. She is eighteen, so they tend to be young party members of the officer class. All the same she is a very nice girl and great fun to be with so I try not to notice her politics."

David found his German was becoming more fluent as he went along. He still had to substitute words he knew for words he would like to say that he didn't know, but he was getting a lot of help from Dieter with his vocabulary. Another month he thought and I shall have forgotten all my English!

Dieter looked at his watch. "Time to get back, we mustn't be late for lunch."

After lunch David went up to his room and put his towel and costume into his knapsack and rejoined Inge and Dieter downstairs. The lake where they were to swim was a leisurely cycle ride of about twenty minutes, and when they arrived there was a small number of young people swimming around in the crystal clear water who waved to them. David put his bike behind one of the bushes, which surrounded the lake, preceded to undress and put on his costume and, having put his clothes neatly into the knapsack, he walked out to find the other two. He had no difficulty in finding them, they were waiting for him by the springboard which was built out over the lake, and they were both stark naked. David halted in surprise. He looked long at Inge standing there, her glorious golden body and blonde hair silhouetted against the pale blue of the water. She was the first naked woman he had seen and he was totally lost for words. Dieter came to the rescue quickly however when he saw his friend's predicament, by now they were firm friends, and hurriedly said, "Inge we should have warned David, perhaps we have embarrassed him. If he is shy this must be quite a shock to him."

Immediately David said, "Please don't worry, I don't mind being without a costume," though what mother and father would have said on the subject I hesitate to think, he said to himself. It was true that David was used to swimming without a costume. At the school baths no one, not even masters, wore anything in the pool. There was the classic incident when the very attractive mother of one of the junior schoolboys had wandered into the gym, which led into the swimming bath, looking for the gym instructor in order to arrange special tuition for her boy who had showed signs of being a first class gymnast. The gym instructor had been a member of the British gymnastics team at the Olympic Games in 1924 and was always looking for boys of special promise to follow in his footsteps. The lady, not finding the gym master, walked past the sign which said, 'Boys only past this point', opened the door, walked into the baths and immediately confronted eighteen-year-old head boy Bates Major, standing totally starkers on the diving board. Bates Major was so put off by this he did a most glorious and painful belly flop into the baths, much to the amusement of the other boys present. The lady, to her credit, just smiled, turned on her heel and walked out again.

David went back to his knapsack and put his costume away and walked back to Inge and Dieter who were still waiting for him. He saw Inge look at him most appreciatively as she said, "Well Dieter, your friend certainly has nothing to be shy about."

Dieter laughed but said, "Inge, behave yourself."

It was a fact that David was up to the front of the queue when they dished out the 'wedding tackle', as Harry once succinctly put it. The vernacular at school was 'He's got a good set of weights', referring of course to the big brass weights greengrocers and butchers used on their scales. However it was the first time that this part of his anatomy was being viewed by the public at large and by an attractive young lady in particular and David did begin to get a little embarrassed. It was Inge that got things moving again, "race you in," she called, and turned and ran to the springboard and the next moment David had the view of her lean tanned buttocks in mid air as she dived into the beautiful clear water.

David followed her and received a terrific shock as he hit the water. When he came up he said, "It's freezing."

Inge laughed and said, "It's warm now compared to the beginning of summer, the water comes down off the mountains and it is really cold then." There were several people swimming around, all in the thirteen to seventeen age group, Inge appeared to be the oldest. They swam over in turn and were introduced to David, shaking hands and being most friendly. They swam around; somebody produced a rubber ball, which they had fun with. All the time one or another walked out of the lake up the small sandy beach and then ran on to the spring board and dived back in. None of them wore costumes, they all acted quite naturally and David found this vastly entertaining.

Eventually Dieter said, "I'm going to sunbathe," to which David said, "I'll join you."

"Me too" said Inge, and they all climbed out of the lake and spread their towels on the grass beyond the beach and lay down in the sun. It was a beautiful warm day and David found himself lying there next to the lovely body of Inge as if he had been doing it all his life.

After a short while a very dark haired girl wandered over and laid her towel beside David saying to the three of them, "May I join you?"

"Yes of course," said Dieter, "you've met David haven't you?"

"Yes," replied the girl but shook hands again. "I am Annalie, called Anni for short." She was probably about sixteen with large breasts, broad shoulders and a strong intelligent face. She was not at all fat, but she was well built, David judged she was a swimmer although he hadn't noticed her performing any startling feats in the water.

She started to speak to David in English, but after a short while Dieter cut in and said, "David is only allowed to speak German while he is here."

"In that case I can speak to him in English and he can answer in German. That way we both get practice."

"Well I suppose that's alright," said Dieter.

She started an animated conversation in very good English with David and again he marvelled that here was this young woman, stark naked, nipples all hard from being in the cold water, goose pimples gradually disappearing in the warmth of the sun, lying beside him and talking as if they were in his drawing room back at Chandlers Lodge. Harry will never believe it he thought...

The shadows were beginning to lengthen. Dieter stood up and suggested it was time they started back. They dressed, shook hands with the others, and got on their bikes and rode off. "Enjoy it?" said Dieter.

"Absolutely marvellous," said David.

"We'll come again later in the week, that's after we get rid of this one here," pointing to Inge.

"You rotters. I shall think of you and envy you like mad."

"Nonsense, you'll be canoodling up with all those randy young diplomats, especially the junior military attaché," said Dieter. David didn't quite get the exact translation of some of the words, but the meaning of them was plain nevertheless.

To carry on the fun he said, "Is that the ugly fellow with the cross eyes that you told me about Dieter?"

"No, that's another one, this one's not as good looking as him, added to which he's Prussian which I know he can't help, but he's a Prussian nevertheless."

Inge chimed in, "I'll deal with both of you later."

The next day they had a sightseeing day in and around Ulm visiting of course the magnificent cathedral, the old city walls, the 16th century Fisherman's Quarters and the narrow streets and alleys of the old town. After a superb lunch they drove to the Wiblingen monastery and afterwards to the Roggenburg monastery both of which impressed David tremendously with their beautiful paintings, statuary and exquisite decoration. That evening would be the last Inge would be with them. They were all a little sad at this, even Inge herself, who one would have guessed would have been excited at the thought of going to Yugoslavia, where no doubt she would be having lots of fun. During the previous two days she had been very friendly towards David, even to the extent of the few occasions when they were alone together, of holding his hand or arm, by which David felt very flattered and which was extremely pleasant. They all retired at about 10.30 after a long day. In his customary manner David hit the pillow and was asleep in no time. He was awakened by his window squeaking and looked across to see a figure in the moonlight climbing in. It was clearly Inge. Realising he was awake she put her finger to her lips, pulled the curtains across the window and walked over to him, fortunately missing the squeaky floorboard in the process. He put the small bedside light on as she reached the bed, but still said nothing. She let her robe drop to the floor and slipped in with him. She was quite naked.

It was like a dream really, David thought afterwards. Neither of them said anything. David had been instantly aroused as she slipped into bed and had at once began to caress him. She moved him from his side to his back and then knelt up and straddled him easing him into her, moving up and down until she was ready to lie down on him. David laid rigid, fighting and fighting not to prematurely end this most wonderful experience. She moved slowly up and down, then from side to side, whispering words of endearment through moist lips buried in his shoulder until she began to give big sobs for what David thought seemed an age. At last David let go of his control and the whole world seemed to explode in his loins and he began to moan, at which Inge put her hand over his mouth and kissed his face and neck. When it was over they lay there without talking until Inge whispered, "I couldn't go without saying goodbye David darling."

"I'm so glad you didn't, that has never happened to me before."

"Are you saying that was the first time you have made love?"

"Yes, I'm afraid it was."

"Oh David, to think I had a lovely virgin David. Oh David I shall never forget you, I shall never forget my virgin David."

She buried her face again into his shoulder and he began to kiss her. He was beginning to leave her, but the excitement of his caressing her and kissing her renewed his passion and again aroused him. He held her close and then rolled over with her. This time he held himself up and looked down on her as he slowly and rhythmically pleasured her. She held her arms up above her head gripping the headboard on the bed. He saw her face was almost contorted with the agony of feeling that possessed her, her breath was coming in little sobs, her eyes tightly closed, her head moving slightly from side to side almost it seemed in desperation until she began to issue little moans as her whole body went absolutely rigid beneath him. As she reached this climax of feeling so he too joined her in an ecstasy even greater than that he had experienced before.

He lowered himself on to her and they both lay there panting with pleasure and satisfaction. He kissed her gently and she held him close.

"David," she said in a whisper, "you're not a boy, you are a man. The woman who eventually gets you will be a very, very lucky lady."

After a while she got up and put her robe back on. She knelt down by the bed and put her arms around David and said, "goodbye darling David," and turned, crossed the room, climbed out onto the veranda and was gone.

They said their formal goodbyes after breakfast the next morning.

They never saw each other again.

Chapter Thirteen

The weeks flashed past. The doktor took David and Dieter twice to visit the city of Munich to see the Royal residence where the kings and queens of Bavaria had lived. They visited the famous Pinakothek art gallery and wandered around the old town of Munich. The Bavarians are a genial friendly people and David enjoyed his visits enormously. The second visit was on a Saturday. They made an early start and had planned to leave for home at about two o'clock and to stop at Augsburg, about half way between Ulm and Munich, for coffee and cakes. When they arrived in Augsburg they saw large crowds assembling, so parking the car they walked to the town centre where they heard there was to be a parade and an address by none other than Herr Goebbels the Reich's propaganda minister.

They got themselves in a good position on one side of the square, at the head of which was a large platform.

Almost immediately the sound of military music could be heard approaching from a side street and suddenly there was an explosion of noise from the emergence of the band and the deafening cheers of the crowd. The band formed into a square from its previous column and slow marched across the square whilst columns of troops repeated the manoeuvre as they emerged in turn. Behind the troops came groups of various organisations, men and women, carrying a multitude of swastika banners and soon the whole square, with the exception of a wide strip in front of the raised platform, was full of feet marching in slow time. The order to halt was given, dressings taken up and the parade stood at ease. After a few minutes, at a signal from an official on the platform, the parade was called to attention again and the band made ready. From another side street a cavalcade of cars drove onto the wide strip, the first ones carrying an assortment of officials, the Burgermeister and his entourage, Army officers, men in brown uniforms and then men in black uniforms. These were followed by several civilians who David judged must be very important as they were the last to take their seats before the big open-topped Mercedes arrived carrying the Reichsminister Goebbels and his aides. As Goebbels mounted the platform and faced the square the band struck up 'Deutschland Uber Alles', whilst Goebbels and all the other dignitaries on the platform stood giving the Nazi salute.

There were speeches of welcome from the Burgermeister, the local party leader, and the commander of the local army unit and then a hush fell as Goebbels stood up to speak. The three previous speakers had all been hefty six footers, so the microphone had to be surreptitiously lowered before the diminutive, club footed Joseph Goebbels began. Once begun though it was plain to see why he held such sway over large audiences. He began quietly tracing the ignominy of the Treaty of Versailles, the rise of communism, the corruption of the Weimar Republic, and as his voice increased in anger he almost screamed his venom about the evils of international Jewry and the German Jews in particular who had bled the country white for so many centuries. While the speech was in progress David looked around at the people in the crowd. Their reactions ranged from ecstasy and enthusiasm, fervent support and blind faith, through the middling people just listening, to a very few who heard what was being said and had fear in their eyes at what all this was leading to. The doktor was one of the latter. David saw the worried frown on his forehead, his lips shut tight. There was no fire in his eyes, only a deep sorrow and foreboding. The Reichsminister having thrown in a few jibes about niggers and nigger music, finished his speech with an impassioned exhortation to the youth of the nation to be true Aryans, to follow the words of the Fuhrer without question and not to rest until all the German peoples were reunited. As he ended and saluted, a deafening chorus of 'Sieg Heil' was taken up by the crowd and after receiving these platitudes for a full five minutes he made to leave the platform, at which the band struck up the national anthem again.

Slowly the crowd broke up. The doktor and the two young men moved slowly through the throng to get back to their car. As they crossed one of the narrow streets two youths wearing armbands called out.

"Herr Doktor, what did you think of the speech?"

They were two of the doktor's senior students.

"Oh, very forceful, very forceful," he said and they passed on. When they got into the car the doktor said to David, "My reply there just shows you the depths to which we have descended when I have to perjure myself to two of my pupils."

The ride home was made in silence until they drove towards the house. "Come in," said the doktor. "Let's cheer ourselves up for your mother's sake. After all most of the day was enjoyable."

That evening after dinner David said to the doktor, "I have been meaning to ask you Herr Doktor how you met Dr Carew, have you known him long?"

The doktor gave a wry smile and said "We met at 7.15pm on February 28th 1917 in the middle of no-mans-land."

David's perplexity showed so clearly on his face that the other three laughed in delight. Dieter and his mother did of course already know the story. "I don't understand," he said.

"Well, we had attacked the British lines that afternoon, just a local affair. The Somerset Light Infantry were opposite us. During the course of the attack I was wounded in the groin and in the leg and fell into a deep shell hole. British artillery rained down on us and my comrades had to retreat back to their own lines, leaving me behind. When it got dark Dr Carew, Captain Carew as he was then, brought a party out to mend the barbed wire, which had been destroyed in our bombardment preceding the attack. He heard me moaning in the shell hole and carried me back to the British lines. I had lost so much blood I was close to death. If he hadn't found me I would certainly have died that night." Frau von Hassellbek held his hand tightly.

"He gave me a packet of cigarettes on which he put his name and home address and said, "Let me know how you get on." I wrote to him from the POW camp and then after the war from here, and we have been good friends ever since. He visits us every two or three years and we go to England when we can. He is a real gentleman and a very, very brave man. All the time he was carrying me Very lights were going up and he was being shot at. The German soldiers didn't know of course he was carrying one of their own officers, yet despite the shots he still walked on when he could easily have dropped me and crawled along in comparative safety."

"May I tell this story at school?" said David, "better still write it as an article in the school magazine."

"By all means," said the doktor, "though he's such a modest man he will probably give you a tanning for doing it."

"It will be more than worth it," grinned David.

At last there was only one week left. They went swimming several times and David had formed a firm friendship with Anni. Although he had thought she was a swimmer, she had such fine strong arms and shoulders; she told him she was a javelin thrower. She was, although only fifteen, the state junior champion, and she was hoping to get into the national team in time for the 1936 Olympic games in Berlin. Although they sat or lay back quite naked by the lake there was never any impropriety between them. David, thinking about it as impartially as he could as he lay in bed one night concluded they must be soul mates otherwise why didn't he get a hard on, as the college venacular went, when they were lying there together. Whatever their relationship was it was very pleasant and he enjoyed her company enormously. She was non-political unlike many of the others, well read, and like him loved music, so they had a lot in common. On the last day at the lake, after they had dressed and were going to get their bikes, Anni held her hand out to shake hands with David, and David pulled her gently to him and kissed her on the lips. She looked at him with her beautiful dark brown eyes and said, "I do so much hope I see you again David."

"So do I," said David and he meant it deep, deep down more than he thought he would have done.

The next day was spent packing ready for an early start the following morning. The doktor and his wife came to the station to see them off and as the train pulled in she very affectionately hugged David and said, "We have so much enjoyed having you David, we did wonder what you would be like and whether we would all get on together, but you have been like another son to us and we would dearly like to see you again." David replied that he truly would like that also and suggested they visit England, perhaps next year.

"We'll see, we'll see," she said.

"Good luck David," said the doktor and to Dieter, "now you behave yourself whilst in England."

Dieter grinned as he embraced his father, "Now you know I can't promise impossible things like that." So the parting was softened with smiles all round as the two lads climbed on to the train and were waved out of the station.

They soon settled back into their seats and began to plan at which points in their journey they would eat their packaged meals. "Your mother has given us enough food to feed the whole train," said David, and continued, "and now my friend, in a few hours you are going to have to start speaking English. Now where will it be? When we get on the boat, or when we get off it? I know, we'll calculate the sailing time and at exactly half way you will start."

Dieter agreed with this arrangement. At the end of the long train ride they arrived at the Hook and transferred to the boat, found their cabin and then explored the vessel, a different one to that which David had travelled on before. Soon, thought David, I shall be speaking English again. He had made tremendous strides in both his vocabulary and speed of talking and, just as the doktor had said, he had developed a South German accent which one day would stand him in very good stead. He was not yet fluent but felt that with a little application and another visit or two to Ulm he might very well become so. Perhaps he would see Inge again. At this thought he got a little glow inside, which he quickly suppressed by thinking of Anni, and then quickly suppressed both of these thoughts by thinking of Pat who he would see tomorrow. At the thought of Pat he had a pang of conscience, he hadn't thought of her as much as he would have expected during that month. Suddenly he had a little panic feeling. "Dieter," he said, they were standing on the deck watching the preparation for departure, "I think it would not be wise to tell the people in England that we all went swimming with no costumes on, particularly Pat my girlfriend."

"Oh, why is that?"

"Well you see, people where we live are very conservative and they think it is very improper. You never ever see people swimming without costumes in England, except at school."

"Well now, what's it worth to keep my mouth shut?"

"I'll throw you off Tower Bridge if you don't and that's a promise."

"I shall have to think about it. I shall have to calculate what the cost will be."

At that David lunged at him and they started to wrestle, much to the amusement of several bystanders, until suddenly the boat lurched either on being released from the dock or by being pulled by a tug, as a result of which they reeled against a hatchway about knee high and both ended up flat on their backs on the hatch cover accompanied by roars of laughter from the spectators. They got up grinning shamefacedly and made their way down to the cabin for their fifth meal of the day.

David hadn't realised when making his calculation as to when Dieter had to start his English that they of course would be asleep at the time. When he awoke therefore, as they approached Harwich after another smooth crossing, he woke Dieter and said, "Good morning."

Dieter put his hand to his forehead and said in German, "Is it time to get up already?"

David stood there as if he hadn't heard him and said, "What language is this person speaking?" to the cabin in general.

They both laughed remembering the same thing had happened to David in Ulm. They collected their belongings and went to the main exit gangway, down through the immigration and customs shed and out towards the station. Through the bustle of people David heard his name called and turned to find Jack Hooper waving to him.

"We've come to collect you," he said, and standing there with him was his mother, Rose and Pat.

After handshaking, embraces, introduction of Dieter and a long kiss to Pat which quite took her breath away, David said, "Why are you here and not at Liverpool Street?"

"I had to come to Colchester yesterday on business so I suggested to your father that your mother and Rose joined Pat and I and we'd come to meet you. We stayed at the George overnight and made an early start for Harwich this morning."

"Well the journey home will certainly be more comfortable than by train sir," said David.

Dieter much admired the beautiful Daimler. It was obvious too that Rose, judging by the sidelong glances she was giving, somewhat admired the clean featured good-looking Dieter. Pat was sitting up front next to her father, and they had the parting window wound down so that they were able to talk to the lads on the occasionals and Ruth and Rose on the back seat. Pat had half turned and laid her arm along the back of the seat behind her father. David held her hand and squeezed it and they smiled at each other. This of course did not go unnoticed by Dieter who in halting English said, "Do you know Pat he has been holding hands with all the girls in Ulm."

"You rotter," said David, thumping him one. "Don't you believe him Pat, he's jealous because you are so beautiful." They all laughed, but Pat felt a glow inside all the same. She had wondered whether David would change towards her and the fact that he had stated as a matter of indisputable fact that she was beautiful made her feel very happy. Ruth sat there watching all this from the rear seat and she too felt very happy that these two young men were obviously such good friends that they could make fun of each other quite naturally, and even more so that David had not lost his feeling for Pat whilst they had been separated. She thought Pat was an adorable girl and had said so to Fred on several occasions, only for Fred to repeat his warning made a long time ago that sooner or later they would probably go their own ways with other partners.

"Well what do you want to do while you are here Dieter?" asked Jack.

Again rather slowly, "I would like to see all the beautiful buildings in London, and Canterbury Cathedral, and the castles at Dover and elsewhere."

"I expect David will get a programme out. I know his father has got a bicycle for you so there's plenty to do and see within easy riding distance of Sandbury, and as for London the train from Sandbury station goes straight to Victoria so you will be able to explore London quite easily."

They made the slow journey through the Blackwall Tunnel, having to stop at each bend to let the oncoming traffic through, a lot of which was in the form of heavy lorries going to the docks and charabancs taking parties from south London to the seaside at Southend and Clacton. Eventually they cleared the tunnel and Dieter asked, "Why did they build the tunnel with so many bends, would it not have been better to have gone straight down and then straight up at the other side?"

"Well," replied Jack, "you have to remember that this tunnel was built to be used by heavy horses and carts to and from the docks before the days of the motor vehicle. As a result the gradients had to be as small as possible. If they had gone straight the road would have been too steep in and out, so they had to zigzag, somewhat like a mountain pass, so that the horses could pull the loads. Have I made that clear?"

"Yes, I understand now, thank you very much sir."

"Look, Rose always calls me Uncle Jack, why don't you two lads do the same. I would be very pleased if you will."

"Yes that would be very nice sir, I mean Uncle Jack."

They all laughed and from then on Uncle Jack it was.

"I think that we are going to enjoy having you with us very much Dieter," said Ruth.

"Yes, I think so too," said Rose, with such emphasis that they all turned to look at her and, realising how forward she had sounded, she blushed furiously.

Dieter in turn said, "I know I shall be very happy here and my mother and father have sent their very best wishes to you and told me to thank you for having me with you."

At last they descended the downs and drove the last few miles into Sandbury. It was Megan's day off and she, Harry along with Fred were all waiting for them as they arrived. Megan had prepared a cold lunch and Fred was to take them all out to dinner at the Angel where he was beginning to become known and welcomed.

The month sped past. The four of them went on the train and explored London several times. They went to Canterbury and Dover, and got on together very well. One day David and Dieter went to Mountfield on their bikes. "I'll show you the farm where we used to live," he said. They reached the Prince of Orange and turned down the lane and stopped outside the house where he had spent his boyhood. Leaning over the gate was a youth of about the same age as the lads. He was a pugnacious looking character with a thick short neck close cropped bristly ginger hair and a pair of piggy little eyes sat very close together which regarded the two lads with undisguised hostility.

"What do you want?" he said.

"We're just looking at the house," said David, "I used to live here."

"Well you don't live here now so piss off."

David was very annoyed at being spoken to in this manner, but nevertheless was not looking for trouble. "There's no reason to be rude," he said, "I have a guest here from overseas surely you can be polite." He realised later what a fatuous thing it was to say to such an oaf.

"Well if he's foreign he can piss off as well, or I'll sort the pair of you out."

"I think you might have a little trouble trying to sort even one of us out let alone both of us," said David, and as he said it the yob swung the gate open, came at David who was nearest to him still sitting on his bike with just his toes touching the ground, and gave him a shove which unbalanced him and toppled him over with his bike on top of him. Dieter in the meantime had moved very quickly. He jumped from his bike and let it fall over and as he turned he saw the yob raising his foot to kick David in the back as he was trying to disentangle himself from his bicycle. He swung his foot and it caught the yob right under the buttocks with such force that he almost left the ground. With a squeal of pain he spun round, little piggy eyes blazing, but before he could move Dieter hit him with his left fist on the jaw with an impact that nearly broke all the bones in his hand. It didn't knock piggy-eyes out, but he was certainly very confused and swung round facing his house. Dieter put the flat of his shoe up on his buttocks and pushed so hard that the yob hurtled across the intervening distance and ended up spread-eagled over the gate, which swung open with the force and deposited him on his own front door step.

"Now you can piss off," said Dieter and turned to David saying, "David, what does piss off mean?"

Further discussion on this subject was halted by George coming out of his cottage next door to see what all the noise was about.

"David," he said, "What a lovely surprise," and then seeing piggy-eyes on the ground said, "What's going on?"

David told him the story and introduced Dieter. George said, "That little bastard has been asking for it ever since he's been here. His parents can't control him; he bullies the kids in the village. One day he's going to end up in real trouble. Anyway, come on in."

The two lads went in and had tea with George in his immaculate home. He left no time in telling Dieter how he owed his life to David, and went on to tell the story of the bull. "Is the bull still here sir?" said Dieter.

"Yes," replied George, "would you like to see him?"

They went off down to the yard and went to the bullpen.

"He looks a very (searching for the word) fearsome and dangerous animal," said Dieter.

"He's that alright," said George, "now lets go back to the house. I've a message I want you to take to your father David."

They went back to the house. There was no sign of piggy-eyes anywhere.

"Now David," said George, "you know I went convalescent to Eastbourne after I was discharged from Sandbury hospital. Well, while I was there I met a war widow lady and we got on very well. We corresponded, she lives in Battle, and she's been here several times, and to cut a long story short, we're going to be married in November."

"George, how marvellous," David exclaimed and both lads pumped Georges hand in congratulation.

"Thank you, thank you both. Now you are all invited to the wedding of course, but I would like to ask your Dad whether you can be my bestman – that's if you want to be of course – because if it wasn't for you there wouldn't be any wedding."

"I'll ask him tonight," said David, "and then drop you a postcard. No on second thoughts I'd better spend three halfpence and make it a letter or Snowy will know, plus half the village, before you do." They laughed uproariously at this and seeing Dieter was puzzled told him about Snowy the postman, and Millie on the switchboard, and how everybody in the village knew all your business even before you did yourselves sometimes. They left the farm and made their way back on the road into the village. After a short ride David said, "I'd like to stop here for just a minute." They were outside Ernie Bolton's house.

He knocked on the door and it was opened by Mrs Bolton, who was so pleased at seeing David she hugged him up and called out, "Ernie come and see who we've got here." David explained he had a German friend with him, could he bring him in. "Of course, of course," she said. David knew it would always be prudent to ask to bring a German into someone's house. So many people had lost dear ones killed by the Germans, only such a very few years ago that it was like yesterday for some, and anti-German feeling ran very high still.

There are some ten thousand villages in England alone, and of that number only around thirty came through the Great War without losing fathers, sons and husbands. In the county of Kent, only one village, the small hamlet of Knowlton, near Canterbury, emerged unscathed. In Mountfield, of the fifty-eight men who went to war, mainly on the Western Front, thirty-one never returned, it was no wonder that the sadness and bitterness survived year after year. However, Dieter was made very welcome, and they had a long chat with Ernie, who as usual was the life and soul of the party. They recalled the hysterical 'Pancake day' which when described to Dieter had him crying real tears of laughter, which in turn started Mrs Bolton off.

Ernie had left school. He couldn't get a job locally and there was no means of transporting a wheelchair by public transport at all, so he was confined to reading, listening to the wireless and wheeling himself around the village. They mentioned their meeting with piggy-eyes. Ernie's face went solemn for the first time. "He has tipped my chair over twice," said Ernie, "Mum had to go and see Crownie who went round to see his parents. They can't do anything with him, but Crownie told him he'd send him to Borstal if he troubled me again. So far he's left me alone."

"Well you've got the consolation that he's got a very sore behind and a throbbing headache at this moment thanks to Dieter," said David, and they all laughed at this thought. It was time to be on their way, so with assurances they would come again before Dieter went home, they rode off back to Sandbury. That evening they had so much to tell the family. Fred readily agreed that David should be George's bestman, so David wrote his letter and got it in that nights' 10 o'clock collection for Snowy the next morning to wonder who was writing to George from Sandbury.

The next day the two lads were wandering around the factory. They had taken to visiting it on occasion, being both very interested in the work that was going on in the workshop. They went into Fred's office and David said to his father, "Dad, I suppose there's nothing we can do for Ernie Bolton is there?"

Fred put down the drawing he was studying and thought for a while. "Lets analyse the situation. First what is he any good at? Second how would he get here to do it? Third how would he get home again? Fourth, how mobile is he without his chair. Now discounting items two, three and four, what is he any good at?"

"Well, I know he's very good at figures and English. He gets on with people very well, he speaks well, and if he was mobile would be an asset to any firm."

As they were talking Harry knocked, walked in, and listened to what they were saying. In the silence that followed David's remarks Harry said, "We want other products for the factory, why not make invalid carriages and Ernie could try out the prototype. I happen to know that Elliott's the coach builders on the other side of town are closing down and will be auctioning off their equipment, perhaps we could use some of it, plus pick up one or two skilled men."

As was his habit, Fred thought deeply while the others waited in silence.

"It's not as daft as it sounds," he eventually said. "I'll have a word with Mr Hooper this evening. In the meantime don't say anything to Ernie if you happen to see him. I could do with an office junior here as it happens, both to learn to do the wages and take that job off Miss Russell, and to help chase up purchasing to help me – but mum's the word for the time being."

The following evening there was a telephone call to the house answered by Ruth. She hurried into the drawing room and said, "David it's for you, its Dr Carew."

David ran to the phone. "Good evening sir."

"Good evening Chandler. I believe young von Hassellbek is with you. I'd like you both to come to tea on Sunday, say four o'clock if your family has no other plans for you."

"May I ask them sir?"

"Yes, I'll hold the line."

David consulted his parents who readily agreed for the lads to go.

"Yes, that's fine sir, we'll be there at four o'clock. Oh sir, would it be possible for me to show Dieter around the school one day next week?"

"Yes, of course, it's open at the moment whilst the decorating and refurbishment is going on, so just wander around."

"Thank you sir."

David rejoined the others. "I shall never live this down," he said.

"What do you mean dear?" said Ruth.

"Having tea with the Head. The rest of the form rags you mercilessly if that ever happens."

"Well perhaps no one will ever find out as it's holiday time."

"Someone will find out don't you worry."

They had tea with Dr Carew and his wife, a pleasant bosomy lady who had years of experience putting boys at ease in the presence of God. David told of his adventures in Germany, noticeably leaving out the swimming episodes and the story the doktor had told him of how he first met Dr Carew – that was for the school magazine. It was a most pleasant visit. Dr Carew instructed Dieter to give his and Mrs Carew's compliments to his family and to say they hoped to visit them next year.

As a result of being responsible for Dieter each day, David had not seen as much of Pat as he would have liked, particularly on her own. They had, with Rose, been about a great deal in a foursome and Pat had been able to arrange her riding school job fairly easily to accommodate these trips. They had discussed the problem together but, as Fred had rightly said a long time before, they were a sensible headed young couple so there was no resentment on Pat's part of Dieter taking centre stage for the time being. Pat had noticed however that on the rare occasions they were alone David's chaste kisses had changed to being a good deal warmer. She didn't object to this by any manner of means, in fact she got considerable pleasure and excitement from them. She put it down to the fact that David was having to bottle up his feelings over days at a time; it would therefore be natural for him to give vent to them when the opportunity arose. She was looking forward to the three days between Dieter's departure and her own return to college so that she would have him entirely to herself, and sometimes her fantasies of what would happen during these three days ran a little wild to the extent she made herself blush to think of them.

At last it was time for Dieter to return. His English had improved tremendously during the month of non-stop talking to all the family, and as they all stood on Liverpool Street station to see him off he shook hands and said to David, "Can we please do this again next year?"

David looked at his father. "As far as I'm concerned young man you can come and stay with us whenever you want to."

The broad smile on Rose's face showed her view on the subject and Ruth hugged him and said, "I now have three boys – four if you count him," pointing to Fred.

As they spoke there was a bellow from down the platform and running towards them they saw Jack. "Couldn't let you go without saying goodbye," he said. "This is for your father, a little present from me to add to those from the Chandlers." It was a large bottle of John Haig. "Let me know if you have to pay any duty and I'll send it to you."

Dieter climbed into the carriage as the departure whistles began to blow and leaned out of the window waving until the train went round the curve and out of sight.

"Do you know Dad," said David, addressing his father but talking to the whole gathering, "I've been with Dieter for eight weeks and we never had a cross word. How many people could you do that with?"

"Very few I would think," said Fred.

"Says a lot for you too though" said Jack.

His mother gave his arm a little hug and said, "I agree with your Uncle Jack."

Chapter Fourteen

As soon as they got home David sped round to the Hollies on his bike to see Pat. She had just arrived back from the stables.

"I'm all smelly," she said. "I'm going to have a bath and then I'll be right down and get us some lunch."

"I'll scrub your back if you like," said David cheekily.

"David Chandler, if you set one foot on those stairs Nannie Westcott would hang, draw and quarter you."

"In that case I'll shin up the drain pipe, she couldn't catch me then."

"She keeps a twelve bore under the sink for people like you."

"Are you telling me there are other people like me?" he asked inching closer to her.

"Oh no you don't," she said realising what he was up to and, just evading his final grasp, she ran up the broad staircase laughing as she went.

After a cold lunch of ham and salad they went out on their bikes. As they left the house David said, "Incidentally, where was Mrs Westcott?"

"Oh she's away today."

"So I could have scrubbed your back anyway? I shall never ever forgive you for that fib," he said in mocking solemnity.

It was a glorious warm early September day and at last they pulled their bikes up into a large field behind a hedge and sat down on the grass together.

"Now tell me everything you did in Germany," said Pat. "We've hardly had a chance to say a word about it since you got back."

It was lucky for David he was facing away from Pat when she sprung this on him. He felt his face going red so he made a lengthy job of getting his cape out of the saddlebag so they had something to sit on.

"Shan't be a minute," he said, rapidly recovering his composure. He spread the cape and they sat down and he took Pat in his arms, laid her back and gave her the longest kiss she had ever experienced in her life.

"That's towards all the kisses I've been missing in the last two months," said David, "and I haven't even started yet."

A little bell of caution rang in Pat's mind. She had no idea of what it was telling her to be cautious about, but instinctively she felt that she had got to ensure that things went no further. On the other hand she was pleased with and excited by this new David and the last thing she wanted was to put him in the wrong in any way.

"David darling, did you miss me?"

Without knowing it she had said exactly the right thing. David had missed her, but he still had this guilty conscience about not having missed her as much or as often as he thought he would or should. Secondly there was the Inge experience, something he would never forget, and thirdly his deep feeling for Anni, which he found even now impossible to analyse. With all this racing through his mind his ardour was somewhat dampened, but he replied in all honesty.

"Yes dearest Pat, I did miss you. I wish you could have been there with me, it was so lovely and you are so lovely, it would have been heaven."

His feelings now had altered from the passionate to the romantic and Pat sensed this and felt happier. They talked on, David telling her about Ulm and Munich and the meeting at Augsburg and listening to Dr Goebbels. Every now and then he would stop and they would have a little kissing session, but in a different tempo to the one when they first arrived.

"Shall we go to the pictures tonight?" said David.

"Yes let's. We ought really to take Rose with us for once," said Pat.

David pulled a long face. "I can't go in the back row with both you and Rose," he said.

"I wouldn't trust being in the back row with you in any event," she said laughingly.

"Alright, we'll take Rose."

Before they went out that evening David said to his father, "Dad I would very much like to take Pat out to dinner tomorrow night, best suit and everything. She goes back to college the day after on Sunday."

"Well what's the problem?"

"Firstly money – how much will it cost me? Second, I don't know much about ordering, can you help me? Third should we have any wine?"

"Right, One – money. If you're going to the Angel it will cost just under a pound for the full works for two people with the tip. Leave two shillings for the tip, that's reasonably generous without being flashy. Next, ordering. Your French is good but don't be afraid to ask the waiter what something means if you're not sure. They always try and blind you with science especially on the sauces. I ask all the time, as my French is non-existent. You don't have to have wine; in fact as you're under age they may not ask you anyway. Have a glass of cider, or you can have just plain water, lots of people do. If you go to the Angel the headwaiter will look after you. He's a very nice old gentleman and knows Uncle Jack and me well. Now, how are you fixed?"

"I've still got three pounds of my holiday money, I spent very little in Ulm, they were all so generous."

"Right then, go and ask the lady and phone the Angel quick, they get pretty booked up most evenings."

He did just that. The headwaiter who answered the phone asked his name and on being told Chandler said, "That's not Mr Chandler senior?"

"No," said David, "He's my father. Mr Hooper's daughter will be my companion."

"Then we shall look forward very much to seeing you both."

They had a pleasant evening at the pictures and Pat was delighted to be asked to go out for dinner. "I shall wear a special dress for the occasion," she said.

Both looking very smart they were dropped off at the Angel by Jack. All the bars and restaurants were crowded although it was only just past seven thirty. After the meal they planned to have a leisurely walk home. Jack having told them that if it was raining to telephone and he would come and pick them up, as he would be back home by nine o'clock.

The meal went very well. They stuck to things they knew and were attentively looked after by the waiter who obviously had been briefed by the headwaiter to take care of them. It was about ten o'clock and turn out time for the pub when David paid the bill, left the tip as instructed by his father, and ushered Pat out on to the little road at the side of the pub which also housed the small car park. As they emerged a gang of rowdies, who appeared to be well drunk, appeared from the public bar and David found himself face to face with none other than piggy-eyes from Home Farm. Instantly recognising him piggy-eyes shouted, "Here's one of the bastards who beat me up," and before David had got his wits together the gang jumped him and started to tear at his clothes, punching and kicking him.

Pat flew at them shouting, "Leave him alone you brutes, leave him alone," until one of the crowd grabbed her and started to fondle her. Piggy-eyes in the meantime had picked up a piece of timber leaning against the wall and swung it hitting David on the back of the neck. He went down pole axed.

"You've killed him you stupid bastard," said one of the mob and promptly took to his heels, closely followed by another. But he hadn't, David came to and started to sit up.

"Get her in the car, we'll take her to the barn," said piggy-eyes. David tried to get up but his legs wouldn't support him and in the meantime the four had bundled Pat into an old Morris Oxford and were driving out towards Mountfield.

By now the landlord and headwaiter, told of the disturbance, had come out to find out what was happening and found David lying in the gravel. "They've taken Pat," he said. "Please phone Mr Hooper and tell him to go to the barn at Home Farm, I think they've taken her there."

The headwaiter raced in and passed a quick account of the incident along with David's message to Mr Hooper. "I'll leave straight away. Please phone Mr Chandler and tell him I'll be there in two minutes and then phone PC Crown and tell him what's happened."

With that he ran out and got the Daimler out of the garage and raced round to collect Fred. As luck would have it Harry was there too, Megan being on night shift. He was still in uniform from being at the Terriers. They ran out when they heard the car, grabbing a couple of torches on the way and in Fred's case a heavy walking stick.

Jack put his foot down all the way and in under five minutes they were turning in the lane by the Prince of Orange, now closed of course. They drove down the lane and into the yard and on the far side could se the barn door left partially open, light from a hurricane lamp inside, and the Oxford parked in the corner. As they burst in, to their horror they saw four rowdies pushing Pat from one to another. They had stripped her naked and her clothes were thrown in all directions. Piggy-eyes had undone his flies and was rampant. As the men burst in he was shouting, "Hold her for me, hold her for me."

Jack hurtled across the intervening space. He was a very big man and he let out a roar that would have frightened the devil himself as he grabbed piggy-eyes round his thick neck, put a hand under his buttocks, lifted him up head height and hurled him onto the ground with a sickening thud. In the meantime another of the rowdies turned with his fists up to Harry. Not being particularly concerned with the niceties of the Queensbury rules at this stage, Harry promptly kicked him in the wedding tackle, as he would have put it, which prostrated him. Fred's attention was directed against one of the gang trying to climb over some bales of straw in an endeavour to get away. The bales kept toppling over which stopped his progress, as a result Fred stood over him with his heavy stick and said, "You move an inch and I'll brain you"- and he meant it, and the yob knew he meant it. The fourth man managed to get out of the door into the yard, but seconds later reappeared firmly grasped by PC Crown. Harry in the meantime had found Pat's coat and wrapped it round her and she was crying hysterically in her father's arms.

"I've phoned for the Black Maria," said Crownie. "I think you'd better get the young lady home sir, we can get a statement from her tomorrow. Don't touch anything here, the Sandbury boy's will want to have a good look round."

They piled back into the Daimler. "I'll drive," said Harry, letting Jack almost lift Pat into the back.

"Do you think it would be better if we let Ruth look after her Jack?" said Fred. "You can stay on as well in the spare room."

"I think that would be a very good idea Fred. I'll stay on with her while you and Harry take the Daimler to the hospital to make sure David is alright."

PC Crown had told them David had been admitted. When they got to the hospital they found David sitting up in a side ward being looked after by Megan. "Is Pat alright?" he said.

"Yes, she's a bit shaken, but otherwise alright." They had decided not to tell him any of the details until later.

David's head was heavily bandaged. "He hit me with a plank of wood," said David.

"Well, good job it was only your head. It could have been serious if it had hit something vital," said Harry.

A sister bustled in. "The police want a statement David, while it is all fresh in your memory. Are you well enough to talk to them?"

"Yes I'm OK now except for a bit of a headache."

"Alright. I'll give them ten minutes and then they must push off and you must get some sleep," and to Fred and Harry, "Doctor will look at him again in the morning but we'll probably let him go by midday."

All clouds have a silver lining. As a result of Pat's ordeal she had another week at home and she and David were able to be together, their pleasure marred only by having to answer countless questions from the police, particularly as to who exactly did what, so that the full charges could be laid against each individual in the gang. They were all eighteen or over, except piggy-eyes, and in PC Crown's words, 'They'll all be away for a very long time'.

Pat quickly recovered from her ordeal although she woke up in tears more than once in the week that followed. She stayed at Chandlers Lodge being nursed by Ruth and Rose through the Sunday and Monday and then went back home. David was a constant and kindly visitor and took her for walks in the neighbouring wood and heath land so that she soon got the colour back into her cheeks again. On the Saturday they were walking along the bridal-path not far from the factory when she stopped and put her arms around David's waist. "We say goodbye tomorrow," she said.

"It will only be till Christmas," David replied.

"David, will you kiss me like you did in the field after Dieter went back?"

"How was that?" said David looking at her in fun, but seeing in her eyes something quite serious that he couldn't quite fathom.

"Like this," she said, pulling his head down she gave him a long passionate kiss that started with her lips and ended with the whole of her body pressing and undulating against him until he had to move away saying, "Stop – stop for goodness sake, you are doing terrible things to me."

"I wanted to do that just once," she said. "I didn't want to lead you on. It was a sort of promise to you that one day we shall be very happy with each other, because I love you David. I know we're both young, but I know my own mind and I love you, and I think you love me. One day we'll be able to show each other how much and that will be wonderful."

David held her close not knowing how to reply so he kept quiet. They walked on a little way in silence and then she said, "Let's go back for tea," and all was back to normal again.

The next day was a sad one for both of them. As he handed Pat into the Daimler he said, "I hope that Gerald bloke is not going to be around this year."

Pat gave a tinkling little laugh and said, "If he is I shall be telling him you're now the heavy weight champion of the south of England."

He smiled and squeezed her hands as he kissed her goodbye, but although he smiled he had a sick feeling of loneliness in the pit of his stomach.

Chapter Fifteen

After the discussion in the office about Ernie Bolton, Fred had phoned Jack to tell him he'd like to speak to him when he had a few minutes, but for various reasons Jack couldn't get to the factory until the day after Pat went back. Fred told him about Ernie, who they would like to help, secondly Harry's idea about the invalid carriages, and thirdly about the closing down of the coachbuilders.

"I wonder if we could pop round there now and see the owner," said Jack, "Mr Elliott isn't it?"

"That's right," said Fred, "It's a very old established business, but it's been going downhill for quite a while I'm told."

They telephoned Mr Elliott who said he'd be delighted to see them.

Mr Elliott was in his late sixties. Apparently he had no family, his manager died a few months back and the works manager was overdue for retirement. They had several skilled craftsmen both in the bodybuilding and the interior fitting department and concentrated mainly on making funeral hearses, although in one shop they did commercial bodies on small van chassis. The premises, which at one time had built horse drawn coaches, were very small and contained a veritable rabbit warren of workshops. There was little space outside the workshops for parking vehicles; the whole impression they received was of Mr Elliott having to get quarts into his pint pots for so long he was glad to be giving up the ghost.

"We could be interested in buying your plant and taking on your men," said Jack, "but first would you have any objection to showing us your books so that we can consider buying the business as a going concern?"

"Not at all," said Mr Elliott. For the next two hours they looked at his orders for the past five years, trying to establish the market he had been in. They looked at the balance sheets and bank statements and finally walked around the shop so that Fred could get an accurate idea of the type of equipment there, its value and the condition of the main pieces of plant.

"Right Mr Elliott. We are going to spend the next couple of hours discussing this and then Fred and I will come and see you again at about five o'clock if that suits you. If we can make you an offer we will, and if we decide we are not interested in proceeding we will come and see you anyway and tell you so."

"You can't be fairer than that," said Mr Elliott and shook hands with them both.

As they left Jack said, "I'll buy you a quick lunch at the Angel if you've nothing else on, we can talk about it there. To be honest I'm missing Pat a bit and could do with the company."

"I'd better give Moira a call," grinned Fred.

"She's coming up at the end of the week," said Jack. "As a matter of fact I nearly drove on to Cardiff when I was down at Gloucester yesterday but I thought I'd better get back, I must be in my office tomorrow."

At the Angel, after they had settled and ordered a meat pie each, Jack said, "Well, what do you think?"

"Two things. First the coach building side is very profitable, albeit the volume is not high. Second, the van bodybuilding side could provide quite a volume of work, at lower individual profit its true, but it needs a lot more space, both inside and outside the building. If we consider this I would suggest moving the whole lot to our works and putting another bay on the building to accommodate it, take in some apprentices to learn Elliott's old boys' skills and actively market our manufacturing capability. Then having done a pukka survey on invalid carriages we could incorporate a small section of the shop for them using the equipment we already have. It occurred to me that if we could buy Elliott's business with the freehold, we could then pull the lot down and get a developer to put shops and flats on the site. It's close to the centre of the town and would lend itself to that sort of use, that could earn us enough to build the bay at least."

Jack was smiling benignly. "My dear Fred, that was the longest speech I've ever heard you make and there wasn't a flaw in it. Now I think you're absolutely right. I think from a commercial point of view we'll carry on the company name, we don't want to endanger Sandbury Engineering if things didn't work according to plan, and it mightn't be a bad idea to offer Mr Elliott the chairmanship of the company. That way we'll keep an Elliott name on the letter heading and the loyalty of his long-serving staff."

And that's how it went. They made Mr Elliott an offer lock, stock and barrel to be in accordance with an agreed valuation, with an extra amount thrown in for goodwill. Mr Elliott was delighted, the workforce of eight men who had been fearful for their jobs were relieved when they were told, even though some of them would have further to go to work, and provisional plans were made for the operation to move to Sandbury Engineering in January 1935.

Before they left the table Jack said, "Now what about this Ernie Bolton. Is there no way of getting him to and from Mountfield?"

"I'll tell you what," said Fred, "How about if we go over and have a pint at the Prince tonight, provided Ruth will give me furlough, and have a chat with Frank Lovell. He knows everybody and if anyone can give Ernie a lift in the mornings, I'll get Harry to run him home in the van at nights."

"You're on, let me know when you've got the boss's permission."

That evening they went over to Mountfield and were most warmly welcomed by Frank and the regulars. Frank spoke for all of them when he said how sorry they were about the two youngsters being set upon at Sandbury. "Only one was from here," said Frank, "and he was a new arrival." (Anyone who hadn't lived in Mountfield for at least five years was counted as a new arrival). As they were talking the door opened and a smallish bespectacled man came in, at whose entry all conversation ceased. Frank quickly whispered to Jack and Fred, "That's the Roper boy's father, he's a decent chap."

Mr Roper came up to the bar. "Good evening Frank, mild and bitter please."

Frank pulled the pint and said, "You ought to know Eddie, these two gentlemen are Mr Chandler and Mr Hooper."

The names took a second or two to register with him, then he turned and said, "In which case I owe you both a deep apology. I cannot tell you how much my wife and I feel for you both and your families at the evil my boy did. He and his gang were thoroughly wicked and I can only hope that the punishment he will get will change him for the better, although in my heart of hearts I don't think he will ever change, I think Satan was born in him." He was almost in tears. Fred stepped over and held out his hand.

"It's not your fault," he said. "You can only do your best for your kids, you can try and teach them right from wrong but if they won't learn there's nothing you can do to make them."

Jack joined them. "I agree with all that," he said, "and anyway we didn't come over to talk about that, we hadn't heard any good jokes lately so we thought we'd come and see this lot to see what's going around."

Conversation buzzed back again and Eddie Roper leaned against the bar with them. At a suitable moment Fred went to one side with Frank and told him in confidence they were thinking of employing Ernie, but they needed someone to give him a lift in the mornings – someone who had a car and worked in Sandbury. "That cuts the possibilities down," said Frank.

"Well I couldn't think of anyone I knew when we were here," said Fred.

"There is one possibility," said Frank. "Eddie Roper's daughter has a good job in the tax office in Sandbury and she's got a little Standard Eight she goes around in. She has to go visiting firms and farmers so she gets an allowance for it."

Fred smiled to himself – everyone knows everybody else's business in Mountfield.

"Lets ask Eddie and see what he thinks," said Frank.

They broached the subject to Eddie and he said he was sure Brenda, his daughter, would be only too pleased to give Ernie a lift. It would be the least she could do in view of the way her brother had been so spiteful to Ernie, to say nothing of the way he had behaved generally in the village. "How long are you going to be here?" he said.

"Oh a little while yet," said Fred. "Jack and I are going to duff up that couple of misfits at darts before we go." Pointing to the two men on the board playing a quick 101 up.

"I'll pop down and ask her now," he said, and scuttled out leaving his beer on the bar. About twenty minutes later he was back. "She'll be pleased to do it," he said, "just let us know when. She leaves here at 8 o'clock and comes back at 5 o'clock from Sandbury in the evening, if you can fit into those times. Her car has a wide door hinged at the back so that will give Ernie plenty of room to get his legs in."

"That's fine," said Fred, "but not a word to Ernie until we've contacted him."

The two men had a pleasant hour with the locals before they moved off back to Sandbury, both pleased with their day's work. When Fred told David what had happened it lifted him out of his despondency as little else could have done. "Well, tomorrow afternoon I'll get Harry to run me over in the van and we'll offer him the job and see what happens," his father said.

"Dad, why don't you learn to drive?"

"What, at my age?"

"Well you're not Methusela are you? In any event the way you're going you will soon be buying your own car and I'm sure you won't be able to afford a chauffeur just yet."

"I'll think about it. I suppose if Harry can manage it I can."

They motored out to Mountfield the next day. Ernie was out in the village. They told Mrs Bolton what they were proposing and asked her whether she thought Ernie would be able to get around alright once he was at work. She said that Mr Bolton had nearly finished making him another chair, so if he took his old chair to the office he could use it there, keeping the new one for going round the village. Ernie came back after a short while and when they asked him whether he would like to go to work he almost cried with delight. They explained what the work entailed and said that David had told them he could do it standing on his head. As they left Mrs Bolton said, "Mr Chandler, you'll never regret doing all this I promise you."

And he never did.

Things were going well at Sandbury Engineering. In August there had been a prolonged heat wave just as the farmers were beginning harvesting. As a result the horses pulling the binders had to be rested during the heat of the day, thus losing a lot of working time. Harry made capital of this by getting Mrs Russell to send a letter to all the farmers in a fifteen mile radius, pointing out that tractors never stopped, they could work a sixteen hour day or longer if there were men to operate them, and when they finished work you just left them to it, you didn't have to unharness, rub down, feed and water them. As a result they sold twenty-two tractors in a month, which is astonishing. At a little over £150 each they were beginning to make a real turnover.

Harry had been to camp for the last week in August and the first week in September and when he came back he was wearing a lance corporals stripe. "Good God," said Fred to the family in general, "Harry's got a laundry mark left on his tunic."

"I'll have you civilian lot standing to attention when you talk to me if you're not careful," said Harry, "this is only a start. I'll be a general one day."

"A general blooming nuisance that's about all," said Fred, but they were all pleased for Harry, particularly as he so enjoyed his Saturday night soldiering.

David went back to school at the end of September, and it was going to be one long slog up until Christmas. This was his last year, there was no way Fred could keep him on to the sixth form and university. The county council made no grants at this level and even if they had, the cost of keeping a young man for five years would have been beyond him. He had asked David what he wanted to do when he left school, and David had said he wanted to come into the business. They had a talk with Jack about this and he suggested it might be a better idea if David got experience elsewhere for a few years before coming into Sandbury Engineering, with that experience he could conceivably bring fresh ideas into the firm to the benefit of them all. "If you get articled to an engineering firm, and at the same time study for a BSc at an evening polytechnic you'll get the best of both worlds," said Jack.

"Do you know any firms that might take him?" asked Fred, "we ought to make enquiries in good time."

"I don't offhand, but I'll look around," said Jack.

He asked around and found that a firm of consulting mechanical engineers named Whitmore, Friend and Company in Victoria Street would have a vacancy in the following September. David went for an interview with Mr Friend Junior, one of the partners, a man of around forty years of age, and was accepted subject to his obtaining matriculation in his end of school examinations, and the payment of £360 as a premium for taking him.

"I think we can take that out of the business," said Jack, "after all we are investing in a future asset to our company."

"Yes, but what happens if he decides to go somewhere else at the end of it all?" said Fred.

"Well it won't be the first and I don't suppose it will be the last investment that's gone down the swannie if he did," said Jack, "but I've got a good idea he'll stick with us."

They put the contract out to build the new bay putting another 1200 square feet on to the factory, the builder promising to have it ready to move into by Christmas. Fred's only comment was, "Yes, but which bloody Christmas?" but in fact it was completed ahead of time and they started to move the stock and pieces of plant they needed from the old factory into the new one ready to start production in the new year. Harry, in the meantime, had been circularising with help of his invaluable Miss Russell, all the Co-op Funeral Furnishing organisations in London and the southeast. They had a particularly nice hearse going through the old works which he invited these prospective customers to come and see, looking after them well at the Angel afterwards as a result of which he had obtained an order from three of them on the understanding that, if all went well, there would be others to follow. The problem was of course the company had to buy the chassis from Daimler to build on, and since the lead-time in completing the coach building was around three months it tied up a lot of cash just sitting on the shop floor.

Reg Church was able to organise an extension to the Elliott coach builder's overdraft and said to Fred, "Right, the quicker you deliver, the less interest we have to pay, so there's an incentive for you."

"I take your point," said Fred, "but you've got to draw a fine balance with this sort of top quality work. Rush it and you may bodge it. I think the thing to do is to keep looking for time saving tools, and by that I don't mean silly gadgets. Let's get Ernie out here in the new year, getting some work-study times going for the different operations. We'll explain fully to the men what we're doing so that we don't upset them and we can then see which jobs are labour intensive. Then we can search for ways of reducing the hours either mechanically or with different materials for the benefit of all of us."

"Sounds logical to me," replied Reg.

During September David wrote his article about Dr Carew for the school magazine, published each term. The practice was that contributors never gave their names, only the editor knew who actually wrote the articles, they signed them with a nom de plume. By this means a boy could write in relative safety for their persons should they be saying anything scathing or humorous about other boys. The first people to grab the magazine were invariably the prefects, who usually were the subjects of some of the entries. The editor of course always ensured that contributions remained at a reasonable level, nothing was allowed to go too far. David started his story with: 'Do you know you pass a hero everyday?' and then went on to tell the story told him by Doktor von Hassellbek, considerably embellished with gore, mud, incessant artillery barrages, star shells, machine guns and so on. It ended with; 'The hero you pass is your Headmaster'.

David signed it Eunuch, and when Jeremy Cartwright, still his best friend at college and the only one in the know as to who wrote it other than the editor, said, "Why did you sign it Eunuch?"

David said, "Well, he'll know I'm the only one in the school who can know the story and there's no doubt in my mind he's going to chew my balls off for writing it."

As it happened Dr Carew couldn't really do that. When the school had assembled for chapel on the morning after publication day, quietly awaiting the masters to file in brought up in the rear by Dr Carew, a chorus of deafening cheers went up when he entered which followed him the whole of his walk down the length of the chapel and for, it seemed, an age after he turned and faced them, when normally they would have been quiet. Even the masters were laughing and clapping until eventually the Head raised his hands and they were at last silent.

"It's a very long time since I was lost for words," he said, and after a minute or two, "if this reception was a result of the article in the magazine yesterday I will tell you there are a number of your masters here who not only carried out unrewarded acts of bravery much greater than the embellished prose of our friend Eunuch. I have a faint idea why he chose that pseudonym (muffled laughter from both staff and boys) but I say to you now in all seriousness, those men carried on the sordid day to day existence in the trenches sometimes for weeks at a time with a fortitude that is beyond all bravery. Most people can be brave on the instant, but fortitude shows the true valour of men. I have a hideous feeling that a number of you will be required to show such fortitude in the years to come. I know you will not forget the example these masters have set you without your even being aware of it up until now."

A lot of boys present had good cause to remember those words in later years in the desert, in the jungle, in the air and on the oceans. David never forgot them or that moment. Other events of significance took place during that September term. Jeremy Cartwright was a frequent visitor to Chandlers Lodge, which gave a good deal of pleasure to them all, especially Rose. Rose was now nearly thirteen and attending a commercial college in Sandbury. She was an attractive, vivacious, well-developed girl, tall for her age. Although she had admired Jeremy from afar since those days back on the farm, Jeremy had never been more than polite and friendly to her, as if she were his younger sister too. David had said to his mother that he would like to learn to dance, "but for goodness sake don't tell Harry, I'll never live it down." She of course was aware ever since the wedding at Carmarthen that Pat was a competent ballroom dancer, so the reason for David's desire to be able to 'trip the light fantastic' was pretty obvious. "Why don't you get Jeremy to go with you on Saturday afternoons," said his mother.

"Could I go as well?" said Rose. "I would love to be able to dance properly."

David broached the subject to Jeremy who was all for it, so it was arranged they would take class lessons, as opposed to individual tuition, on Saturday afternoons at one shilling and sixpence a two hour session. The lessons gave Rose an opportunity to pair up with Jeremy and after three or four weeks it was obvious that, not only were they getting on well together with their dancing, but they were also getting on well together full stop! The Chandlers had no concern at this obvious state of affairs, Jeremy was a decent lad, Rose was bound to find boyfriends and if they were all like Jeremy they felt they would have little to worry about. The other person taking lessons was Fred. He had bought a second-hand Rover and Harry took him out in it during the lunch hour whenever they could manage it. In no time at all he was driving competently, so that by the end of the year he was able to apply to be tested, which he passed without difficulty.

The final event of significance concerned Jack and Moira. One evening sitting with Ruth and Fred, Jack said, "I would like Moira to come up over Christmas. She has several days leave to come and I could take a few days at the same time."

"Then she'd better come here," Ruth said immediately.

"I've always said you're an angel Ruth," said Jack, "that is exactly what I hoped you would say."

They all understood without anyone having to say it that Moira couldn't stay at The Hollies, even though Pat would be there. You just could not be too careful at this stage when Jack's decree absolute was so near. It was settled therefore that Moira would join them on the 21st and go back on New Year's Day. They would spend Christmas at Chandlers Lodge, Jack would then take them all out on Boxing night as usual and they would find a party for all to go to on New Year's Eve.

Later that evening as they were undressing for bed Ruth said,

"You know Fred, everything is going so well for us all, I get a funny feeling sometimes that it can't stay like this, that something will happen to spoil it all."

"I'm no Gypsy Rose Lee to be able to tell your future," said Fred, "for one thing I've got the wrong fittings. All I can say with all fingers crossed is that I can't think of anything that might upset things. If something does happen we'll just have to face it like everyone else has to, but it's no good worrying about it in advance. Now come here and give me a cuddle." And as an after thought, "Now if I was to put you in the family way again would you count that as a disaster?"

"Fred Chandler you wouldn't know how."

"Oh wouldn't I – hold on to your nightie."

The special occasion was of course George's wedding. It was a quiet affair held at Mountfield as George's Elizabeth had no relatives and only a few friends at Battle. David was very proud standing as bestman for the first time. He had always admired George, as a gentle man of high integrity who rarely raised his voice, and to David's knowledge had never spoken ill of another person, except perhaps sadly about the Roper boy. They had a reception in the clubroom at the Prince of Orange afterwards and it was a most pleasant and jolly occasion. Elizabeth was a comely woman and the general opinion was they were ideally suited.

During the course of the evening George asked David if he would call for silence, as his wife would like to say just a few words. In all innocence David rapped loudly on the table and asked the assembled company for silence for Mrs George Tanner who wanted to say a few words. Along with the other guests David was expecting Elizabeth to say how pleased she was to meet them all etc etc, but to his astonishment she took his hand and led him to the middle of the floor. "Ladies and gentlemen," she said in a soft Sussex burr, "I would not be here today and have made so many new friends if it had not been for the bravery of one young man, in fact our bestman today, who was the one who brought my George to me." David was beginning to blush furiously. "George and I therefore," George had joined them and had put his arm around David's shoulders, "would like to present this gift to him in your presence in gratitude for firstly saving George's life and secondly for giving me another life which I never expected to enjoy again." With that she presented him with a box which appeared magically from George's inside pocket and which when opened contained a beautiful gold wristlet watch, inscribed on the back of which was: 'To David for bravery in 1931'. She then folded David to her ample bosom and kissed him, followed by George pumping his hand till he thought it would never recover.

Everyone cheered and clapped, and Harry started the chorus of, "He's a jolly good fellow," all much to David's acute embarrassment.

When the hubbub subsided someone said, "Speech," at which David just said, "I shall treasure this always, it is beautiful, and I am very happy for you both."

The party ended at ten o'clock. George and Elizabeth walked to their cottage down the lane. George had only got the weekend off, he had to start milking again on Monday, but that was the way of things if you worked on a farm.

Chapter Sixteen

They had a wonderful Christmas. In addition to all the family and Moira, Jack and Pat, David brought home two boys who where having to stay at the college over Christmas. Their fathers were both doctor missionaries in China and for one reason or another they had no relatives able to have them in England over the holidays. They were two lively lads, both vying for Rose's company despite the fact that David told them Jeremy would give them a good thumping when he came back in the new term. "He can't thump us," said one of them, "we're both pacifists."

"Yes but there you have a problem, Jeremy isn't."

Over the holiday David broached with his father the subject of going to Germany again in 1935. During the September term David had been receiving special instruction in two by two-hourly sessions each week with a German master named Herr Grunberg, in place of the usual German lessons. Herr Grunberg was one of the seventy thousand German Jews who had been able to emigrate since the Nazi's came to power. The greatest proportion of this number settled in France, Belgium and Holland, where of course ultimately most of them fell victim to the extermination camps. Those that reached Britain and the United States were the lucky ones, although they all arrived penniless with only the clothes on they stood up in, at least they were safe.

As David was leaving school in July he suggested to his father that he went to Ulm over Easter, and then Dieter could come back in mid-July for one month before David started work in the first week of September. The answer he received was totally expected. "I'll have to think about it. But if you go at Easter you won't see Pat for six months you know, have you thought about that?"

"We'll keep in touch, we'll be alright," said David.

Fred discussed it with Ruth and they decided it was the best plan. It would be all too much of a rush if they tried to get both visits to take place in July and August. David wrote to Herr Doktor therefore, who agreed quite readily and it was all arranged.

On New Year's Day Jack proposed to Moira who immediately accepted on the understanding she should carry on with her work, which as she said to Jack was becoming even more important. However there was no problem in this respect as she had applied for a transfer to the War Office in London and, not only had this been approved, but she had also been given a higher grade which put her in charge of the section she had been working in and which placed her as one of the top women in the department. They decided they would marry in Sandbury, provided the vicar there would countenance having a divorcee marry again in church.

In the event Jack had a long talk with the vicar who said that normally it would be impossible for him to conduct such a service but, as Jack had been the innocent party in the divorce and was known as a man of high principles in the community, albeit a 'not too regular attender at church', this latter remark made not without some emphasis, he would bend the rules and allow the ceremony. The same four girls who had been bridesmaids at Megan's wedding would be asked to be attendants at Moira's and it was decided it would take place on Easter Saturday.

Moira and Jack went round to Chandlers Lodge for lunch, which also included Megan and Harry and the two visitors from college. When they were seated Jack stood up and immediately all went quiet, sensing something important was to be said.

"Pat, my dear friends, I am most pleased to tell you that I have asked Moira to marry me and she has graciously said she will," and then promptly sat down. There was quiet for a moment and then there was bedlam. Pat ran round the table and kissed Moira and her father, Fred knocked a chair over in his haste to congratulate both of them, the boys and Rose clapped and cheered.

Megan and Harry waited impatiently for their turn to express their good wishes and finally Ruth, when all the noise subsided, kissed them both and as practical as she always was said, "And when and where is this happy event to be?"

Jack filled in all the details. The girls were thrilled to be bridesmaids again, and he would be honoured if Fred would be bestman, to which Fred readily assured him it would be a great privilege, but he felt that Jack must know many more people more highly qualified for the job than he. Jack's reply was instant and sincere. "Nobody has been a greater friend to me and made me more welcome than you and your family at a time when most other people didn't want to know. That I shall never forget."

They sat down again for a cold lunch and there was a general buzz of conversation. "What will you wear?"

"Will the Lloyds' be coming?" Moira's answer seemed to indicate that half of Carmarthen would be invited.

"Where will you honeymoon?"

David was busy checking the date with his proposed departure for Germany and found that it was three days before he left. That meant he would have Pat for a few days at least. In the event they had found that David could only go for three weeks since it was essential he was back on time for the final summer term.

The move into the new bay at the factory went reasonably well, the men appreciating more spacious and better lit conditions. Ernie Bolton settled in well. The transport arrangements worked most of the time, but on the odd occasions when Miss Roper couldn't give Ernie a lift Harry stepped in, and on one occasion Jack took him home in the Daimler, which made Ernie feel very important indeed. During the term David had 'mock-matric' as it was known. Questions were taken from previous matric papers and the examination conditions were the same as for the real examination to come in mid-June. He passed everything with flying colours, "which doesn't mean you are going to get such easy questions in June, so don't slacken off – keep revising," said his form master. He'd seen boys before get too confident as a result of a good 'mock' and then fall flat on their faces when the real thing arrived.

Soon it was Easter. "Could Jeremy come to the wedding?" said Rose to her mother.

"You'll have to ask Uncle Jack," Ruth replied, "but I'm sure he'll say yes. Jeremy will have to bunk in with David if he does come."

Uncle Jack was asked and said, "Of course, of course," in his usual genial way, "and I'll make sure when Moira throws her bouquet it comes in your direction!"

Rose blushed, "We're great friends," she said, "nothing more."

"You can't kid me you haven't got designs on the poor fellow," joked Uncle Jack, "he doesn't know of course but he'll be caught in the snare like the rest of us."

"I'll tell Moira what you said," said Rose with a laugh. She had noticed recently how the rest of the family were beginning to talk to her as a grown-up rather than as a child; and she liked the feeling of being one of them. Even Harry, who was always fiercely protective of his sister and never said a word out of place in front of her, now sometimes said saucy things to her asking her how her love life was going and making other such remarks, which he certainly wouldn't have done a few months ago. She had her thirteenth birthday in January, and Ruth had long and frank talks with her about love and sex, and what was allowed with a relationship with boys and what was not, the reasons for these rules and the difficulties in keeping to them sometimes. Unlike many mothers and daughters she and Ruth had the greatest blessing of being able to talk to each other of these things. She knew what a boy looked like, she had seen David undressing many times when he was younger, but it was the feelings a boy might have and the feelings that they might generate in her that she could not envisage and about which Ruth did her best to describe in plain words so that she would know when to say 'stop'. In this Ruth was eminently sensible. She recalled her own courtship with Fred when many times she could have been a 'fallen woman' as she said to Rose with a conspiratorial smile, they waited and it was well worth the waiting. After their talks she had said to Fred, "Well, I've read her the gospel, there's not much more I can do."

"We can keep an eye on who she goes out with I suppose."

"In the long run you've just got to trust her, you can't be with her all the time," replied Ruth, "I think she'll be alright though."

One evening Jack called round. Harry happened to be there, and they started talking again about Germany, particularly as David would soon be going there again.

"I'm quite worried about what's happening there," said Fred. "Hitler made himself president and chancellor last year, at the beginning of this year he abolished all the powers of the German states, now his army has marched back into Sarr and today I read he's started conscription. He's forming," looking at the Daily Express, "thirty-six divisions, half a million men. He's now formed an air force, which is illegal under the Treaty of Versailles. He justifies this by saying that the Soviet Union has over a hundred divisions and a million men under arms threatening him from the east."

"I think he's got his eye on the west not the east," said Jack. "He's going to get all his old territory back mark my words, even if he is risking a war with France and ourselves."

"I wonder if Baldwin has got the message?" said Harry, "it looks as though he might have, he's announced a general rearmament this week. Knowing him that probably means three new tanks and four field guns."

"Well, if re-arming means reducing the two and a half million unemployed perhaps we should welcome it," said Jack, "though the thought of lads like you," nodding to Harry, "blowing each other to bits again for the second time in twenty odd years fills me with horror."

"Perhaps he's bluffing," said Harry. "By the way I heard last night our company is to send a detachment to the Jubilee parade on May 6th and I'm in it. Seems a good time to ask for the day off since you're talking about soldiers."

"I've told you before Harry, you can't really call the Service Corps soldiers, you've got to be in the Hampshires to be one of those."

"Or the Royal Artillery," said Jack.

"Now you lot would starve to death or have no ammunition to fire if it wasn't for the Service Corps driving through shot and shell to reach you," said Harry. "Anyway King George sent a special message for us to be there to show those guardsmen how to march properly, he's apparently fed up with them always being out of step on the changing of the guard."

"Well it will certainly be a good experience for you," said Jack, "and we'll have to come and watch you."

"We'll know which one he is," said Fred. "He'll be the only one in step. I tell you what, why don't we invite old Hitler over to see what he's up against."

"Anyway, what about my day off?"

"Well as it's for the call to king and country I suppose we can't say no," said Fred. "As it happens everybody is getting a day off anyway, I thought you already knew."

Easter came and with it the wedding. As Moira had said it looked as though half the population of Carmarthen was there, along with many of Jack's city colleagues. The Welsh contingent nearly raised the church roof singing the hymns, it was wonderful. Jack had the reception at the Angel, they went off at about 7.30 to stay overnight at the Grosvenor and then to catch the boat train from Victoria in the morning for a ten day honeymoon in Nice. Pat was to stay with Ruth until they returned.

On the Tuesday after the wedding David left for his second visit to Ulm. He had spent most of the previous five days that Pat had been at home with her, although most of the time they were in a foursome with Rose and Jeremy. Jeremy had come up on the train on the Saturday morning and stayed over until Easter Monday evening.

Pat came with Fred, Ruth and Rose to Liverpool Street, the latter three turning their backs as David gave Pat a lingering farewell kiss from the doorway of the train. They waved him out of the station and when they were out of sight he sat back feeling rather empty, which feeling persisted until eventually the train was clanking slowly over the points at Harwich docks. The crossing was a little choppy but caused David no great discomfort. The train journey was uneventful, although going through the German towns en route David noticed nearly all the buildings of any size, even the churches, flew the swastika flag. He recollected the Englishman's comments in the train on his first visit about the armband industry and smiled at himself when he considered that the flag industry was doing even better by the looks of things.

At last he reached Ulm and there waiting for him were the doktor and his wife and of course his friend Dieter. They all shook hands and once again David had to launch into his German. "My goodness," said the doktor, "your German is now very good, but you've lost the accent you went away with."

"I've had a teacher from Dusseldorf all this year," said David. "I suppose I've taken on his accent."

"Never mind," said Frau von Hassellbek, "We'll soon get you speaking properly."

When they got home and had been greeted again warmly by

Susanne and Hans, the doktor said, "We must telephone your mother. I'll book the call again while you wash in your room and then we'll have a talk."

The room was exactly as he had left it. He said to Dieter, "It's like coming to a second home."

Dieter clapped him on the back and said, "It is your second home, always remember that."

The telephone call was eventually put through and David was able to speak to his mother, father and Rose, also a few words to Pat. He promised to telephone again the following week.

When they were all seated for dinner David asked whether Inge would be here during his stay. There was a moment's silence, until the doktor said, "I'm afraid not David. As you know Inge is an ardent National Socialist. When she was in Belgrade on holiday last year she met an SS major, a young man twenty-seven years old, a relative of Herr Himmler. They married in January and she now works for the party in Berlin. We went to the wedding, but I have to tell you that we were so sickened by the debauchery that took place after Herr Himmler left the reception that we couldn't get back here fast enough. I know we are only country cousins but these people are uncouth animals and yet they hold the power." He paused for a little while. "David, I have said some things to you that I should not have said. Please do not ever repeat them."

"You may rely on that absolutely Herr Doktor," said David, saddened that such nice people were divided by this political dogma, although he of course could have no conception of the depths of depravity this dogma was going to spew upon the world.

They had two days of cold and rain, but on the third day it was sunny and warm. "When I was here last Dieter, Inge told me the water in the lake was very cold in April and May. Is it too cold to go swimming?"

"All I can say to you is that you won't stay in very long, and if you're very long when you go in you'll be very short when you come out."

The young men laughed uproariously at the joke.

"Let's try it this afternoon," continued Dieter, "you'll see what I mean then."

When they arrived at the lake there were only two couples there. David was secretly disappointed not to see Anni, but said nothing to Dieter. Three out of four already there had not met David before, so they clambered out and ran to greet him, shaking hands with wet, cold hands. The fourth, a young man of seventeen or eighteen came out more slowly and was introduced by Dieter.

"You are English?" he said.

"Yes"

"The English killed my father, I never knew him."

"I am terribly sorry," said David, "I really am terribly sorry."

The young man looked at David with cold eyes. "Well one day I may avenge him."

David said nothing but Dieter protested, "Johann, that is most unkind to our guest."

Johann paused and then turned and ran up the springboard back into the lake. David and Dieter looked at each other, both shrugged and went off to the bushes to get undressed. David was first into the lake and the cold water hit him like a sledgehammer to such an extent that he let out a bellow that set the others laughing. He swam around furiously for a minute or two until he called to Dieter, "I must go out and get warm again – I don't know how you can stand it so cold."

"You'll get used to it," said one of the girls.

He ran up the sandy stretch and as he reached the grass he turned and started to do PT exercises to get his circulation going. At this Dieter called out, "You weren't in very long."

David waved his fist at him and ran back up the board. This time the cold did not come as quite a shock as before, but all the same after five minutes he had to come out and this time Dieter came with him.

"Rub yourself down hard and put your clothes on straight away and you'll feel marvellous," said Dieter, which is exactly what he did and he felt a glorious glow creeping through him as he sat and watched the other four still in the water.

When the others came out and were dressed again they all sat for a while gossiping, although it was noticeable that Johann had very little to say.

That evening at dinner David told the story of his article for the school magazine and particularly how the whole school cheered and clapped Dr Carew when he walked into chapel the morning after publication.

"But you didn't get a tanning I understand," said the doktor.

"How do you know that Herr Doktor?" said David.

"Ah well, the weekend after the incident Dr Carew telephoned me and said, 'I hear you've been telling tales out of school'. I professed total innocence of course until he said, 'Oh I know it was young Chandler it couldn't be anyone else', and then I told him that I had in fact told you the story. I can tell you David that although he probably showed no emotion in front of you boys he was deeply touched indeed by the affection the whole school showed to him that morning. I can tell you from my own experience that being a headmaster is a very lonely life.

You are not only the headmaster of the boys, you are also the headmaster of the staff. It's like being the colonel of a battalion of soldiers, you cannot have the love and respect of all those people just by being in charge, you have to earn it and when you are the one who has to lay down the discipline and do unpopular things at times, it is extremely difficult to know whether you have succeeded or not. That spontaneous show of affection and admiration showed Dr Carew that he had succeeded, and the memory of it will stay with him all his days, just as it would with me if I had been so fortunate as to have it happen to me."

"It was a wonderful morning Herr Doktor," said David, and he went on to describe the whole episode in detail, in such detail in fact that Frau von Hassellbek was in tears at the emotion of it all.

"We must go to England soon and see the doctor and Mrs Carew," said Frau von Hassellbek.

"Yes, please do and come and see us as well. Why don't you come over when Dieter is with me, we would all like that very much."

"Well we'll certainly give it a lot of thought," said the doktor.

The days sped past. They went to the lake every two or three days and at dinner after one of these visits David said to Dieter, "We haven't seen Anni at the lake this year, does she go to work or something?"

There was a silence, and the doktor elected to answer his question. "David, again I am going to have to ask you not to repeat what I am going to say to you. Unfortunately Anni cannot now mix with her old friends." David looked blank and his puzzlement showed clearly all over his face. The doktor continued. "Anni's mother is half Jewish. In addition she was a trade union activist. Anni's father has a small business here in Neudorf, he is a very pleasant man. The mother has been arrested and is to be taken to Dachau. Legislation will soon be in force which allows Aryans to divorce their Jewish partners because they are Jews, and the Nazi's have decreed that anyone that has one Jewish grandparent is himself or herself a Jew. This puts Anni into a very difficult position."

"But I thought Anni was hoping to get into the Olympic Games team next year in Berlin?"

"She can no longer compete anywhere, she is Jewish. Because she is Jewish she will find it difficult to get any meaningful work. In the meantime her father will almost certainly have to divorce her mother to save his own life, and if there is a round-up of Jews as many people are saying there might be, then he would lose Anni as well."

"Wouldn't it be possible to get Anni out of the country?"

"If she had somewhere to go – yes. They have not stopped Jews from leaving yet, although they cannot take wealth with them."

"She can come to us."

"Now that's very noble of you David, but before you even consider that you must have a long talk with your parents. And David, please again remember that nothing we have said in here this evening must be repeated outside. I would also like you to know that we are all patriotic Germans, we love our country as you do yours, but there are things the National Socialist clique are doing that many of us feel that we are heading for the greatest disaster in history."

The Herr Doktor could not have known how prophetic his words were.

Chapter Seventeen

The three weeks soon sped past. There was plenty to do and see. They travelled around on their bikes, took train rides to other towns, and one weekend they all piled in to the Mercedes and spent three days touring round the Black Forest, staying one night in the beautiful town of Freiburg and another in a small village near the Swiss border. David loved this country so much, and all the people he met were so friendly he found it difficult to understand why there should be this undercurrent of uncertainty and apprehension on the part of such people as the Herr Doktor. He knew, as everybody did, that the National Socialists were making whipping boys of the Jews and the communists. With the regard to the communists he could understand that, even have some sympathy with it, bearing in mind his own upbringing in a solidly conservative family, and the horror of the knowledge that the communists murdered in cold blood our own King's cousin and all his family at Ekaterinaberg still fresh in people's minds. But he couldn't understand this hatred of the Jews. He personally had never known a Jewish family so he was hardly an expert on the subject. He had two Jewish friends at school, Levy and Nathan, but the only difference between them and the rest of the boys was they didn't go to chapel, otherwise they were the same as everybody else as far as he could see. An announcement had been made from Goebbels' headquarters only the previous day that in future all non-Aryans were to be banned from publishing literary work in Germany. The doctor's comment was, 'another step to total dictatorship'. David said to himself, 'He won't be able to say that to anybody but us', and then he realised fully that what he had just thought was exactly the cause of all this apprehension. Fear was being instilled into ordinary people. In time no one would know who they could or could not talk to, the doktor and his kind of thinking person were realising this already, with others it would take a lot longer, and many others, perhaps the majority, would never realise it, they would accept it as the norm

"You're far away David," said Frau von Hassellbek.

"Oh I was just thinking what a beautiful country Germany is," said David.

"Like everywhere else, some parts are nicer than others," she said, "but it is very beautiful in the south."

"Like the people," said David looking at her with a smile.

She squeezed his arm. "I think this young man is flattering me," she said to her husband.

"And why shouldn't he recognise a beautiful woman when he sees one," said the doktor laughingly.

On the eve of his departure David again raised the question of Anni. "If I get permission from my parents should I contact you, or should I contact Anni's father direct?"

He saw the doktor and his wife look at each other. "I really think it would be best if you weren't involved Herr Doktor. After all, I assume Anni's father would have sufficient money to send her to us for a holiday wouldn't he? If the holiday gets more and more extended who will care – except her father of course, he's bound to miss her terribly. Perhaps when her mother is released we can get her away too. I am sure my parents or Uncle Jack will be able to find them work and somewhere to live."

The doktor thought for a while. "I know you are thinking of us," he said. "What a sad state of affairs it is to be sure. Well yes, contact Herr Reisner direct, I will have a word with him in the meantime to tell him what's happening so that you don't have to give long explanations over the telephone and I'll let him know that you are a good family so that he will not worry about Anni's welfare."

"Thank you Herr Doktor," said David. "You know I'm beginning to feel a bit like the Scarlet Pimpernel already!" They laughed, but there was an undertone of sadness in their laughter.

When they saw him off the next morning Frau von Hasselbek embraced him for a long time saying, "David, I do hope this is not the last time we shall see you here. You know that you and your family are always welcome here, you have become very dear to us."

"Quite so David," said the doktor.

"I hate the sight of him," joked Dieter, but nevertheless hugged David and helped him on the train with his case and Mr Salmon's knapsack.

"I do hope you can both come with Dieter in August. Why not drive, then you will be able to tour around England?"

"That's not a bad idea," said the doktor, "The problem is you drive on the wrong side of the road."

The train was beginning to pull out.

"No we don't sir – you do." They all laughed and David watched until the three figures disappeared from view.

The journey back to Liverpool Street, apart from a rougher crossing than he had previously experienced, was uneventful.

Again he was fed to bursting with cold meats, black bread, fruit and cakes Frau von Hasselbek had packed for him, but he still had some left when he got back home. He was met by his father, his mother and Rose who were all patently pleased to see him.

"We'll want to know all about Germany and old Hitler and his lot as soon as you've drawn breath," said Fred.

"There is an enormous amount to tell," said David.

"Well you relax now," said his mother, "that can wait till you've had a good meal."

David was just going to cry out, 'I couldn't eat a thing' when he realised his mother had probably killed the fatted calf for him, and he hoped by the time he got home the food he had eaten would have gone down. In the event of course it had, and he did full justice to a meat pie, which had been left in the Aga for them. That evening he told them what was happening to the Jews in Germany and in particular the case of Anni Reisner. Ruth and Rose were horrified at the story. "I had no idea things were going as far," said Ruth.

"There is no doubt that Nazi policy as already stated by Streicher and others is the elimination of the Jews, so I am told," said David, "and the people I have discussed this with are not given to wild exaggerations."

"Well, Uncle Jack and I were discussing this some little while ago," said his father, "but we couldn't really believe the German people would do things like that."

"As I understand it," said David, "it's not the German people, it's a clique of evil men influencing a mob of fanatics. The bulk of the people who actively oppose what is going on are called communists and put into camps, like Dachau near Munich."

"Well getting back to your friend Anni, I'll talk it all over with your mother and we'll decide if anything can be done and let you know tomorrow."

"Thank you Dad, she really is a very nice girl – you'd love her."

"He'd better not," said his mother with a pseudo stern face, "come to that neither had you better be too complimentary in certain quarters!"

David laughed. "She's just a nice girl, that's all, and anyway she knows all about Pat."

It took a little while, even though he was really tired and full of food for David to get off to sleep that night. He hoped and hoped they could get Anni away and then he thought of all the thousands of other Annis' there must be that would be unable to get away and what would happen to them, but in his wildest nightmare he could never have imagined what was to happen to them and millions like them.

The next evening at supper his father said, "David, your mother and I have been talking about Anni and we have decided she can come here. You say she is nearly seventeen and speaks good English so it shouldn't be too difficult for her to get a job. Anyway that will all wait until she gets here. Now if you can telephone the doktor and see how the land lies out there, we can then put a call through to Herr Reisner

147

and see what he says or has organised."

"Right, I'll book the call right away."

It was only a quarter of an hour before the telephone rang.

"Your call to Germany."

"Herr Doktor, how are you all?"

"The same as we were when you phoned us yesterday."

David laughed at this. He had of course given a brief call to Dieter to let them know he had arrived safely.

"We are just going to phone our mutual friend and wondered if you had spoken to him?"

"Yes, he is expecting your call and has made some plans."

"Very good, goodbye now and regards to you all from us. By the way my parents say they will be delighted to put you up in August, so let us know your arrangements."

"Thank you very much, goodbye."

Ruth and Fred had been listening to David with a mixture of pride and amazement at his obvious fluency. It was the first time they had heard him talking in German and they were most impressed.

"Well?" said Fred

"Well what Dad?"

"What did you say and what did he say to you lummock?"

"Oh of course," said David realising it was all double Dutch to them, or at least double German. He did a rapid translation and then asked his father if he should phone Herr Reisner.

"Best get it done quickly, don't you think Mother?" said Fred. Ruth was surprised, he hadn't called her mother for months.

David booked the call to the Reisner number, which took rather longer to come through than the previous call – nearly forty minutes. Herr Reisner must have been told that a caller from England was on the line because, as soon as David said "Herr Reisner?" he answered quickly before anything more could be said.

"Herr Chandler, good evening, your colleague here has told me of your requirement. I am going to Paris to a trade fair on Thursday week and I will put the goods on the boat train arriving at 8pm at Victoria on Friday evening. Will that be alright?"

David instantly fell in with the line of conversation and said, "That is most kind of you Herr Reisner, we'll pick the goods up at Victoria."

"Thank you very much Herr Chandler. Best wishes to your family, goodnight now," and he rang off.

David excitedly turned round to his parents. "That didn't take long," said Fred.

"I think he was afraid someone was listening to the call," said David and proceeded to recount the conversation.

"Well, he's no fool, I'll hand that to him," said Fred, "although to think that someone is going to listen in to your calls in this day and age takes some understanding."

David was very pleased at the outcome of their planning and found himself looking forward very much to seeing Anni again. One of the first things he must tell her is not to say anything about the nude swimming. What his mother and father or Pat for that matter would think if they knew he had lain naked for hours next to this attractive young lady didn't bear thinking about. Oh well, we'll cross that bridge when we come to it he thought.

The next day he was back at school. For the next months there were to be few set lessons, revision, revision, revision, ready for matric in June, the masters were very good in that if a boy felt he needed some special coaching in a particular item they would take him on one side and give him individual attention. This could sometimes make all the difference between passing and failing. The curse of the matriculation exam was that you had to pass maths, a five-hour paper in two parts. English another five-hour paper in three parts and then a language, a science subject, history or geography. If you did brilliantly in all papers but failed on the language for example, you failed the whole exam, and it had happened many times. David felt quietly confident about it all, but he knew only too well that it was possible, particularly in his case in chemistry, to get questions on which he could come unstuck, on the other hand he was strong on physics. "Oh well, it's no use worrying, I can always be a road sweeper," he said to his parents.

"I doubt it," said his father," you'd fall off the broom inside ten minutes."

He worked hard during May. On May 6th they all went to London to see the King George V Jubilee procession, and to see of course Harry marching with the Territorial contingent. And see him they did, in fact he passed within six feet of them but to his credit kept his eyes straight in front, uniform pressed with knife-edged creases in the trousers and sleeves. "Megan made a good job of that uniform," said Fred.

"They look as good as the guards any day," said Ruth. David, Megan and Rose were cheering like mad and so were Moira and Jack. Then came the King and Queen Mary, the King in his ermine robes waving to them from his side of the state coach. Then came the Household Cavalry and finally the police horses. With all the bands and the bunting and the cheering it was an amazing experience for them all.

"Nobody does this sort of thing like we do," said Fred proudly. "Makes you want to be a soldier again."

"What would they do with a broken-down old warhorse like you?" said Ruth.

The others not listening Fred said, "You may live to regret saying that young lady. On the other hand knowing you, you wouldn't regret it."

She squeezed his arm, 'I'm a lucky woman', she thought.

That evening Megan and Harry came to supper and they all fell to talking about Anni's arrival on the following Friday.

"I'm on early turn next week," said Megan, "So if you go and meet her I'll come in and get supper for us all. You should be home here by half past nine provided there's no delay." And so it was arranged. They all congratulated Harry on his turnout and marching, David saying the RASC band was the best of the lot.

"Well we've been up since four o'clock this morning," said Harry, "so if you'll excuse us we'll be off to bed."

After they had gone Rose and David went to bed. Fred started to make peculiar whinnying noises. "What on earth is that racket?" said Ruth.

"It's that old warhorse you were talking about this morning. I told you, you might live to regret your remarks, looks as though he's got the bit between his teeth and nothing will hold him back from a certain filly he's had his eye on all day. So you'd better get up those stairs if you don't want someone walking in on your being dealt with in the kitchen." He moved quickly towards her – she spun round and raced up the stairs, the mood he was in he was likely to carry out his threat!

On the following Friday David hurried home from school, changed from uniform into ordinary clothes and patiently waited for his father and mother and Rose to get ready. When his mother came down into the sitting room, quietly but elegantly dressed in her black suit with white and gold trimmings, David thought, not for the first time, my mother is a very handsome woman. She caught him looking at her and said. "As the girl in the sweetshop said, have you had your pennorth?"

David grinned. "I was just thinking what an attractive piece of stuff you are."

"*You* have been listening to Harry too much."

"No I mean it."

"Well, you are a cheeky little devil, but thanks anyway."

"Thanks for what?" Fred asked as he walked in.

"He reckons I'm an attractive piece of stuff."

"Cheeky little blighter. To be fair though he's perfectly right. I reckon you're an attractive piece of stuff. I doubt very much whether I shall trade you in for a while yet, provided you continue to behave yourself of course."

"Now I know where he gets it all from," said Ruth.

"Where's Rose got to?" said Fred. "Oh here she comes. Come on out to the car." And out they went.

When they were driving up to London Fred said, "You know it's going to be a big wrench for that girl, it's not going to be easy for her to settle in to a new way of life. She may be a bit difficult at first, not knowing what terrible things could be happening to her mother, knowing the agony her father must be in losing his family. It really doesn't bear thinking about."

"I think," said Ruth, "that we must be very kind to her and keep her busy so that she doesn't get time to brood. It won't take the hurt away but it will hopefully give her less time to think about it."

They parked in the forecourt of Victoria Station and Fred gave the attendant a shilling to look after the car. They were early, so they walked across and looked in the windows of the Army and Navy store and then strolled back to the buffet and had a pot of tea served by a young Scottish waitress with a most engaging smile and highland accent. David in the meantime had gone to the enquiry desk to see if the boat train was on time and was told it was ten minutes early, which meant it would arrive in about ten minutes. He raced back to the buffet to warn the others, gulped down the cup of tea that had been poured for him, and they went out to the platform to wait for the train. In a cloud of steam, the mighty engine slowly approached the buffers stopping about six feet from the huge rams, which looked so enormous until you saw this giant locomotive against them. Doors started to be thrown open, dozens of porters with their trolleys who were stationed along the platform moved forward to collect the baggage. Senior porters at the first class section, juniors at the third, and in an instant the whole platform seemed to be in a state of total chaos.

Suddenly through the milling crowds of porters, trolleys, beautifully furred women, elegant men and some not so elegant, David saw Anni, looking thinner than when he last saw her, clutching a small weekend case looking anxiously down the platform, and when he waved she saw him and started quickly towards them. As she reached them she held out her hand to shake hands with David. He took her hand but put his other hand on her shoulder and pulled her to him giving her a light kiss on the cheek. Then he turned and introduced her to his mother and Rose and his father who said, "Tell her David, welcome to London."

"Oh didn't I tell you, Anni speaks very good English indeed."

"Well that will be a great help," said Ruth. "I was worried that we might have difficulty in speaking to each other." Ruth gave her a kiss on the cheek, she shook hands with Fred and they all made their way out to the Rover on the forecourt. There was not too much traffic as they dodged the trams over Vauxhall Bridge and out through Camberwell and Lewisham to get on to the Sidcup by-pass out to Kent. Anni was very quiet, and Rose and Ruth who were sitting either side of her on the back seat linked their arms through hers so as to let her know she was wanted.

"Can we telephone your father to let him know you have arrived safely," said Ruth, speaking slowly as she had to Dieter when he first arrived.

"Yes please," she said, "I have the hotel number and his room number, and he is going to stay in after dinner all the evening to hear from me."

"Good we'll phone as soon as we get home, I expect he's missing you already."

"He will be," said Anni, "he will be, and I miss him. Why are they being so cruel, why are they so terribly cruel. When he said goodbye in Paris he stood on the platform and he cried and cried and couldn't stop even when he was waving goodbye to me. I never ever saw my father cry before, but he cried and cried, and so did I, and a French lady on the train was very kind and I told her what they had done to us all, my mother, my father and me, and then she cried too."

And then the floodgates opened as the memory of it all, combined with the anxiety and tiredness, and the thought of her mother enduring she knew not what, combined to produce such despair that she sobbed deep uncontrollable sobs. Ruth folded her into her arms and held her close, making little soothing noises containing no intelligent words and Rose held one of her hands in both of hers and was herself in tears. Rose had never seen anyone suffer such a deep agony of unhappiness as this poor girl was experiencing and her heart went out to her. The two men at the front looked grimly ahead, trying as men always do not to be seen to be piping their eye under such emotional circumstances, and in David's case, probably because of his fondness of Anni, not succeeding very well. In a low voice Fred said to David, "That bastard Hitler has got a lot to answer for."

"Perhaps he will answer for it one day," said David.

Gradually Anni stopped sobbing. Fred had passed over a clean white handkerchief out of his top breast pocket, which Rose had unfolded and given to Anni. In a little while she said, "I'm sorry to have caused you that trouble."

Ruth again gave her a big hug and said, "After all you've been through we think you're very brave. From now on you must think of all of us as your family, if you have troubles come to us, if you are sad or lonely or want to talk to someone we are all here. And when you get to Sandbury and you meet Harry and Megan and Uncle Jack and Auntie Moira it will be the same with them. From now on you will be surrounded by people who will love and care for you, and when your father is able to visit you he will be made welcome and when they release your mother she can come and live here as well."

"Oh thank you, thank you so much," said Anni, and cried again, but only softly and only for a short while.

But she never did see her mother again.

Chapter Eighteen

When they reached Chandlers Lodge, Harry and Megan and Jack and Moira were waiting and greeted her warmly. They could tell she had been crying and her hair was dishevelled where she had been cuddled up by Ruth, so they made a special point of keeping the conversation going. Rose and David took her up to her room, David carrying her one small suitcase. When David left the room she washed in the washbasin in the corner where Megan had put a large jug of warm water, set her hair up again and when she was ready to go down for supper she was looking more like her old self. They booked the call to her father, which came during supper. Anni did not stay on long but gave the Chandlers number to her father so that he could telephone her when he was able. After supper, during which Anni started to make conversation giving David a few butterflies in case she mentioned the swimming parties, Moira and Jack and Megan and Harry left, all four shaking hands and kissing Anni.

"How very kind they all are," said Anni.

"Now my love," said Fred "it's off to bed with you and you can have a lie in in the morning."

"What is this lie in?" said Anni.

"That means you can get up any time you want to," said Ruth.

"I have some things to discuss with Herr Chandler when it is convenient."

"Well I'll be home at 12.30 being Saturday," said Fred, "we can sort them out then. In the meantime you can call us Auntie Ruth and Uncle Fred – you are now part of the family."

"How will I ever repay your kindness to me?"

"Well all you do," said Fred, "is marry a millionaire one day and make us all rich." They all laughed and Rose led her off to her room.

"Your room is next to mine so if you need anything just come and see me. In the morning, if I'm not in my room, come down to the kitchen and we'll be there."

Anni took some time to get to sleep, but eventually it overcame her and she slept soundly until 8.30am when she woke and went to Rose's room. Finding it empty she went back to her own room, but on the way she was hailed by David coming up the stairs.

"Good morning Anni, did you sleep well?"

"Yes thank you, what time is it? My watch has stopped."

"It's nine o'clock, come down and have some breakfast, your dressing gown is OK."

She turned and went down stairs, following David into the

kitchen. "Mum and Rose have gone down to the corner shop, they won't be long," said David, "which gives me a chance of telling you how very pleased I am to see you again. We will get lots of time to talk, but there is one thing I must ask you before the others get back."

"Yes David, of course, what is it?"

"It's about when we all went swimming. Here my family, in fact everybody, is very conservative about wearing bathing suits for swimming, they would be very shocked if they knew that we swam with nothing on. I would be very grateful if you did not mention it."

"I shan't say a word," she said with a mischievous smile, "but I have to say David I thought you looked very lovely without your clothes."

David reddened a little, "Not nearly as lovely as you were," he said, seriously meaning it.

The conversation was interrupted by the back door latch being lifted and Ruth and Rose arriving carrying brown carrier bags full of groceries.

"Did you sleep well dear?" said Ruth, giving her arm a little squeeze.

"Yes thank you Mrs Chandler"

"Now then, you know what Uncle Fred said."

"I'm sorry Auntie Ruth."

"Right now, breakfast – porridge or Shredded Wheat, eggs and bacon, fried bread and fried potatoes, toast and marmalade, tea or coffee."

"That is an English breakfast?"

"That's one of them, otherwise you can have kippers."

"Kippers, what are kippers?"

In the fun of trying to explain what kippers were Ruth said, "Well we haven't got any anyway, so it will be eggs and bacon."

Anni elected tea to drink on the basis when in Rome etc. She had never seen it made in a big family tea pot before and certainly had no idea of the religious procedure of warming the pot, letting it stand, tea cosy on, water absolutely boiling, one for each person and one for the pot, milk in the cups first.

She found it utterly fascinating, so much so that when she eventually received her cup of tea all eyes were on her to see whether she liked it or not. She sipped the brew and pronounced it was the finest she had ever tasted.

They spent the morning showing her the house and then they walked over to the Hollies and had morning coffee with Moira, Jack having gone into town to see about his new car. When they got home Fred had arrived home from the factory.

"May I now talk to you Uncle Fred?" said Anni.

"Yes of course love, is it private?"

"No, no, it's for everyone to know, but will you excuse me for a moment." She went off upstairs and returned with her suitcase.

"Please Auntie Ruth, do you have some scissors," she asked.

Ruth went to one of the cupboards and got them for her. She opened her case. "First of all, this case is all I could bring. If I had brought a large suitcase with all my clothes in someone may have informed on me and they would possibly have stopped me going to France."

They all wondered who would have informed, who would have stopped her and why, but they all kept silent to allow her to continue. Answers to their questions would undoubtedly come in due course. She continued, "If anyone had stopped us I was going to the trade fair to help my father. My father has a small business as a clock maker and was exhibiting there. First of all he asked me to give you this. A small gift to show just a little of how he is so grateful to you." From her case she removed a black velvet package which, by the way she handled it was, although small, very heavy. She laid it on the table and snipped the chord tying it, gently unwrapped the black velvet and removed a most exquisite clock. The case was obviously solid silver, with the most beautiful filigree work surrounding it in a dozen different interwoven designs. On the top of the filigree was formed a mass of flowers with delicate leaves and with small semi-precious stones forming the centre of each flower. It was about six inches high by three inches wide and quite, quite beautiful.

They all looked at it in silence.

"I have never seen anything so beautiful ever before," said Ruth her eyes brimming with tears, which prompted Fred to step in quickly and say, "Anni, this must be a very valuable clock; your father is far, far too generous." He didn't want to appear ungracious but to have a gift of this nature was far beyond anything he had ever experienced or would be likely to experience again.

"My father said you were doing more for him than he could ever repay, it is nothing compared to that. The clock is about one hundred years old and was made by a famous maker, whose name is on the dial, in the city of Freiburg. It is for you as a family." She was lost among the four of them all hugging her at once.

"Next, my father has sent me money to give to you to pay for my food and so on and to buy me some clothes." With that she took the scissors and cut the lining in the lid of the suitcase and to their astonishment there were packets of French and German banknotes all secured by gummed paper to the lid of the case. She took it out packet by packet and handed them one by one to Fred.

"You've got forty thousand francs and seven thousand marks here," said Fred. "Come on brains," (to David), "you know what the exchange rates are, how much is that in sterling?"

David did some quick calculations. "There are about seventy-five francs to the pound and twelve marks, so it's well over a thousand pounds," he said. "You could buy three houses with that."

"Right now," said Fred, "this money goes straight into the bank on Monday and will only be used in an emergency. We will have a clear understanding. You are now part of the family, you do not pay for your food or clothes until you go to work and then part of your wages you will give to Auntie Ruth for what we call your keep. Is that clear to you?"

"Yes Uncle Fred, but why are you all so kind when you don't even know me, and I'm not even from your family?" she was near to tears again.

"Because there is so little we can do about what is happening over there, and anyway you are adopted family so that's the reason. Besides that you are going to marry a millionaire aren't you, and make us all rich."

They all smiled and Rose put her arm around her. "It'll be nice having a sister," she said, "Brothers are such a nuisance."

There was a moment's quiet as once more Anni dived into her suitcase and produced a large manila envelope. "In here my father has written a letter for you Uncle Fred and also there is my birth registration, the deeds of ownership of his house and workshop, and his will which leaves everything to me. He said the letter explains everything."

Fred took the letter, only two pages written in neat gothic script and gave it to David to read and translate. It thanked all the family for taking Anni into safety, it explained he was enclosing the deeds of his properties, along with his will so that if one day the government of Germany was to be changed Anni could claim what was legally hers. It also said that in a codicil to the will, should anything happen to Anni, then the properties would be inherited by Mr Fredrick Chandler or his heirs, on the understanding that he or she would take care of Frau Reisner should she succeed him.

"Well I think we'd better take this lot for safe keeping to Alan Porter on Monday," said Fred, "and get some advice as to whether it's straightforward. Do you think your father will be able to come and see us all?"

"He is hoping to be able to come to a trade fair in Birmingham next summer," said Anni.

"In that case we'll keep our fingers crossed. David will you do a written translation as far as you can of the letter and documents so that we don't have to pay Alan Porter a small fortune to get them done?" David readily agreed.

"Well now," said Ruth, who had remained silent through all the previous discussions, "if we're all finished we'll have lunch."

Anni soon got used to the routine of the house. She was a quiet amenable girl and got on with Rose very well indeed, although Rose was three years younger. Harry made a fuss of her and made her laugh so that after a week or so the sadness left her face for most of the time. She saw little of David since all of his time was now taken up with preparing for matric. His mother always insisted he stopped for an hour during the evening and had supper with them all, otherwise he was fully committed to his studies. The only exception to this was the Saturday afternoon dance lessons, for which Jeremy could come from school with David at lunchtime, have lunch with the family and then go on to the dance studio. This routine had been interrupted by Anni's arrival, but the following Saturday David, having told Anni what they were going to do, asked her if she would care to join them.

"But I do not dance at all," said Anni.

"That's all right," said David, "you would come with us and then leave us and go to the beginner's class as we did last year, and then for the last forty-five minutes there is general dancing when you could rejoin us. Jeremy and Rose dance together and we could dance together. The instructors still come round and help you if you ask, otherwise it's just fun."

When they arrived at the studio David took Anni to the principal and introduced her. When they met up again at the interval before the general dancing he said, "Well, how did you get on?"

"It is not as easy as it looks."

"Oh you'll soon get the hang of it, we all felt like that when we started."

They moved slowly around the floor in the general dancing that followed, Anni not saying very much until David said, "Cat got your tongue?" laughingly.

"What does that mean?" she said puzzled.

"It's a silly English saying that you address to people who are not talking very much."

"Oh I'm sorry."

"No, don't be sorry, I was only joking," and he gave her a little squeeze. There was a pause.

"David you have a girlfriend I believe, she is called Pat?"

"Yes that's right. She's away at college at present but will be home at the end of July for two months then she goes to Switzerland for one year."

"You must miss her."

"Yes I do."

"I want you to know, and I want her to know that I would never try to come between you just because I am here and she is not, even though I do like you very much."

"You are a very, very nice person Anni."

Two things happened to Anni as a result of the week that followed. Firstly she said at supper one evening she would like to get a job. Fred said that he didn't know quite what the procedure was for someone of refugee status to register for employment, but he would get Miss Russell to find out and then they could take the matter further.

"But first of all," he said, "what sort of work would you like to do?"

"I'd like to be a nurse like Megan, but Megan says you have to be eighteen years old so I won't be able to do that yet."

"Alright, what's your next choice?"

"Well I did a commercial course at school so I can type quite well, but I can't do shorthand. I could do ordinary office work."

"We'll look in the local Chronicle at the weekend and see what's going," said Fred. "I'd offer you a job with Miss Russell at Sandbury Engineering but I think it would be much better for you to have other interests outside the family."

When the Chronicle came on Friday they looked through the situations vacant and found three possible chances. One was general clerical work at the local Water Board, a second was for a wages clerk at the Mid-Kent Cooperative Society and the third was assistant to the secretary of the Sandbury Golf Club (established 1804). She telephoned for an interview to each and obtained an appointment to go and see each of them. Ruth went with her for the first two interviews. She acquitted herself well and was told as always that there were other people to see and 'we will let you know'.

"It's a start," said Ruth, "at least you know what it's like to be interviewed now."

The Golf Club interview was for 5.30pm so it was decided that Fred would go with her whilst Ruth got on with the family's supper, particularly since Megan and Harry were joining them that evening.

They arrived promptly, asked for the secretary Mr Robbins-Smythe, and were shown into a beautifully furnished office with large picture windows looking out on to the magnificent Sandbury Golf Course, stretching into the distance on all sides. They stood waiting for a moment or two looking at the glorious panorama, when in bustled Mr

159

Robbins-Smythe, hand outstretched, his whole body wobbling with bonhomie.

"Good afternoon Mr Reisner."

"I'm afraid you've got the wrong end of the stick Mr Robbins-Smythe, my name is Chandler this is Miss Reisner, my ward."

"Oh, I do apologise for the mistake, I jumped at the wrong gun – what? Now please sit down."

They sat down in front of his huge mahogany desk. He was a small man with a white clipped military style moustache, a most affected Oxford accent and a constant smile, which somehow rarely seemed to reach his eyes. He had small white effeminate hands, which he held in front of him with his fingers together, showing beautifully manicured nails. Bit of a ponce this bloke, thought Fred unkindly.

"Right now young lady, you've applied for this position, tell me something about yourself."

Anni began to tell him how she was a refugee from Germany, how she had only newly arrived and was being cared for by Mr and Mrs Chandler.

"Why are you a refugee?" said Robbins-Smythe in a tone that started to grate on Fred. He asked the question as if it was something one should be ashamed of, in fact it was said in quite an aggressive manner. Fred had by now had some experience of interviewing people for jobs, and he had always found that you get far more out of a candidate by being friendly and by helping them along than you do by trying to make them look small or by putting them at a disadvantage in any way.

Anni looked at Fred questioningly.

Fred said, "Anni's mother is Jewish, therefore Anni was put at risk. That is why her father sent her to me."

Robbins-Smythe sank his head onto his pigeon chest.

Suddenly he looked up. "Would you like to come over to the window with me Mr Chandler. Chandler, Chandler, are you the gentleman that owns Sandbury Engineering and has taken Elliott's over?"

"Yes, I own it with a partner, Mr Jack Hooper."

"Oh well perhaps we can entice both of you to join our club at sometime. I'm sure there would be no problems with proposers etc, etc," and then in a much quieter voice, "we have a problem Mr Chandler – with Anni being Jewish you understand."

"No I don't understand," said Fred bluntly.

"Well you see old boy," Fred's teeth grated at the 'old boy', "we don't have Jews as members of the club do you see, therefore it would be difficult to employ someone Jewish to help run it. I have to tell you we are of course not alone in this."

Fred's hackles were rising. Although he personally had no direct Jewish friends, or even acquaintances, the smug assumption by Robbins-Smythe that he would readily see the difficulty and understand it was beginning to make him very annoyed indeed. He hated injustice of any kind, which was why he hated Hitler and his gang, and he could see that this smarmy little twit would be one of the first to volunteer to run a concentration camp given the opportunity.

"Are you saying that if I was a member here and I proposed a decent honest Jewish friend for membership you wouldn't accept him?" he asked.

"If you could find one," smirked Robbins-Smythe, "he'd be blackballed – not that of course you would in the first place."

"Anni – we're going," said Fred, "before I put this nasty little man's nose back between his ears. And as for you Mr Robins-Smythe, I suggest you go to Germany, they've got some good jobs for people like you."

He stormed out, Anni following at a near gallop behind him. When they got in the car and had driven for a while Anni deemed it safe to ask what it was all about.

"That man is a fascist," said Fred. He had never used the word before, but it now summed up in his mind everything offensive in the racial conduct of Hitler and Robbins-Smythe. Anni questioned him no further.

When they got home Megan and Harry were there and Jack had popped in to leave a message from Moira to ask if Ruth could go shopping with her to Cuff's on the following Saturday. Ruth immediately sensed that something was definitely 'up' with Fred. As Anni went up to her room Ruth said, "How did you get on?"

"I very nearly ran the chance of being locked up for assault and battery," said Fred, still looking very serious indeed, and went on to tell them of the episode with Robbins-Smythe. There were exclamations of disbelief, anger and from Harry

"I'll get a bucket of golf balls and stick them up his backside one by one if I get the chance," which they all knew was Harry's way of saying he was more than a little offended by the outrageous incident.

There was a slight pause, and Jack said, "It's not uncommon. Jewish friends of mine in the city find it very difficult to get into some of the clubs. We have some colonial colleagues from India and Malaya who have the same problem. I didn't realise it had spread down to Sandbury though."

The conversation passed on to other things through the meal and in the post the next morning Anni received letters from both the Water

Board and the Co-op offering her the job, and after discussions with Ruth and Fred decided she would join the Co-op, starting the following Monday.

As a result of her starting at the Co-op, she was approached on her third day by a fresh faced young woman of about twenty-one years old asking her whether she did any sports or athletics as the Sandbury Co-op had a first class sports ground. This young lady, Hazel Butler, was the area sports organiser and it was part of her job to talk to all the new employees to find out their sporting interests. When Anni told her she was a javelin thrower Hazel was most enthusiastic. "Oh do please come and train with us, we haven't anyone on the javelin." Anni therefore arranged to join them on the following Saturday, although she made it clear it would take a little while for her to get back into serious training as she had been unable to train for the past nine months. "Oh, why was that?" said Hazel suspecting Anni had possibly had an injury. Anni said she would explain it all next time they met.

She liked her job at the Co-op, but she had terrible trouble at first with pounds, shillings and pence. In particular if say someone was on one and fourpence half penny an hour and they did overtime at time and a third for one and a half hours, she was lost. After a while though she began to get the hang of it all. There were ten women and ten men in the office, with an office manager Mr Croft who was kindness itself. As the end of the first week she drew her own first pay packet and proudly took it back to Chandlers Lodge unopened and gave it to Ruth. Rose put her arms round her and danced them both round, all the time singing 'the breadwinner's home, the breadwinners home'. The three of them were laughing with the excitement of it all when Fred walked into he kitchen.

"Now what's going on?" he said.

"Anni has just brought home her first pay packet," said Ruth.

At this, probably because of the excitement of it all, and because Ruth had said 'brought home', Anni suddenly burst into tears. "It is my home isn't it, Auntie Ruth, it really is isn't it?"

"Yes, of course it is my dear," said Ruth cuddling her up, "of course it is and it will be for as long as you want it to be. We all love you dearly, it is your home, it always will be."

Anni stopped crying. "I'm sorry," she said, "I don't know what made me do that. I am silly."

"You're not silly my love," said Fred, "You've brought all that money home, now I can retire and grow mushrooms."

They all laughed at this effort to bring Anni back to her normal, cheerful self, at which they saw he was gradually succeeding.

"Anyway," said Fred, "Auntie Ruth is the chief cashier in the establishment, so Rose and I will leave you to talk to her about money.

This high finance is beyond ordinary mortals like us, isn't it love?" With that he put his arm around Rose and they walked off into the sitting room.

"How much have you after you've paid your sickness and unemployment money?" said Ruth.

"Well my pay is one pound, ten shillings a week and I pay three pence sickness and ten pence unemployment at my age. I elected to join the sports club so I pay threepence a week which means I get to use all the club facilities. The threepence per week goes up each year to a shilling a week when you're twenty-one. So that leaves me twenty-nine shillings and two pence in the pay packet."

"Right," said Ruth, "I will take ten shillings a week for your keep. You will save five shillings a week for clothes and holidays in a box we will keep here in the kitchen. I've got an Oxo tin we can cut a slot in which will be ideal for the purpose. You will put five shillings a week in the Post Office to keep for a rainy day. You get sixpence in the pound interest every year on that, you keep your own book, but if you want to withdraw money at any time see us first in case we can find a different way. Don't touch your Post Office book unless you can help it. Finally the other nine shillings and fivepence you keep for spending money, fares and other things. And remember one thing, if you are ever needing money for any reason at all come to me first. No one else will know and if I can help I will."

Anni hugged her impulsively, "I think you should take more for my, what did Uncle Fred call it? I know my keep. It doesn't seem nearly enough."

"It's enough, as you get on we'll take a bit more but thats enough for now. Do you know that an old age pensioner only has ten shillings a week to live on to cover everything, heating, food, rent the lot. How the poor souls do it I don't know."

And so it was decided. Later that night before they went to sleep Ruth told Fred that she would put the ten shillings keep money aside for Anni to have at some time in the future. It might be a useful nest egg for her one day.

"Does that mean I'm giving you so much housekeeping money you can feed another mouth without worrying about it?" said Fred.

"Well, I can manage alright," she said seriously answering his question.

"In that case I reckon I'm entitled to a share in your goodies," he said. "Have you got anything put aside for me for the future – by that I mean for the immediate future, like now for example?"

"Fred Chandler, you get worse as you get older."

"No I don't, I get better, and I'll prove it to you."

And he did, and she had to agree.

Chapter Nineteen

In June David hardly spoke a word to anyone he was so wrapped up in his books. He still found time to telephone Pat twice a week, but was sidetracked by little else. Even when Harry came in one evening and said he'd backed the Derby winner Bahram owned by the Aga Khan, he hardly showed any interest at all. Apparently Harry had bet a 'treble' for Bahram to win the Derby, Two Thousand Guineas and the St Leger in September. If he came in on all of them, even though the odds would get progressively shorter on the days, he would still make a nice little sum as he had got fixed odds to start with. Fred took him up on this. "I didn't know you'd gone into betting," he said.

"Well I don't back a horse from one year's end to another," said Harry. "It's a right mug's game if you ask me. But the sergeant at the Drill Hall ran a sweep for the Derby and I drew Bahram, so when I heard he was entered for the other two races I thought I'd have a flutter. Anyway I've won the sweep which has netted me thirty bob, so I shan't be out of pocket if he does fall over in the other two races."

The last week of the month was the start of the exams, which lasted over two weeks. On the days on which there were no examinations David was allowed to stay at home and revise. After each paper he came home and was virtually greeted with 'What was it like? How did you get on?'

Mostly he was able to say, "I think I did alright," but like most people taking examination he was superstitious about saying he thought he'd done well in case it brought him bad luck. On the afternoon after the last exam he arrived home full of relief, feeling ravenously hungry, talking nineteen to the dozen and unable to sit down for more than a minute at a time. Only his mother was home, Rose not yet in from school and his father and Anni would not be in until about 6 o'clock.

"What's for dinner tonight Mum, I'm starving."

"Oh, I haven't bothered about anything. Your father has had a meal out at lunchtime, Rose had a school dinner and Anni was going to try the staff canteen. I expect I'll get a few sandwiches later on for you and me."

He walked into the kitchen and sure enough nothing was bubbling on the AGA and no signs of any preparation going on anywhere. At that moment Rose arrived, "There's no dinner for me," said David.

"I had a school dinner, it was lovely," said Rose.

David's spirits began to sink rapidly. He went up to his room to put his books away and change from his school uniform. When he came down it was about ten to six and both his father and Anni had arrived home.

"Did you have a good lunch Dad?" was David's first greeting.

"Yes very nice indeed thank you. Why do you ask?"

"What about you Anni?"

"Yes, it was Lancashire hot pot – I didn't know what that was so I thought I'd try it – it was delicious."

"You're a rotten lot. I'm not getting any dinner."

At this the others all looked at each other and burst out laughing. "You're going to get a dinner alright old son," said Fred. "We're all taking you to the Angel to celebrate the end of your exams, but we thought we'd pull your leg first."

"If you weren't my Dad I'd thump you," said David, but Rose and Anni took one of his arms each and hugged him.

When they arrived at the Angel they were surprised to meet Moira and Jack, who had also decided to have a meal out. The headwaiter swiftly organised a table for all of them and they spent a very pleasant evening, although as Fred said, "This is to celebrate the finish of David Chandler's school days, and the conclusion of his examinations. The only thing is, if he hasn't passed his matric then he is going to have to refund the money we've spent on the meal this evening."

"There will be no fear of that," said Jack. "No fear whatsoever."

It was to be about three weeks before the result of the exam would be known. The weeks dragged by due to the fact there was little work to do at school along with no revision, and these two factors alone needed some getting used to. However, he had two things to look forward to. Pat would be home in two weeks and Dieter would be here in three weeks, so he set to planning an eight-day cycling tour of the south coast. Anni could only get one week's holiday without pay because she hadn't been at the Co-op long enough to be entitled to paid holiday, so it was arranged she would take her holiday in the second week in August to coincide with the cycling tour. When Jeremy heard of the plans he asked if he could join in, so David took the whole plan to his mother and father for approval. There would be six of them. They would stay at youth hostels where there would be separate accommodation. David emphasised this to his parents. True to form Fred said, "We'll think about it and let you know tomorrow."

That night when they had got to bed Fred said to Ruth, "Why don't we have a holiday on our own while they are away? As long as Jack and Moira are here, and Megan and Harry, they've always got someone to contact if they get in any trouble. Harry doesn't go to camp until the third week in the month so he can look after the factory."

"What a marvellous idea," said Ruth, "where would you like to go?"

"How about Paris?"

Ruth was utterly dumbfounded. Had he said Worthing or Cliftonville or even as far away as Bournemouth she would not have been surprised. But Paris?

"Are you serious?" she said.

"Yes, I'm serious. While we're there I'd like to take an excursion out to the battlefields again and see the war cemeteries. I know that sounds a bit sombre but I'd like to go and pay my respects, and it would only be one day out of the week, the rest of the time we can see all the sights of Paris."

"Like the Folies Bergeres I suppose."

"The thought hadn't crossed my mind," said Fred giving her a hug. "So it's on then?"

"Oh yes please," said Ruth. "Won't the children be surprised. You are a nice man Fred Chandler."

"In that case come and be nice to me."

The next morning they gave David the go-ahead to organise his plans in detail. He then casually said, "Oh by the way your mother and I will be taking a holiday while you're away."

"Where are you going Mummy?" asked Rose.

In a superbly casual reply Ruth said "Oh – Paris."

"Where?" there was a chorus from the three youngsters. "Paris – you know, that little place on the other side of the channel."

There was pandemonium for a minute, then David said "But Dad, you always told me that Paris was the place you went to without your wife. Still I suppose it's safe for you to go back there now after all these years."

"You cheeky little devil – you're not too old to get a clip round the ear even now," said Fred laughingly.

"Ah but you'd have to catch me first," said David.

Rose was the practical one on this occasion, "But you'll have to have some new clothes and new hats won't you Mummy?"

"Don't start putting ideas into her head you nitwit," said Fred.

"Well it's only a week, so two or three should be enough," said Ruth. "You two can come and help me choose them."

A couple of days later Jeremy said to David, "I spoke to my mother and father on the telephone last evening, and since we shall be on school holiday when the tour starts, he'll bring me up in the car to Sandbury with my bike on the back. Then they suggest that if you haven't organised anything to the contrary we could end up at Romsey at our house for two days, we've plenty of room, we can use that as our base and then at the end you can put your bikes in the guard's van and take the train back to Waterloo."

David thought this over and said it was a rattling idea. So he planned it that on –

Day One – Sandbury – Brighton – fifty miles.
Day Two – Brighton all day.
Day Three – Brighton – Portsmouth via Arundel and Chichester – forty miles.
Day Four – At Portsmouth.
Day Five – To Winchester and on to Romsey – forty miles.
Days Six and Seven – Stay with Jeremy. Visit Salisbury or Bournemouth.
Day Eight – Back to Waterloo and Sandbury.

When they discussed the plan that evening Fred said, "I'll get Harry to pick you up at Waterloo in the firm's van to bring you and your bikes back home." And then as an afterthought, "It will be interesting meeting Buffy Cartwright again after all these years." It was strange really that, even though he and Ruth had become more cosmopolitan over the last few years, they still hadn't attended the school's parents' day in the summer terms. "We should have done," he said to Ruth on several occasions.

At the end of the second week in July, Anni brought home two pay packets and gave them to Ruth. "What have you got here?" said Ruth.

"It's my divi – what does it mean, divi?"

"It's short for dividend, the amount of money you get every year on any company shares you may own."

"Well they explained to me that at the Co-op all the customers save up the little tin discs they are given when they buy anything, and then they hand them in and they get one and sixpence in the pound for their divi. Apparently the staff all get the same divi on their wages, so if someone is earning say one hundred pounds a year, they get three pounds and fifteen shillings for divi each six months."

"Well let's see what enormous divi you've got – you've not been there five minutes."

They opened up the packet in which was a hand written calculation slip, which showed that Anni had earned six pounds in that half year and that her divi was therefore nine shillings.

"You're nine shillings better off than you thought you were," said Ruth.

"I shan't be able to sleep tonight wondering how to spend it," said Anni. All the family were pleased for Anni, even though it was so little. It was another example that she was making progress in her new life, she was laughing more, the care lines were seen less frequently and, as only she herself knew, she was waking up and crying much less frequently than when she had first arrived.

The next week Pat came home and was introduced to Anni. David made what he hoped was a not too obvious fuss of Pat in front of Anni, and Anni was intelligent enough to realise what he was doing. In the event the girls hit it off quite well. During one of their conversations Anni told Pat that she was in training and about the Co-op sports club. Pat asked if she could go with her, she had for the past year been doing very well in the long jump and would like to keep in practice. When Anni asked Hazel Butler if it would be alright she answered with an enthusiastic 'yes' saying Pat could become an associate member on payment of half a crown. The following Saturday they spent the afternoon at the sports ground and when they were having tea, after having showered and changed, Anni took the opportunity to tell Pat what she had said to David. "I like David very much Pat, but I promise you that never would I try to come between you, not that for one moment do I think I could." Pat squeezed her hand, nothing more was said and they were both very glad that there would be no hidden feeling between them.

Tuesday would be the last day of term. It was also the dreadful results day. At chapel that morning Dr Carew said goodbye to those that were leaving, wished everyone a happy holiday and a safe journey to all those travelling long journeys home. Finally he gave a little homily about exam results. "Some of you may not have passed," he said, "but courage in a man is shown when he can pick himself up from the floor and go out and prove himself despite a setback." He went on a little more in that vein. All the time David was getting butterflies in his stomach at the thought of having to go home after five years of slogging hard to tell them he had failed. He could readily see for the first time how people could even be driven to suicide at such an enormous disappointment, particularly if they were ultra-sensitive or had parents who had driven them hard all those years. Then he found himself standing up with the others as Dr Carew swept out, and then made his way back to the form room. There was excited, even agitated conversation going on for several minutes until the deputy head master strode in carrying an important looking folder under his arm. They all stood and were told to be seated.

"So as not to prolong the agony any longer I am pleased to tell you that every member of this form has passed his matriculation," he said, "details of the exact results will be posted to you in due course. Congratulations to you all, this is the first time this has happened in the fifteen years I have been here," and he strode off again. There was pandemonium following this announcement, hand shakes, back slapping, dancing on the desks, desk lids banging, tears on some shamefaced countenances, and an enormous feeling of relief all round. David and Jeremy did an old fashioned waltz in front of the desks, knocking the blackboard over in the process. It was bedlam.

Eventually they all calmed down and began to pack their bags and say their goodbyes. David and Jeremy went out together through the enormous front door and down the imposing flight of steps David had first climbed in short trousers with sixpence in his pocket over five years ago. At the bottom of the steps Jeremy stopped, "End of an era, what?" he said. David nodded. He was sad he would no longer be a 'college boy'. He had got to love this place despite the occasional brush with authority, usually in the form of scummy prefects trying to make a name for themselves.

"What time will your Dad be here?" said David.

"He said about lunchtime, he came up in our car yesterday and stayed overnight at his club."

"Well, have a good journey home and see you in two weeks."

They shook hands and David went off to the bike sheds to pack all his belongings onto the carrier mounted over the Raleigh's rear wheel. When he got home Rose and Ruth were there, and Megan had called in as she was on late shift. He walked in without saying anything whilst they stood and looked at him.

"Well?" said his mother.

"Yes thank you Mum, very well thank you. Could I have a cup of chocolate do you think?"

"You little monster, you'll get nothing till you tell us."

"Tell you what Mum, I haven't done anything."

Rose ran across and kicked him lightly on the shin, "Tell us or I'll do it harder," she said.

"You may be interested to know I have passed my matriculation," said David.

His mother crushed him up and said all sorts of unconnected things including, "I'm so pleased – you are clever – you worked very hard," and then finally "I'll get you some chocolate."

Harry and Fred came in for lunch. "He's passed, Dad!" said Rose.

"Congratulations – well done," said Fred.

"Yes, jolly well done," said Harry and then as an afterthought, "do you think he'd be able to get us dry wood now Dad if he had to?"

"I doubt it very much," said his father.

The next week Dieter arrived. He had filled out a little from the previous year and was strikingly blonde and good-looking. Anni was a little apprehensive as to how he would accept her. After all, young men of his age were the main targets of the Nazi brainwashing that was going on regarding the Aryan super race, how they were to destroy the sub-human Jews and the inferior niggers. When they used to go swimming he was always very friendly with her, liking her as a person and enjoying her company without either of them having any sort of serious feeling toward each other. She was afraid he might have changed, particularly knowing the reason for her being here. In the event she had no cause for concern. He was already at Chandlers Lodge when she came home from work on the Friday evening, and when she walked in he jumped up, hugged her to him, kissed her warmly in front of all the others, and stood with his arm around her shoulders. With the emotion of it all she burst into tears, something she hadn't done for several weeks, but Dieter hugged her up and quickly she was apologising and wiping her eyes. Dieter joked with her, "I'm supposed to make you happy not make you cry – am I that ugly?" they all laughed and she was her old self again.

The week passed quickly, with their overhauling their bikes and getting their clothing and knapsacks ready. It had been decided that Jeremy's father would bring him on the Friday evening so that they could all make an early start for Brighton on the Saturday. They had just finished dinner, Jack, Moira and Pat had joined them, when a big chauffeur driven Wolseley arrived. Out got Jeremy and a somewhat rotund gentleman with a very well fed jolly face who was obviously his father. His first words to Fred were, "You haven't changed a bit, I'd know you anywhere," shaking his hand vigorously, and continued with, "I seem to have put on a pound or two since we last saw each other, all these city lunches don't you know." It was obvious he was genuinely pleased to see his comrade in arms.

"Let me introduce you," said Fred, and one, by one he shook hands, the youngsters last. They went into the sitting room where Ruth, as practical as ever, asked if she could get them a meal.

"No thank you very much," said Mr Cartwright. "Jeremy and I ate on the way up."

"Right then, you'll have a drink Mr Cartwright," said Fred.

"Now look here, I'm sure you lot all call each other by your christian names, so I'd be most grateful if I could be included in this, I've always had the nickname Buffy, so if you'll do me the honour of calling me that I shall be very pleased. Oh, whisky please," on answering Fred's question.

"I can tell you one thing," said Fred with a laugh, "I've called you that many times, but never to your face!"

"You know we go back to South Africa and the Mons lot," said Buffy to the assembled company, pointing at Fred. "I could tell you some stories about this man, but most of them wouldn't fit into this polite society. So you've got everything organised young man have you?" he said to David.

"Well I hope so sir," said David.

They talked generally about the proposed trip until Fred stood up and asked for quiet. "What I am going to say is serious," he said. "I thought I'd wait until you were all here before I made this little speech. It's to do with rules and regulations you must all observe while you are away. One – travelling, on main roads you ride in pairs about fifteen yards apart. On narrow roads and lanes you ride single file. The man rides on the outside when in pairs.

Two – you ride at the speed of the slowest rider.

Three – when one dismounts on a hill you all dismount.

Four – you stay together. One person wandering off can cause havoc.

Five – we shall be away tomorrow early so shan't be here all next week, you've got three numbers you call in emergency, plus the factory number. Emergencies don't include asking for more spending money incidentally.

Now any questions?" There were none, so he concluded with, "well, we all hope you have a lot of fun."

"Not as much as they'll have in Paris I bet," said David in a low voice to Pat, but not so low that Buffy didn't hear it.

"What's this Fred?" he asked, "going to Paris, you're taking a chance aren't you? Still I suppose it's safe for you to go back there now."

There was laughter at this, but Fred said, "That's what David said, but if it comes to telling tales I know one or two people in the Hampshires who didn't put everything they were doing in their letters home!"

Buffy roared. "You're right there, but you do realise," to the company in general, "he is definitely not including me in that number."

After more conversation and a couple more drinks Buffy stood up and said, "Well I really must be going. Thompson and I have to get back to Romsey." He shook hands all round and Ruth and Fred walked with him to the car, the door of which Thompson was holding open.

"Our lads seem to have got on very well over the past five years haven't they? And Jeremy seems quite fond of young Rose, by Jove she is a pretty little thing, I can quite understand it. Anyway, perhaps later in the year you could all find a long weekend to come down to us at Romsey, we'd be delighted to have you."

"That's most kind," said Ruth. "It would be wonderful if we could."

171

"Well get it organised Fred and have a super weekend," and with that the car door was closed behind him, Thompson climbed in the front and the Wolseley swept away out of the drive.

"What a very nice man," said Ruth.

"Yes, he did seem genuinely pleased to see us didn't he?" said Fred. "If he was just being nice for the sake of the children I don't think he would have invited us down."

The next morning everyone was up at the crack of dawn. Jack was taking Ruth and Fred to the station to get the train for Victoria and there was much cheering and waving as they were driven away. The youngsters finished packing their panniers slung over the back wheel carrier, slung their knapsacks and by the time Jack got back they were ready to go.

"God, think of the peace we're going to have for a whole week," said Harry.

"Away you go then," said Jack, "and don't forget what Uncle Fred told you last night." They mounted their bikes, and ringing their bells furiously moved slowly towards the gate.

"Do you know which way to turn at the gate?" yelled Harry. There was a suspicion of two fingers being raised in his direction as David commenced the turn, and then they were gone.

The countryside was beautiful as they made their way steadily through Tunbridge Wells, Uckfield and Lewes, stopping from time to time for a drink and to 'water the horses' as uncle Jack would have said. By late afternoon they had reached the youth hostel outside Brighton and booked in for two nights. The next day was a fine one which they spent on the beach and wondering around the old town. Being Sunday there were lots of day-trippers and the hostel was packed to capacity with youngsters coming down for the weekend to swim or walk over the Downs.

The next day they took the coast road to Worthing and then on to Arundel where they spent an hour looking around the castle and Arundel's quaint streets. Then the short ride to Chichester where they visited the cathedral, and then on to the hostel at Portsmouth, where again they booked in for two nights.

They all got on remarkably well. There was very little 'pairing off'. David had discussed this with Pat before they left and they had decided that if they set the example of mixing in with the others at all times it would give the lead. "After all," David said, "there's nothing worse than being in a party and having two of the party spooning all the time, it's sick making."

"Spooning, what is spooning?" teased Pat.

"When we get home from this holiday I will demonstrate to you a dozen different examples of the art of spooning," replied David.

"Oh and where did you learn them may I ask?"

"Young hot-blooded fellas like me don't have to learn them, they come naturally you'll see."

They thoroughly enjoyed their stay at Portsmouth, swimming at Hayling Island, and then visiting the Victory and other sights in this mighty naval town. The next day they were off across country to Bishops Waltham and Twyford, and eventually arrived at Winchester. There was an enormous amount to see there. "We shan't see it all," said Jeremy, "perhaps we can come back in again later. But first of all Dieter you must see the cathedral. I'm told by David you have the tallest spire in the world at Ulm, we have the longest nave in Europe in our cathedral."

At four o'clock they headed for Romsey and arrived a little saddle-sore in about an hour to be warmly welcomed by Jeremy's mother and father.

"Well now," said Buffy, "any problems?"

"Apart from the fact that David got us lost half a dozen times, no," said Jeremy.

"And how did you manage riding on the correct side of the road for a change?" he said to Dieter.

"I managed very well thank you, sir" said Dieter, "better than David did when he first came to Ulm – he was going around in circles until he got used to it."

"That's two of you I've got to sort out," said David. Jeremy's mother was very amused at all this banter. Her life, with her son away at boarding school and her husband going to London nearly every day was really very lonely, and she had been looking forward so much to having them all, even though it was only for a short time.

"Right, unload your stuff and put your bikes in the garage, then come on in and we'll show you your rooms. You can freshen up and then we'll have tea. Dinner is at 7.30."

Dinner was served by two rather pretty local girls. David found himself looking at one of them for longer than a cursory glance until he got a smart kick on the ankle from Pat sitting next to him. "What's that for? He whispered.

"That's just for looking," she said. He grinned amiably. The next day Buffy suggested they ditched their bikes and drive to Bournemouth and have a picnic lunch on the beach. Cook and the two girls got a hamper together which Thompson strapped on to the back luggage grid. "How are we all going to get in?" said Jeremy.

"Well you lot can pile in the Wolseley with Thompson," said Buffy, "and your mother and I will follow in the Triumph."

"That's fine," said Jeremy, "as long as we've got the food. You'd better keep up or we'll woof it all before you arrive."

"You'll go head first in the briny if you do my lad. I'm looking forward to some of that pork pie. Your mother made that for you with her own fair hands, to the utter astonishment of cook, I would add, who probably thought she couldn't even boil water."

They had great fun on the beach and to their surprise Buffy pulled out two bottles of champagne and gave them each a glass. "And it's a very special occasion," he said, "don't expect it with every meal."

Whilst Jeremy was sitting with his mother on the beach during the afternoon he said, "Mummy, do you think Rose could stay on a few days when the others go back?"

She looked at him intently. "You're not getting too fond of her are you Jeremy, after all there are lots of other girls around."

"Mummy, I like her enormously. We get on so well together. There's nothing soppy about it, it's not that we've got a silly crush on each other, it's just that I do so enjoy being with her."

"Well I must say I haven't had a chance to get to know her yet. She gives me the impression of being an extremely open and honest girl, but she is only thirteen."

Jeremy butted in, "Nearly fourteen Mummy."

"Well nearly fourteen then, I know a few months are terribly important at that age. Anyhow, as I was saying, she strikes me as being as charming a girl as one could wish to meet. I'll ask your father. He will have to contact Mr Chandler and ask if she can stay for one week, though I presume she hasn't many clothes having been on a cycling holiday."

"Oh, we'll manage somehow."

That evening Buffy was approached and readily agreed. "I'll contact Harry straight away," he said. Harry said that he knew she was in good hands and to tell her to have a lovely time, so all was settled, except that they still hadn't mentioned it to Rose! Jeremy found Rose in the billiard room with the others, watching David and Dieter playing snooker. He asked her to come outside.

"Rose, would you like to stay on for a week when the others go back on Saturday?"

"But I've no clothes."

"Then you can walk around in nothing."

"That, Mr Cartwright, is a very forward thing to say to a young lady."

"Please, would you stay," holding her hands and looking earnestly into her eyes.

"Dearest Jeremy there is nothing I would like more." And she put her arms round his neck and kissed him very gently. They had known each other since she was an eight-year-old, they had been dancing, walking, cycling, playing tennis together, but they had never kissed before, and it was beautiful.

"We'd better get back in or they'll send a search party," said Jeremy. "Am I your dearest?"

"Yes, yes you are – shall I tell everyone?"

"They'll find out soon enough," and he kissed her lightly again.

Saturday came and it was time for departure. It had been decided that the four going home would ride to Romsey station and the others would come down in the car to see them off. Mrs Cartwright had had a small hamper of sandwiches and fruit packed, as she said 'for the journey' to which Buffy commented, "I make that so called journey two or three times a week and no one packs me any sandwiches!"

"Oh, but you're different," said his wife. He mused over this pronouncement for a few moments but, not being able to see any logic in the statement, decided not to pursue the discussion further.

When the train pulled in and the bicycles were stowed in the guard's van they climbed aboard, but not before David had said to Jeremy, "Now you take good care of Rose do you hear."

"Yes big brother," said Jeremy "you may rest assured she's utterly safe in my hands."

"You keep your hands off her you horrible man you," he said playfully pounding him in the ribs.

But there was no one else in the world he would have trusted his sister with more than Jeremy Cartwright.

Chapter Twenty

Harry met them at Waterloo as arranged and took them home, first dropping Pat off and then the other three back at Chandlers Lodge. Moira had cooked dinner for them back at the Hollies, and after dinner Harry was to take the Rover up to Victoria to pick up Ruth and Fred, Megan being on duty that evening.

Jack and Moira were anxious to know how they'd been, where they'd been, what they'd seen, what it was like at Romsey and so on, and of course when Harry arrived back at about 9.45 with Ruth and Fred everyone wanted to know about their trip, so it was nearly midnight before they left for Chandlers Lodge.

As they turned into the short drive Fred said, "Hang on Harry, someone's just ran out across the back lawn, lets go after him."

"We'll go, you stay here with the girls," said Harry, and the younger ones ran like hares round the side of the house and across the wide expanse of lawn at the back towards a small wood.

In the meantime Fred had got down from the car, followed by Anni, and watched the others disappearing towards the copse. It was a bright moonlit night and suddenly Anni saw a running figure who had obviously doubled back out of the copse and was heading towards the front gateway of the house no more than fifty yards away. In a second or two it was obvious why he had done this, he went down the bank by the side of the road and was reappearing with a bicycle, which he had obviously hidden there. Before Fred could say a word Anni had taken off. Although not a runner she was an athlete and was used to short powerful sprints that javelin throwers have to use in their run up. In seconds, whilst the intruder was scooting the bicycle along to get on, she was out of the gate and across the road. Just as he got on the saddle she hit him full force, which sent him and the bicycle careering down the bank into the ditch below. Anni herself had bounced off sideways and ended up on her rear end on the rough, newly gritted tarmac road, much to the detriment of her dress, and later as she was painfully to discover, the skin of her bottom as well.

In the meantime Fred, yelling all the way for the others, had caught up and jumping down the bank fell on the intruder forcing him into the ditch again. With four hefty men surrounding him he would have been a lunatic to have tried to get away so he dragged himself out of the muddy water and scrambled up the bank.

While the intruder was climbing out of the ditch Dieter had gone over to Anni, who was now suffering reaction from what she had done and from the pain which was now beginning, and lifted her up. He put her arm around his shoulders and with his arm around her waist started to lead her limping badly back to the house. Fred immediately left the other two to go over and put his arm round from the other side. "That was a brave thing to do Anni, I don't think even now he knows what hit him."

When they got to the car Ruth took over from the two men while Fred unlocked the house, put the lights on and telephoned for the police. The intruder, a man in his early thirties was carrying a sort of carpetbag with a noose type top, which he had slung across his shoulder. "You make sure he doesn't move," said Fred. "I'll have a quick look around the house." When he came back he was white with temper, none of them had seen him look like this, and when the intruder saw him walking towards him he looked round for somewhere to run. Ruth immediately pushed in front of him.

"What's the matter dear, please, what's the matter?"

"The swine has stolen Anni's clock," he said, and pushing past Ruth he grabbed him by his throat and the front of his sodden coat and said, "where is it or I'll swing for you."

"It's in here," he said, and from a large padded inside pocket of his jacket he pulled the clock. One or two parts of the filigree had been bent in the collision with Anni but otherwise it was still working.

"Put it down there you thieving swine," pointing to a side table, "don't touch it anyone, perhaps the police will want fingerprints from it."

Ruth pulled Fred's coat sleeve and said, "I'm going up to see Anni." When she went into her room Anni had taken her top clothes off, but the blood from the cuts and abrasions she had received had started to congeal, so Ruth had to cut away her underwear and gently sponged her bottom until she had cleaned the wounds. "I don't know whether we should call the doctor," said Ruth.

"Oh that's not necessary," said Anni.

"It's such a large area I can't even see how we can dress it with what we have. It must be terribly painful. I think you're wonderfully brave. I know, I'll ring Megan at the hospital, perhaps Harry can pop over and pick up some dressings."

She rang Megan who said she was just going off on her mid-shift break. If Harry came over and collected her she could bring some dressings back with her and see whether they needed to get the doctor or not. Harry was despatched and ten minutes later they were both back. When Megan saw the damage she said, "Well as long as we keep the wounds free from infection you can stay here, otherwise we'll have you in the hospital. I'll come in twice a day for the next few days to keep an eye on you and to change the dressings. I've brought you a mild sleeping draught for tonight but I don't want you to keep having them. I'm afraid though you're going to be sleeping on your tummy for a few nights."

Anni smiled wanly, "What is that David says? – worse things happen at sea."

As soon as the police had left and taken the intruder away, telling Fred they would come back the next day and take statements, they all went up to see Anni. She was drowsy so they stayed only a few minutes saying goodnight. When they came down Fred said to them, "You should have seen her go – she was like a ruddy rocket. By God she's got some guts. That swine had the surprise of his life. One minute he thinks he's got away with it, the next minute a thunderbolt hits him and he's in the ditch."

"Well I think we'd all better get to bed," said Ruth, "it's been a very long day for all of us."

The next morning a policeman called and apologised for disturbing them on a Sunday. He was very pleased to tell them that not only would they not have to go to court to give evidence but, in addition to stating he would plead guilty to the offence of the previous evening, the burglar admitted to twenty-seven other offences in the past eighteen months. On searching his home a considerable quantity of goods recently stolen had been recovered, some of which carried a reward from the insurance companies, which would be shared among them.

"Oh no it won't," said Fred. "That's Anni's – if she hadn't had the guts and initiative to go for him he would have got away."

There was a chorus of approval at this. The policeman then went on to say that he was unable to say how much the reward would be, it was normally about ten percent of the value of the articles recovered. However, three of the items of jewellery were quite valuable which the thief had hung on to because he had obviously found it difficult to get them fenced locally, so it could be in the order of two or three hundred pounds. There were whistles from Dieter and David, and Harry said, "I reckon I'd risk a sore bum for that sort of money," which utterance was followed by a smart cuff from Megan.

"Was he a local man?" said Fred.

"Yes sir, and the amusing thing about it is his name is Sykes."

There was general laughter at this. When the policeman had gone they all went up to see Anni. After all the excitement she had slept quite well despite the pain. This morning the wounds were giving her some discomfort, but she put a brave face on it asking Megan how long before she could get up. "Whenever you feel like it," said Megan, "just wear your nightie and dressing gown. You'll have to eat your meals off the mantelpiece. I'll come and see to the dressings this evening."

"Oh and by the way," said Fred, "you're in the money."

"How do you mean, I am in the money Uncle Fred?" Anni replied.

"The police have told us they have recovered a lot of stolen property from this man and there will be a reward. Since you caught him – it's yours. They think it could be two to three hundred pounds."

Anni was wide-eyed, "But that's more than a year's wages."

"Well perhaps you'd better change your job and go out and catch burglars," said Harry, "you'll be a millionairess in no time and then you won't have to marry one to keep us all in luxury."

When the men had gone, Megan and Ruth stayed behind and having changed the dressings helped Anni to slide off the bed on her tummy and stood her up to put her dressing gown on. "Try walking across the room," said Megan. It was obviously very painful for the poor girl, so Megan suggested she lay on her side for that day and to try walking tomorrow.

"I've got to be better in two weeks, we've got our big sports meeting – I don't want to miss that."

"Oh you'll mend fast in a few days," said Megan.

"Yes but I shan't be able to train," said Anni.

"Well we'll see how you are by the end of the week. You should be able to do some training in the following week, provided it doesn't re-open the cuts."

Everyone was looking forward to the sports day. It was an inter Co-op event held every year between the two south London Co-ops, the Royal Arsenal and the South Suburban, the Medway Co-op from Chatham district and the Thanet Co-op from Ramsgate and Canterbury, along of course with their own Mid-Kent Co-op. Each team was the host in turn, and they all tried to out do each other in the welcome and on the presentation of the event. The standard of the athletes was very high, the frontrunners invariably being the Royal Arsenal who had won the event for seven of the past eight years. This year it was being held at Sandbury.

The Saturday of the meeting dawned fine and clear. Anni had been able to get some training in during the previous evenings, although she was not back at work yet since she still found it uncomfortable to sit down for long. Pat went with her and, combined with the practise and the coaching of Hazel Butler, had added over a foot to her previous best in the long jump.

"You could be up among the medals with a bit of luck," said Hazel, which spurred Pat on to even further efforts.

"You've really got the bug," said David, after her third night out in a row, "You sure you've not got a fancy for one of those hulking great shot putters down there."

"It's a hammer thrower actually," said Pat, "he's gorgeous."

The girls and David and Dieter went off early. Fred and Ruth were coming for lunch, which was to be laid out and provided by the Co-op catering service in a huge marquee. The event was opened by the mayor, but prior to this there had been a marching display by the band of the Queens Own Royal West Kent Regiment, affectionately known because they were the 50th foot, as 'the blind half hundred'. No one there watching the display could have imagined the glory the regiment was to bring on itself a few years later at Imphal when they were the key factor in stopping the Japanese from invading India. Many things were to happen between this glorious day and the valour and sacrifice of Imphal.

Following the marching display by the band, the teams marched past the mayor and dignitaries from the various societies and by eleven o'clock the events began. Both Anni and Pat qualified for the finals to be held in the afternoon to great applause from David and Dieter, and then they all wandered over to the refreshment area to meet the families and tell them the good news. Jack insisted the lunch was on him, so he organised a table for ten. By now the first results were coming in and to the surprise of most people Thanet were in the lead followed by Mid-Kent with RACS third.

"Don't let that fool you," Hazel Butler had said as she passed their table and had been introduced, "there's a long way to go yet, but if you two do well we're in with a chance."

After lunch Thanet dropped away and for a short spell Mid-Kent were in the lead. Then they had a poor patch in the middle distance finals in the men's events and let RACS slip into the lead. Then the ladies middle distance and relay teams performed a miracle for Mid-Kent and beat all comers knocking RACS back into third place again. Then it was the ladies' long jump. Pat put everything she knew into her final jump and managed to reach second place thereby accumulating valuable points. Then came Anni, and on her final throw she almost got back to her old form at Ulm. As Jack said afterwards, "That javelin soared and soared, I thought it was never going to come down." It was a magnificent throw reaching over ten feet past the nearest competitor. More valuable points. They all eagerly awaited the last finals to be staged. Scores were fairly evenly matched over the top three teams as before, with Mid-Kent slightly in the lead. The ladies 800 yards was won by Mid-Kent who also got a third which meant if they could get one place in the final of the men's mile they were the overall winners. The race was run in tense excitement, the crowd all-willing on the two Mid-Kent runners. They ran a great technical race and were first and second on the last lap, but at the final run in an unknown from south

Suburban sailed past them as if he were just starting, not just finishing, and won by six clear yards. However overall victory for Mid-Kent, the first time in ten years, was assured to cheering that could be heard back in the town centre.

All the younger ones went to a dance given by the Co-op at the Town Hall that evening, having been given an early supper by Ruth before they went. The others had their meal with Ruth and Fred at about eight o'clock, still talking about the day's events. During the conversation Harry asked Jack whether he had got his new car yet.

"Well no," said Jack. "I changed my mind. I was going to have a new Daimler but I thought I'd get something a little bit smaller so that Moira could drive it as well. So I've ordered that new car that's coming out called a Jaguar. I don't know the price yet but I believe it could be around £600 hundred odd pounds. It should be ready by the end of September."

"That's a lot of money," said Harry. "I see the new Ford V8 pilot is going to be £225, and the new Rolls Royce V12 £1800 – fancy paying that much money for a motor car!"

"Well I suppose you have to pay for perfection when you want anything," said Jack, "look at the money Moira cost me."

They all smiled at this little pleasantry, they all liked Moira very much. She was obviously very intelligent yet she was always friendly and chatty to the other ladies and she treated Pat like a sister rather than as a stepmother. Inevitably the subject came up as to whether anything had been heard of Anni's mother.

"Nothing at all," said Ruth. "David spoke to Mr Reisner the other day when he phoned from Switzerland but he is not even sure which camp she is in."

"The poor girl," said Moira. "Oh I do feel so sorry for her. I'm so glad she has found such kind people as you to care for her."

Fred, in one of his rare moments of sentiment, said, "she's one of our family now until she can go back to her father."

"You say back to her father, but what about her mother?" said Jack.

"I think most of us, knowing what those evil swine are doing over there, think it's unlikely she'll ever come out of that camp alive. They're actively purging the city of Berlin from all Jews and communists now, and we all know what purging means. I saw today that any Aryan seen with a Jew means both will be taken to concentration camps, and as you know already anyone with one Jewish grandparent is classified as a Jew. You can bet a lot of old scores are being settled by people informing on people they don't like very much by saying they're of Jewish descent whether they are or not."

They were all solemn at Fred's remarks. Moira said, "What does Dieter think about all this?"

"He doesn't say much and we really don't like to ask too much," said Ruth. "When David was over there he was left in no doubt that they thought very little of the Nazis, but of course their position is made more difficult by Dieter's sister being married to one of the top party officials and being a fervent Nazi herself. What we do know is that they are such nice people it seems inconceivable that other people of the same race and background, even their own family, can be doing such terrible things. He has the added problem of being called up for army service in a year or so which I gather he is not looking forward to at all!"

"Well enough of this gloom after such a great day," said Jack, and the conversation went on to other things.

The next day Dieter had to pack to go home and on the Monday they saw him off on the boat train again, liberally supplied as always with enough goodies to last him a week. "See you next year," called Fred as the train pulled away. They were all sad to see him go; he too like Anni was now almost part of the family.

Chapter Twenty-one

The days slipped past and September came, which brought with it the beginning of David's adult life. No longer was he a schoolboy not, as he well knew, that he had stopped learning, there was still plenty of that to be done. He was made very welcome at Whitmore, Friend and Co. and put under the wing of Mr Phillips who was a senior design engineer mainly concerned with mechanical handling systems. His first job was with a section of a large coal handling and washing plant being jointly developed with a German firm for a coalmine complex in the Ruhr. Mr Phillips told him that the main difficulty with the project was that the German partners lettered all their drawings in their own language, which meant there was always a delay in getting the translations done before they could be incorporated into the British drawings. Apparently they were sent out to an agency for this purpose.

"If you like Mr Phillips I could do that for you."

Phillips looked at him intently. "You speak German?" he said.

"Yes sir, I am almost fluent except possibly for some of the more technical terms which I may have to look up."

"You and I are going to get on very well young Mr Chandler I can see that."

And they did. When in a month or so several engineers came over from Dusseldorf, Mr Phillips said, "I'd like you to sit in on the meetings as an observer, not to say anything unless I ask you, but to keep a check on whether the translations are accurate or not – can you do that?"

"I'll do my best sir."

David found the work very interesting. It stretched his mind considerably, but when he got stuck he was always able to talk to Mr Phillips who showed infinite patience in not only answering his questions but also pointing him in the right direction regarding reading material relating to the problem in hand. His parents, sensing that he felt he was starting a career, not just doing a job, were more than pleased to be making the further sacrifice of having to support him to a certain extent for some little while yet. Pat went off to finishing school much to David's dismay.

"Only till Christmas," she said. "I'll be home for a month then."

"Well don't start falling for any Swiss bankers just because they've got pots of money," said David.

"If I do I'll make sure he gives you some of it," she laughed.

"You know Pat I can't imagine life without you."

"If you were a bit older I would take that as a proposal."

"If I were a bit older it certainly would be."

She kissed him tenderly and at length. "We have plenty of time," she said.

Jack and Moira and Fred and Ruth were talking together on the evening that Pat had been seen off at Victoria. She was going to Lausanne in the company of four other young ladies and a female chaperone who Jack swore looked like Lucretia Borgia. "She was hideous," he said, "but I would think the ideal chaperone. No young man in his right mind would think of getting anywhere near her charges."

Ruth said, "I expect she and David will miss each other again for a while. Although he doesn't make it public in any shape or form, I know that deep down David feels the separation deeply."

Jack replied. "Moira and I were only talking about this coming back from Victoria. They've been best friends, or whatever youngsters call this relationship these modern days, for several years now and as far as we know haven't seriously looked at anyone else in that time. To a lesser extent young Rose and Jeremy are the same. It's so unusual. I was always off with the old and on with the new at their age – what about you Fred?"

"I am certainly not going to incriminate myself in that respect, but as we've said before it seems to work with them. Whether it's because they're apart for a few months, and then back together again for a while which makes it all new and exciting I don't know. Young Rose of course is too young to know her own mind yet, but Jeremy's a good lad and will take care of her, so we've no worries there."

"Wouldn't it be nice to be young again," said Ruth.

"Only if you knew what you know now," said Jack.

Changing the subject Fred said "By the way did you know Harry has backed Bahram on a treble for the Derby, Two Thousand Guineas and the St. Leger? Well the first two have come up and the St Leger is being run this week. I expect it will be on short odds but all the same he should make a few pounds if it does win."

It did win the St Leger. Harry won quite a few pounds. Not as much as the Aga Khan did who owned it or Freddie Fox who rode it, but enough to be able to buy a second-hand Austin Ten, which thereafter became his pride and joy. As he said "It won't do 300 mph like Malcolm Campbell has just done, but it will keep me dry on a wet day."

The months rolled on towards Christmas. David got into the routine of catching the 7.40 Victoria train to get into the office in good time for a 9 o'clock start, and back on the 5.20 which meant he was indoors, having left his bike at the station, by half past six. He had taken to buying a German newspaper at Victoria each day, which he and Anni found interesting. Almost every week some new restriction was being placed on the Jews. In October they read that non-belief in National Socialism was now grounds for divorce. He had one or two odd looks passed at him as he sat reading the paper in the train home, but nothing was said at any time. Mr Phillips used his knowledge continuously, but rarely spoke to David about himself, or his home life and friends.

In November the public elected a Tory government despite the highly regarded Clem Atlee having recently been made leader of the Labour Party. The new government had a mandate for big increases in defence spending which prompted Jack and Fred to discuss whether they could move into the manufacture of equipment for the armed services on a subcontract basis. They were both in a moral dilemma in respect of this proposed venture. They had a soldiers' sickening disgust of war profiteers who made fortunes out of other people being blown to bits. On the other hand if they could provide components of the highest quality at a realistic cost which would help to ensure that our fighting men, soldiers, sailors and airmen could rely on them possibly for their lives, then they would be working in a good cause. The latter view prevailed, but not without honest misgivings on both their parts. Harry, as usual, made the blunt observation that since he would probably be one of the first to be at the sharp end if there was a war, he'd rather have well made stuff than back street rubbish to soldier with. As a result they decided to start looking for work in the manufacture of special vehicle bodies for the Forces and Civil Defence units.

As Jack said, "I read an article by James Garvin, editor of the Observer, last weekend. He said there will be peace if Britain is strong and known to be. There will be war if she is weak and thought to be, and I agree with him."

A week before Christmas Pat arrived home. When David rushed round that evening to see her, he found a somewhat different Pat to the one who left him in September. Having given her a big welcoming kiss and a long hug, quite unembarrassed by the presence of Moira and Jack, he held her at arms length to get a good look at her. He then dropped his arms and slowly walked around her, and having completed the circle he stopped and said, "What an elegant young woman we have here to be sure," and that just about summed her up. From the tip of her superbly coiffured hair, to her subtly made up features, her classically cut suit which emphasised her shapely figure, to her sheer silk stockinged legs and medium high-heeled patent court shoes, she could have come off the front cover of Vogue. "Well I've told you before and I'll say it again," said David, "you are beautiful – isn't she?" he said turning to Jack and Moira.

"We think so," said Jack, "but then we're prejudiced aren't we.

Let's say she's not so bad and improving."

"Now you've seen me all poshed up I'm going to get into something more comfortable," Pat said and went off up to her room. In a few minutes she was down in a jumper and skirt and flat shoes, but David had to admit she still looked so sophisticated he had this funny feeling he was being left behind somehow.

"I'm coming up to town tomorrow to do some Christmas shopping. What if I meet you at Victoria and we come back on the train together?" she said.

"Better still why not meet at the Coventry Street Corner House and we'll have a meal and then come home if you won't be too tired by then," said David. "We'll miss the rush hour that way."

It was soon time for David to go home. Pat saw him to the door and after a few lingering goodnight kisses he jumped on his bike and pedalled away. Then the reality of life hit him. He had invited Pat to have supper at the Corner House and he knew for a fact that he only had eight shillings and some odd coppers to his name. Only that day one of the men at the office pulled his handkerchief out of his pocket and with it came a stream of loose change, which rolled in all directions over the polished linoleum floor. The others all helped to pick it up and on giving it back someone said, "Have you got it all?" the reply came, "I don't know, I don't know how much money I had in my pocket in the first place."

David had thought to himself, "How marvellous it must be to have so much money you didn't know how much you'd got." He knew to the penny most of the time exactly what he had and it was never very much. When he got home his mother and father asked how Pat was and about Lausanne. David told them about his evening and then said, "Pat is coming to London for Christmas shopping tomorrow and I suggested we met up and had supper at the Corner House."

Quick as a flash Fred said, "Then you wished you'd kept your mouth shut because you're skint – right?"

"Absolutely right," said David, a little down in the dumps.

"In which case we'd better let him have a pound, no make it thirty bob in case, don't you agree mother?"

"You really are a couple of sports," said David. "One day I'll pay you both back."

"Don't worry," said Fred, "I'm keeping tabs in the back of my diary for when you're rich. So far you're down for about five thousand."

Pat and David met as arranged at the Corner House. They had a very pleasant evening and then got the bus down to Victoria, walking right to the end of the platform to make sure they got into an empty compartment, pulling the blinds down once they were in. After a spell of serious canoodling David said, "Now I've really said hello again properly, tell me what you get up to at this finishing school."

Pat then described her daily life. They were constantly chaperoned. Their lessons consisted mainly of literature and languages, they could take which ones of the latter they wanted, but most of the work was oral. As a result her French conversation was becoming quite good, though her German wasn't so hot. Then they studied social behaviour, dress sense, the use of make-up and hair styling, and silly things like how to get in and out of different cars from MGs to Rolls Royces without as she said, 'Showing your knickers'. They were being taught bridge and the object of the whole exercise was to turn out a young woman able to present herself properly, to have poise, and to be able to converse with all ages and ranks of people, "except the working class of course – they don't know there is a working class or if it exists it is not to be considered."

"Well that's let me out then."

She giggled and made a grab at him round his neck, showing a considerable amount stocking in the process, and as she did so the door from the corridor opened and a voice said, "Tickets please." Without blinking an eyelid, he'd seen it all before and a lot more besides, the benign ticket collector clipped their little bits of cardboard and went on his way. The two went in to a fit of giggles and cuddled up close. "You haven't learnt much at school so far," David said, "you were definitely showing your knickers then."

Soon it was Christmas and they stuck to the usual arrangement. Christmas Day at Chandlers Lodge, Boxing Day at The Hollies and then out to a show in the evening. On Christmas day they all sat around the wireless to hear the King's Christmas message. Ruth said, "He doesn't sound very well to me." There was general agreement on this.

Harry said, "I suppose we shall soon be able to have television down here, then perhaps we'll be able to see him as well as hear him."

"I think that's going to be a while yet," said Jack "although I read that a chap in Belgium named Dumas or Damas has invented colour television. Just imagine being able to sit here and see the Changing of the Guard or something like that in colour!"

"I'll believe it when I see it," said Fred.

Nineteen thirty-six came in very cold. In Germany a new edict forbade firms to employ Jewish women under the age of thirty-five, followed by Hitler telling the League of Nations in Geneva to mind its own business regarding German treatment of the Jews.

"Shows how effective the League of Nations is," said Fred. "They ought to wind that bloody lot up." Because of their fondness for Anni, and their concern over her mother, Fred felt all these indignities inflicted on the Jews almost personally. The frustration of knowing that the whole of the rest of the world could do nothing made him see red as little else did. At the end of the second week in January Pat went back to Lausanne, which plunged David into his usual gloom. However Mr Phillips kept him very busy at the office. And then the whole nation was plunged into mourning with the death of George V. The King and Queen Mary were much loved, Queen Mary particularly by the East Enders of London who she regularly visited. Add to the sadness of losing the King, the unhappy feeling many people had regarding the new King's association with Wallis Simpson, many people were concerned for the stability of the crown. "We'll have to wait and see," said Jack, "but I have great fears of what may happen."

In February David was seventeen. He was doing well at Whitmore Friend and was now taking special instruction twice a week in draughtsmanship. The chief draughtsman was a Mr Parker, one of the old school for whom nothing but perfection would be accepted. David enjoyed these lessons and the simple detail drawings he was being instructed to carry out. He was amazed to learn how the most elementary things that the normal person took for granted, say a cogwheel or a bearing, required such detailed calculation and design knowledge for them to be manufactured to suit a particular purpose. He was talking enthusiastically to his father one evening about a machine being designed in the office to fill tubes with glue. The technology and know-how required was far beyond anything an ordinary person buying a tube of glue would ever envisage, even if they thought about it in the first place.

"When you design a machine to fill bottles of whisky you can bring me home a few samples," said his father, but behind the banter he was very pleased that the boy was not just 'going to work', he could already sense he was getting immersed in the projects, giving him the sort of enquiring mind that would stand him in good stead in the future, and hopefully bring benefit to Sandbury Engineering eventually.

In early March the papers were full of the first flight of the new fighter plane, named the Spitfire. "What a beauty," Harry had said, and had a big picture of it on his office wall.

"If it is as good as it looks," said Fred, "it will be a real winner." No one at that time could have envisaged in their wildest dreams how much of a winner it would be.

A couple of days later in spite of the Versailles Treaty forbidding their doing so, the Germans marched back into the Rhineland. "We're going to need those Spitfires a lot sooner than we thought I reckon," said Fred. "I see they had a national plebiscite and 99% of the people who voted backed Hitler in what he was doing. It must be the result of fear, never in any country in the world would you get 99% of the population voting for the same thing at the same time."

"I also read," said David, "that those people who abstained lost their jobs."

"In that case," his father said, "I wouldn't give much for the chances of the one percent who voted against him would you?"

Easter came and Pat came home. Rose went to stay at Romsey for a week. Jeremy had stayed for the occasional weekend at Chandlers Lodge since leaving school and going to work in his father's offices. On Easter Sunday Harry and Megan came to lunch, to which also Moira and Jack had been invited. When they were all seated Harry stood up and in very solemn tones said, "I know I am rarely credited with saying anything serious, but today I have a very serious statement to make to my mother and father."

There was complete silence as they all, thoroughly taken in by this solemn demeanour, waited for the rest of his statement.

He went on, "I'm afraid they are very shortly to have to be called Granny and Granddad."

Everybody spoke at once and when the excitement subsided it was established that the happy event would be in November, that Megan would get six months leave from the hospital, two months before and four months after the confinement. "I must phone Rose," said Ruth, "she'll be so excited at being an Auntie."

"Now we know for sure," said Megan, "we're going to see Mr Salmon at Cuff's again to fit out the small room as a nursery."

"In that case I suggest you make out a list, like a wedding list, only this is a christening list. We all would like to chip in something towards the new arrival," said Fred.

"What a good idea," said Jack, "I thoroughly second the motion."

"I'll buy the potty," said David.

"Clip his ear someone," said Harry. Pat playfully complied with the order.

When later David and Pat were strolling through the woods nearby, Pat said, "Aren't Harry and Megan lucky."

"Well, yes I suppose they are," said David, "but had you any particular reason in mind?"

"Having a baby of course, dunderhead," she answered.

"Well, I'm told it's not too difficult," said David teasingly, and at the same time slipping his arm round her waist.

"I'm serious," she said pushing his arm away, and when he looked into her eyes he could see they were quite misty. He just didn't know what to say, he was completely out of his depth, and recognising that, he thought it would be politic to say nothing. After a while she was her old lively self. David didn't mention the incident again, but he thought about it many times and wondered if all girls got this longing feeling, or whatever it was, when babies were mentioned or when one was on display. As far as he could see they made noise at one end and pongs the other, there was very little that one should start getting emotional or sentimental about.

Chapter Twenty-two

Anni's mother was arrested in February the previous year, 1935. At four o'clock in the morning a thunderous knocking at the Reisner door preceded her being bundled into a van with a small suitcase into which she was allowed to put a few belongings, and taken off to the prison at Ulm where she was housed with a score or more Jewish women and known communists. On the second day she was taken in front of a small immaculately dressed, bland faced man of about forty-five, who merely said to her, "You are Jewish and a communist, do you deny this?"

"I am part Jewish, but I am a trade unionist not a communist."

"We believe you are a communist or a communist sympathiser. Do you deny you have associated with communists? For example..." And he read out a list of names of known communists in her union who she of course knew and had worked with.

"I know these people but I am not a communist."

"Take her away."

And that's all there was to her trial and her incarceration in Dachau. When she got to Dachau she found the section she was taken to was guarded by SS troops. Going through the reception area where she and her small suitcase were searched and all her valuables removed, including her wedding ring, she was pointed in the direction of a store, where she was issued her prison uniform.

Standing in the store was a tall, not unhandsome officer, probably in his early forties. Whilst drawing her uniform from the trustee behind the counter she looked through into the next room to see the women being sat on stools and having their hair cut off. It was a sickening sight to her, she had always been proud of her luxurious black hair. She was a most handsome woman, full in the figure, with dark limpid eyes and a flawless complexion. Her hair was her crowning glory and the thought of losing it sent such terror into her that she almost screamed. When she looked up she saw that the officer was watching her intently and for a moment she looked deep into his eyes, her own showing the depth of the horror she felt at being mutilated in this way. The officer looked across at the female guard in charge.

"This one will do," he said, pointing to Anni's mother, turned on his heel and walked out.

The guard walked to the counter. "Wait there, Jewish cow," she said. In a few minutes she returned with another trustee.

"Take this to the major's quarters," she said pointing to Frau Reisner, and handing a pass to the trustee.

When they were clear of the guard the trustee said in what Frau

191

Reisner was to learn was the standard camp whisper, "You're the lucky one aren't you."

"Why am I lucky?"

"You'll work in the major's house, sleep in a bed, be in the warm, have decent food and you won't be beaten if you behave yourself."

They passed through the inner gateway, the trustee showing the pass to the soldiers on the gate. "I wouldn't mind having this one in my bunk tonight," said one of the soldiers.

"She's too old for a young rookie like you," said the corporal of the guard. "She needs a real man to satisfy her, you can see that plainly enough."

"Maybe that's what the Major's got in mind."

"He'll be slipping if he hasn't."

At the sound of the coarse laughter that followed them they made their way to a small detached bungalow-type building situated just inside the outer perimeter, but obscured from the camp itself by a row of closely planted conifers. The two women went through the front entrance and into a small office just inside the door where a civilian typist was working.

"Woman to look after the Major," said the trustee.

The civilian, who looked to be in her mid-forties, studied Frau Reisner intently for several seconds. "You can go," she said to the trustee.

"You can cook and clean properly?" she said in a not unkind voice. "Your name is Reisner, aren't you Jewish?"

"My mother was half Jewish, I am Catholic. I have always been a competent housewife."

"Very well, come with me."

She took Frau Reisner and showed her the house, which comprised a kitchen and outhouse, large sitting room and small dining room, a bedroom with a double bed, bathroom and a small bedroom also with a double bed. At the rear of the ground floor there was a flight of wooden stairs, which led up to a small room in the apex of the building, which was Frau Reisner's room. It had it's own washstand complete with a luxury she had missed since she was first taken to prison, a mirror. She put her small suitcase on the bed and they went back downstairs to the kitchen.

"Your duties are simple. You keep the house and the office thoroughly clean and polished. You wake the Major at 6.30 with coffee, there is an alarm clock in your room. You make him breakfast. Mostly he has lunches and his evening meal at the officers dining room. Sometimes he will eat here but will let you know in advance. He is an easy man to cater for. He has a manservant who comes in during the day who takes care of his uniform and boots, but you will do all his washing and bed linen. You will do the ironing and provide me with coffee during the day and a light lunch. I am not here on Saturdays or Sundays unless something important is happening. You will eat in the kitchen. You are not allowed to touch the drink in the dining room nor the wine in the outhouse, you will go straight back to the main camp if you act in any way improperly. Similarly you will not go into the office unless you are told and under no circumstances will you go into any drawers, cupboards or files. For that you would face the severest punishment. Now have you any questions?"

"Why was the previous woman sent back?"

"She wasn't, she was released."

"I thought..."

"You thought no one is ever released? Some are, it depends on whether they are able to realise the great opportunity our Fuhrer is bringing to the people of the Third Reich and to wholeheartedly give themselves to him." Her eyes were shining with an evangelical fervour, which seemed to be changing her whole appearance. Frau Reisner kept quiet. The woman's features then resumed their normal appearance as she thought to herself, 'But that doesn't apply to Jews'.

"Anything else?"

"How do I get the food, cleaning materials and things like that?"

"You give me a list of your requirements and I give the money to Hans, the Major's servant, and he gets it."

"I haven't any other questions."

"Well I shall be going home shortly, make us some coffee, then look around so that you know where everything is, cook yourself something for the evening meal and go to bed. The Major will not be in until late tonight. By the way, when I've gone lock the doors and windows. Although we're in a prison neither the guards nor the trustees are to be trusted."

She heard the major come home around midnight and fearfully wondered whether there would be any footsteps on her stairway, but soon there was silence and she went off soundly to sleep. She woke up feeling cold. The house had been warm when she went to bed, but as the heat dissipated, the space where she was under the roof got colder and colder with the temperature at well below freezing outside. There was no more bedding in the room so she put all her clothes, except the top uniform, back on and again crawled back into bed. It was better but she was still not warm and was glad when the alarm went at six o'clock so that she could go down into the kitchen and stoke up the coal range.

Promptly at six thirty she took in his coffee. She got him breakfast when he came into the kitchen and then left to clean the bathroom. The routine gradually took shape. The major rarely spoke more than a few words. His servant was an old soldier who kept himself to himself. The secretary was more talkative sometimes than at others. All in all she considered herself very fortunate indeed to have such a good job even though her underlying resentment at being in prison at all was still there, particularly when she remembered the hideous sight of those women having their hair cut off. She could have no inkling of the real horrors being perpetrated only a few hundred yards away, compared to which having one's hair cut off was absolutely nothing.

At the end of March, the major came back to the house in the middle of the day and asked for a light lunch. Frau Reisner prepared him a vegetable omelette with some cheese, biscuits and coffee, and waited on him whilst he ate in the small dining room. She had made his bed and tidied his bedroom early in the morning, after which Hans appeared and took an iron and ironing stand from the kitchen into the bedroom to do some pressing. He would never bring uniforms into the kitchen in case he got something spilt on them.

After lunch, the major retired to his bedroom. She heard him moving around for some time, during which he called to her to let him know when his car arrived. After about an hour a small staff car arrived and Frau Reisner knocked on the door to tell him it was there.

He called out, "Will you fix this for me, Reisner?"

She went into the bedroom and saw he was dressed in an entirely different dress uniform. He really looked magnificent, his tall lean figure, strong face and dark hair greying at the temples being shown to the greatest advantage in the pale blue uniform with the maroon facings and solid silver dress-daggers, buttons and collar motifs. He wore his Iron Cross from the Great War, and his other medals on the left side of his chest. He looked every inch a soldier.

Without thinking she stopped in her tracks and said, "You look magnificent in that uniform," and them stumbled on, "I'm sorry sir, I didn't mean to be presumptuous.

He smiled, it was the first real smile he had ever given her. "That's alright Reisner. I tell you I feel like a soldier in this uniform. It's my old regiment, we have a reunion tonight in Munich. Now, I can't fix this collar." It was a very high collar on the dress uniform, and was fastened at the front by hooks and eyes.

'God knows how men with short necks can wear a collar like this', thought Frau Reisner. As he was so tall, she got a footstool to stand on and found that one of the hooks had got compressed as Hans did his pressing and would therefore not engage in its eye.

"Just one minute sir," she said, and went off to the kitchen to get a knife to prise it open. She stood back on the footstool and asked him to come a little closer.

"I hope you're not going to cut my throat Reisner?" he said, with another slow smile. She didn't answer, but eased the knife-edge into the hook, levering it open, but in doing so she over balanced. Instinctively the major held her tight to prevent her falling. The stood for one or two minutes looking into each other's eyes which, because of the footstool, were at the same level, until he released her and let her stand on the floor.

"Thank you Reisner. I shall be late. I'll try not to disturb you," and off he went to his staff car.

After he had gone, she tried to analyse what if anything, had happened between them. She was a married woman, married to a solid, respectable, if unexciting clockmaker. Although she had travelled in the course of her union duties and stayed in hotels with men colleagues, and had had innumerable invitations to share a room, she had always been faithful to her husband and had really never felt sexually attracted to any of them. She decided that if any chemistry did take place when she was fixing the major's collar, it was probably due to the fact that she had had no contact with her husband for what seemed an eternity. The major himself, seemed so forlorn at times as to be almost a prisoner himself, and he was undoubtedly very handsome.

Before the typist left, Frau Reisner asked her casually, "Is the Major married?" to which she got a very short and emphatic answer.

"It's a subject you mind your own business about, and one which will land you in very deep trouble if you mention it – understand?"

"I'm sorry, I didn't mean to offend." But she was more curious than ever.

At about one o'clock in the morning she heard the staff car return, the sound of voices as the driver and the major entered the house, a cheery goodnight from the driver and then silence for some little while. Then there was a solid thump as if something heavy had fallen. She wondered whether to go down or not and with some misgivings eventually decided she would. Slipping on a robe the major's secretary had brought in for her, she crept down the stairway and into the living room. Spread-eagled half on, half off, an armchair was the major, still fully dressed and breathing heavily. He was obviously quite drunk. She wondered whether to try and make him more comfortable or to try to get him into his bedroom. She decided the latter would be far too difficult so gradually she tugged at him until he was at least lying fully in the armchair. She unfastened the high collar, unbuttoned his tunic and took off his belt. She then unfastened his boot buckles and with some difficulty pulled the boots off. She then pulled another low armchair over and lifted his legs up on to it. Finally she got a pillow and eiderdown off the bed and made his head comfortable and covered him with the eiderdown.

"There, you'll do until the morning," she said, "but I wouldn't like to have your head tomorrow," and with that she quite involuntarily bent over and kissed his forehead and went back to bed.

At 6.30 she took him his coffee and he woke up with a start, realised where he was and that someone had obviously looked after him. He said "Did you do this for me?"

"Yes Herr Major, you were very tired."

A slow smile appeared fleetingly, "That's a good word for it, you should be a politician. I'm very grateful."

"Thank you sir," she said and went back to the kitchen.

When he reappeared she left him to eat his breakfast and when he left for the day he said, "I shall eat in this evening, something light."

During the day Hans arrived and looking at the crumpled uniform said, "Good God look at this, you would think he'd slept in it." Frau Reisner smiled to herself but made no answer. She never knew how to take Hans. He was not rude or aggressive to her but she had the feeling that he despised her because she was a prisoner and at the same time was jealous of her because she attended to his master's needs. One day she had asked him whether he had been with the major long. "We were in the trenches together," he had said, "We were real soldiers then. He didn't need any other servants those days."

That evening she prepared a light meal of soup, schnitzel and chocolate cake, which he enjoyed. When she gave him his coffee in the sitting room and asked if he required her anymore he said, "Will you please sit down Frau Reisner."

It was the first time he had ever addressed her other than plain Reisner. She sat on the low chair she had put his feet on the previous night and waited.

"I would like to thank you again for looking after me last night. As you know I went to a regimental reunion, not that there are many of us left of the wartime cadre. I am afraid we all got a little depressed about one thing and another and had too much to drink, hence my condition when I got home." Frau Reisner did a little smile and gave a shrug but remained silent. "Tell me about yourself, you are obviously from a good family."

Frau Reisner outlined to him her background. Her father was a doctor who was killed in action in the war, her mother was a concert singer. She was married to a clock manufacturer who had a small business in Ulm and she had one daughter still at school. She had worked for a trade union and was herself a democrat, certainly not a communist. "I don't really know why I am here," she said in conclusion.

"You are Jewish and you are a democrat, that is enough for them I'm afraid," said the major in a low despondent voice. She gathered from the latter remark that whilst he was one of them he wasn't necessarily for them.

"Well I'm going to bed now," he continued. "I'm not really feeling up to scratch – I suppose it's last night catching up on me."

She gave him a little smile and rose to leave. As she passed him he took her hand. "Tell me one thing. When you left me last night did I imagine it or did you kiss me?"

"I thought you were asleep."

"Please do it to me again, nothing else nice seems to happen to me these days."

She bent over and kissed his forehead. He let go her hand and she went off to bed. His feeling 'not up to scratch' however was not due to the previous night's activities. In the morning he had a high fever. Frau Berg summoned the staff doctor who pronounced he had a virulent form of influenza, which was going through the camp. "I will try and get a nurse to come in but we are so heavily committed at the moment," the doctor said to Frau Berg.

Frau Reisner was standing near by and said, "I can help Herr Doktor, my father was a doctor and I had basic nurse training."

The doctor was somewhat taken aback at this turn of events. Here was a camp inmate volunteering to nurse an SS major, somehow it didn't seem to add up. He looked questioningly at Frau Berg. She said, "Reisner has proved to be very responsible since she has been here, and very loyal to the Major. If you could look in each day to make sure everything is alright I'm sure it would be satisfactory, she does of course live-in so is at hand at night."

"Very well, we'll try it out."

For five days the major fought against the influenza, which had brought on double pneumonia. With the exception of an hour or two during the day when Frau Berg volunteered to sit by him and Frau Reisner could go to bed, she watched over him day and night, washed him, constantly changed his bed linen and night shirt, gave him his medicines, coaxed him to eat the soups she made and to drink as much as she could persuade him to swallow. The doctor was extremely worried, losing five hundred women in the camp was one thing, but to lose an SS major would be a vastly different thing altogether. On the fifth night the major was delirious at times, but by the sixth morning he had quietened and when Frau Reisner moved him to wash him he awoke and said, "How long have I been ill?" she was so pleased to hear his voice, faint and distant though it sounded, that she burst into sobs of relief, holding his hand so tightly and kissing it and holding it to her

197

breast. When she recovered herself she saw that he had gone off to sleep again, but his breathing was noticeably easier and his colour a little bit more normal.

She finished washing him and Hans came in to help her change the bed linen. He immediately noticed the improvement and grunted, "Look's as though he'll get over it."

She smiled at him and said, "Yes it does doesn't it." He answered her with the nearest thing to a smile she had ever seen registered on his face, and she got the feeling that from now on they were friends.

The major made rapid strides from then on. He had a number of visitors shown in by Frau Berg and when they were there Frau Reisner disappeared to her room or to the kitchen or outhouse. On the second day of his recovery she got him out of bed and into an armchair so that with Hans' help she could put all of his bedding out in the yard to air. When they came back Hans said to him, using the paternal, gruff manner in which an old soldier servant is able to talk to his master, "You'd have been a gonner if it hadn't been for her."

Frau Reisner said, "Oh don't be silly," and walked off to the kitchen to carry on with her work. Before he left, Hans helped her get the bedding back in and remake the major's bed. She made a light meal on a tray, which he ate, it was the first solid food he'd had for over a week. "Now we must build you up again," she said. When she had cleared away she went back into the sitting room to see if he wanted to go back to bed yet.

He asked her to come and sit with him on the sofa. "Frau Reisner" he said, "What is your name?"

She told him – "Trudi."

"Trudi, would you think it ridiculous if I told you that I had grown very fond of you over the past weeks you have been here?"

"Patients always fall for their nurse," she said with a smile.

"No, it was before I was a patient," he said. "I think it was from the time I saw the horror in your face at the women's hair being cut off. You see, in reality, it is essential the hair is removed because of the conditions under which they have to live, but it is evil that human beings should have to live like that in the first place. I have told you I am a soldier. I was seconded to the SS for these duties, these are not duties for a soldier, but I have to do what I'm ordered to do." He paused in deep thought for a while and then put his arm around her shoulder. "Thank you for all you've done for me. It is many, many years since I've experienced such care and kindness. I think I would like to go back to bed now."

She helped him back into bed and asked if he would like some hot milk. Having drunk the milk he lay back on the pillows and took her hand as she sat on the bed beside him. She held it close and felt a great pity for this man who was having to compromise his honour and principles in the course of obeying orders from people he obviously despised. It didn't occur to her that her own principles were infinitely worse and that if anyone deserved pity it was her, but then in fairness she had no conception either of the evils being perpetrated on the other side of those screens of conifers she looked out on every day.

His eyes closed and after a while Trudi put his arm back under the coverlet, kissed him gently on the forehead, put the nightlight on and went to her attic to prepare for bed. Before finally going to bed she thought she would have one last check that the major was settled down properly so she put on her gown and crept down the stairs into his bedroom. Seeing that he was comfortable she turned to leave when he said, "Trudi."

"Yes Major?"

"Would you come in with me tonight, I would like that very much."

Without a word she slipped off her robe and laid it on the chair and slid under the covers beside him. He put one of his arms around her cupping her breast with the other hand and whispered, "goodnight Trudi," and in no time at all was sound asleep. Once during the night they awoke and clung to each other, each having their own need for the closeness of another human being, each having been denied physical contact with a loving partner for so long.

Each night thereafter, even when the major was fully recovered, Trudi joined him, but it was nearly three weeks before they became lovers. Trudi tried to analyse why she felt no shame in being unfaithful to her husband. Perhaps she felt in her heart of hearts that this love between her and the major was taking place in a different world between two different people, not her and her husband, but another Trudi and another husband. In the first week of their sleeping together the major had told Trudi of his wife, of how one afternoon he had arrived back unexpectedly at his married quarters at Potsdam where he was stationed and found her in bed with two teenage girls. In front of the girls she told him that in the ten years they had been married she had been revolted by him and now he had found out her real tastes he could do what he liked about it. She was very well off, she was not dependant on him, divorce in his regiment was forbidden so he got a transfer to the SS were such things didn't matter and had not seen or spoken to her for nearly three years.

Her heart ached for him as he told her of his humiliation that the fact he had to leave the regiment he loved and in which both his father and grandfather had served. "I think we're two lost souls together," she said.

Their strange liaison continued all through the summer and through the winter into 1936. They had both blotted out the fact that it couldn't last, sooner or later either the major would be moved or the camp authorities would put Trudi elsewhere. There was a rumour that an all-woman camp was being built at a place called Ravensbruck and they might be sent there. What they did know was that they deeply and truly loved each other. The horrific facts were that only the major knew what went on beyond the conifers, whereas Trudi lived more or less in ignorance of what beastiality some members of the human race could do and were doing to others. She couldn't know how the inmates were being worked to death, their living conditions so appalling that the slightest illness became a death sentence. She had adapted to the situation of not being allowed past the front door of the bungalow and to the confinement of the small rear yard where she could hang out the washing and occasionally sit in the sun. She consoled herself that she was far better off than the other prisoners, and even if she wasn't free, everyday she spent in the comfort of the bungalow and in the love of the major was a day off her sentence. She had no way of knowing that you cannot subtract from infinity.

In early April the major came home one evening and said he had to go to Berlin for a top level conference lasting for three or four days. He then intended to visit his parents for a couple of days who live in Mecklenburg, taking the journey time he would be away to about ten days. The days dragged while he was away and it was with great joy she welcomed his return, although she had to suppress it for a while whilst Hans, who had been with him, unpacked his valise and hung out his clothes leaving his laundry in a bag for Trudi to attend to in due course. When the coast was clear she flew into his arms and they clung together as if they had been apart for a year. Eventually he let her go and they made the usual preparations for bed, and although he made love to her with all the fervour she had enjoyed for these past months, when she was eventually lying beside him she felt that all was not well. She had not asked how the conference had gone, that would not have been the thing to do at all. In the quiet she said, "Did you see your parents, are they well?"

"Yes they are well, but my father is not happy with what I am doing."

"But he must know you have to obey orders."

"Yes, but he rightly says there comes a time when you have to put personal honour before everything."

"I'm sorry darling. I don't understand," but in the pit of her stomach there was a cold fear beginning to make itself known. She said no more but held herself to him in a supreme endeavour to comfort them both, and eventually they went to sleep wrapped as close as it is possible for two human beings to be entwined.

He was very quiet and reserved the next morning and in saying goodbye held her a little closer and for a little longer than he normally did. Trudi still had this premonition of something happening to change the happiness she had experienced in the last few months. That evening the major arrived home and they ate their meal silently together, until eventually she said, "Darling, there is something troubling you beyond what your father said, can't you tell me about it or is it to do with your duties?"

He took her hand and led her to the sofa. "It is to do with us," he said, "and there is no way I can delay telling you about it. At the conference I heard the most appalling news, news that I could not even pass to my father. The Nazi's have a master plan to exterminate all Jews. They call it the final solution. Because I have volunteered for this evil organisation I am to play a major part in it. I am to be promoted and sent to Berlin where I am to organise the systematic rounding up of all Jews to go into the new camps being built. They are already gassing mental defectives, rapists and other deviants, and the next stage will be the elimination of all Jews, men women and children. I could easily cut and run, but that would be dishonourable. I therefore have come to the only solution an officer and a gentleman could arrive at and that is to take my own life."

She gave a suppressed scream of anguish but said nothing.

They were silent for a long time.

"I will join you," she said very quietly but very firmly. "If you leave me here they will come for me and I would die anyway, perhaps horribly for all I know. If I died in your arms, I know despite the great sin we have committed, I shall see you in heaven."

He held her very close for a long time. Then he went to the kitchen and got two glasses of wine, from his pocket he took a small pillbox containing two tablets and gave her one. "These will act very quickly," he said, "goodbye my darling Trudi."

They washed the tablets down with wine, placed the glasses on the side table and sat down on the sofa with their arms around each other and with Trudi's head on the major's shoulder. And that was how Frau Deig found them the next morning.

Chapter Twenty-three

Pat went back to Switzerland for her final term in Lausanne leaving David in his usual state of gloom. This was added to by the fact that he never seemed to have any money. He realised that he was costing his parents a fortune, not just as a result of the £360 debenture money, but his fares and pocket money, clothes and books he had to buy all added up to an appreciable sum. He consoled himself with 'it can't last forever' but even so was secretly a bit worried as to how he would manage to keep Pat happy in his present impecunious state when she came home for good.

Anni had started serious training again which kept her out a couple of evenings a week. "She doesn't seem to have any boyfriends," remarked Fred one evening. Ruth looked at him with a look, which said, 'and don't you know why?'

"What's that quizzical look meant to convey?" he said.

"It would have to be someone very special indeed to tempt Anni," said Ruth.

"Why's that?"

"Don't you know how she feels about David?"

"About David? David's got Pat."

"I know, and Anni knows too, and Pat knows how Anni feels about David, and Anni knows how David feels about Pat."

"This is all too damned complicated for me. Are you saying Anni is in love with David and no one else will do?"

"Exactly that. That's why I say it will have to be someone very special."

"God how these kids complicate their lives. I'm sure I was never like that. If someone wasn't interested in me it was their hard luck."

"Well you always were a modest little violet."

At that moment the phone rang which Fred answered. "There is a long distance call from Germany," said the operator, "for Miss Anni Reisner."

"She's not here but we will take the call," and yelling upstairs called, "David, Herr Reisner on the phone."

David came downstairs two at a time and took the phone just as Herr Reisner was connected.

Immediately he told Anni's father that she was at the sports field, could he take a message. "Ask her to telephone me as soon as she comes in, with your father's permission." He said.

"Yes of course Herr Reisner," and rang off.

Half an hour later Anni arrived and a call was put in to Ulm.

When it was through Anni took it. She said very little, but when she came back into the drawing room her face was streaming with tears. Ruth ran to her, "Come and sit down dear, what is the matter?"

She asked the question but instinctively knew the answer. She held Anni close. Rose sat on the sofa with them holding Anni's hand whilst Fred and David stood helplessly by waiting for her to regain her composure. Eventually she sobbed, "My mother is dead."

"Oh you poor dear girl, do you know what happened?"

She became a little more in control and said, "My father just had a letter from Dachau saying that she had died from pneumonia," she paused, "but the terrible thing is they simply say she was cremated and the ashes disposed of," and with a high pitched cry of anguish, "we can't even go to her funeral, we shall never know where her ashes were placed, my father is desolate." She broke into further sobs which rent the hearts of all of them. Fred and David went out into the kitchen and left the girls with Ruth.

"Can you imagine what sort of bastards wouldn't send the ashes home for a decent disposal," said Fred.

"Can you imagine what sort of bastards would have put her in the camp in the first place," said David.

They were both very angry, angry at their own impotence as much as anything else, angry at the realisation that they would never know the truth and angry at the heartache into which thoroughly decent people were being plunged. It was a wicked evil world these people were making.

Ruth phoned Mr Croft, Anni's immediate boss, first thing in the morning and gave him the tragic news. He was most sympathetic and said she could take as long as she liked before returning. He asked when the funeral was and would Anni be able to go. Ruth could sense the horror with which he greeted the news there would be no funeral and the circumstances, which brought this about. "Oh my God Mrs Chandler," he said, "what the poor girl must be suffering. I know there's little enough we can do, but I am a lay preacher and I will have prayers said in my church on Sunday for her mother, as well as for her father and herself and yourselves who must be suffering so with her."

Ruth went back into the kitchen and found Anni had come downstairs. "What a dear kind man your Mr Croft is," she said to Anni. "He said you must take as long as you want before you go back, and he is going to lead prayers for your mother and father and yourself on Sunday."

Anni had a little more colour and appeared to have got over the first shock of the news. "Could I please phone my father again this evening to tell him I'm alright?" she asked.

"Of course, you can do it now if you want to. It will probably take longer during the day to go through but by all means try if you would like to."

She thanked Ruth with a little hug and said she would like to. The call in fact was through quite quickly and when she had finished her conversation she came back into the kitchen.

"He is feeling more settled today," she said, "but he was worried about me. He said I was to thank you Auntie Ruth and all the family for being so wonderfully kind to me yet again, and I do, I thank you so very much."

Ruth could see she was about to cry again so she held her tight and said, "No more tears, you are part of our family as we've said before. You will grieve for your poor mother for a long time, and that is only right. Now you must, for your father's sake, be brave. Knowing you I know you will be. Now I'm going to make you some porridge."

Anni insisted on going back to work the next day. Mr Croft had told the staff not to fuss her, but they were all very kind. They had read or heard second-hand about 'concentration camps' but to them they involved other people, nobody they knew or were likely to know, but now suddenly they were, if only peripherally, a part of this evil.

A totally unexpected occurrence was the arrival at the house, on the day she was away from work, of a beautiful posy of violets and primroses for Anni. "Who is it from?" said Rose excitedly.

Anni opened the little envelope and withdrew the card. It says: 'Your friends are thinking of you – Ernie Bolton'.

Anni had been to the factory on a number of occasions and had been introduced to Ernie by David as one of his oldest and best friends. She had immediately liked the irrepressible Ernie, and as she had told David she admired so much the way he overcame his handicap. Whenever she had cause to go there she always looked into 'Ernie's den' as he called his little office, and laughed and joked with him. "What a very kind thing to do," said Anni. "I shall have to go and thank him, in fact I'd better go this afternoon as I shan't have the chance again this week."

That afternoon she got on her bike and pedalled down to Sandbury Engineering. Fred was quite surprised to see her as Miss Russell fussed her into his office. "Can I get you a cup of tea dear, would you like biscuits?"

"Of course, we would like tea and biscuits, wouldn't we love?" said Fred and then as an aside, "I'm glad you called in, the only way I get a second cup of tea in the afternoon is if we have an unexpected visitor." Anni laughed and said she'd love a cup and then told Fred of the arrival of the flowers from Ernie and that she had come down to thank him. "He's out in the body shop at the moment doing some time and motion work," said Fred, "so we can't interrupt that. He'll be back in about a quarter of an hour now I should think, he's been out there over an hour."

Anni asked him what was time and motion study, and Fred said, "Well it's a way of improving the method you do things, but I'll let Ernie tell you if you're interested, although he's young he's a dab hand at it. To do the job properly you have to have a great attention to detail and an aptitude for creating better ways of doing things. On the other hand you have to have the courage to say sometimes we're already doing it the best way so leave well alone. If you've been working on a project for a couple of hours and at the end of it you say 'we're not going to change anything' that takes as much guts as changing the whole factory around. Now, you've got me talking about work and I'll bore you to tears in ten minutes flat!! Anyway, how are you feeling now?"

"I've accepted all that's happened, but I can't understand why. My mother was a dear kind person, why would they want to lock her away?"

"It's a form of terrorism really, lock away all the potential dissidents and you halve your problems. What they can't see is they create more enemies, particularly abroad, with behaviour like that. But that's how police states work, and Germany now is a police state, I'm sad to say. Hang on, Ernie has just driven into his office, if you've finished your tea I'll take you in."

"Don't worry I know the way, and thank you for the tea."

She went down the corridor, knocked on Ernie's door and walked in. Ernie looked up and seeing Anni flushed up to his eyebrows. He shook hands with her and asked her to sit down. He had a warm friendly handshake, and as he greeted her he looked straight into her eyes searching to find whether she was still deep in sorrow in a effort to say the right thing. He need not have been apprehensive because she immediately said, "I came to thank you for the lovely flowers, it was a very kind thought and I was most touched."

He was quiet for a moment or two, and then in a solemn voice uncharacteristic of him began, "I just wanted you to know I felt very deeply for you in the loss of your mother, I know how terrible I would feel if it happened to me. I have always admired your courage since you came here and had to start a whole new life with people you hardly knew. You are lucky perhaps that you could not be with finer people than the Chandlers, but even so I have watched your loneliness sometimes, even though you are surrounded by loving people. I would like you to consider me among those people." He looked away for a moment or two, and then turned to her again with his familiar contagious smile. "I'm just sorry I can't take you dancing or no one else would stand a chance."

"Oh Ernie, you really are a dear," she said and she leaned forward and took his hand and kissed him on the cheek. "Those flowers did help so much, you'll never know."

They sat talking for another ten minutes until Anni said, "I must go or Mr Chandler will give you the sack."

"He can't do that," said Ernie, "the factory would fold up if I wasn't hear to run it."

"I'll see you again soon," and once more leaning forward and kissing Ernie on the cheek she got up and went out to her bike leaving Ernie in a state of euphoria. It was the first time a most attractive girl had ever kissed him, and she had done it twice!!

When she got home Ruth could see she was brighter in spirit and asked how she had got on. She explained she'd been able to get uncle Fred another cup of tea and a biscuit as a result of her visit. "He's an old kidder," said Ruth, "he's only got to blink his eyelids at Miss Russell and she'd run all the way to Sandbury and back for him." Ruth laughed at the thought of the somewhat robust figure of Miss Russell running to Sandbury and back.

"But apart from Uncle Fred, how did you get on with Ernie?"

"I thanked him for the flowers. He was a bit embarrassed at first, but he's such a naturally nice person he soon had me smiling at him. He thinks the world of you, you know."

"Well he and David have been friends since they were little. David always took on the job of protecting him against the odd bullyboy that you get in any school or village who wanted to pick on such an easy target."

"It's a pity about his legs. He's so good looking and intelligent he must feel bitter about not being able to compete physically with the others."

"If he does feel bitter I've never seen him show it. Neither have I ever seen him being sorry for himself. That means one of two things. Whether he's come to terms with his disability or he has a mastery of the face he puts upon the world. All I know is that he is one of the nicest, most amusing people I know. I think his biggest problem will be when he falls in love with someone. How is he going to progress it? He can't go dancing, go for walks, show off like young fellows do. Furthermore he would find it difficult to think that someone could love him knowing the problems she would inherit. She would have to be a very special person I think. Do you know Anni dear, I think that would be the biggest problem of all, he could think that no one could love him and be petrified to even make advances in case they rebuffed him or felt sorry for him. Poor Ernie, he's such a lovely chap."

When Anni went to bed that night it was some little while before she went to sleep. Thinking of her darling mother, thinking of Ernie, at last she gave a little sob, pulled her knees up under her chin to go to sleep only to think, Ernie can't do this.

The next evening Harry called round. David, Anni and Rose were out together. Fred opened a quart of Whitbread's as Ruth began telling them about Anni and Ernie. "I think they like each other," she said, "but the problem is how on earth can they ever get together at all? Ernie has no means of getting from one place to another. I know he gets a lift to and from work, but once he's either at home or at Sandbury he's stuck."

"Well it happens we've got a problem there," said Fred, "Ernie told me today that as from September Brenda Roper, the girl who gives him the lift and has been an absolute 100% reliable brick to him, has got promotion and is moving to Croydon, and he's pretty worried thinking he might be out of a job. I've told him not to worry about that, we'd find a way somehow."

There was silence while they digested this news.

"I had some thoughts about this a little while ago," said Harry. "Supposing he had a motorbike and a sidecar. He's nearly seventeen and a half now so he can take his test. I don't suppose they've got any regulations covering people like him, but I would have thought if he was in perfect control of a vehicle, driven entirely with hand operated controls he would be alright."

"That's feasible, but where does he buy such a vehicle?" said Fred.

"We'll adapt one for him. Let's take a sequence of his daily routine. He gets up and uses his crutches. He can't stand unaided but his legs will just take his weight as he swings his crutches, that we know. He gets to his motorbike, sits backwards on the saddle, lifts with his hands one leg over the petrol tank on the left side and then lifts the other leg on the footrest on the right side. What we've got to do in the works is to make a saddle mounting to turn through ninety degrees and lock so he can swing round, a hand brake instead of the usual foot brake, a mounting in the side of the side car to take his crutches, and a lever positioned somewhere that he can pull instead of using a kick start. In fact it wouldn't be beyond the bounds of possibility to put a battery in the back of the sidecar and use an electric self-starter. With the sidecar he would not only have stability, but he could also take Anni out snogging if he felt like it."

Fred indulged in his usual contemplative silence. "Not as daft as it sounds," he said, "but first of all we've got to find out whether he can afford the motorbike. I expect his father would help him. I'll put it to him in the morning. You know we always said we'd look into the business of building invalid carriages, we'll have to take a look at them again when we've got a few minutes. The problem with them as I can see it is that they cater for the invalid and not for the invalid's companion. I think we should perhaps try and look at it from that point of view."

When it was broached to Ernie the next morning he was very enthusiastic. I've got a bit saved up he said, and with a grin, "after all I don't get a lot of a chance to go out and spend my money do I."

"Well mention it to your father and we'll talk again tomorrow."

And so it was that the 'Ernie Bike Mark One', as it was dubbed in the factory, appeared on the production line. Ernie and his father provided the money and they shopped around and bought a Royal Enfield 500 with a hand gear change fitted with a Swallow sidecar. The fitters in Sandbury Engineering checked out all the mechanical parts and made the modifications, and the coachbuilders and painters in the Elliott's section made a superb job of the paintwork. A number of parts like the exhaust pipes and rear springs were taken away and chromed and when the complete machine was ready it was an absolute picture. Ernie was very popular throughout the factory and everybody had really pulled out the stops to make a great job of it for him.

In the meantime Ernie's father, who was a tool maker by trade, had designed and built a folding chair constructed almost entirely of aluminium which fitted on to two bayonet fixings between the bike and the sidecar so that it in no way impeded the driver when he was moving the handlebars. Between them all they had made the utmost use of all the space available, although when the chair was fixed on there was no room for a pillion passenger. As Ernie said, "As long as I can put someone in the sidecar that's all that matters!"

On the Saturday morning when it was all finished Harry tried the combination out on the concrete hard standing to the cheers of all the men. The beautiful deep pop popping of the Royal Enfield engine was music in the ears of Ernie as it made it's triumphant first lap round the haymaking machinery, drills and rollers on show at the front of the factory. There was a burst of applause as Harry returned to the start point. It was arranged that Harry would stay on after lunch and give Ernie his first lesson, not only on how to ride the machine, but firstly how to get on and off it. The swivelling saddle idea worked very well after a bit of practice. Lifting his leg over the petrol tank was a bit difficult in the beginning but he soon got the hang of it. The chair tended to run away a couple of times at first. "I'll have to get Dad to fit a brake or something, we hadn't thought of that," said Ernie.

After practising the on/off procedure and mounting and

dismounting the chair, which of course he would have to do sitting on the bike, Harry said, "Right, we'll leave the chair behind, I'll get on the pillion and off we go." He showed Ernie how to operate the controls, and off they went, very sedately, not getting out of first gear for one lap, then going on to second on the second lap. "We won't go into top until we can get a longer run," said Harry. "I think we'll call it a day now and I'll run you home in the car. If you practise in your dinner hour every day next week by the following weekend we'll be able to go out on the road."

And that is how Ernie first became really mobile. He was not of course allowed to take passengers other than qualified drivers until he passed his test, but in six weeks he went for his test and passed with no problems at all.

During May and June, Anni had called in at the factory at least once a week on her way home and spent some time with Ernie. Up until now that would not have been possible as Brenda Roper collected him each day at 5 o'clock. Now that Ernie was himself mobile, even if he could still not carry unqualified passengers, he was able to hang on until 5.15 until Anni arrived. Her Saturdays were taken up again with athletics, either at Sandbury Co-op sports field or in competitive events elsewhere. One afternoon when Anni called in, Ernie asked if he could come and watch her competing at the Co-op field on Saturday. She said she'd be delighted to see him there.

"You won't feel odd among all those athletes being with someone like me?" he queried. He spoke casually but she could sense a deep anguish inside him. He was sitting on the bike looking a little way from her. She turned his head and shoulders to her and kissed him fully on the lips for several seconds. He in turn put his arms around her and crushed her to him, with years of having to carry his weight from his arms and shoulders he was enormously strong.

She eased back from him "Does that answer you?" she said, "because if it doesn't I shall have to do it again."

"I wasn't fully convinced," he said and again held her to him and kissed her.

What neither of them knew was that Fred just happened to look out of office window at that moment, which prompted him to pick up the phone and telephone Ruth. His cryptic message which had her seething with curiosity was, "I'm on my way home and by the way, I think Anni has got over our David." And promptly put the receiver down.

Ernie's visit to the sports ground was to mark a turning point in his life. Anni was waiting for him at the forecourt and once he had parked his bike and transferred himself to his chair she pushed him round to the front of the pavilion where they met Hazel Butler, and where he was introduced to a number of the other athletes. Anni was obviously very popular. Without exception they all treated him as one of them, in talking to him there was no trying to evade the point that he had no use of his legs and above all they spoke entirely without condescension. In fact one of the bigger field sportsmen said, "There's a very damp patch over by the javelin and long jump areas you have to cross. I reckon your wheels will sink in, so when you're ready to go give Billy and me a shout and we'll lift you over it – don't want you getting bogged down on your first visit."

Ernie laughed at this friendly offer and said, "That's very well but how do I get back?"

"Oh, we leave you there, then we can persuade Anni to come out with us."

This sort of banter was the lifeblood of Ernie's relationship with the lads at Mountfield, and later the men at the factory. It gave him the feeling of belonging when he could easily have been left to vegetate on the sidelines.

"Well if you drop me I'll sue you."

He had a wonderful afternoon out in the open air and during the tea interval Hazel Butler brought over a short, stocky enormously powerful looking man who Ernie judged to be in his mid-thirties and introduced him.

"Ernie, I'd like you to meet Freddie Booth. Freddie is a qualified physiotherapist who not only helps the AAA Kent team, but also works for Sandbury Town Football Club, and in his spare time works at the Sandbury Hospital."

"She's kidding Ernie. Most of the time I'm at the hospital, the rest of the time I try and look after this lot's aches and pains – real and imaginary."

"Oh then you would know Staff Nurse Chandler," said Ernie.

"Of course, she's gorgeous. How do you know her?"

"Her husband is one of my bosses."

"Well now. Anni was telling me about you and it's possible we can do something to help you. If you can come to the club here on Wednesday evening when I do the midweek session, I'd like to have a look at your legs. I'm always 'John Blunt', so I'm telling you now don't expect miracles but we may be able to improve things with a lot of hard work and dedication on your part and a bit of know-how on ours. By the way, do you swim?"

"No, living cooped up in a little village I've never really had the opportunity to learn. Anyway how can you swim without legs?"

"The answer to that is, easily. So Anni, take him to the baths two nights a week and teach him to swim. Don't worry if people look at you, after a while they'll be admiring your guts, and if they don't, ignore them, they'll be morons not worth concerning yourself about."

He stood up and shook hands with an enormous hand the size, Ernie thought, of a dinner plate, and said, "Right, Wednesday night 7 o'clock,"

Ernie was quiet for a few seconds. He then took Anni's hand. "Look Anni, he's rather taking you for granted. I don't really expect you to give up two evenings a week to teach me to swim, after all you must have lots of other things to do."

Although they were surrounded by people most of whom knew Anni, she leaned forward, kissed him lightly on the cheek and said, "One – I like going swimming, two – I like you, so it will be fun for both of us."

"You're an angel, I really mean that."

Chapter Twenty-four

Megan was nearly five months pregnant. Being at the hospital she had the best of attention and all of both families were pleased that everything was going so well. She had been positively forbidden by matron to do any heavy or awkward work, in particular lifting patients was definitely out and the occasional bed making she helped with when they were short-staffed was forbidden.

She was making the rounds with another nurse giving out the evening pills and medicines, which duty required the supervision of either a sister or staff nurse. As she examined the bed chart of one patient to establish the medication required and then checked it against the list on the mobile cabinet they were pushing around, she looked across the ward to where a probationer was making a patient comfortable. This patient had severe respiratory problems and had therefore to be supported by pillows so that he partially sat up rather than lie flat. He was very poorly and he was a very heavy man, which made the probationer's job even more difficult. However having successfully accomplished her task she moved on to another patient at the end of the ward. What she had neglected to do and Megan immediately spotted, was that she had not replaced the side frame on the bed, which acted as a safeguard to prevent rolling off the pillow frame and possibly out of bed. Without further thought Megan moved across the ward to fix the frame but as she started to cross the patient started to roll over. She moved quickly but even so did not reach him until he was almost out of bed. She put her arms round him but in doing so slipped and she found herself on the floor halfway under the bed with the weight of the patient across her stomach. The pain was intense. "My baby, my baby," she cried out. In the meantime the other nurses and one or two of the mobile patients arrived and lifted the patient back into bed.

The poor probationer realising she was the cause of all the trouble was sobbing uncontrollably, sister came running from her office saying "Don't move her," and organised a pillow for her head. "Get the casualty doctor quick and stop blubbering," she snapped at the probationer. They took her to a side ward and she lost her baby an hour later. Harry had been telephoned and was waiting in the corridor outside. The doctor came out to see him and told him the appalling news.

Matron was most kind to him and said, "You can come in and see her for a little while, then she must sleep, but you can come back again whenever you want tomorrow." They held hands, Harry crying for the first time for more years than he could remember.

Megan soothed him and said, "We have plenty of time darling Harry, we have plenty of time."

Harry went back to Chandlers Lodge where Jack and Moira had joined the family to await his arrival. When they saw his face they knew immediately the outcome. "Will you phone Carmarthen or would you like me to do it?" said Moira.

"It's for me to do I think," said Harry, "but thank you very much for offering."

They were all looking at Harry so far removed from the usual 'life and soul of the party' Harry they all knew and loved that it didn't seem possible it was the same man. He went and made the painful telephone call and said he would report again the next day.

"You'd better stay here tonight," said Ruth.

"No, no. I'm used to being on my own when Megan is on night duty, I'll be alright now I've got over the first shock." said Harry. "I think I shall feel better when I'm getting on with the routine things I have to do at home."

Three days later Megan came home. She appeared fit and well again but no one could know the heartache she was suffering, as indeed do all those who lose their babies before they ever know them. Harry took her away to Littlehampton for three days. They walked the grassy spaces and along the beach and by the time they came home they had come to terms with their loss and had resolved only to look to the future.

Chapter Twenty-five

It had already been arranged that David would go to Ulm again in the summer for two weeks and that Dieter would come back with him for two weeks. At the beginning of June Pat telephoned her father to say the school was closing two weeks earlier than had been expected, they were having to carry out urgent structural repairs. This meant that she would be leaving for home on the same day that David would leave for Germany. When Jack told him this David said, "Would you have any objections to Pat joining me at Ulm? She can go direct from Lausanne I'm sure," and then an afterthought "Herr and Frau von Hassellbek would take good care of her and see that she was alright."

Jack replied, "Well yes, alright, but first clear it with the von Hassellbeks and your parents, and then you can send Pat a telegram to see if she would like to join you."

That evening David telephoned Dieter who said he'd telephone him back. He did this an hour later and said, "My mother and father would be delighted to have Pat as well, and we wondered if Rose and Jeremy would like to come with you, and we can do some cycling here. We had such fun when we ended up at Romsey."

David immediately broached the subject to his mother and father ending with, "You'll have no worries about Rose, we'll all see she's looked after."

"And who's going to look after you I wonder?" said Fred.

David then telephoned Jeremy at his lodgings in London and found him in. Jeremy said he'd love to join them and that he was not bound to any set holiday dates so that side of it was no problem. Finally he sent a telegram off to Pat and the next day, having received an enthusiastic affirmation from Pat, telephoned Dieter again and all was arranged for the third week in July. His final words with Dieter, in German of course, since he was in earshot of the family, were that they would not be able to do their usual swimming with Rose and Pat present. This was greeted with a roar of laughter from Dieter who finally indicated he knew another lake where older people went and where they all wore costumes so 'not to lose any sleep'.

When the great day of departure arrived Thompson drove Jeremy and his mother and father up to Liverpool Street, meeting Fred and Ruth there with the pre-arranged intention of their all having lunch together after they'd seen the youngsters off on the boat train. As they were standing on the platform the familiar burly figure of Jack appeared running along and waving. When they had waved the youngsters goodbye Jack said, "I'm collecting Moira at 12.30 from the War Office, will you all join me for lunch at my club?" Fred and Buffy looked at each other and obviously being in agreement thanked him for the offer. They all climbed into the big Wolseley and headed for Whitehall to pick up Moira, which they did at 12.30 on the dot. It was only a short journey to the club in Pall Mall. A liveried doorman opened the rear door for the ladies to alight, holding the arm of each one in turn. They went up the stairs into the club and Ruth and Fred, both unused to such establishments, were immediately struck by the intense quiet after the hurly burly of Pall Mall outside. To fit in with the ambience Jack's and Buffy's normally very robust voices sunk almost to a whisper as they were ushered along to the special dining room reserved for members with lady guests.

"This is one of the few clubs in the West End where you can eat the food," said Jack with a laugh. "Having said that I hope they don't let me down today."

The conversation was evenly shared all through the meal, both Fred and Ruth rapidly becoming acclimatised to their surroundings. The high vaulted ornamental ceilings, the beautiful carpets and the panelled walls with what were obviously original paintings hung on them, all added to the pleasure they were obtaining from the company, the wines and the food. Jack, seeing Ruth looking around in obvious pleasure at the surroundings, said, "Like it?"

"Jack I could very easily develop a taste for all this," she said and squeezed his hand resting on the table beside her.

"Yes it's very nice," he said, "but you know I wouldn't change it for Chandlers Lodge for all the tea in China," and turning to Buffy and Rita Cartwright said, "these two dear people have done more for me than you could ever imagine."

There was a pause for a few seconds and then Buffy said, "Fred we were going to ask if Ruth and yourself could come down to Romsey next weekend whilst the children are away. There is a Hampshires open day at Winchester on Saturday, which I thought we could go to." He turned to Jack and Moira, "It occurs to me that if you and Moira have nothing on perhaps you would care to come as well?"

Ruth spoke first. "I am sure we would love to come," she said. It was the first time that she could ever remember in all their married life that she had made a decision which affected them both without asking Fred first. It had swiftly passed through her mind that Fred might well be conscious of the sergeant/officer situation to the extent he might make an excuse not to go. Having given her answer she then turned to Fred.

"Wouldn't we dear?"

"Well, yes of course, very much."

Jack then answered Buffy's question by asking Moira, "Have we anything on dear? And can you get Friday and Monday off?"

"That would be no problem, I have lots of time due to me."

"That's settled then. We'll meet you off the train and you can come back on the Monday midday service," said Buffy, "the only problem is, I understand you were a gunner Jack. I think we'll probably have to get you a special dispensation to get you into the Hampshires. I don't doubt Fred will put a word in for you."

They all laughed at this sally, but Jack speedily answered, "I can't see that putting a bit of class into the occasion would raise objections."

"They never grow up do they," said Rita. "It will be lovely having you all, it's so long since we had a full house."

The following Friday Harry took them to Waterloo in Jack's Jaguar for the journey to Romsey. They dined at home on Friday evening and over dinner Buffy outlined the programme for the following day, which by all accounts was to be quite hectic. They had been told to bring evening dress and the men to bring their medals and miniatures for the following evening. The morning comprised massed bands, led by the Hampshires, which was followed by a march past by the Old Comrades in which Buffy and Fred took part. After a buffet lunch splendidly laid out, as only the army can do, they went back to the stands to see demonstrations and displays of drill, battle tactics, PT and finally the massed bands again. At 4.30 they made their way back to Romsey to get dressed for the cocktail party at the Officers Mess, Fred and Ruth, Jack and Moira of course being the guests of Buffy and Rita, to be followed by dinner and speeches. It was a wonderful day for all of them, made even more memorable by the Colonel of the Regiment approaching their party, looking straight at Fred and saying, "I remember you – we boxed each other in Ireland and you beat me – remember?" and then looking at his decorations said – "Military medal and Mons Star eh?? Not many of us wearing the Mons Star around now, what? Buffy, nice to see you, have a super evening all of you," and he was off to the next group.

"What a memory he's got," said Fred. "He was only a Lieutenant when we fought."

"What I shall never understand about men," said Ruth to Moira and Rita, "is that when they meet after nearly thirty years the first thing they talk about is when they were knocking the daylights out of each other."

The weekend flew by but the high point so far as Fred was concerned was the fact that Ruth and he had been accepted into the society of what he would have called the officer class, without having any feelings of inferiority whatsoever. He was particularly happy about this for Ruth's sake. The other ladies obviously liked her enormously and she more than held her own in the conversation stakes. As they were being seen off from Romsey, Fred said to the Cartwrights, "We'll have to arrange a weekend at Sandbury in the autumn." To which invitation came the reply that they would look forward to that.

As they were travelling back Moira said, "I wonder how the children are getting on."

They were in fact getting on very well. The von Hassellbeks met them as usual, and the following day the immaculately groomed figure of Pat arrived to be welcomed with a huge kiss from David and introduced to Dieter's mother and father. As they were walking to the car David said in a low voice, "You look utterly gorgeous." She smiled and squeezed his arm. Frau von Hassellbek made a little speech that evening at dinner saying how thrilled she was to have such a nice lot of young people in the house. Tomorrow they would be joined by Dieter's cousin, Rosemarie, from Munich, so they would have a Rose and a Rosa, as she is called, and I think she added that when you see Rosa you will have a little surprise! And surprise it was. When she arrived Rosa was almost the double of Pat, same height, same figure, same colouring and very similar features. They could have been sisters – almost twins in fact. When they were introduced they both looked at one another and burst into laughter, which was quickly echoed by the others. They spent the remainder of the holiday riding around on hired bicycles, swimming, in the costumed lake of course! visiting the sights of Ulm, Augsburg and Munich in the car with the doktor and, as he said afterwards, how they all got in he will never know, until finally it was time to go. On the day before departure David managed to get Dieter on one side to ask about Inge. Dieter was obviously upset at having to answer. He told David that she was closely involved with the concentration camp programme, but he knew little more than that.

"Quite frankly David," he said, "I know only what my father tells me and he is so appalled at what is happening that he says very little. He loves Inge of course, but I think by not finding out what she is doing he hopes to blot it out of his mind. He and my mother are deeply unhappy about it all. Inge telephones every now and then and they just chat, it's all very sad and no one knows where it will end."

David put his arm around Dieter's shoulder. "Tell them I think of them," he said, and continued, "now to more cheerful things. Would it be possible for Rosa to come to England with us tomorrow? I'll phone my parents and get their approval."

"It's very short notice, I don't know if she has a passport."

"Well, find out if it can be done, otherwise we shall have to find you an English girlfriend when we get home."

"Oh, what's happened to Anni?"

"I'm afraid Anni is spoken for," and he went on to tell him about Ernie Bolton and the Erniebike.

Having got enthusiastic approval from Ruth and Fred they approached Frau von Hassellbek who said she would telephone Rosa's parents. There was no problem with the passport as she had brought it with her in case they made a visit to Switzerland.

Rosa's parents, assured that Rosa would be very well looked after, readily agreed and arranged with the doktor to give her money to take with her, which they would then send on to him. The boat ticket was the only problem as all the berths were taken, but David said they'd sort that out when they got aboard – a pound in the right pocket could do wonders he was sure. In the event there were several berths not taken up so there was no problem and, after a reasonably calm crossing, they arrived at Harwich for the boat train to Liverpool Street.

On the way they decided they would have a little game when they arrived in London. Pat and Rosa did their hair in an identical manner, put on a little identical make-up and Pat put on a short jerkin that Dieter was wearing, it was big for her but they pulled it in at the back and put in a safety pin. Rosa's jerkin was a very similar colour they each had on a dark skirt so the final picture was one of almost identical twins.

As the train shuddered to a stop in the big, sooty, gloomy station David leaning out of the window waved to his parents and to Jack and Moira standing some way down the platform. Leaving 'the twins' on the train, the others jumped on to the platform to hugs and kisses all round until David said, "Now we would like to introduce the Sandbury twins," at which point the girls descended and stood shoulder to shoulder in the artificial manner beloved of mannequins on the cover of Vogue.

"I don't know which one to kiss," bellowed Jack to the great amusement of not only the welcoming party but to passers-by heading for the exit, "so I'll kiss them both!"

"Any excuse," said Moira, "I think I give him too much red meat."

David and Jeremy spent the next week with the others but then had to return to work. Dieter and the three girls explored London several times, meeting the other two for lunch, but it was all over much too quickly and it was with sadness they made their way back to Liverpool Street to wave Rosa and Dieter goodbye.

The months moved on towards Christmas. In August the Olympic Games were held in Berlin. Attempts throughout the world athletics movement were made to get the games moved since Berlin had been awarded them prior to Hitler becoming Fuhrer, but to no avail. There were one or two token Jewish entries in the German team, but these fooled nobody. When Jesse Owens, America's super athlete won four gold medals Hitler would not meet him, the crowd however rose to him in spontaneous applause, at which Hitler rose leaving the stadium stating that that the United States were using 'black mercenaries'.

Mosley Blackshirts continued to cause trouble, particularly in the East End of London where there was a large Jewish population, culminating in what was to be called the 'Battle of Cable Street' where ten thousand fascists rioted and at one point threw a Jewish tailor and his son through their own plate glass shop window. Then in December Edward VIII, not yet officially crowned, abdicated to marry Wallis Simpson and precipitated a constitutional crisis, which many thought would be the end of the monarchy. On December 12th, King George the VI was proclaimed King and was to devote the rest of his life to his family and his people to a degree few if any British monarchs had done before him.

While all this was happening David and Jeremy decided to join the Terriers. One evening David had gone home having discussed the project at a number of lunchtime meetings with Jeremy, and asked his father if he would allow him to join. He could join at seventeen and three quarters, but had to have his father's permission. "We want to join the Rifles," said David.

"A blooming black buttoned mob?" said his father. "Why can't you find a decent regiment that marches properly instead of running along like startled hares."

"Well, we could go in the Fusiliers or the Queens, but you wouldn't want us to sink that low would you?"

"Alright you can go, mainly because in three months time I couldn't stop you anyway and in any event I think it will be a good experience for you – it certainly hasn't done Harry any harm."

And so they were attested in the middle of November. Most of the Rifles were young city gents with a sprinkling of tradesmen and artisans. Many of them like David and Jeremy could probably have applied for a commission in one of the County Regiments surrounding London, but there was a cachet in belonging to the Rifles, the officers coming mainly from the aristocracy and from Members of Parliament. Unlike Harry, they were Friday night not Saturday night soldiers and as drill finished late they decided that they would ask Jeremy's landlady to put David up for the night each week, which she readily agreed to do. They would then go home on the Saturday morning. When they arrived for their second drill the regular drill sergeant told them he wanted 'a bit extra' tonight as the battalion second in command was paying them a visit.

"So bags of swank you lot, and don't forget if he stops to talk to you when he inspects the company, don't look at him – look straight ahead."

In due course their visitor arrived and watched the foot drill, they hadn't as yet graduated to rifle drill of course, and as the column turned about David and Jeremy sneaked a look at the visitor, to their astonishment saw it was none other than their old school master Mr Scott-Calder, or Major Scott-Calder as he should be properly addressed, complete with Great War medal ribbons and MC to boot. The drill sergeant halted them, turned them into line, open order march, right dress, eyes front, and then marched up to the major and saluted, "Company ready for your inspection – sir!!!"

David and Jeremy were next to each other in the centre rank. As the major went along he spoke a word or two here and there, corrected dress faults imaginary or otherwise as all inspecting officers do, and eventually found himself in front of his ex-pupils.

"Well, well, what have we here Sergeant Molloy?"

"Two new recruits sir."

"How are they shaping Sergeant?"

"They're getting the hang of it sir."

"Well keep them hard at it."

"Yes sir, certainly sir," and they passed on down the parade. When the inspection was over they were all dismissed for a ten-minute break, after which the new recruits were given instruction in basic rifle drill by a corporal. During the break the sergeant came over to them. "You know the Major?"

"Yes Sergeant, he taught us at school."

"Well then, you're going to have to do better than everybody else because he'll be watching you, and if he's watching you, the company Commander will be watching you, and believe me, because they're watching you I'll be watching you. But I'll tell you this, as far as I'm concerned, that man is next to God. I was in France with him in the Rifle Brigade and he was the finest officer I ever served with. They just don't make them like him anymore."

The next morning they both went down to Sandbury as Rita and Buffy had come up for their weekend stay. There was a big dinner party at the Angel on Saturday evening, which had posed a minor problem. Anni was of course one of the family, but it was obvious that she was now going steady with Ernie. They could hardly include Anni without inviting Ernie, but Ernie was one of their employees. Ruth decided the problem emphatically when they discussed it a few nights before. "If he's Anni's boyfriend, he comes. It wouldn't matter if he was a dustman."

Fred looked at her with a twinkle in his eye. "Do I denote a feeling that madam is putting her foot down after nearly thirty years of servitude?"

"Anni's friends are our friends, that's all."

"And well said too," was Fred's rejoinder. So with Megan and Harry they had a party of fourteen at dinner who adjourned afterwards to Chandlers Lodge until well after midnight. On Sunday morning the youngsters all went for a walk through the woods, except Anni, who was collected by Ernie to go on a visit to his aunt at Uckfield in Sussex.

It was the first opportunity Buffy had had to look at the Erniebike and he was tickled pink by it. "By Jove Ernie," he said, "you must feel like king of the road on that, it must be the love of your life."

Ernie pondered for a minute, and quietly and seriously said, "No sir, it's the second love of my life."

Buffy said nothing in reply but clapped him on the back and then said, "Good for you old son, good for you." Afterwards when he and Fred were enjoying a pre-lunch drink over at The Hollies he said, "What a rattling good chap that Ernie is – I think you two have got a real winner in the stable with him."

With all the youngsters out and the men over at The Hollies, Ruth and Rita were left at Chandlers Lodge. Ruth had said she would start preparing the dinner and perhaps Rita would like to listen to the wireless in the sitting room. Rita immediately said, "Not likely, if you'll allow me, I'll help with the cooking, I get so little chance to do it so please find me a pinny and give me my orders." This agreed they worked until Rita said, "Ruth, do you mind Jeremy seeing Rose, she is a lot younger than he is."

"Well Fred and I talked about it and we came to the conclusion that Jeremy was a nice decent boy, Rose knew the facts of life and what is and isn't allowed. They are both so open and honest we can't see any problems, quite the reverse in fact, we couldn't wish for her to have a nicer boyfriend. Of course as Fred said, they will probably both be off with the old and on with the new, but to be honest I hope they stay friends. They have one advantage in that they're not in each other's pockets, so absence perhaps may make the heart grow fonder! Anyway I've chuntered on – how do you feel about it?"

"Well, Buffy fell for Rose the minute he saw her, and I can tell you in these four walls that he read the riot act to Jeremy about taking care of her or he would have to deal with him in no uncertain terms. I think Jeremy was a bit mystified at what he was getting at – they're a bit backwards at these public schools you know. I personally think of her as one of the nicest, sweetest girls I've ever met, but when it comes down to it we have to leave them to sort out their own relationships."

They left that subject, Ruth following with, "What do you and Buffy think about the boys going into the Rifles?"

"Well like you we know our sons will be taken from us to fight if there is another war. If we have strong reserve forces, as well as our regular forces perhaps Hitler will think twice about starting one. I lost a brother, two very dear cousins and an uncle in the last war, I pray to God we don't all have to go through that again. It's a bit of a game to them at the moment I suppose, let's hope they don't have to grow up to face the reality."

The weekend flew past and the Cartwrights went off on Monday having issued an invitation for all to come and spend Easter at Romsey next year – "Make it a long break – it'll be fun," said Buffy. After their departure everyone was busy catching up on things that had been neglected in the past few days, all except Pat that is. She had still not decided what sort of a job she would like to do. Her father had said she could wait until after Christmas, then she would have to make up her mind. She had long talks with David as they walked through the woods with their arms around each other.

She had no desire to take up a professional career, she really didn't want to work in an office, she loved horses but realised the impracticality of working in stables and to start a stables would be a risky business. David had added quite impulsively, "Not only that, I want you elegant as you are now, not all horsy."

"That's very unfair," laughed Pat, "Lots of people I know are both horsy as you put it, and elegant, some even at the same time."

"Then why don't you start a boutique selling all elegant clothes including elegant horsy clothes?" said David. "I can't think of one in Sandbury."

They stopped. "What a brilliant idea," she said. "Let's go home and talk to Daddy about it."

"Kiss me first because I thought about it." She needed no second bidding.

When they broached the subject to Jack and Moira they were quite taken by it. "I'll be your first customer," she said, and continued, "you know Jack, I can never buy anything in Sandbury – there is a first class ladies tailor in the High Street and a couple of dress shops, but nowhere can you buy good quality country clothes or something a bit up-market. It could be a profitable little venture."

"Well Pat you've got all the time in the world," her father said, "so, start doing your homework. You'll need premises, look around, see the agents, see what's going on. Find out rents and rates and what you need to fit the shop out. Find out the cost of stocking it. Go to Maidstone and see what level of stocks a similar shop carries there, in other words think of everything and put it down on paper, then we'll try and work out if it's a goer. Oh and don't forget you'll be borrowing the money for it from me and I shall want the same interest on it as I get on deposit now."

"Oh Jack," said Moira.

"No, start as you mean to go on," said Jack. "If she went to the bank – not that they'd look at her at her age and experience, or rather the lack of it – they'd charge her interest so it's only right she lives in the real world from the word go."

The following Saturday she and David went off to Maidstone and spent the day 'on reconnaissance' as David put it, and by Christmas Pat had got most of the facts and figures she needed but still hadn't found any premises. On the Friday before Christmas there was the usual party at the factory to which David and Pat were invited. During their visit they started a conversation with Mr Elliott during which Pat said, "You must know everyone in Sandbury Mr Elliott, do you know anyone near the centre of town who is giving up their shop? I'm looking for premises to start a boutique," and at his puzzled look on hearing the word, "you know a ladies fashion shop."

"Well, there isn't one to my knowledge, except of course the ladies dress shop by the clock tower may be a possibility. Mrs Draper who owns it has been saying for a long time she'd like to give up. The rates and everything keep going up and I think she's finding it all a bit much."

"Does she own it or lease it?" asked David.

"Oh yes, she owns it, but it's too small for one of the multiples to want it, and a bit too big these days for one person to run on her own, particularly as she's getting on a bit as she is. Anyway we're very good friends, we go to whist drives together since my wife died. I'll ask her about it if you like."

"Oh yes, please do. We would buy it from her at an agreed price, and even if she wanted to stay on part-time we'd be glad for her to do so. Just one thing Mr Elliott, I would be altering things a bit to do what we want to do, so it's best she knows that from the beginning. Thank you very much indeed for all your help."

After the Christmas break Pat had a telephone call from Mrs Draper asking her if she would care to come in and talk to her. From this meeting she established that Mrs Draper would like to sell the business, and secondly would like to keep her hand in on say Thursday, Friday and Saturday each week for a modest sum. She was a pleasant woman of matronly appearance, but dressed in a neat sober style to suit her age and figure. Pat told her of the way she proposed to alter the image of the shop and asked her if that would present any problems from a selling point of view and was assured that it would be a challenge that she would look forward to with enthusiasm. Pat got all the details regarding prices, rates, heating costs, necessary refurbishments immediately required (she noticed the carpets in the fitting rooms were very worn), and asked what the two upper floors were used for. The answer for this was, "Oh just general storage." When she went upstairs she found the 'general storage' to be old broken window dressing dummies and equipment dating back she guessed to Queen Victoria's days, and it occurred to her immediately that, with a little modification and considerable redecoration it could be made into office accommodation and sub-let. It was after all a prime site in the centre of town. As her father had instructed she got everything down on paper and the following Friday afternoon Jack asked Reg Church, the accountant, to come along and then gave Fred a call at the factory to ask if he could come up and join them. The meeting got under way with Fred saying he was delighted to be there, curious in fact, but what had a dress shop got to do with him?

"Well it could involve Sandbury Properties Ltd, if we decide to go along that road," said Jack. Sandbury Properties Ltd was the company they had formed to build the shops with flats above on the site of the old Elliott factory they had bought and demolished. Fred had a 30% stake in this company.

"I'm going to suggest," said Jack, "that Sandbury Properties Ltd buys the freehold of Mrs Draper's shop, she is incidentally asking a very reasonable price for it, we then lease it to Pat's company and then if Pat goes bust we've still got the property."

"I don't intend to go bust," said Pat in high dudgeon.

"This is a very imperfect world," said Jack, "we could be involved in another slump, we could even be at war, so we've got to think well ahead."

"It's a very sound suggestion," said Reg.

"Now," continued Jack, "the company can pay for the premises to be redecorated and refurbished so that Pat can start with a clean sheet. As she has shrewdly noticed the upstairs can be leased to either solicitors or accountants, or someone solid like that, which brings in an income making Pat's rent more reasonable and affordable and still give us a good return."

"Well count me in," said Fred. "Now if you don't want me anymore, I'll go and do some work." He got up to leave and Pat jumped up and gave him a kiss saying, "thank you Uncle Fred you're a darling."

"All the girls tell me that," he said and walked out grinning.

Having spent a couple of hours discussing the project they decided to instruct solicitors and get the whole thing in operation on March quarter day – "if the solicitors get a move on," said Reg.

"They'll have my toe behind them if they don't," said Jack.

When Jack was sitting on the settee with Moira later that evening he was strangely quiet. "Penny for them," said Moira.

"I was just thinking how lucky it was that young David stopped to chat up Pat that day. At that time she was the only one who stopped me literally from packing it all in."

"You don't mean…"

"Yes I do."

"Oh you poor darling."

"Then I met the Chandlers, they showed me what family life was all about. I got a new interest in life working with them getting Sandbury Engineering off the ground. As a result of that we got Sandbury Properties going. Then the greatest thing of all I went to Harry Chandler's wedding and met my darling Moira, and now we're going to have the excitement of watching Pat try and make her way in life. God has been very good to me these last five years."

There was a long pause until Moira said, "Darling I don't want to spoil your evening."

"What's the matter, is anything wrong?"

"Well not exactly but I have had it confirmed today that I am, as they say, with child. Don't ask me how it happened but we slipped up somewhere!!"

Jack had gone completely white with shock.

"But Moira, I'm so excited I don't know what to say. I'm thrilled, delighted, but darling did the doctor say it would be alright, I mean I don't know quite how to say it…"

"You're saying is it alright at my age, what's going to happen about my job, when is it due – isn't that right?"

"Yes darling, but before you tell me that I am so thrilled I could go around breaking windows. But you're sure the doctor said it would be alright? Hadn't you better stop working, and particularly travelling, all that bumping around and cold platforms and climbing all those stairs at the Ministry and missing lunch breaks like you sometimes have to, that will have to stop won't it." He could hardly get the words out fast enough he was in such an unholy tizz. She took his enormous hands and pressed them together.

"Now steady up. Firstly I'm having a baby not becoming an invalid. Secondly the doctor says I do have to be a little more careful than a younger woman. Thirdly the baby is due at the end of August. I'm to go on half time from the end of April and on six months leave from the end of June. While I am on leave certain work, which only I can do, will be brought to me here by messenger. I am to have two safes installed to keep it in and an assistant will travel with the messenger to be with me while I work on the documents. She will have a second key to the safes."

"Golly this must be high-powered stuff."

"Yes I'm afraid it is."

"I honestly didn't realise you were so important."

"Perhaps I'm not, put it down to the Minister's overwhelming obsession with security."

"I'd rather it was that way than any other. Now tell me all about this Dr Wallah and then tell me how we're going to tell Pat – God I wonder how she'll take it? After all she's been the only apple in the basket for so many years, how will she feel about sharing?"

"If I know Pat she'll love the baby and when you come to think of it she may have some of her own in the not too distant future."

"God that's a thought – I'll be a Granddad." Then he turned to Moira, "Darling, darling Moira, I'm so proud of you. We must make sure everything stays alright."

"You're thinking of poor Megan aren't you?"

"Yes I was."

"Well that was just a terrible piece of bad luck so don't let it worry you. The doctor at the War Office is going to see me every week, at the slightest problem he has told me he will personally take me round to a great friend of his at Charing Cross Hospital, and in any event will have me there from March onwards every week. So I couldn't be in better hands."

As she spoke they heard the outside door close and a few seconds later Pat put her head round the door. "I'm going to get some cocoa, would you like any?"

"Could you spare a minute first dear?" said Jack.

"Certainly, what's up?"

Jack looked at Moira, Moira looked at Jack.

"Come on, tell me what have I done?" said Pat, curiosity showing all over her face.

"You haven't done anything darling," said Moira,

"quite the reverse in fact. I'm going to have a baby."

"You're not? I mean how wonderful, oh I am so pleased for you, both of you, and come to that me as well. I shall have a sister or brother perhaps both I don't know."

She, like her father, was so excited she didn't really know what she was saying. She ran over to the settee and kissed Moira and her father. "Oh won't everyone be pleased," she said.

"I think one or two might be surprised," said Jack, "particularly down in Carmarthen. Now I don't want you to say anything to anyone. We'll have the Chandlers over for a drink before dinner tomorrow night and burst it on them then, and then we'll phone Carmarthen. God, I hope their hearts are in better shape than mine, mine nearly stopped when I heard the news."

"Daddy, how do you think Megan will take it?"

Jack thought for a moment, but it was Moira who answered.

"I've known Megan since she was a little girl, she will be happy for us, she would never let her own sadness stand in the way of her feeling happiness for others."

"I think you're right," said Pat, "she has a lovely nature."

"And the way you've taken it shows that you have too," said Moira and hugged her close.

Chapter Twenty-six

Christmas came and went and early in the New Year, David broached the subject that had been giving him cause for private concern ever since Pat returned from Germany with him. One Sunday afternoon whilst they were out for their usual walk in the woods he stopped by a large fallen tree trunk sat down and gently pulled Pat on his lap. "Darling Pat," he said, "you know I love you very much don't you?"

"I love you to – I wonder why we've never told each other before?"

"I think it's probably because we've been in love for so long that we've automatically assumed we've each known it. Not only that when you're younger it probably sounds a bit soppy being in love, but we're both eighteen almost now, and we've both seen a little of the outside world so perhaps we can say we've grown up. After all I could be a soldier tomorrow and you could be a businesswoman."

She kissed him with a long lingering kiss that spoke volumes.

"The problem is that I can't be as generous to you in taking you out as I would like to. I would love to take you to shows and concerts and have supper afterwards and all that sort of thing, but it just isn't possible and I was so desperately afraid that you might find someone else who could and I would lose you."

"David darling, if we were both at university, as we easily could have been, we'd have been as poor as church mice, and we would have been apart for another three years, except for vacations. At least we see each other regularly, we're both very busy and we've got time on our side." She paused for a while. "I have a problem too. Sometimes I want you so very much I can hardly stand it."

He looked at her in total astonishment and at last held her close to him and whispered, "I'm the same, but the problem with me is it shows."

"We've got to be sensible darling. I don't want to make love properly until we're married. Does that sound silly and old fashioned?"

"No it doesn't. I feel the same though it nearly chokes me to say it. If all things were equal would you marry me?"

"Yes darling David."

"In that case when it's possible will you marry me?"

"Yes darling David."

There was a long silence until Pat lifted her head from David's shoulder and said, "Do we tell anyone yet?"

"Let's wait until we're both eighteen – it's only a couple of weeks now, but it sounds more grown up at eighteen."

A month later after their Sunday walk David went to Jack and asked his permission to become engaged to Pat, telling him they would not think of marrying until they were twenty-one. Jack didn't hesitate. "Couldn't think of anyone I'd want more for a son-in-law" he said, "absolutely delighted." When David and Pat then went to Chandlers Lodge and stood together with their arms around each other while David told them all – Megan and Harry were there – that he asked Pat to marry him when they are twenty-one and that Jack had given his blessing, they were showered with hugs and kisses and handshakes from the delighted family, which were repeated an hour or so later when Anni and Ernie arrived and were given the news.

"We'll have to stop all these popsies from phoning you up now won't we old lad," said Harry. "Do you know Pat sometimes there are half a dozen in one evening. They used to sit outside on their bicycles just for a glimpse of him when you were away in Switzerland."

"One more word from you older brother and I'll start telling tales of what used to go on in Mountfield."

"OK, OK," said Harry using the vernacular he had picked up in the Sandbury cinema. "You keep your trap shut and I'll do the same."

Later that night when they were preparing for bed Ruth said, "When those two stood there with their arms round each other I thought they were the most handsome couple I have ever seen."

"Yes they are very well suited, we're all very lucky."

As Pat had said they were both very busy. Pat threw herself into the organising of the shop and to letting the upper premises, the first floor to a dental surgeon who wished to start a practice in Sandbury and the second floor to a well-established hire purchase company wishing to open up locally. Having leased these parts of the premises most of their lease payments to Sandbury Properties and the rates were covered which meant a much reduced overhead burden on the shop itself.

Having organised a new junior and advertised successfully for a part-time alteration hand, she and Mrs Draper started to interview travellers to see what was available and to establish which lines at which prices they should stock to catch the summer trade. Although Mrs Draper had not sold the quality of goods that Pat was aiming for, she nevertheless had a world of experience in handling travellers and agents and in driving bargains with them which Pat on her own would never have been able to do. In no time at all Pat had found herself being propositioned by one or two smart alecs until they retreated in confusion on finding that she was the owner of the business, but she didn't hold it against them and in the main, the travellers were a helpful, informative and jolly lot.

Mrs Draper had told her, "If a traveller calls, try and see him. If he hasn't got what you want don't be afraid to tell him. On the other hand he may have just what you are looking for so it will be a few minutes well spent."

She opened on Easter Saturday and true to her promise Moira called at nine o'clock and was her first customer, buying a plaid skirt, two jumpers, one light lambswool for indoors and a heavier one for outdoors, and a Burberry raincoat, Pat having successfully obtained the agency for these renowned products. Ruth, Rose and Megan came in the afternoon along with Fred and Harry. They each made purchases paid for by the men, with the comment by Fred that this was the first time he had ever been dragged out shopping and hoped that it would not be too regular an occurrence.

Pat was quick with her rejoinder, "There's no problem Uncle Fred, I'll give Rose and Auntie Ruth a credit account, then they can come in on their own and choose things without bothering you, and the same with Megan – I'm sure Harry will be delighted."

Jack came in at the end of the day with David and said, "We're going to the Angel tonight to celebrate." Which rounded off an exciting but thoroughly strenuous day.

David in the meantime had been putting his German to good use. His firm had received another contract from Germany to design an iron ore installation. The very size of the project made David's eyes boggle but Mr Phillips was able to break it down for him so that not only was it less frightening, but in fact he could begin to see how they would go about detailing it all. Again David's knowledge of German was invaluable. He still took the German newspaper everyday, readily available at Victoria Station, and frequently practised for an hour at a time with Anni so that instead of forgetting what he had learned he was in fact improving on it. One day Mr Phillips said, "Is your passport in order David?" and when David replied in the affirmative he said, "Right, we've got to go to a site meeting in Dusseldorf next Monday for a week. I shall arrange all the tickets and expenses, so you won't have to find any money whatsoever." He knew that someone in David's position would be disastrously hard up. "Come in as usual on Monday and we'll go on the night ferry via Ostend."

David was looking forward to this, his first 'business' trip abroad. In fact he felt quite important. Despite the fact that all expenses would be paid, his father gave him £20 to keep by 'just in case – not for lecherous living – understand?' David was very grateful to his father for thinking about him in this way. He knew that his being in his normal impecunious state would prevent his even being able to buy a round of drinks if the situation arose, and it was very gratifying that his father, busy though he was, would take the time to put himself in David's shoes and realise he could suffer embarrassment.

On the Monday of the departure day Mr Phillips told David he would be leaving before lunch to go to a call in the West End. David was to collect two rolls of drawings from the print room at two o'clock and then take them to Mr Phillips apartment just off Vauxhall Bridge Road, where he would check them, and if there were any missing, they would still have time to get them run off before David then met him at six o'clock at Victoria for the boat train.

David duly arrived at Rochester Close and was admitted by Mr Phillips. Inside the front door there was a spacious entrance hall with a wide flight of carpeted stairs in front of the doorway. To the left there was a set of double doors, which Mr Phillips pushed open and which opened into a large, high ceilinged, comfortably furnished drawing room with a mahogany table in the centre.

"Put them on the table David while I get my glasses," he said running briskly up the stairway. David looked around, much appreciating the good taste shown in the decoration of the panelled walls and the intricacies of the Adam ceiling. He turned when he heard Mr Phillips coming down the stairs, and at the same moment he heard the front door open and close. Looking through the drawing room doorway he saw Mr Phillips had reached the bottom of the stairway and that a young man had quickly taken the few paces from the front door and was throwing his arms around Mr Phillips neck. As David stood motionless watching this young man was saying, "Peter, Peter dear they have accepted my designs," and to his astonishment kissed Mr Phillips fully on the lips. Mr Phillips stood frozen to the floor. The young man sensing that something dreadful had happened looked over his shoulder and saw David through the doorway. "Oh Peter, Peter I am so sorry," he said with a sob, and laid his head against Mr Phillips shoulder. With only the short look that David had had of the young man he made an immediate impression on him of being quite the most handsome person he had ever seen. Probably around twenty-five years of age, long lustrous black wavy hair, an olive complexion and the most striking thing of all, large violet blue eyes of great beauty.

"Reuben, don't worry," said Mr Phillips, "go on upstairs and I'll see you later." He put his arm round the young mans shoulders and walked the first few stairs with him. David was most upset at being part of this little drama and was inwardly confused as to how to conduct himself with Mr Phillips when he returned. It was no use pretending he hadn't seen anything, on the other hand since he worked so closely with Mr Phillips, and would in particular be even more close over the next few days, something would have to be said. In the event the more experienced man took the initiative.

"David, I'm sorry you've been embarrassed in this matter. Reuben is my chum, and has been for the past three years. I have found you to be in every way a person of honour, so what I am to tell you I would ask, provided your conscience will allow, to be strictly between us. Reuben and I live here together. If our relationship were known we, as you know, would be liable to prosecution and imprisonment. My father is a very senior civil servant, Reuben's father is a Rabbi, so again if our relationship was known all of us would be open to blackmail from the evil parasites that find out these things and then live by the proceeds. Finally Mr Friend is a particularly puritanical person and there is no doubt he would dispense with my services if he knew. Reuben and I live for each other, we harm no one, we wish to be in peace. I would therefore be grateful for your discretion in this matter even if you don't approve of the situation as you find it."

David didn't hesitate for a moment, but held out his hand and said, "Mr Phillips, I don't pretend to understand but you have my word that no one will ever hear anything from me."

Mr Phillips took his hand and shook it warmly. "Reuben will be so relieved," he said, "he's absolutely distraught that his impulsiveness might cause me harm, I must go and tell him."

David didn't know why he had said it, he thought afterwards it was probably without knowing it he was curious and wanted to have a closer look at this beautiful young man. "Perhaps he would care to come down and meet me so that he knows all is well."

"What a good idea. Sit down and I will make some tea."

After five minutes or so they both reappeared, Reuben a little red-eyed, he had obviously been in tears.

"Reuben, this is my friend, David Chandler, who is my indentured apprentice, and who is coming to Germany with me. I would add that David is betrothed to the most engagingly beautiful young lady named Pat, who I once had the privilege of meeting." David wondered afterwards whether the latter piece of information was designed to ensure that Reuben was not jealous of his going away with Mr Phillips for a week.

A slow really beautiful smile passed over Reuben's face as he extended his hand. David, half expecting a limp clasp, was pleasantly surprised by a strong grip, followed by Reuben placing his left hand on their clasped hands and saying, "I shall always be grateful for your kindness to us David."

There was no doubt about it thought David, this young man is quite the most beautiful man I have ever met, with his voice as melodious as his features were handsome he could have captivated any woman. I'll never understand it thought David.

"You were saying your designs had been accepted – what were they for?" said David.

"Oh well, I've been designing the sets and backcloths for the new production of 'Traviata' at Sadlers Wells. I took the sketches about a month ago, which they were pleased with, and was told to do large colour layouts for presentation today. They were delighted with them. I have to tell you that Peter helped me with the draughtsmanship, anyway they all loved them so now I shall get the contract to work with the scenery people."

"I've never seen 'Traviata' – I'd love to see it."

"Then you shall – I will give Peter two complimentary tickets for you for the opening performance, and you can bring Pat and we'll all have supper afterwards," and then as an afterthought, "will that be alright Peter?"

Peter, who was scanning the drawings David had brought said, "Yes of course we shall be delighted to entertain them." David and Reuben chatted on, mainly about the theatre and opera while Peter finished looking through the drawings. David found himself liking this highly intelligent, articulate and obviously very talented young man more and more. When Mr Phillips had finished looking at the drawings, and had given David instructions to get two more copies of several of them – "They'll be useful to their electricians," he had said, he said he would meet David at Victoria as arranged. They walked to the door together and Reuben quite spontaneously linked arms with both of them, relinquishing David's and shaking hands again as Mr Phillips opened the door.

"Have a good trip David and look after this one for me won't you?"

David made the short walk back to Victoria Street thinking over the afternoon's events, ending in his saying out loud to himself, "Well, we do see life, Chandler my son," to the total astonishment of an elderly lady who happened to be passing at the time.

Their journey to and from Dusseldorf and their stay in the city were uneventful, but to David intensely interesting. The Germans he met were unfailingly courteous and congratulated him on his command of the language. In fact on two occasions he was asked which part of the south did he come from, they couldn't quite place the accent. On the way back Mr Phillips said, "I think this contact with Germany may soon be put a stop to," and when David asked him why he said that, although this was an iron ore processing plant, that was the first stage of making steel and steel made armaments and the armaments could be used against us.

"But the people we deal with are so friendly and cooperative," said

David.

"Yes, but for the first time ever in the years I've been coming here I have noticed there were parts of the huge plant which had been enclosed and 'entry forbidden' signs up. All that is new. One wonders what is going on behind those guarded gates. At this very moment Hitler is building the Siegfried Line opposite the Maginot Line. He has closed all the Catholic schools, there are now only Nazi state schools designed to indoctrinate the children from an early age. All of this must be for one purpose – war, but whether it is against France and ourselves, or as I see it more likely against the Soviet Union, we don't know. After all, Hitler sent the Condor Legion to Spain during the winter. There is no doubt that it is as much designed to get battle experience against the other major belligerent the Soviet Union as it is to help Franco, and of course his Luftwaffe is operating widely there in support of Franco's air force. We could be their next target."

They looked out of the window as the train sped through the Kent countryside both wondering what the immediate future held in store. It seemed inconceivable that in the midst of all this beauty two armies were slaughtering each other only a few hundred miles away. Soon after Easter they heard the news of the Luftwaffe raid on Guernica, which became the first city in Europe to be totally destroyed from the air. It was certainly not to be the last.

Harry was getting ready for another big parade. Again he had been lucky to be included in the Coronation procession of King George VI. "If we had a television you could see me on it," said Harry.

The Coronation on May 12th was to be the BBC's first outside broadcast. Televisions could be bought now for sixty guineas, a big reduction on 1936 prices, and rumour had it that GEC would shortly be marketing one for under £50. They only broadcast for about one hour a day and reception was very poor in some districts. "I'll stick to the wireless and the Pathe News for the time being," Fred had proclaimed to the family when Rose had asked wasn't it about time they got one. In the event they all went to see the procession, although this time Harry was marching on the other side of the road to the one on which they were standing.

In due course Harry received the Coronation medal to add to his Jubilee medal which prompted Fred to say, "Two blooming medals already and he hasn't seen a shot fired in anger yet." Nevertheless they were proud of him. He was a smart upright soldier, unlike many others in his company who looked as though they'd had their uniforms thrown on them from ten yards away. He looked the part, felt the part, and was a credit to his unit. It was soon after the Coronation that Megan and Harry announced to the family that she was pregnant again with Harry affirming that this time she was to take a whole year off, or he would 'tie her down'.

The baby was due on Christmas Day and she would stop working at the end of June, this would coincide with Moira being at home, so as Megan said, "We can parade our bumps around Sandbury – at least for a little while until the end of August when Auntie Moira's is due. I can pick up all the tips from Auntie Moira as to how to cope."

Pat's Easter season had gone quite well, and despite the fact that occasionally they got an unpleasant, even rude prospective customer, she enjoyed the work and the challenge. She had got some quite revealing swimwear in for the summer and found that a number of the better off young ladies were attracted by these garments and stayed to buy other things. In her spare time she roughed out advertisements to go into the local Chronicle. The advertising representative who came to see her said that he would get the editor to call round with a view to running a full page feature on the new enterprise, particularly as her family was so well-known in the town. This would be supported by advertisements from her nationally famous brand name suppliers, all of which would be to the benefit of everybody. In the event it gave a great deal of the right type of publicity resulting in visits from people way out of Sandbury, many of them as Mrs Draper said, 'just blackening their noses'. Nevertheless it all helped to put 'Country Style' on the map, for after much thought that was the name Pat had ultimately settled on.

There was a side effect to Pat having the shop, two in fact. Firstly they stayed open until eight o'clock on Saturday nights, so by the time she had closed the books and banked up she was fit for nothing but to put her feet up. As a result not only did David not have to lay out for entertainment on that evening, but also as everything in Kent was dead on Sundays the whole weekend was very light on his pocket, which secretly suited him down to the ground under his present circumstances.

Secondly, Pat felt guilty at being so worn out on the Saturday night that she didn't feel like going anywhere, so on Sundays during their walks out she was even more affectionate to make up for her lack of energy the previous day, to which David had to say to her, "Pat Hooper, if you don't want to end up like Moira and Megan you'd better walk on the other side of the road at least for the next ten minutes," Pat gave a trilling little laugh and immediately did as she was told. It was at this moment that Ernie and Anni swung round the corner on the Erniebike and passed them, Anni craning her neck round to see why they were walking so much apart. When Pat and David reached home, Anni and Ernie were there and the first question from Ernie was, "You two have an argument?"

Pat and David looked at each other and burst into laughter, which in Pat's case continued with fits of giggles for several minutes. Anni and Ernie looked at each other until Ernie said, "They're both overworking – going into a nervous decline or something. They'll get over it in time, if they don't we'll send for the ambulance."

Chapter Twenty-seven

When Ernie became the proud owner of the Royal Enfield combination the previous year, he could have had no conception of the way his life would be transformed. Combined with that, to find that instead of admiring Anni from afar as he had done for the past months, he was now her 'one and only' was totally beyond belief. He visited Freddie Booth as arranged so that Freddie could evaluate what muscle strength he had, and where. At that first visit Anni had said, "I'll wait outside, call me when you want me."

"Not on your life," said Freddie, "you can come in here and you can see what I do, and maybe you'll be able to help in due course. You don't mind her seeing you with no trousers on do you?" Freddie asked Ernie.

Ernie's emotions were mixed to say the least. Firstly he was a bit shy of Anni seeing him without trousers, secondly he was fearful that when she saw his emaciated legs they might revolt her, thirdly if Freddie said, 'There's nothing I can do' it might make her not want to carry on with him. On his motorbike, at his desk, even in his chair he was a person in control if not absolutely fully, but on that treatment table lying back with no trousers on he was useless, a nobody. Anni saved the situation.

"We shall lift him on the table," she said, "and I will take his trousers off. I've never taken a man's trousers off before so it will be good practice for the future."

Freddie roared with laughter at this and Ernie, relieved at having the tension broken joined in. They lifted him up on the table and Anni got him a pillow. Ernie undid his belt and fly buttons. "At least I can do this bit," he joked and Anni pulled his trousers off. Freddie spent a good half-hour feeling the muscles in each leg whilst the other two waited in silence. At last he stood back. "Well," said Ernie, "tell us the worst."

"The worst is that there's going to be a lot of work needed over a long period of time just to improve you. I'll tell you now you will never be as mobile as other people, but with a lot of work every day, and I mean every day, it's my opinion you will stand on your own two feet even if you can't play football."

Anni clapped her hands with delight and then threw her arms round Freddie's neck and kissed him on the cheek. Freddie held her arm.

"I'm telling you now that in the excitement of this moment everything seems rosy to you, but I want to warn you, that in six months you may not see any improvement whatsoever and that's when you're both going to need all the guts you've got to keep going. It may be twelve months before you notice any difference at all, so much so you may feel like giving up. Only you can handle that side of things. What I will do is give you an hour every Wednesday evening. I will give you a chart of exercises to do every day at home and I mean *everyday*. You are to go swimming at least two nights a week. *Do not* go beyond the times I indicate for swimming or exercise each day or you'll overdo it, and cause problems. Finally I will show Anni certain basic treatment that she can carry out on you after the swimming. There is a table in the clubroom at the baths. I will arrange for you to be able to use it."

And that's how the long slog started. It wasn't all work however. Shortly after Ernie had got his licence he took Anni to his home to meet his mother and father and the very pretty sister Rebecca, three years older than Ernie, who all the village lads fancied when they were at school, and a good many since if the truth were known, Rebecca remaining strictly unattached. Mr and Mrs Bolton were ordinary country folk who were really not at all sure what to expect when they were to meet Anni. Ernie had of course told them she was German, that her mother was Jewish and had died in a concentration camp. If Ernie had bought a girl home who was a Methodist instead of C of E it would have been cause enough for a little consternation, but a German Jewess? The parents and Rebecca were of course deeply, deeply grateful to Anni for having organised his therapy and even more for becoming fond of Ernie. He obviously adored her so they were determined that even if she arrived with two heads or was as ugly as sin they would make her welcome. There were however butterflies in all tummies when the great day arrived, and when Anni got out of the side car and took off her tight-fitting leather hat she wore and they saw what an attractive looking girl Ernie had been fortunate enough to find for himself, the fact that she was German and Jewish just went by the board and they took to her instantly.

Most Saturday afternoons, up until the beginning of September, Ernie drove Anni to sports meetings. The annual Co-op meeting was at Croydon this year and Mid-Kent retained the title they had won the year before, Anni again winning the javelin. At the beginning of September the Mid-Kent entered a team in the Kent AAA championships and did very well indeed considering it was the first time they had entered. Anni had to be satisfied with a very close second to the winner who was the British AAA champion and came from Margate, but was pleased all the same to be getting into the senior events.

All through the winter they carried on with their routine. Ernie became a competent swimmer and enjoyed himself in the pool as more or less an equal with all the others. Freddie had devised a series of exercises to be carried out in the water and he was thrilled to find he could stand in the water without support. But after six months as Freddie had warned them he was still not able to support his own weight out of the pool, although a lot of the muscle was building up. "We've all just got to keep at it – Rome wasn't built in a day," admonished Freddie.

Ernie thought to himself, 'He's said that a few times before, I bet'. It was Easter 1937 that Ernie accidentally found he was making headway. He was walking around at home on his crutches when he released his grip from one for a second or two to pick up a newspaper from the table. Inadvertently he let the crutch slip from under his arm and it fell to the floor. Under normal circumstances this would have been a minor disaster as he couldn't take his weight with the aid of only one crutch. His mother came running to pick up the crutch having had the problem many times before but stopped in astonishment to see Ernie standing still, his weight partially on one crutch and steadying himself with his hand on the table. Apart from this small assistance he was standing on his own two feet, which were carrying the bulk of his weight. He had the sense not to be too ambitious and try to put a foot forward, but for two or three exciting and precious minutes he had done something he had not been able to do for over ten years. After his mother handed him the fallen crutch he made his way to his chair and sat down. He was trembling a little, but he smiled at his mother and said, "We're getting somewhere at last." She was so delighted she started to cry until Ernie said, "if you do that when I've only stood still for two minutes, what are you going to do when I run up the road?"

She laughed through her tears and said, "Oh, how Anni will be pleased."

"Yes, we owe it all to her Mother. You know I'm going to marry her one day if she'll be fool enough to have me, don't you?"

"Your father and I both knew that the day you brought her home," said Mrs Bolton. "Oh I do hope it all stays well between you."

"And you don't mind that she's German?"

"For all she's done for you I wouldn't care if she was a mix of double Dutch and Chinese," replied his mother, not being able to think of anything more unusual than a mixture of that complexity.

After that he threw himself into the exercising and swimming with renewed enthusiasm. Despite being only eighteen he was accepting more and more responsibility at the factory and Fred and Harry found that, as Buffy Cartwright had said, they really had a winner there.

Work was building up. The firm had applied for government work, particularly on the building of specialist vehicle bodies, and had been recognised by the AID, the INO, and the CIA which were the three bodies who established the credentials and maintained the quality of inspection of equipment for the RAF the Royal Navy and the Army respectively. Elliott's had always had a good name for quality hearses and now that the operating circumstances were more effective their prices became more competitive and this bought them more work. They were even making them on Rolls Royces selling overseas so all in all the vehicle side was doing very well. On the agricultural side they had got the new ranges of tractors, which included pneumatic tyres and lighting and had started a plumber and mate to look after the installation of milking parlours. Milking machines had been around for some time, particularly in the big dairying counties like Cheshire and Somerset, but had been slow to catch on in the South East.

Harry had investigated the possibility of their taking an agency with a big Swedish company and had established that selling the milking equipment would not make their fortune, but there was money to be made in installing it, running all the pipe work and supplying the storage tanks and supporting steelwork. He put his findings to the directors at one of the Friday meetings and Reg Church said he would do his sums and report the following week. As the main overhead would be the pipe fitter and mate, he suggested they take on a self-employed pair initially, so that when there was no work they wouldn't have to pay wages. Conversely of course they would have to take their place in the queue when they wanted work done. It was hoped that by giving the pair regular work they would get some sort of preference when it was needed. He further suggested that if they kept a spares counter this could be a useful sideline – as he said, "You can charge what you like for spares," and seeing Fred's disapproving look continued, "within reason of course." With all the work they were getting the labour force had gone up to over thirty.

In early June Fred was having an evening drink at home with Moira and Jack. Ruth and Moira went off to see some drapes she had bought for Rose's room, so Fred took the opportunity to talk a bit of shop with Jack, something which they generally avoided when the ladies were present. He told Jack they were bulging at the seams at the moment, and if they got more orders from the RAF, which looked on the cards, they would shortly have to consider building another bay or even two. In addition it was essential they built a paint shop. At the moment the painting was being done where the vehicles were finished, which was far from satisfactory from both a health point of view and the risk of fire.

"How much room have we got?" asked Jack.

"We could find room for another three bays, a thousand feet a bay, three thousand feet."

"You know what I'm thinking Fred?"

"No – fire away."

"That field next door, it might be a good idea to buy it. If we're going to get more and more ministry work and we've got plenty of space it could go in our favour. What do you think?"

"I think it's a very good idea. It won't cost a lot because it's not much good there for a farmer and there's plenty of other housing land around."

"Well look, lets bring it up on Friday and get Reg to cost out the extension and the land purchase. He can also find out from one of his mates in the valuation department in the council whether they'd have any objections to another factory going up there. I can't think they would, after all we're next door and there's a furniture factory only half a mile down the road."

So it was that by the end of the summer they'd got the RAF order which would last over twelve months, they'd put the extra bays contract out to a builder, and the land was quietly bought for a very reasonable price by a nominee, ostensibly for grazing. When Reg presented them with their revised overhead schedule to take into account the new purchases, he also reminded them that from next year they were going to have to give two weeks holiday pay to all employees, not just to staff as they did at present. In addition to that overtime rates were increased for the first two hours to time and a third instead of time and a quarter as at present, which had to be taken into account.

Fred's reaction was, "God – the bloody unions will break us yet."

"You know, you're becoming a right true blue capitalist," joked Jack. Fred secretly pondered on this remark and inwardly had to agree.

In the meantime Sadlers Wells had reopened their Italian Opera season and, true to his word, Reuben had sent two stall tickets to David via Peter Phillips. David had asked for them to be on the Wednesday as this was the half-day that Pat closed her shop. Peter said to David that as Reuben was taking them to supper afterwards would it not be a good idea if they stayed – they'd be too late for the last train to Sandbury. Peter had two guestrooms in his flat and would be most pleased to have them. David's immediate thoughts were 'what a good idea' and then he wondered if uncle Jack would much like the idea, even though they were engaged. When he broached the subject Pat was enthusiastic about it and felt sure her father would have no objections. Her feelings were absolutely correct because his reply was that he was very pleased that she had asked him, but they were eighteen now, and engaged, and really were capable of making their own decisions adding that he had absolute trust in both of them to make the right ones.

David told Mr Phillips he would be most grateful to accept his kind offer and it was arranged for the two of them to leave an hour early on the day, go to Victoria and meet Pat off the train, and walk to the flat to join Reuben for tea. They would then get a cab to Sadlers Wells.

They met Pat from the train and David re-introduced her to Mr Phillips, although they had met once before, very briefly.

"Look David," said Mr Phillips, "We've both been working together for nearly two years, I think it's about time you started calling me Peter, and that goes for you too Pat if you'd be so kind." And Peter it became, except in the office in front of other people where David still maintained the courtesies.

Reuben opened the door to them when they arrived at Rochester Close and greeted David warmly. He was doubly charming to Pat who David could see was most impressed by his almost beautiful good looks and impeccable manners. "Tea is almost ready," he said, "so please come into the drawing room." They had their tea, Reuben producing a silver tray of wafer thin cucumber sandwiches and another tray with small iced cakes on it. "I made the sandwiches," he said, "but I must confess I bought the cakes at Fortnum and Mason." He went on to talk excitedly about the production that evening, addressing his conversation mainly to Pat but occasionally bringing in David and Peter. He explained that it was a traditional presentation, the trouble with a lot of productions lately had been that people had tried tinkering about with the settings of the plots to try and modernise them or give them a new slant. His view was that, although he was much younger than a lot of people in the business and therefore less experienced, he felt that if you have a good product you should stick to it and not mess it about. Pat asked him whether there was another side to the coin in that the way it had been done could be improved upon, and secondly young people might be tempted to see a production because it had been modernised or had a more modern setting. This led to an earnest and interesting conversation between the two, with the occasional friendly smile to Peter and David from Reuben, almost an apology for his having hogged the conversation.

They had a wonderful evening. Pat and David took particular note of the scenery in order to be able to talk intelligently to Reuben and Peter over supper. Reuben took them to the Café Royal and eventually they arrived at Rochester Close at about 12.30. "Well now," said Peter, "I shall have breakfast ready at 8.30, which will give us enough time to eat it and walk Pat to Victoria for the 9.30 train. By the way, I hope someone is opening the shop."

"Oh yes, I've organised Mrs Draper to do that. I shall be in soon after eleven so she won't be too long on her own.

"Well you won't see me in the morning so I'll say my goodbye's now," said Reuben, kissing Pat on the cheek and shaking hands with David.

"It's been a wonderful evening, I do hope we can all do it again soon," and with that he went upstairs.

"Now the breakfast room is in here," said Peter, indicating to a door at the end of the entry hall behind the stairway. "If you would like to go up, I'll check round and lock up and see you in the morning."

When they first arrived at the house they had been shown their rooms on the first floor landing, which were separated by a bathroom, which had a door opening into each room. They went upstairs and David followed Pat into her room, closed the door behind them and turned the key.

"Mr Chandler, what are you up to?" said Pat.

"I'm going to undress you and put you to bed," said David.

Her voice changed to almost a whisper, "David darling, you mustn't. I can't be responsible for my actions if you do."

David was holding her close to him. Her dress had buttons, which opened down the back. He began to undo them until he was able to slide it off her shoulders and gently pull it down one arm at a time, until it fell into a crumpled heap around her feet. Next he slipped off the silk underslip and that fell on top of the dress.

"David darling," she said, her head buried in his shoulders, "you agreed we would wait until our wedding."

"And I shall keep my word love, but tonight I am going to undress you and put you to bed."

She clung to him tightly as he kissed her shoulders, neck and ears. He had a little difficulty in undoing her brassiere, but in due course it slid off and she was left standing in her cami-knickers, suspender belt and stockings. He then picked her up bodily, leaving the dress and other garments on the floor where she had stood and carried her to the bed. He laid her gently on the bed and knelt beside her kissing her gently on the lips, on the neck and then on her firm round breasts while she lay back panting in the excitement of all that was happening to her. After a while he moved down the bed and slid her shoes off, unfastened the stockings from the suspender belt and slid them off and then, putting one hand on either side of her waist, he swiftly whisked away the cami-knickers and suspender belt in one movement, she aiding him momentarily by lifting her bottom off the bed.

As he kissed her stomach and the tops of her thighs, she put her hand down in a not so serious attempt to stop him, nevertheless he raised his head and said, "And now I am going to put you to bed." He walked to the other side of the bed and pulled down the covers and then walked back looking down at her as she lay there. "You really are the most beautiful picture I have ever seen," he said, and he bent down, picked her up and carried her round, laid her gently on the bed and pulled the covers over her. He again knelt down beside her, kissed her on the lips and said, "Good night Pat darling," and went to his room.

Thinking about it in bed afterwards he marvelled at his being able to walk away when he was bursting with desire for this creature he adored. He wondered how Pat would feel, would she be grateful to him for being strong, or would she be frustrated at being left as she was. He went to sleep on a cloud.

Chapter Twenty-eight

The summer moved on. Moira was moved into Charing Cross Hospital a month before the expected delivery because of blood pressure complications, but on August 30th she produced a beautiful seven pound baby boy and they were both well, although as Moira said, "Never again!" They named the baby plain John Hooper. Pat loved him, which was an immense relief to both Moira and Jack, and with the fuss that Rose, Ruth and Megan made of him Jack was prompted to say, "Well it looks as though we shall never be short of babysitters."

Both David and Harry were away at camp when the baby arrived. David was on Salisbury Plain where they were to be introduced to the new role the Rifles were to play in the modern army. When they were originally formed at the beginning of the Peninsular War their role was to act as rearguards to cover a retreat. 'The Rifles are first in and last out', they were told, and in the Peninsular War, the Crimea, the Indian Mutiny, the North West Frontier and the Boer War they showed their skill. Every rifleman, always armed with the latest weapon, had to be a crack shot. He was trained to use every rock, every hillock of grass, every scrap of cover to enable him to see without being seen, to kill without being killed and to use every round of ammunition to best effect. Now with what would be a mobile war, if war came, they were to continue with this role but instead of marching half as fast again as the ordinary infantry in order to get out in front, they would ride in small trucks as part of an armoured brigade. When the tanks were halted the Rifles would speedily de-buss and clear the way ahead supported by the firepower of the tanks. Having completed their task they would get back into their trucks whilst the tanks pushed on. The main problem in 1937 was that there were precious few trucks and even fewer tanks for them to practise with, as a result most of the exercises simulated the fact they had just met opposition and had debussed, were being supported by the non-existent tanks, and were carrying out various forms of attack against a non-existent enemy. As Jeremy said to David, "It's all good fun old boy, but it certainly isn't war."

"You never know," said David, "you may have too much war one of these days." He couldn't know how prophetic he was being.

Harry's fortnight consisted of driving to Catterick and then taking part in a divisional exercise at Barnard Castle. They were the largest manoeuvres in which they had ever taken part and with live firing and the participation of some twelve thousand troops, they all learnt a lot about having the right ammunition and the right food in the right place at the right time. With so many vehicles employed they had to make instant decisions when vehicles broke down. If a three-tonner laden with twenty-five pounder shells broke down, it would not be long before the Royal Artillery would be screaming, but even more so if the KOYLI's ration wagon broke down there would be a number of well chosen words directed at the Royal Army Service chaps. It did give them an introduction to what real war would be like, particularly when the umpires jumped on a wagon and said, 'You've just been shelled and blown to bits', which they did at fairly regular intervals, giving all sorts of logistical nightmares to the support troop commanders.

Their fortnight over, they came back to see the baby and to go back to work. David was sad that he had been unable to go to Ulm this year. He probably would have organised it somehow, but Dieter was waiting to be called up for army service, which he expected to start in August or September and immediately applied to be an officer. He wrote to David before he left for Berlin and said that his letters would now be censored, but he hoped they would see each other in a year's time when his officer training would be finished and he would come back to civilian life, he hoped for a very long time! Unfortunately Herr Hitler caused it to be otherwise and it was many years before David saw Dieter again.

At the end of September Anni had a telephone call from her father in Switzerland. It was a long and obviously exciting call. She ran into the drawing room where Ruth, Fred, David and Rose were listening to the wireless, and in a torrent of words told them her father was coming to England, not just for a visit, but to stay.

"What about the business?" said Fred.

"He has sold it to a Swiss clockmaker and has leased the house to a young couple belonging to a relative and he's coming to live here."

"Ruth stood up and hugged her. "We're all so happy for you," she said, "He must come here with us until you both find a place to live. We've plenty of room and he can stay as long as you like, but oh Anni – we shall miss you so much, we shall all miss you."

Anni had been so excited at her father's news it just hadn't occurred to her that she would be losing this family which she had grown to love in the nearly two and a half years she had been living at Chandlers Lodge.

"Oh Auntie Ruth," she said, "I don't want to leave you all, I love you all so much."

"Now look my love. Very soon you would probably be leaving us anyway. You're not going to stay single all your life. Harry's gone, David and Rose will go, and so will you – that's the way of the world and Uncle Fred and I will be left rattling around this place on our own like two peas in a pod, except of course when you all visit us and bring your children with you. Then we'll have great fun with the children without having the work and responsibility, so don't be sad, it's just another chapter in all our lives. Above all, think how happy your father will be when he's with you and when he becomes part of our family as well."

"Auntie Ruth, you always make me feel better when I talk to you. I do wish my mother could have met you, she would have loved you too."

"Now let's be practical. When is your father coming and what will he bring with him?"

"He is coming in two weeks time and he has asked if he can send some crates of belongings to Chandlers Lodge. As he is not Jewish they probably will not stop him doing that. He thinks he will arrive at Croydon Airport at 4 o'clock in the afternoon of the 14th and would be grateful if we could organise a taxi to bring him here. He said he would stay in a hotel, but if you really can put him up for a few days I would be very grateful."

Fred took up the conversation. "Don't worry about taxis. You, Auntie Ruth and I will go in the Humber (Fred had traded in his Rover) and meet him, and he can come here for as long as he likes, as Auntie Ruth says. One thing you've got to think about though is you will now have to divide your time, so you'd better talk it over with Ernie – it's going to come as a bit of a shock to him although he's got plenty of sense and I've no doubt he will take it all in his stride. I'll say nothing until you've had a chance to talk to him."

The next evening Ernie picked Anni up to go to the swimming baths and, after the session in the pool and then on the massage table, Anni said, "Ernie, could we go and have a quiet drink somewhere?"

"Of course," said Ernie, "but don't tell me you've started hitting the bottle."

"No, nothing like that. I have something important to tell you."

They went into the Crown and Cushion near the baths and when they had got their drinks and were seated Ernie said, "Right, what's it all about?"

"My father is coming to live here permanently," she said, and went on to tell him the full story. He was silent for a while after she had finished.

"What's the matter, dear Ernie?"

"I am very happy for you, so very happy my love, but I was just thinking when he sees me whether he'll think I'm a suitable person for you."

She gave a little sob and held his arm tight burrowing her head on his shoulder.

"Darling Ernie," she said, "when he sees you, and sees how much I love you he'll be very happy for us both. I've told him all about you, he knows how I feel about you, and I know he will like you – everybody does who meets you, he'll be no exception."

The cheerful Ernie face reappeared, "Now you're giving me a big head," he said. She kissed him on the cheek.

"Once he's here we can keep to our routine, there will be no need to change anything except perhaps at the weekends, but we'll cross that bridge when we get to it."

Karl Reisner arrived on time at Croydon Airport from Zurich, despite a strong headwind, which gave them all a bumpy flight. When he came through customs there was an ecstatic welcome from Anni, laughing and crying at the same time, until at last she calmed down sufficiently enough to be able to introduce him to Fred and Ruth. He shook hands warmly with Fred and then he held Ruth to him and with tears in his eyes said in German, which Anni translated when he had finished speaking, "My dear Mrs Chandler I will never, never be able to thank you enough for taking my Anni into your family and being a mother to her."

Anni having translated he went on, "I am sure you have saved her life." When Anni translated this both she and Ruth were visibly shocked, but Ruth quickly recovered her composure and said that now they were both together they would be able to start a new life.

Fred and Anni picked up the two cases that Mr Reisner had brought with him and they all moved to the tarmac at the front of the low reception building where they had parked the Humber and, having strapped the luggage on to the capacious luggage rack, they set off for Sandbury. When Mr Reisner had recovered from the emotion of the first meeting he began to speak in halting English. "I am sorry my English is not very good, I shall have to learn quickly ja?"

"Anni will be a good teacher," said Ruth. "Her English was very good when she arrived but now it's perfect." Anni translated 'perfect' which had puzzled Herr Reisner.

Karl Reisner was a man of medium build, probably around fifty, Fred had thought, with a studious, kindly look, thinning grey hair and wearing rimless glasses. They had seen from photographs that Anni was like her mother, handsome, full breasted, and with lustrous dark hair. As they drove along Fred was thinking they'd never had a cross word with Anni. It wasn't that she was docile, she stood her corner in arguments with Rose and David from time to time, but she never showed aggression and was rarely out of sorts with the world. And the way she'd taken Ernie on makes her something special thought Fred, and she could have had her pick of most of those athletic types she meets at the sports ground and AAA meetings. There's no accounting for love I suppose, he was thinking when a voice said, "Fred you daydreaming or something?" it was Ruth saying, "Mr Reisner said how far is Sandbury from London."

Fred immediately jerked himself back into the present and gave the information, apologising for letting his thoughts wander. When they got home Ruth said, "Now Mr Reisner the first thing that happens in any English house when you get home is you have a cup of tea, would you care for a cup?"

"Yes please very much. Anni has told me about your tea. It is very good. And will you please call me Karl, it is much more friendly."

"Right then, Anni will show you your room and I'll make the tea."

When David arrived home Karl made a tremendous fuss of him.

"This is the man I have to thank for my daughter's safety," he said again in German, "and I will never forget it," Anni translated.

After dinner Harry and Megan came, and shortly after, Moira, Jack and Pat arrived to welcome Karl to his new home, if only temporary. As they were talking Karl said to Anni, "Is not your Ernie coming this evening?"

Anni said, "No, he thought it would be better for you to meet all the family first and then he would come and see you tomorrow evening. He is a little shy at meeting you, being handicapped in the way he is."

"If he means everything to you, he will mean everything to me, and that is a promise."

Anni hugged him. "I'm so happy you are here, we've so much to talk about and I've so much to show you."

After a while Jack said, "Well all you nice people I'm afraid we've got to make tracks, I've got a baby to feed."

"That'll be the day," said Fred to general laughter, Anni explaining to Karl that Jack and Moira had a month old baby, and that Megan's was due at Christmas. At that the evening broke up, David walking Pat home, leaving the five of them sitting and talking, Ruth saying that it had been an exciting day and would they all like a cup of cocoa before they went to bed.

Karl soon settled in. He met Ernie the next evening before the two young ones went to the baths, and after the first shock of seeing Ernie swinging his way along on crutches, was soon charmed by Ernie's friendliness and personality. He was intrigued too when he saw the masterly way Ernie handled the combination when he mounted and moved off, saying to Ruth and Fred, "Very nice boy." While Anni was out that evening he said to Fred that he would like to have a talk with Ruth and himself, with David present to help with the translation. David was out that evening, so it was arranged for the next evening when again Ernie and Anni would be with Freddie Booth at the Sports Club. In the meantime he would walk around the town. "That won't take long," joked Fred.

The next evening Karl explained why he wanted to have a talk with them. He told them that he had been lucky in selling his business to a Swiss firm he had known for many years, and that they had paid him in Swiss Francs, which payment was now on deposit in Zurich, this meant that he was quite well off financially. His house he had leased to a distant relative from the north of Germany who would pay the modest rent he had agreed into his bank account in Ulm. One day he hoped the Nazis would be kicked out and he would be able to recover that money, but if he didn't then he would gladly sacrifice it to have his daughter safe and to be with her, or near her. He had always realised, that like all parents, he would probably lose her in the not too distant future anyway, but at least he would be able to see her. He then went on sadly about her mother, saying that no one will ever know how and why she died, and that he was bitterly ashamed of what was being done in his country in the persecution of Jews and others. Only in August, he said, Himmler had opened a new all women camp at Buchenwald – "Why do they need to lock up thousands of women?" he said, the anguish showing on his sensitive face. In order to keep himself occupied he thought he would start up a small business doing watch and clock repairs. With the interest from his Zurich deposit he didn't need to work but he had always worked and he would be bored to tears doing nothing – after all he was still quite a young man he said with a smile.

"Well we can do with a repair shop in Sandbury," said David.

"If you take a watch to the jewellers here they send it away somewhere."

"I'll look around for some premises," said Karl, "perhaps I'll find something with living accommodation above. After all I don't need a big house, I could be quite happy in a flat."

"Reg Church might know of somewhere," said Fred, "he's our accountant."

"Perhaps I could meet him. I shall need an accountant and a bank and probably a lawyer as well. Perhaps you could introduce me to some people. I used to belong to a Rotary Club in Ulm, perhaps I could join one here once I get to know the town more and can speak better English."

"Again, Reg is a Rotarian, I'll get him to give you the information. As a matter of fact I was going to ask him about joining myself, they do a lot of good work in the town, and I get a bit more time to myself these days than I used to."

Fred arranged the meeting for the following Friday directly after the usual factory meeting. Karl came to the factory about an hour before the appointed time and Ernie got into his chair and gave him a guided tour. He found it very interesting, although Ernie said, "Unlike you and your clocks, we are not precision engineers – we work to the nearest thumbnail." The joke didn't register with Karl leaving his face blank, so Ernie went on, "I'll get Anni to translate that when she arrives."

Anni arrived just after five o'clock to help in the meeting. Reg said he felt sure there would be premises available, somewhere that would suit Karl, probably not in the high street, but then he wouldn't want to pay the high street prices. He would make enquires. When they discussed the Rotary Club, Reg said there would be no problem if Karl had his membership card from Ulm, even if it was out of date, he would be delighted to propose him. Fred then repeated what he had said about asking to join, and again he said he would put his name forward. Jack said that if he had been able to make the lunch meeting on Monday, which was when the Sandbury Club had it's weekly gathering, he would have like to join, but Monday was mostly out of the question. "Good job it is," said Fred, "someone would have blackballed you anyway." Everyone except Karl laughed at this while Anni endeavoured to translate for her father's benefit, but finding it difficult to explain the practice of 'blackballing'.

Karl settled in quickly at Chandlers Lodge and proved to be a most congenial guest. He insisted on paying his way, being very firm with Ruth which prompted Fred to remark that he might look meek and mild but he must be pretty tough to put one over on Ruth, when they were talking to Jack and Moira one evening. Through Reg he got himself organised at the bank who arranged for him to have a drawing account from his Swiss deposit, and as the bank manager was also a Rotarian, he invited Karl, along with Fred, to the next meeting which they enjoyed immensely, not least because of the very warm welcome everyone of the thirty odd members gave them. Karl would have enjoyed it much more, as he confessed to the family afterwards, if his English was better, but they all reassured him that in a few months, with Anni and David's help he would be speaking like a true man of Kent.

The next day the papers were full of pictures of Hitler welcoming the Duke and Duchess of Windsor to Berlin. "By God, what does he think he's doing?" roared Jack. "The Duke must be mad – can't he see how he's helping to build up the vanity of the nasty little man – what does he hope to gain by it." It was a very rare occurrence to see Jack so livid, in fact as Fred said to Ruth later when they were alone, he'd only seen him like it once before and that was when he picked up the Roper boy and threw him across the barn. There was widespread criticism of this visit, with all the evil this man Hitler was preaching, with the fact he was a complete dictator, that he was building one new concentration camp after another, then to be gilded by the seal of approval from a royal Duke was monstrous. Little did anyone realise that at the back of his scheming mind Hitler had already dreamt of conquering the United Kingdom and having a puppet king on the throne in the form of Edward, Duke of Windsor. A few days later a professor at Princeton University, Joachim Prinz, was forecasting that German Jewry would be extinct in ten years. How horribly, horribly right he nearly was.

Chapter Twenty-nine

Winter came. Pat got her Christmas stock in, they had had quite a good summer, they'd made some mistakes but as Mrs Draper said, 'You'll always buy something in that you think is marvellous only to find nobody else wants it'. Pat got on well most of the time with Mrs Draper, and she learnt an awful lot from her. They were beginning to attract people from way out of town, the word having got around that if you want something out of the ordinary, go to Country Style. Pat looked forward to her Wednesdays off. She and Mrs Draper had agreed that they would have either Monday afternoon or Wednesday morning off in alternate weeks. This meant that every fortnight she could have a lovely lie in, and then generally she would go up town and go to a film with David, a Corner House supper afterwards and then home on the last train. One night when they hadn't kept an eye on the time they had to run to catch the train, which prompted David to say as they sat panting in the compartment when the train pulled out, "You know we could always have asked Peter to put us up if we'd missed the train."

She gave him a long look which said, 'If you ever do that again we shall not wait until we're married'. He gave her a little kiss on the cheek to the fond amusement of an elderly lady sitting opposite.

Ernie was making good progress. He could now stand unaided, but still could not walk. As a result Freddie Booth said, "We're going to stop my Wednesday night therapy now. I want you to come in the gym, (the Co-op had a well equipped gymnasium at the sports club, which doubled as netball pitches for the ladies section), "and start walking the parallel bars."

"If I can't walk on the floor how do you expect me to walk up on the bars," said Ernie.

"No, you nut. What you do is you take your weight on your forearms on the bars and you then walk from one end to the other, turn round and walk back. After about a thousand times you'll get the hang of it."

"Sounds wildly exciting – haven't got any good treadmills knocking around I suppose?"

"That's not a bad idea – I'll look around and see if I can find one."

It was monotonous, hard work but gradually Ernie could feel the improvement. One evening Anni asked if her father could come and see the treatment, and when he saw the tremendous effort Ernie had to make, and experienced how kind everyone was to him knowing he was a refugee, he was very touched and said to Ernie, "I have seen many brave men but you are the bravest. My Anni is a very lucky girl."

"Mr Reisner," said Ernie seeing Anni was on the other side of the room talking to Freddie, "I would like to ask your permission to become engaged to Anni." Karl was not quite sure what engaged was, and Ernie realising this went on, "I mean I want to ask her to marry me. Not for a year or two yet, but if we are engaged it means we have agreed we are going to get married one day."

"My dear boy," said Karl, "if Anni says yes, that is good enough for me. I will help you both all I can."

"Well when the time is right I will ask her," said Ernie, "but you won't say anything will you?"

"No, of course not."

The following Friday evening Ernie popped the question, was greeted with an ecstatic affirmation, they bought the engagement ring on the Saturday afternoon and spent the rest of the weekend showing it off to both families, all members of which were as thrilled for them as themselves.

David had another trip to Germany in November. Peter had called him in and said the people they designed the glue plant for had made two plants for German firms to manufacture under licence, one in Munich and one in Berlin. To make doubly sure everything was assembled correctly, some parts having been made in Germany and some in the UK, they wanted the original designers to check before their own commissioning engineers started the plant going. After all, as the managing director said to Peter, if a glue plant goes wrong, your batting on a very sticky wicket!

They flew to Munich from Croydon Airport on the Monday morning flight and arrived after a couple of stops at about 4.30 in the afternoon. The work went very well, the German plant engineers were highly competent, so much so that when one or two snags did arise over the next couple of days they very quickly dismantled components, re-machined some faces and reassembled without causing any alarm or consternation.

As a result they were finished on Thursday evening and were not due to fly to Berlin until Monday morning. David asked Peter if he would like to come to Ulm with him to visit the von Hassellbeks. He said he'd be most pleased, so David phoned the doktor who said they'd be delighted to have them for the weekend. It is roughly eighty miles from Munich to Ulm so they decided to hire a car, drive on Friday afternoon and come back after lunch on Sunday. They had a most pleasant time, visiting the opera on Saturday evening, and for the rest of the time talking and gossiping. Peter was a splendid conversationalist. He was not only a first class engineer, but also a great lover of the theatre, particularly Shakespeare and the Greek tragedies where he found a kindred spirit with the doktor. Out of deference to their hosts they steered clear of politics, although one or two not too plainly veiled remarks from the doktor left them in no doubt where his sympathies didn't lie!

Dieter telephoned on the Friday evening.

The doktor said, "I have a person here who wants to talk to you about income tax or something."

"My income tax? I don't earn enough to pay income tax."

"Well there is some you should have paid apparently, so after you have finished your military service he says you may have to go to prison."

"You just put him on – I'll tell him a thing or two." David took the receiver and with a disguised voice carried on with the joke.

"I understand you owe five thousand marks in back tax."

"Absolute nonsense – hey wait a minute someone's pulling my leg."

David then spoke in his normal voice to the great excitement of Dieter at the other end. David said he was coming to Berlin next week, could they meet for dinner one evening. To his great disappointment Dieter said that was unfortunately impossible, they had an exercise on at Luneberg all the week and he would be away from Sunday to Sunday. David asked how he enjoyed being a cadet, to which Dieter replied it was a great life, he was really beginning to enjoy all the comradeship. "We have some good long serving officers teaching us," he said. "I love the tradition and discipline – we'll have to talk about it more some time."

During the visit when David had the doktor to himself he asked after Inge. "She came to see us a month ago," said the doktor, "she is such a beautiful, intelligent girl yet she is blinded by National Socialism. With her connections in the Himmler family she is making great progress in her job. She is now a deputy director in the new Buchenwald concentration camp. I think her main problem is with her having her husband in Berlin she is not there to be able to keep an eye on him, except at weekends when she flies home. I understand that like most of the top Nazis his morals are something akin to those of an alley cat, I think Inge just turns a blind eye and lives for the party."

When they left on Sunday Peter produced two presents, "from David and I for a memorable weekend," he said, although in fact David neither knew about nor had contributed to them. He had bought a pure silk tie and matching scarf for the doktor and a beautiful cameo broach for Frau von Hassellbek. They were in such exquisite taste that the doktor said, "Peter – I think you must be an artist in disguise."

The drive back to Munich was uneventful as also was the Monday morning flight to Berlin. The plant commissioning went well, as a result of which they were finished by Thursday lunchtime, so they flew home on Friday, a day early. David went to meet Pat at the shop at closing time, seven o'clock on Fridays, and was welcomed with the inevitable question, "David, what are you doing here?"

"I'm just checking up that you've not got another bloke in tow while I'm away, that's all. Anyway, since you haven't, I'm taking you to the Angel for dinner – it's all arranged."

"Oh how lovely – you can tell me about your trip – how is Peter, and did he talk about Reuben at all?"

Over dinner David told her about the von Hassellbeks, including Dieter and Inge, as a result of which the subject of concentration camps arose. Whilst they were in Berlin an edict had been issued to the effect that all children were to be raised in the Nazi ideology. Parents who objected to this, pacifists and extreme religious groups, would have the children taken from them and fostered out to 'suitable foster parents'.

"Oh isn't it appalling," said Pat. "I'm so thankful Anni has escaped all that persecution, how could they do it to so many innocent people? Don't you feel awkward having to work and talk to them as if nothing is happening?"

David said it was very difficult, and yet because most people were not involved they blotted it out of their minds as if it were going on somewhere else, with the exception of the fanatics of course, who existed in all stratas of German society, and who you could recognise straight away. "It's the herd instinct I suppose," David continued. "If a lion brings down a zebra on the edge of the herd, the others keep on feeding because they know they are safe, at least for the time being. Anyway enough about such serious things, I'm happy because I'm dining out with the most beautiful girl in Kent."

"Only Kent?"

"Well Kent and perhaps part of Surrey as well."

She gave him a little kick under the table.

Megan's baby was due on Christmas Day. By the end of November she was very large, as a result the visiting consultant gynaecologist suggested she had an X-ray to see if she was going to have twins, and to her mixed delight and consternation they confirmed that this in fact was to be the case. The consternation was caused by the fact that she had bought only one of everything, including one cot. The pram was a large one and would accommodate the two, except that they had to take it back to the factory at Woolwich to have a second hood fitted. The family had a conference and decided to chip in and duplicate everything that was on Megan's original list. Karl, Anni and Ernie insisted on being included and on the following Saturday Ruth, Rose and Anni went off to do all the necessary purchasing from the two baby stores in Sandbury, Anni having been advised by Ernie to keep her eyes open because she might need to be doing the exercise for herself in the not too distant future.

Anni blushed and said to the other two, "He's getting very cheeky now he can walk up and down, goodness knows what he'll be like when he's able to run."

"Then you'll really have to watch yourself," replied Ernie.

"I think he's getting more like Harry everyday," said Ruth.

With a swift change of mood Ernie said seriously, "If I was to get like Harry, not physically I mean, but if I was to have Harry's nature I'd be more than happy."

"You're lovely as you are," said Ruth and to the surprise of them all bent over and kissed Ernie on the cheek, much to his embarrassment. She had always been fond of the brave little boy, knowing him as she did from the time he could run around with the others, only to be struck down when he was eight, and despite all the pain and discomfort, the inability to take part fully with the other lads, still to remain cheerful and cheeky most of the time. She was so happy when he came to work at Sandbury Engineering and happier still when she was told by Fred and Harry what an asset he was making of himself, and most of all she was happy that he had found someone like Anni to love and plan for.

Megan's babies arrived a week early, a boy and a girl, the girl making twice as much noise as the boy, as Harry was told when he was allowed in to visit. "Well that's proof that it's born in them," he said, "as if any of us men needed proof." They were named Mark Trevor and Elizabeth Ruth. He was enormously proud of his twins and went round the factory giving each of the workers a cigar and to those who didn't smoke he said, "Well take it home for your mother."

Megan came through the ordeal without fuss and was rewarded with a constant stream of visitors. Matron had had her put in a side ward, which was readily accessible from the main entrance, and was a frequent visitor herself. "These are the first hospital twins we've had in years," she said, "so we're going to make a fuss of them."

Harry went to dinner at Chandlers Lodge in high dudgeon one evening after visiting Megan. When asked what the problem was he said, "That Matron. She thinks that because one of her staff has presented the hospital with twins she's got the paternal rights, that's if a female can have paternal rights. Anyway, what did she have to do with it, that's what I'd like to know."

David said, "Well with that good looking milkman around that calls on you, how do you know if you had anything to do with it?"

There was the usual squaring up between them, much to the

amusement of Karl in particular, during which Ruth noted that David was filling out to be much taller than Harry and a good deal thicker set. Harry was lean and muscular like his father whereas David was bigger boned and would eventually be a hefty young man.

As it was Christmas Eve when Megan came home, they brought her back to Chandlers Lodge where they stayed until the New Year. It was a jolly Christmas, the house seemed to be teeming with people with the four Hoopers calling in and Ernie coming on Boxing Day. When they sat down at Ruth's big kitchen table there were fifteen plus the three babies, Jeremy and his parents having travelled up on Boxing Day morning and staying at Jack's house since Chandlers Lodge was bursting at the seams. The festivities over, and the visitors all gone the place seemed empty although there were still six of them. This was not to be for long though. Over the holiday period Reg Church and his wife and daughter called in and told Karl he had heard of some premises just off the high street which would be coming available. One of his Rotarian friends was an estate agent with premises comprising a small shop front, which had originally been the front room of the house. When he moved in after the Great War he had extended the house backwards into the garden and used the front room for his business. Now he was going upmarket and buying for himself a new house built not far from Chandlers Lodge and taking over larger lock-up shop premises actually in the high street.

Karl and Anni went to see it with Reg, Anni saying on the way that it needed to have access for Ernie's chair. "I don't think that's a problem from what I remember," said Reg, "the front entrance is at pavement level, and there is quite wide access at the side to the living quarters at the back, even wide enough, once the fences were modified, to take the Royal Enfield."

This proved to be the case, so after establishing the accommodation was suitable, there were two good sized double bedrooms, bathroom, drawing room, dining room and kitchen, Karl said it was just what he wanted and he would get the money drafted as soon as the solicitors could make the necessary arrangements. They decided to take possession on March quarter day, but as the shop section had already moved, Vic Moore, the current owner said Karl could come in as soon as he wanted to in order to fit it out, and to get the front sign altered. All through January they made lists of household goods and furniture, which would be needed.

Harry suggested they spend a day with Mr Salmon at Cuffs and go through the store with him, which they did. Mr Salmon was his usual courteous and helpful self. He noted that no mention had been made of a Mrs Reisner but being the gentleman he was did not comment. When they were lunching together at the Star and Garter Anni told him that her mother had died at Dachau and Mr Salmon, whose family had many Jewish friends in Germany, was most distressed. Karl relieved the gloom by saying, "You know Anni is engaged? It will not be long before they are here to chose a home – ja?" Karl's English was improving but he still used 'ja' and 'nein' and 'nicht war' quite a lot.

When they left, Mr Salmon presented Anni with a cut glass bowl, similar to the one he had given to Megan when they visited him back in 1934. Like Megan, Anni was so thrilled at the first present destined for her eventual home that she too kissed Mr Salmon, to his embarrassment and Karl's amusement.

In February Hitler appointed himself Supreme Commander of all the Reich's armed forces. "More evidence that he means war," said Fred. "I think it is because he cannot fully trust his generals if he is only a civilian," said Karl. "As Supreme Commander they are on oath to obey whatever he says."

Sure enough in March 1938 Hitler invaded Austria. Key Jewish citizens were sent to Dachau, others were given seven days to get out. Pastor Niemoller, who had been preaching against Nazi ideology, was sent to Sachsenhausen, people like Richard Tauber were kicked out, the head of the Rothschild Bank seized. Although there was no mobilisation yet in Britain all Territorial units were put on alert, and as the summer progressed so the army council ordered that exercises this year were to take on a new significance and be the most extensive ever seen in peace time. In June the new Bren gun came into service although the City Rifles were told, "It will be a long time before you even see one let alone fire one," so they had to stick to their Lewis guns, for which in fact most of them had some affection.

During May Fred came home one evening and said to Ruth, "Thomas Cook are running an eight day holiday on the Riviera for eight pounds seventeen and sixpence – why don't we go? If things do blow up later in the year we may not get the chance again."

They had had holidays from time to time, usually four or five days at the most, but never a long holiday. "I'm going to see if they can extend that for a week so that we can get two weeks away. Rose can come and so can Jeremy if he can fix his holidays at that time and is not involved in camp. If we go at the end of July he would be back in good time for camp anyway I should think."

Ruth was thrilled to bits. "Imagine me on the Riviera," she said.

"Well don't say anything to Rose until I find out if they've got vacancies," said Fred.

He got it all confirmed the next day. Rose was delighted and ran out to telephone Jeremy who said he was sure it would be alright at the office, but would confirm from the office in the morning. He confirmed as arranged and said he would send his money straight away. With all the loose ends tied up Fred booked for the two weeks David and Harry would be away at camp, Jack saying he would keep in touch with Karl and Anni to make sure all was well with them at the house. Jeremy was able to miss camp by electing to go on four long weekend signalling courses in September and October, "though how David will be able to manage without me I don't know – he hardly knows how to do his own boots up."

It was decided that by leaving Ernie in charge at the factory it would give him some experience in decision making, it would be a quiet time anyway and he would have the support of Reg Church and Mr Elliott if he needed any help.

The talk of war increased day by day fuelled by the news coming from both the continent and from the home front. In May Hitler visited Mussolini and inspected the Italian Fleet. The least that could be interpreted by this was that in the event of war Italy would be a friendly neutral, but Hitler obviously had designs on the use of Italian ports in which to base his submarines to attack shipping through the Mediterranean. The German press and wireless each day mounted its attack on Czechoslovakia. Approximately 20% of the Czech population, mainly in the western area, were of German origin. They were told they would soon be free. At home the Essential Commodities Bill was presented to parliament. When Fred asked Jack what it was all about, Jack explained that commodity buyers were being given grants or loans to buy in as much as they could of food and materials essential for war. "It looks as though the government for once in its life is seeing a bit beyond the end of its collective nose," said Jack. The government, having formed the Air Raid Precautions Organisation (ARP) the previous year now formed the Women's Voluntary Service under the Dowager Lady Reading to mobilise women who would not normally serve in one of the forces. This was to be a force, which did magnificent work, not only during the war but in the peace that followed as well. It was announced in July that thirty five million gas masks were ready to be issued from strategically placed depots throughout the country.

In Europe Hitler announced prohibited zones, which included the whole of the Baden area down to Ulm, the Black Forest and many other parts of Germany, particularly along the Rhine. At the same time that David and Harry were at camp, the German army held manoeuvres putting one and a half million men under arms, and operating right up to the French and Polish borders. A chill feeling was being experienced by millions of people, particularly mothers and wives with sons and husbands of military age. In July the government ordered another one thousand Spitfires, and then in August to relieve the gloom Len Hutton scored 364 at the Oval against Australia to give an innings total of 903 for 7.

In September there was considerable unrest in Sudetenland the part of Czechoslovakia heavily populated by Germans, so much so the Czech Government declared martial law. On September 15th Chamberlain flew to Berchtesgaden to see Hitler to discuss Czechoslovakia. He came back the next day with Hitler's demands, went back again to Bad Godesberg for further talks and then returned. After discussions with the French he again went back to see Hitler and capitulated to virtually all Hitler's demands, on the promise from Hitler that he had 'no further territorial ambitions'. He flew back to Heston and appeared from the aircraft waving the now famous piece of paper saying 'Peace in our time'. The next day Hitler marched into Sudetenland and a large chunk of Czechoslovakia was ceded to the Third Reich. Feelings in Britain were mixed. Some thought it had given us a breathing space to prepare for the war, which was bound to come. Others were disgusted and sickened by our running out on our ally. Some genuinely believed we had been saved from the abyss. Fred and Jack both had a combination of feelings of disgust but being hardheaded ex-soldiers themselves, welcomed the breathing space to prepare. "As long as the silly sods do take advantage of the time they've been given instead of believing a word that hypocritical criminal says," said Jack.

Anti-Semitism increased by leaps and bounds in both Germany and Austria. In Austria there was confiscation of property owned by Jews with forced eviction. Thousands were rounded up in dawn raids and sent to concentration camps. Children in schools were segregated and it was illegal for Jews to employ Aryans.

In Munich all Jews were told to quit Germany or go to concentration camps, but first they had to pay a tax before they could leave which effectively meant that most of them had to stay. On November 9th in Berlin, the infamous 'Kristal Nacht' took place, organised by the Nazi party. Seven thousand Jewish shops were looted, hundreds of synagogues were burnt down and thousands of Jews injured and killed. Hermann Goering, commenting on the night's work, and mindful of the fact plate glass was mainly imported to Germany and therefore used up valuable hard currency, was reported as saying, 'They should have killed more Jews and broken less glass'. Chamberlain in the meantime had offered a home in Rhodesia to the German Jews and in the former German colony of Tanganyika, Britain having already taken eleven thousand to settle here, but this of course admirable though it was, was only nibbling at the problem.

Altogether 1938 was a year the Chandlers would never forget, but as Christmas approached and plans were being made for all the family festivities, there was fear in Ruth's heart in particular as to whether this would be the last time they would enjoy such a gathering. From what she had heard about more and more orders coming in to the factory from the government, including fitting out a new type of radio receiver van, making chassis components for mobile guns and searchlight mountings, all indicated steps in only one direction, preparing for war. If war came, her two sons and the boyfriend of her daughter would be among the first to be called.

David in the meantime had completed his indentures with Whitmore, Friend and Co at the end of September, and they, most unusually, offered him a permanent job on the staff. He discussed this with his father who asked Jack to come over and give them his views on the subject. After a good deal of talk they all came to the conclusion that a few more years spent at Victoria Street would not do any harm. The experience already gained there would be invaluable. The prospect which now arose of his being in charge of a small section in a year or so, and of being involved in other projects literally worldwide, would give him a sound project management background. If after he decided to leave Whitmore and Friend he did courses in such subjects as commercial accountancy, industrial relations and the like it would fit him out for eventual management along side his brother. David was offered a particularly good salary which would be increased in the following February and substantially increased in February 1940.

But things don't always go according to plan. Adolf Hitler was to put a spoke in the wheel of all their plans, but one plan David was determined to raise at this meeting, and when all the other subjects were exhausted, decisions made, and the Whitbread Light Ales topped up, David said, "Now I am a fully employed working man, may I ask you two gentlemen a question?"

Given the go-ahead he continued, "When can I marry my Pat?"

There was a moment or two of complete silence.

"But you've nothing saved yet," said Fred.

"I will have by next summer," he said, "and I've always put my Terriers pay by, not that that's a fortune, and at the end of my debentures Mr Friend gave me back £100 for all the original work I did for them, so I've got nearly £200 now, and I reckon by next summer I will have saved another £200, that will be enough to get us started, particularly as we will both be earning."

"But you won't be twenty-one for over a year yet," said Fred, and then, "what do you think Jack?"

"Well, this is a strange situation for me to find myself in," said Jack, "first of all strictly speaking this is a family matter. On the other hand it's my daughter he's proposing to marry – or at least I assume it is?" they all laughed, and the initial tension resulting from David's first remark on the subject faded away.

"But seriously," said Jack "they've both proved themselves in every respect, so as far as I'm concerned it's a green light all the way."

"You've obviously thought about it – have you discussed it with Pat? The proposed date I mean?" said Fred.

"No not yet, but if I get the all clear now, I shall tonight. I thought midsummer would be ideal. That would give us time to find somewhere to live and for all other arrangements to be made."

"How would that suit you Jack? After all you're the one to be landed with all the organising," and then Fred added "not that we won't chip in of course."

"Oh no you won't my old son," said Jack, "this is my do. I'm going to see that my only daughter has a right good send-off, just as you will when Rose takes flight."

"Well, with respect, when you two stop arguing, what's the answer?" said David.

The two older men looked at each other and without a further word shook hands with David and then with each other.

"I think all three of us must go and be the bearers of good tidings to our respective loved ones," said Jack.

"And good luck to the pair of you," said Fred.

"Hear hear," said Jack.

Chapter Thirty

In the New Year Pat and David started house hunting. They decided it would be something quite modest so that it was easily managed. They further decided between themselves that as they were so young they would wait a while before they had children, and when and if this happened they could then look around for a bigger place. Jack and Moira had a discussion with Ruth and Fred about giving them a start off. Jack said he had considered buying a place for them, but he wondered whether this would be a wise thing to do. Fred said that if David was the only child he would have agreed to that and gone half with Jack, but he hadn't been able to do that for Harry, he still had Rose to think about and he felt it would be unfair to the other two to make a special case of David. "They won't exactly be short of cash," said Moira, "after all Pat is doing quite well at the shop, and paying her loan commitments on time, and as I understand it David is now getting a good salary for his age."

"How about if we pay a decent deposit on the house between us, they can get a mortgage from the Woolwich Equitable for the remainder. That will make them understand that things are not too easily come by without making them have to look at every penny."

At this suggestion from Fred, the others were in ready agreement. "This will be outside what we give them for a wedding present of course," added Fred, to which again they all readily agreed. They decided to say nothing to Pat and David until they had in fact decided on a property. This subject of course had been occupying the young couple's minds ever since David had told an ecstatic Pat of his meeting with the two fathers. Would Pat prefer a small cottage in the country, would it be better to have a small house in town, or one of the flats in a new development just off the high street, or a semi on the outskirts. All properties had their advantages and disadvantages. They had no car and no likelihood of getting one yet so they ought to be fairly near the town and the station, or at least on a bus route. Some places were ideal from an access point of view but suffered disadvantages from other reasons.

One beautiful small cottage was right next door to an abattoir. "The thought of seeing lorry loads of animals going in there every day would have soon made me a vegetarian," said David. Another very nice semi was on a corner where they discovered lorries detoured to miss the high street traffic, causing noise and fumes. Like many people before them and since, they quickly got used to seeing through the frothy descriptions from the agents and looking beyond just the property itself. Eventually they read an advertisement in the local paper for a bungalow for sale. No description – just bungalow for sale. They wrote to the box number and received an invitation to call any evening. The property was about a mile out of town and about two hundred yards off the main road. It was tucked away behind high yew hedges with a garden surrounding it, which although it was February nevertheless showed ample proof of the love and care that had been lavished upon it over a very long period of time. The door was opened by an immaculately dressed lady, probably in her late sixties who welcomed them in and offered them tea, which was served in exquisite china cups from the most elegant of teapots. Everything about the bungalow indicated a degree of care echoing what they had seen in the garden. David looked at Pat, Pat looked at David, they both knew this would be ideal.

"My name is Mrs Treharne," said the lady, "my husband and I settled here after the war. He was a career officer and served mainly in India until after the war. We have a lovely daughter who lives in north London, and since my husband died three years ago she has been trying to persuade me to go and live with her and her husband, who is a doctor in Hampstead. I have at last decided I will go provided I can sell the house to someone who will love it and take care of it as I do, and will also have my cat Susie, because it would be cruel to uproot her from here, particularly as my daughter has both a dog and a cat. I have to be sure that whoever I sell to will love Susie."

"Could we see the other rooms do you think?" said Pat.

"Yes of course." As Pat expected, the other rooms, including the small conservatory at the rear, were immaculate. The whole place was light, airy and smelt sweet, so unlike some of the dank premises they had looked at.

When they went back to the sitting room Pat said, "When would you like someone to take the premises?" Mrs Treharne said that there was no set time scale as far as she was concerned.

"I take it you're not married yet?" she said to Pat.

"No, we're engaged to be married on the third Saturday in June, another four months, but if you wanted to complete at any time there would be no problem."

"I shall be taking most of my furniture as my son-in-law is building an extension to their house for me to live in, and that will be all ready after Easter, so it would be clear by say May Day." She paused for a moment or two, "You know we're talking like this and you haven't even asked how much."

The three of them laughed at this.

"And neither have we met Susie yet," said David. "So tell us the worst – how much?"

"I have been advised to ask for £750," and then as an after

thought, "oh, but I do hate talking about money."

"Done," said David.

Pat looked at him in complete astonishment. Mrs Treharne for the first time probably in many years lost her imperturbable bearing, and the silence was broken by David taking out his cheque book and saying, "I'll leave you a cheque as a deposit for £50 subject to contract and we'll hope to have everything settled for May 1st. If you will tell me your solicitors I'll start getting it organised tomorrow. Two more things, firstly Pat and I would be delighted for you to visit us here at anytime so that you can see we are keeping up the high standards you have set, secondly can we now be introduced to our cat."

Mrs Treharne got up without a word to go into the conservatory where Susie was asleep in her basket. While she was gone Pat looked at David and said, "I do love masterful men," in an ironic manner, which belied the love shining from her eyes. When Mrs Treharne returned with Susie they immediately adored this gorgeous tortoise shell cat and realised what a terrible wrench it was going to be for Mrs Treharne to leave her behind.

"Mrs Treharne you must come and see Susie from time to time, you will be very welcome, and you have our word she will be loved and cared for at all times."

They went home bursting with excitement having asked Mrs Treharne's permission to bring their respective parents at the weekend to see her beautiful home, to which she readily agreed.

Although he said little to Pat, at the back of his mind David wondered how long it would be before he had to leave her alone in the bungalow – and they weren't even in it yet! He still read his German paper every day and the news in that and in the British press was getting more ominous by the day.

In January 1939 the German paper reported that all women in the Reich under twenty-five years of age were to be called for one year's service either in the armed forces or in the factories. Further restrictions were being placed on Jews. No longer could they practise as dentists, veterinary surgeons or pharmacists. They could no longer hold driving licenses. They were banned from cinemas and concerts and people who allowed them to attend were to be punished as well. In February all Jews in Berlin had to give up their precious stones and metals, it was a systematic method of destroying Jewry through poverty, so much so that the only way many were surviving was by the efforts of international aid organisations, particularly from America. At the end of 1938 the British Government had ordered ten million air raid shelters to be constructed. By March 1939 they were beginning to be delivered to the most vulnerable areas first, and then to the urban and country areas.

They were called the Anderson shelter, named after the home secretary and were six feet long, six feet high and four feet six inches wide. They were designed to be sunk three feet into the ground, and the earth that was excavated to accommodate this was piled on top of the arched roof to add to the protection.

In March 1939 the Territorial Army was doubled in size. Both David and Jeremy had been made lance corporals back in the summer of 1938, and in March 1939 they became corporals as a result of the general promotion of NCO's to train the new intakes. They were still in the same platoon together, but as each commanded a section of ten men they now had a friendly rivalry between them. Harry who now had nearly six years service had been made a sergeant. One evening Ruth got some photos taken of Fred when he was a sergeant just before the Great War and the likeliness between him and Harry in uniform was staggering, "Only I'm just that bit better looking," being the not unexpected comment from Harry.

"I just hope this lot is going to blow over," said Fred. "I wouldn't want either of you to have to go through what we had to."

Harry was serious for a moment, "Well we all live in hopes, but if Chamberlain does what he says he will do I'm afraid war is inevitable."

In March Hitler marched into the Bohemia department of Czechoslovakia. Memel, part of Lithuania was ceded to the Germans and another part of Czechoslovakia was occupied by the Hungarians. Finally Hitler announced that the rest of Czechoslovakia not yet occupied would be a protectorate of the Third Reich. Czechoslovakia ceased to exist. In London, Neville Chamberlain re-pledged our full intention to defend Poland should Germany attack that country. "Though how the hell we defend a country on the other side of Europe I fail to understand," said Jack. As a result of Chamberlain's statement Britain, France and Poland signed a mutual assistance pact, which was promptly denounced by Hitler, who used it as an excuse to tear up the 1934 Naval Treaty which had limited the number of ships and submarines he could build.

In May the Conscription Bill was introduced and passed at the end of the month, which affected all twenty year old men, the first of which presented themselves to their depots at the beginning of June. The term of service was for six months plus time in the Territorial Army on completion. Those men who joined in June 1939 spent a very great deal longer in the army than they had ever expected to, those that is who eventually came back. They were to be paid one shilling and sixpence a day, wives if any would get seventeen shillings per week. Amid all this gloom and despondency Anni and her father were in a strange position. They were aliens in a land that could soon be at war with their country, which would make them enemy aliens. What would happen to them? Mr Reisner was doing quite well with his watch and clock business and at Rotary. Anni thought of herself almost as English having been here for four years. They were discussing this with Ernie one evening, the uncertainty of it all bringing a blight on the good news that had been theirs for the past eighteen months with Karl's arrival, Anni's engagement, Ernie's steady progress to responsibility at the factory and above all dramatic improvement over the last six months in his walking ability. He could now, with the aid of just sticks to maintain his balance, walk considerable distances, although in the factory in order to get around more quickly he still used his chair.

In the middle of the conversation Ernie said, "I think we should marry as soon as possible after Pat and David, then you at least will be English."

Karl looked at them both. "That is a very good plan," he said. "I cannot become naturalised for seven years, so there is no way I can escape being an enemy alien. That doesn't mean to say they will lock us all up. The English are very civilised people particularly with regards to refugees."

Anni sank to her knees beside his chair, "But supposing they do take you away. Can't you go to Switzerland or America?"

"My dear child, I would rather be here and know that I am not far from you both, and for all I know be able to see you from time to time, than to go to some other country where I have nobody. No, I am going to stay in England and one day I too will become English and I shall do all I can to pay back the kindness this country has done to me in accepting my daughter, in giving her such a fine husband and even if they do lock me up for a while, in giving me a home as well."

Anni smiled through her tears at Ernie and said, "Father has spoken, and when he speaks like that nothing will change him."

"In that case, when do we get married?" asked Ernie.

"Pat and David are marrying on 17th June, let's make it the first Saturday in August, but we do have a problem of course. You know I am a Catholic, a lapsed Catholic it is true, but still a Catholic."

"Well there's no reason why we can't marry at the Sandbury Registry Office, if you and your father don't object," said Ernie. "You'll look as beautiful there as in any church."

They both looked at Karl. "Anni's mother was a Catholic," he said, "We were married at City Hall."

There was a silence for a few moments broken by Anni who said, "We'd better go along and get it organised tomorrow then hadn't we?" she hugged Ernie and then her father and said "There'll be so much to do, organising the reception and all the other things I shan't know where to start. And we haven't even thought of where we are going to live!"

Karl took her hand. "I think at first if you live here it would be best. I will keep out of your way, and then if there was a war you could stay and look after the place while I am away. In any case we shall have a grand wedding and I shall settle £5,000 on you as my wedding present, but nobody is to know that please, except of course Mr and Mrs Bolton and Ruth and Fred – you will want to tell them naturally."

They were both overwhelmed at this momentous announcement, protesting together that this was too generous, but Karl showed the same firmness that he had used when negotiating terms with Ruth – no mean adversary – overriding their protestations with humour and decisive finality. So the 5th August would be the great day and the two young newly weds would be off to a fine start thanks to Karl.

Summer came. First Pat and David went to see Mr Salmon and with his genial guidance bought all the necessities for their new home. Mrs Treharne said that since her new windows were a lot larger than those at the bungalow she would leave all the curtains for them – that is if they were suitable of course! They were of very good quality and in excellent condition, so Pat said she would be pleased to have them. When David asked how much she was quite shocked. "I wouldn't dream of taking anything for them," she said. "I am so pleased that a couple like you are taking over my house," and as an after thought, "I turned two couples away before you came you know – they were not people I would have liked to live here."

David put his arm round her shoulder and gave her a little hug. "You will come to the wedding won't you?" he said, "and then come and visit us and Susie afterwards."

Mrs Treharne was quite touched, it was not often these days anyone was so kind to her, not that anyone was unkind to her, and it was just that like a lot of other people her circle of friends had diminished. When her husband died, as a widow she was asked out less and less, her family were away up in north London, as a result she was left more and more on her own. "I shall be delighted to come to your wedding," she said, "and to visit you later, you really are very kind. I knew when I left here I would miss Susie terribly, it would be almost like parting with a child, but the thought that she will be safe and well and that I can come and see her now and then would make all the difference to me. Now, I would like to give you a wedding present if you would like it. If you don't like it please don't be afraid that you will offend me by saying so, I assure you absolutely that you won't."

She led them into the spare bedroom where there was a tapestry rug lying over a chest of some sort. She pulled the cover off to reveal a most beautifully ornamented sandalwood box, about three feet six inches long by eighteen inches wide by a little over two feet high, with heavy brass hinges and a lock on the face. She opened it. It was empty and on being opened gave out a most subtle and delicate perfume. Pat fell in love with it immediately. "It is beautiful," she said, "but surely much too valuable to give away."

"If you really like it, it is yours," said Mrs Treharne.

Pat hugged her and said they would always treasure it. It was their first wedding present and they were both thrilled at such a beautiful gift knowing as they did how much it must have meant to Mrs Treharne.

Mrs Treharne moved a day or so after May Day and in the following week Mr Salmon had the young couple's home delivered to them. There was so much to do in sending out the invitations and making all the last minute arrangements for bridesmaids dresses, reception details and so on. Moira was having to work long hours at the ministry, sometimes not being able to even come home at night. She had employed a first class nanny to look after the young John, but she was deeply apologetic to Pat and David in not being able to help as she would have liked in sharing the enormous amount of work there was to be done. However Ruth was as always her calm organised self and readily available to do everything she could in making sure nothing was forgotten or left to the last minute, and in helping Pat at the bungalow, which as Pat had for years thought of auntie Ruth as a second mother was very greatly appreciated.

The wedding was to be a 'top hat do' as Harry called it. Harry of course was to be Best man and much looking forward to the task. It was decided that young John and the twins would be too young to be attendants, although they would be brought to the wedding and then cared for by John's nanny, who loved the twins and often looked after them. The guest list grew day by day as friends and relatives from both families sent in their acceptances. The Lord Lieutenant of the county and Lady Houghton accepted, both old friends of Jack's family. Two old army friends of Jack's, both now lieutenant generals also were coming, the folk from Wales would be massively represented. The managers and senior staff at the factory were not forgotten. The shop would be shut for the day and Mrs Draper, so expert at advising other people what to wear, was in absolute lather of indecision as to what to buy 'for the wedding'. The Cartwrights of course were coming so also were some senior ministerial colleagues of Moira.

A huge marquee was to be erected in the garden of The Hollies, which required the levelling of one complete flower bed, readily sacrificed for the big occasion, and a band from London organised to provide the music for the evening celebrations. The honeymoon destination had been kept secret except to a select few, they were in fact spending their wedding night at the Grosvenor Gardens Hotel, to go on to the Grand at Torquay for ten days afterwards. The days flew past to the great day. David held his stag party at the Angel on the Thursday evening 'otherwise if we have it on Friday Harry will still be three parts cut and swaying all over the place when he is trying to find the ring'. Even so many of David's Terrier friends made the journey to Sandbury as also to his great pleasure did Peter Phillips and Reuben, the latter surprising David by drinking pints of bitter!

The great day dawned fine and sunny. David and Harry made their way to the old 16th century church in Harry's new Riley, which Harry then parked in the Angel car park. "I doubt if I shall be fit to drive that home tonight," he said, "so it will be safe there."

"As long as you remember where you left it," replied David.

"Still half an hour to kick off," said Harry, "fancy a quick one?"

"Alright, but only one," said David. "I don't suppose the vicar here will be like the one in Carmarthen. We don't want to blow booze all over him."

"At Carmarthen it was the other way round," said Harry. "Do you remember, he was blowing it all over us!"

They laughed heartily at this recollection as they made their way into the saloon bar, where instantly they were hailed by a trio of David's pals from the Rifles, who had arrived early from London.

"Surround him you blokes," said Corporal English, "if we keep him here it'll save him from a fate worse than death."

"One drink and one only," said David.

"Right, treble whisky Mr Barman please."

The banter went on, but they let him get off with one light ale, after which they all drank up and formed up outside as if escorting a prisoner for CO's orders.

"Escort and accused, by the left, quick march," bellowed Harry, and in this manner they marched across the road into the churchyard and up to the church door, to the great amusement of a number of guests arriving for the ceremony.

"Party halt, prisoner and Best man fall out" and with that they made their ways to their positions inside the church. David had asked the vicar if Miss Parnell from Mountfield, provided she was able, could come and play at his wedding. The vicar readily agreed. He knew her quite well as she occasionally came to his church as a guest organist. As a result David telephoned her and asked if he and Pat could come and see her. She took to Pat straight away and said she'd be delighted to come. David tactfully raised the question of her fee which she immediately squashed by saying there was no question of payment. David had helped her enough times when he was a boy – 'although they've got an electric bellows at Mountfield now so I don't need a boy to pump it up or fall asleep in the loft'– this latter reference to the time David had allowed the mighty instrument to run out of wind.

Miss Parnell had great fun relating this incident, with embellishments to Pat, who said, "You will come to the reception afterwards won't you?"

"Yes please do," said David. "There will be people there you know." Little did he know how prophetic he was being. As David arrived in his allotted seat, Miss Parnell was playing some of her own variations on a piece by Elgar and seeing him now a grown man and being able to play at his wedding gave her enormous pleasure.

The church filled, David looked at his watch. "Five minutes to kick off," whispered Harry, "you've still got time to duck out."

"Would you if you were in my shoes?"

"You've got a point there."

"Have you got the ring?"

"Why does every idiot ask the Best man if he's got the ring?"

"Because he can't think of anything else intelligent to say."

"Well I have – I think – it was here a minute ago – where can it be?"

"I'll get you for this."

Pat was ten whole minutes late – it seemed like a lifetime. Miss Parnell kept a watchful eye on her mirror but she was an old hand at weddings and knew only too well that for every ceremony that started on time a score didn't. The choir had filed in from their vestry in the meantime and were sitting patiently looking at the order of service. At last the vicar appeared. "Any minute now," whispered Harry, overheard by the vicar wearing his Great War ribbons who gave David an understanding grin. And the whole magnificent church came to life with the playing of the Wagner wedding march as the vision of loveliness who was Pat slowly paced the aisle on the arm of her so proud father. The rest of the proceedings were somewhat of a dream to David but eventually he found himself with a small coterie of relatives and in-laws signing the register, while the choir sang an anthem David had sung many times at other weddings. Then a little wait before they emerged again to walk down the aisle to the music of Mendelssohn to emerge into the brilliant June sunlight – it was a wonderful June that year – for the inevitable and to David endless photographic session. At last they were being pelted with confetti, Pat threw her bouquet, which was neatly caught by Rose, and they were in the car and away.

"You are the most beautiful bride that ever was Mrs Chandler," said David.

Pat leaned across and gave him a long kiss, studiously ignored by the driver who was looking straight ahead and not into his mirror.

All the staff who had been hired by Jack for the reception were standing outside the marquee as they arrived and there were gasps of appreciation of the brides beautiful gown and the lovely picture she made. They were professional people, well used to catering at such functions, but there were still a number who became quite emotional at the sight of the handsome young man and his beautiful bride.

The reception was superb. Jack had given strict orders to the caterers that no one was to be seen with an empty glass, "get em' all a bit tiddly – that's the way to do it," he had said to Ruth and Fred and Moira when they were doing the planning. "This is the only time this is going to happen to me and I intend people will remember it. God knows what is going to happen in the not too distant future to stop celebrations of this nature anyway, but let's not dwell on that."

There was the well-known formula of witty speeches, the giving of presents to the attendants, the bridegroom saying 'my wife and I' to thunderous applause and the reading of telegrams until eventually Harry rose and said there would be a break of one hour whilst the tables were cleared and the floor laid for dancing. During this time guests would be free to walk in the garden and the bride and groom would hope to be able to talk to each of them either during the break or during the evening. They would be leaving at nine o'clock, but the band was booked until midnight and there were limitless supplies of lubricating fluids of all types which must be consumed as the suppliers flatly refused to take anything back, this latter remark to general laughter and spontaneous applause.

Whilst the meal was in progress, Miss Parnell sitting on the centre spring, caught a side view of one of Jack's general friends, in civilian clothes of course, sitting with his back to her further down one of the outer sprigs. Although it was twenty-five years since she last saw him, just before he went off to war, it was unmistakably him. He was sitting between two ladies somewhat younger than him and was chatting to each in turn, and she found herself saying to herself, 'I wonder which one is his wife?' with a pang that she thought had left her many, many years ago.

Miss Parnell's father, a wealthy man, had died when she was only ten and she had missed him terribly over all the years ever since. When she was just seventeen, in 1911, she had been introduced to a newly promoted Captain Fredrick Earnshaw, by her brother who was a lieutenant in the same regiment, the Green Howard's. They fell in love with one another and at the end of that year Freddie, as he was known, was being posted to India for four years, and asked Miss Parnell's mother for permission to marry her daughter so that she could go with him. Mrs Parnell flatly refused on the grounds that the girl wasn't old enough, she didn't want her traipsing around all over the globe like a camp follower and that frankly he wasn't good enough for her, his parents not being landed gentry. Freddie left, was posted to India, then the middle east, and did not return to England until 1916 then being sent to command a battalion in France. They saw each other three times before he was sent to France but then drifted apart. Miss Parnell's brother had been killed in early 1915, as a result Miss Parnell felt she could not leave her grieving mother whose life had been desolated by the loss of her only son who had been the life and soul of her being, so she felt her duty lay at home.

When the break in the reception came, Miss Parnell joined the throng moving to the garden. On emerging she saw Jack talking to General Earnshaw, and on seeing that she was on her own he called her over. "Oh, Miss Parnell, may I introduce my friend General Sir Frederick Earnshaw," and to Sir Frederick, "This is Miss Parnell."

To Jacks total surprise the general turned and took Miss Parnell's outstretched hand in both of his and raised it to his lips saying, "Kate – is it really you? You haven't altered one little bit."

"I'm afraid you flatter me Freddie, but yes it is really me."

He was still holding her hand and looking with such intense pleasure into her eyes that Miss Parnell blushed a little.

"Would you mind telling me what's going on here?" asked Jack, a true romantic at heart.

"This lady is the reason I never married," said Freddie. "I could never find another who would begin to compare."

"But the ladies at the table?" queried Kate, speaking without thinking.

"Which table was that?"

"At the reception you had a lady on either side, I rather thought..." And then broke off.

"You rather thought...?"

"Yes I did, it was silly of me."

Jack by now was intrigued by this chance meeting. He had been bosom pals with Freddie when they were in the Middle East and had continued their friendship ever since. He had often wondered why Freddie had not married. He was tall, lean good-looking chap in a rugged sort of way, and would have been considered 'a good catch' one would have thought.

"Well now," said Jack, "I have an awful lot of people to talk to. Can I leave Miss Parnell in your tender care Freddie while I do the rounds?"

"The fact is old boy, that if you dare try and interrupt us for the rest of the evening I'll flatten you." Jack walked off laughing heartily leaving them to spend the evening renewing the closeness they had enjoyed only too briefly twenty-five years before.

Pat and David made the rounds of all guests, the Cartwrights, the Boltons, the Lloyds, Anni and Ernie and her father talking to Mrs Treharne, Mr Scott-Calder talking to Dr and Mrs Carew and many others one or the other of them didn't know. When they came to Anni, still dressed in her bridesmaid dress – Rose of course was the other attendant – Pat said, "You'll be next Anni." When they came to Dr Carew he asked them if they had heard from the von Hassellbeks, apart from the telegram which had been read out. David said that they had received letters from both the doktor and from Dieter, posted in Switzerland, which apparently the doktor was visiting. Dieter had ended his letter by saying, 'I don't know what will happen in the future but you can be sure always of the undying friendship of me and my family and Rosa, to whom I have become very attached, for you and Pat and your families'.

"That's probably why they were posted in Switzerland – it's terribly sad," said Dr Carew. "Anyway, you be off, no sad thoughts today," and they moved on to talk to Miss Parnell and the general.

At half past eight they went into the house to change. As they went in Harry said to them, "Now if you are longer than fifteen minutes I'll come and get you." David swung a mock punch at him, and they made their way to the two rooms where their clothes were laid out ready. Pat's were in her own room, and as the two bridesmaids helped her out of her gown and Moira made one or two adjustments to her hair, Pat looked around at the room which had been her home for most of her twenty years. Her teddy still sat on her pillow; it was all so familiar, what was the future to hold for her?

Would it all be as wonderful as she had dreamt it would be?

Would they really be everything to each other as she had imagined?

Moira's voice spoke softy to her. "Getting a few collywobbles now is it?" She often lapsed into her native accent and vocabulary when she was not being what Jack called her 'ministry self'.

"Not really," said Pat. "I was just thinking, this isn't my room anymore."

"You have another room now which you will share and be happy in, take my word."

Pat squeezed her hand and pronounced herself ready to go. Moira went into the room in which David waited with Fred and they all then went off downstairs and out through the throng surrounding the car which was to take them to London.

There followed ten days of bliss until they arrived back at Paddington to be met by Jack and ferried home, firstly to The Hollies and then to the bungalow. They received an enthusiastic welcome from Susie. After Mrs Treharne had moved to Hampstead Pat had visited at least twice a day to look after her and, as she had a cat flap into the conservatory, she was quite happy. While they were on honeymoon Ruth, Rose and occasionally Jack organised visits to make sure she was alright and to make a fuss of her, but when Pat and David arrived she purred to such effect that David said, "Hey, you'll bust your boiler if you're not careful." Perhaps she knew she was going to have so little time with this new master to whom she had became so attached that she had to show how happy she was with him. Cats know all sorts of things we humans don't know, as any cat lover will tell you.

Chapter Thirty-one

One evening while the young ones were away Rose had gone to London for a theatre visit with Jeremy prior to catching the last train back to Sandbury, Jack and Moira called round to see Ruth and Fred. Inevitably the conversation turned to what most thinking people considered, 'the approaching war'.

"Everything's gaining momentum," said Jack. "I hear that all the plans are laid and will be announced soon for the wartime control of the various railway companies, and that they are stocking food in dozens of different reception areas in case of heavy bombing and the subsequent breakdown of communications. I'm afraid that, unlike the Great War, the civilian population in the big towns here is going to be in the front line as much as the soldiers."

"And yet the Labour Party is still opposing conscription," said Fred. "Do they really believe that Hitler is going to stay put after getting as far as he has already without a war? Not likely, Poland is next, then Russia, then us, or then us and then Russia. Certainly it's Poland next and I bet he's thinking that despite all our huffing and puffing we'll just sit on our backsides and let him do it, as we did with Czechoslovakia."

Ruth said very little during these conversations, but inside she dreaded the inevitability of her two sons being uprooted at a time when they had everything to live for. And there was Rose too, so much in love with her Jeremy who, with David, would also be whisked away from them if war was thrust upon them. She looked so sad and crestfallen that Jack said, "All this war talk depressing you Ruth?"

He had rarely seen Ruth looking other than her imperturbable collected self but now tears were brimming as she said, "I was thinking of how the children will all be taken from us, Harry, David and Jeremy, just when they have everything to live for. It seems so wicked. And not only us, millions of other mothers not only here, but in France and Germany, even will be thinking the same thing. I've never hated anyone as far as I know in all my life, but I hate that evil man Hitler for all he's done and for all the heartache he's going to cause."

Fred put his arm around her shoulder, but all he could find to say was, "Well perhaps when he sees what he's up against he'll pull back," but to himself he said that he wouldn't back next week's wages on it.

August soon came and with it Anni's wedding day. She had had long discussions with Ruth and Rose as to what to wear and eventually they opted for the traditional white wedding, but without a long train. Ernie had stipulated it would be a top hat affair even though it was to be held at Sandbury Registry Office – he said that looking as handsome as he had at David's wedding nothing else would do. Karl provided a reception at the Angel for over seventy friends and relatives, but the great event of the day was Ernie walking unaided, other than by the strong arm of Anni, out from the ceremony and into the waiting car. As he said to David during the evening, "I swore I'd do that on my wedding day and I did." The newly-weds were only to have a short honeymoon. With the amount of work they had at Sandbury Engineering and with Ernie now being one of the lynchpins, time was a precious commodity. Anni fully understood and was proud that Ernie was such a key factor in an enterprise, which was doing so much in helping to get the country into a state of readiness to combat the evil, which had killed her mother. The factory was now running two shifts, and at the last Friday management meeting it had been mooted by Ernie that they should consider Saturday working all day and even Sunday. Fred was in principle against Sunday working, reckoning that men would soon get overtired and stale if they did not have a day off. "Six days shalt they labour wasn't done for religious reasons," he opined. "I reckon it was just good sense, if we've to get a rush job out I think it might be justified, but not as a regular thing."

Jack, who attended these meetings whenever he could, suggested it might be a good idea to buy in as many spares as they could locate for agricultural equipment, and in addition to buy as cheaply as possible as many second-hand and broken down items as they could find. "If the war does come there is going to be a great need to keep all farm implements going, and we'll certainly find shortages of parts. If we can cannibalise old broken down tractors and so on we'll be doing a great service to the country and earn a few bob at the same time."

It was decided therefore that Harry would have an intensive fortnight on the road visiting his customers. This operation proved most successful to the extent that he got a lot of bits and pieces for nothing or just scrap value, a great deal of which proved to be useful later on, and that which was of no use eventually ended up in one of the various scrap metal drives, to be made into munitions.

Rumours of the German Army massing on the Polish border came in daily as August progressed and it was therefore no surprise whatsoever when, on September 1st, news flashed around the world that Hitler had invaded. Division after division poured across the frontiers from Germany in the west and Czechoslovakia in the South. Prime Minister Chamberlain ordered Germany to withdraw or Britain and France would declare war. There being no satisfactory reply from Hitler, on Sunday September 3rd war was declared, beginning a conflict in which it is estimated twenty five million people would eventually perish worldwide.

That evening the King broadcast to his people and in solemn tones of great sadness said that the task facing us would be hard, there would be dark days ahead, but with God's help we would prevail – God bless us all. Later that day Australia, New Zealand and South Africa and the next day Canada, all declared war on Germany.

The first things to affect everybody were the obliteration of place names on shop fronts, milestones etc, removal of all signposts, and then painting out of telephone exchange names. The Sandbury Engineering signboard was removed and put away in stores, few thought it would be over five years before it was replaced, and then in a very different world. Immediate blackout was ordered. In houses, and even in shops like Pat's, it was not too difficult to comply with, but in the factory, which had a great expanse of glass in the roof in each of the bays it was extremely difficult. On the Monday morning it was all hands to the deck, or in this case the roof, in coating the glass with tar and any kind of paint, all mixed up together, that they could lay their hands on. The optimists were all saying, 'the war would be over by Christmas' upon which Fred commented, 'It had better be, I don't think some of that paint will last that long'.

At the end of the week both Harry and David received telegrams ordering them to report to their units immediately, David at Colchester, Harry at Bulford on the Salisbury Plain. They both said their goodbyes to their colleagues at work on the Friday, on the Sunday everyone met for Sunday lunch at Chandlers Lodge none knowing when they would ever meet again like this. When they had finished lunch Jack stood up and said he would like to make a short speech, and to general assent proceeded to say how proud they all were of their three soldiers, "and here I include our dear friend Jeremy, who is almost one of the family. I'm not going to be jingoistic," he continued, "but we have a tyrant to face who is so evil that only the force of arms will unseat him and give us the lasting peace that Fred and I thought wrongly we had achieved twenty odd years ago. There is no doubt in my mind that right is on our side, therefore we must prevail. We wish you two young men, and Jeremy as well, a safe passage through all the dangers you may be facing in the coming months and years, and that you will always be secure in the knowledge that we here at home will be supporting you with our love and our thoughts until you return."

There was a deep silence as Jack finished until Harry rose and said, "Thank you Uncle Jack, these words mean a lot to young David and me and will to Jeremy when they are passed on I'm sure. We are very fortunate to belong to such lovely people as all of you and in my case the Lloyds as well, you may trust us never to let you down."

Another silence followed until Harry continued in typical Harry fashion, "Though how the hell you're going to run 'Blacked Out Engineering' without me God alone knows."

The laughter was a relief after the tension of the two speeches but when Ruth said goodbye to the two boys, as she still thought of them, when they made their way home that evening tears were in her eyes as they were in both Rose's and Moira's. These would not be the last tears they would shed over these young men, like millions of wives, mothers, sisters and girlfriends all over the world for the next six years or more.

David and Harry were seen off at Sandbury on Monday morning and travelled together to Victoria. They went as far as the embankment on the Innercircle Line together, where Harry had to change to get to Waterloo, whilst David had to go on to Liverpool Street. They shook hands.

"Take care of yourself – don't forget you're an old married man now."

"Yes Sergeant, and you too Sergeant," and with a little grin at each other the soldier brothers said farewell with no fuss, no histrionics, but a deep knowledge of the love and comradeship that existed between them.

Arriving at Liverpool Street, David went up onto the main line station and was walking across the concourse to find out which platform he was to leave from, and there to meet Jeremy, when a bellow came from a military policeman, a lance corporal, directed at David.

"Hey you – where you going to?"

David put his kitbag down and turned to the redcap. It was then the redcap saw that David was a full corporal.

"Sorry Corporal" he said, "didn't see you were a Corporal. Why are you improperly dressed with stripes only on one arm?"

"In our regiment we only wear them on the right arm, so I suggest if you see more of our lot you watch who you're talking to. If you talk to a Sergeant or Sergeant Major like you've just addressed me, you could be in it up to here."

The redcap mumbled an apology and David walked on to the departures board which indicated the train to Colchester would leave from platform 6. Jeremy was already at the gate so, as they had plenty of time they went over to a Salvation Army canteen van for tea and 'a wad'. The journey to Colchester was uneventful, the train being full of a mixture of army, navy and RAF men, some young, some obvious regulars and reservists, a few militiamen coming back off leave and a few in civilian clothes, having newly joined up, going to the depot to be kitted out. When they arrived at Colchester a regimental policeman indicated they should board one of the trucks standing by to take them to their camp, where having reported to the CSM at A company office they would be told which hut they were in.

"You're still in 2 platoon, you've got a new Sergeant, Sergeant Harris," said the sergeant major, "better report to him and make yourselves known, then there'll be a company parade at nine o'clock in the morning to see who is here and who isn't."

They went to their hut, which could house a complete platoon of thirty-six men. The sergeant had a separate room at the entry to the hut, at which they knocked. A bellow from inside told them to come in and they found themselves in the presence of a red faced, ginger haired, stocky, thick necked individual with close set eyes who immediately reminded David with a shock of piggy-eyes at Home Farm.

"Corporals Cartwright and Chandler reporting Sergeant," said Jeremy in his usual polite upper middle class accent.

"What have we got here then, another couple of bloody useless college boys eh? Good God almighty I've got to get a platoon together to fight a war and they send me a couple of bloody corporals straight out of the kindergarten. How much service have you got in?"

"Three years, Sergeant" said Jeremy.

"Do you know what this means?" said the sergeant pointing to a medal ribbon on his left breast.

"Yes Sergeant," said Jeremy, "It's the Long Service and Good Conduct Medal. We have always been told it is very highly regarded and one should always listen to what a holder of such an award has to say."

David gulped back an attack of mild hysteria the subtle Mickey-taking had brought upon him.

"You taking the piss out of me?"

"Good Lord, no Sergeant, absolutely not."

He obviously wasn't satisfied.

"And what's the matter with you corporal, haven't you got a tongue in your bleeding head?" this remark directed at David.

"Oh yes Sergeant, it's just that Corporal Cartwright is the senior by one number."

"What do you mean by one number?"

"Well Sergeant, we're the same age, joined the same day, or night to be precise, were promoted on the same day, but he happens to be 695 and I happen to be 696, so he's the senior."

The sergeant, he with the medal for eighteen years undiscovered crime, still couldn't be sure if they were having him on so he said, "Right, you take the first double bunk inside the door, I want my corporals where I can get at them in a hurry. And I want you to get the names of the men as they arrive, divide them into sections and platoon HQ and then bring the list to me before parade tomorrow morning –

understood?"

"Yes Sergeant."

They took a pace back, right about turned and marched out.

When they got into the barrack room David said, "You silly sod, you nearly made me choke."

"I think we may be going to have some trouble with that one," said Jeremy, "and he's a lazy devil, it's his job to work out the platoon structure, not ours."

They made themselves known to the new arrivals who had come from other units and from the depot, and said cheery hellos to their old comrades from the City Rifles. By supper time that evening they had thirty-one, including themselves, so they made up the sections as far as they could, and at nine o'clock Jeremy knocked on the sergeant's door with the lists. There was no answer. He tried again at nine thirty, still no answer. Lights out was at ten o'clock so at ten to ten he tried again and a bellow from within said he should enter. When he went in the sergeant was sitting on the edge of his bunk obviously very much the worse for drink.

"What do you want?"

"Here are the lists you asked for Sergeant. Platoon strength thirty-one at present. Who is to be our officer, do you know?"

"No I don't. Some pissy arse one pipper I expect straight out of school with his diapers still on."

He took the list but his eyes wouldn't focus properly, so he threw them on to the cabinet by the side of the bed.

"Call me at 7.30," he said, starting to undress. Jeremy left quickly to get to bed before the bugle blew lights out.

They all soon settled in. Their platoon officer turned out to be a full lieutenant from the depot named Austen. His family was a famous brewing family so he was obviously very well off as the Jaguar SS sports that he arrived in indicated. He was a charming man, softly spoken in direct contrast to the bellicose red-necked sergeant, but despite the fact he rarely raised his voice it soon became obvious that he was going to run 2 platoon and not Sergeant Harris, eighteen years service or no eighteen years.

The first weeks were taken up by the normal routine of morning PT, foot drill, occasional guard duty, endless route marches starting at six miles and going up to fifteen miles before lunchtime at rifleman's pace, initially with light packs and working up to full marching order. Rarely did the men finish the day needing anyone to rock them to sleep. All the time Mr Austen was at the front working as hard as the others, and to give him credit, although an 'old man' of thirty-seven years of age, so did the sergeant. Around the camp the men had constructed sandbag enclosures which were manned with their Lewis guns – they still only had one Bren gun in the company – whenever there was a stand-to. The magazines for immediate use for 2 platoon Lewis guns were housed in a locked cupboard in the sergeant's room and it was his responsibility in the event of a stand-to, real or practice, to bring them out to the section corporal for issue to the gun teams as they left the hut.

'A' Company Commander Major Grant, a Great War veteran confided to the sergeant major one Saturday morning that he thought it might be a good idea to have a practice stand-to at two o'clock on Sunday morning. "I know half of them will have been down to the village pubs all the evening, so there will be some thick heads about, but if we get a parachute drop on us you can bet your bottom dollar they'd do it at the time we least expect it. Oh, and by the way you don't tell the platoon officers, I know what they're like at trying to beat each other and they'll tip the wink to the platoons if we're not careful."

Sure enough at two o'clock on Sunday morning the major, 2nd in command and CSM each marched into a platoon barrack block bellowing, "Stand-to – stand-to," and then went outside to see which platoon was the quickest in manning their emplacements.

David and Jeremy fell out of bed and speedily dressed, complete with greatcoats, steel helmets and respirators, David having first given a thunderous knocking on Sergeant Harris's door. They dressed very quickly and went to the sergeant's room to collect the magazines, only to find him still in his bed, snoring loudly and obviously still very drunk. His keys were on the cabinet so they quickly unlocked it and handed out the magazines so that the guns would be properly manned.

"Quick," said David, "lets get his trousers and greatcoat on." They pulled his blankets back, swung his legs round, put his trousers on and each slipped a bare foot into a boot and laced them so that they wouldn't slip off. They pulled him into his greatcoat, put his tin hat on, swung his gas mask round his neck and lifted him up. And then with one of his arms round each of them they half carried, half dragged him to the hut door. A quick look outside to see that they could get to the emplacement, and they'd got him leaning against the sandbags mumbling, "What the bloody hell's going on?"

The combination of the cold night air and of being man handled had the effect of quickly, if not of sobering him up, of at least enabling him to stand on his own two feet, and in five minutes time being able to announce to the newly arrived Mr Austen, "2 platoon stood-to sir."

In the event 3 platoon had beaten them, but only by a short head, so they were not disgraced. In a quarter of an hour they got the 'stand down' and all went back to bed. That morning when they came back from breakfast the sergeant called them in as they passed his door.

"Did you get me dressed and out last night?"

Jeremy answered "Yes Sergeant." There was a pause.

"If you'd left me there and I'd been absent off stand-to I would have been right in it – even busted to corporal."

They didn't answer.

"Well why did you do it, you didn't owe me any favours, why didn't you leave me there?"

Jeremy again, "In a good platoon one doesn't do that sort of thing does one?"

The sergeant didn't know how to answer that.

David thought he would go in with both feet, "Sergeant Harris," he said, "can I ask you a question strictly in these four walls without you bawling us out?"

"Well since I owe you go ahead."

"You're a damned good, capable sergeant and you know the game from A to Z, why do you spoil it all by being on the booze whenever you get the chance? You must know that the people like the RSM will notice, which means you'll never make CSM and if you're pissed on a real stand-to you'll be finished."

They waited for the explosion, but after a certain reddening of the face and neck, to their surprise the sergeant said, "Obvious as that is it?" and then followed with, "Alright, point taken, fall out."

Back in the hut Jeremy said, "crikey David you took a chance didn't you?"

"Well let's hope it comes off," said David, and whether his words had done the trick, or merely triggered off what the sergeant, knowing he was drinking too much, was trying to plan for himself, they never knew, but rarely did they see him after a skinful, except on one or two occasions when he had a Saturday night out with the RSM. It was well known in the battalion that keeping up with the RSM was a very difficult task indeed.

Chapter Thirty-two

When Harry left David at the Embankment Station on September 11th, he had a premonition it would be a long time before he saw him once more. In fact it wasn't such a long time as wars go, but in his wildest dreams he could not have envisaged the experiences they were both to undergo before they shook hands again. The journey from Waterloo to Bulford in a special troop train, with only a handful of RAF uniforms to enliven the drab sea of khaki serge, was uneventful and he reached his barracks during the afternoon. This was a peacetime camp; as a result the sergeant's mess, and his quarters, were very comfortable and well furnished. As he remarked to his staff sergeant friend who he had bumped into on the train, "Well, this will do me for the rest of the war."

"Enjoy it now my son, I don't think it will last for long."

And neither did it. They spent the next three weeks getting their vehicles ready and being kitted out on a war basis, and on October 12th they were given forty-eight hours notice to move for embarkation to Weymouth. On the 14th the long convoy of three-tonners and attendant utility vans and motor cyclist outriders began the slow journey to the port, and having taken a complete twenty-four hours to embark all the vehicles they sailed to their destination of Cherbourg, which was a military secret but which everybody seemed to know about. Even the 'dockies' who came on and off the ship as she was being loaded could tell them when they were leaving and what time they would arrive. So much for official secrets!

Once they were under way they were briefed as to their destination and what they were going to do. Their base would be at Le Mans in a huge arms and equipment dump made available by the French army. They would then either be involved in collecting supplies from the various ports in Normandy and Brittany and bringing them to Le Mans, or from here they would make the three hundred mile journey to the British divisions sent to man the Maginot Line way over on the German frontier. This return trip in convoy would take six days, the men sleeping in their trucks most of the time. Harry enjoyed this 'phoney war' as it was subsequently to become known. The people of Le Mans were friendly and welcoming as were those at stopover points en route to the Maginot Line, and their pay went a long way at French prices, particularly for food, although he had problems with some of the drivers in keeping them off the cheap wine that was available everywhere. He enjoyed wandering around Le Mans especially the old town and the huge cathedral with its memorial inside to the British soldiers killed in the Great War in the defence of France. He visited

Chartres on one of his days off, and with a weekend pass he and his staff sergeant pal Willy Freeman went to Paris. He wrote regularly to Megan, his parents and Rose, and David at his camp at the village outside Colchester, so all in all time passed quickly.

At the end of September Warsaw fell to the Germans and on October 1st hostilities ceased in Poland. On October 6th Hitler positively assured Belgium and Holland of his friendship for the two countries.

"Do you think anyone believes him?" said Jack.

"They'd be mad if they do," was the general rejoinder.

Karl Reisner and Anni, and all their friends were waiting to see what would happen to enemy aliens, who of course had already been registered. In October Karl had to attend a tribunal to establish whether he as an enemy alien should be interned, set free, or in some cases involving sickness, old age etcetera be repatriated. Statements provided by a number of people in Sandbury, including Fred, Jack and several Rotarians as to his character and sympathies, the fact that he has a married daughter who is now English, and that his wife had died in Dachau all produced overwhelming evidence that he should be allowed to carry on in the community. As a result he was sent home to the great joy of all who had supported him, and to make the statement, "I shall be proud one day to call myself British."

Rose had finished at her technical college in July and had taken at the end of August a job on the administrative side of the Sandbury Hospital, where in addition to routine letters on behalf of the hospital administrator she soon became involved in typing reports for case histories etc., for visiting consultants. Both her shorthand and typing were of a very good standard and quickly won the approval of the hypercritical medical staff. It was apparent too that not only her typing was winning approval. Several of the younger doctors seemed to be finding even more ingenious excuses for visiting the admin block, a place they would normally steer clear of, because there was no doubt that Rose, in addition to being friendly and vivacious, was as one young houseman put it 'a very lovely piece of crackling'.

On one occasion three of them were talking in the corridor about this vision of beauty when Megan, by now a sister, overheard them.

"I'm sorry to have to tell you gentlemen, but that young lady is my sister-in-law and I can tell you she is spoken for by a very wealthy young man."

"Oh," said one, "what does he do for a living?"

"He's a Corporal in the army."

"Well, if he's away in the army she must get very lonely, so I shall have to try and cheer her up. I mean, it's the best one can do for one of our fighting men isn't it? After all he wouldn't want her moping around, or getting mixed up with people like these two," indicating the other white-coated couple.

"You don't stand a chance," said Megan with a smile.

"By the way Sister, I believe your husband is called up?" said another.

"Yes, he was a Territorial."

"In that case the same must apply to you. If at any time you would like me to take you for a drink or to the flicks I would consider it a privilege."

"I'll think about it, as long as I can bring my twins with me."

There was general laughter at this. Megan was very popular although a stickler for discipline who would stand no nonsense or sloppiness from her nurses. The story was told how a man of forty odd was bought into the ward having had an accident. He was from the East End of London – a real cockney, and it was the first time he'd ever been in hospital. He had been settled in his bed having been patched up in casualty, and was taking in his new and unfamiliar surroundings, when sister Chandler walked through the ward, spoke to one of the patients, and walked back again. A minute or two later she had to repeat this passage of the ward, her trim figure, starched headdress and cuffs and blue uniform obviously fascinated the new arrival, since as she passed in front of him his head moved with her, like a slow motion version of a spectator at Wimbledon. On her return the second time he could contain himself no longer.

"Sister," he said.

"Yes Mr Brown."

"Sister, are you a real Sister?"

"Well of course I am Mr Brown, why do you ask?"

"Well I always thought a Sister was a right bleeding old battleaxe, but you're a corker."

Incidents like this in a ward cause near hysteria. Megan smiled and said, "Thank you Mr Brown," and swept on. The story soon got around and several young doctors were heard afterwards saying to each other when Megan was in earshot "Seen any battleaxes around lately doctor?"

The factory was going full blast almost twenty-four hours a day. They started to recruit women to train for semi-skilled work and found them very adaptable and willing to learn. Most of their male staff of military age were classified as having reserved occupations, which meant they would not at least for the present be called up into the forces, although as Fred said to Jack at one of their meetings, "That won't stop some of them from getting the bug and volunteering," hence the need to train replacements. The air raids the government had expected did not materialise. It had been expected by the government that one hundred thousand casualties would have been suffered in the first weeks of the war but to date not a bomb had been dropped. Most of our raids on Germany had consisted of dropping millions of leaflets telling the Germans what a nasty man Mr Hitler was and that Britain and France only wanted peace. "Fat lot of bloody use that is," was Fred's exasperated comment, "risking our men and machines on stupid propaganda."

In October Hitler made a peace offer to the allies. It was refused and he was furious. Intelligence gathered from a crashed German plane, blown off its course in bad weather into Belgium, revealed plans to invade Holland and Belgium, but Belgium would still not allow allied troops onto her territory to help defend her. In the event as a result of atrocious weather the attack did not come, although one and a half million men were reported assembled on the Dutch and Belgian borders and on the German North Sea coast.

At home rationing food began on November 1st. Initially bacon and ham and butter were the first to be affected. When Ruth got her first butter ration she cut off Fred's allowance and showed it to him. "That is your ration for a week," she said, "as I see it, the way you eat butter, you can have one slice of toast with Sunday breakfast, or two scones for Sunday tea, the rest of the week you'll be on margarine."

"I'm sure there will be many things that I shall not be happy with while this war lasts," said Fred, "but you know it's strictly against my religion to eat margarine, I had enough of that in the army. However long hostilities last it will seem endless without butter."

"You are happy with your two rashers then?"

"Only two rashers? I shall never survive."

But survive on rations they did.

On November 8th news leaked out via Sweden of the first attempt on Hitler's life. He visited the Munich Beer Cellar where the movement all began, to give his annual speech. He deliberately cut the speech short because of war commitments and a few minutes after he left a bomb exploded in a briefcase left behind the platform. There were a number of Party officials killed and the resultant round-up of Jews, Bavarian monarchists and Catholics resulted in thousands being executed or sent to concentration camps. If his speech had been of its usual duration who knows what a difference it would have made to millions of people. At home, as a result of Sir Freddie meeting Kate Parnell at Pat and David's wedding, the general, who was stationed at the War Office, made frequent visits to Mountfield and on the last Saturday of September as they sat in Kate's drawing room drinking their coffee he put his cup and saucer down, reached over and held Kate's hand and said, "Kate dear, I cannot go through another war without you – will you marry me? Please say yes, please do. I know it wont be easy for you, your having been on your own for so long, to have to put up with my funny ways, but please say you will, will you Kate?"

"General Sir Frederick Earnshaw – will you let me get a word in edgeways?"

"I'm sorry my dear, I've got into a bit of a tiz-woz, if you know what I mean. But will you marry me?"

"Yes, dear Freddie, I will."

He stood up and pulled her gently up to him and kissed her long and ardently. When he released her she said, "You know I am only doing this so that I shall be a Lady – don't you?"

"And you'll be the fairest 'Lady' in the land," said Freddie.

They spent the rest of the evening planning when and where, as all couples do and opted for a simple ceremony at Mountfied Church for the third Saturday in December, with just a short honeymoon in the west country over Christmas. Moira and Jack and Pat and David were invited along with a few relatives and other friends and the reception was to be held at the Angel.

David and Jeremy got their first weekend pass the second week in November. David phoned his mother and father and asked, since Jeremy desperately wanted to be with Rose, and of course his parents would like to see Jeremy, whether they could invite Buffy and Rita up for the weekend so that they could have at least one evening all together at Chandlers Lodge. Ruth and Fred enthusiastically agreed so it was all arranged. Mrs Draper suggested to Pat that she should leave early on Friday as David expected to be at Sandbury Station just after four o'clock, and that she should have Saturday off. "After all I expect you'll have far more important things to do than sell dresses," with a sidelong look which spoke volumes.

The weekend passed like a flash from the time Pat and Rose met them off the train until they saw them back on again on Sunday. They all went to Chandlers Lodge for David just to say hello to his parents, and then Pat and David went on to the bungalow, where he was ecstatically welcomed by Susie. On Saturday evening they all sat down to a superb meal of roast pheasant, Duffy having brought six brace up from Romsey for the occasion, and Jack brought over two bottles of champagne. "And I'm saving the rest of the case for Victory night," he boomed, "and you're all invited to see them off."

"Have you got a date for that, so I can put it in my diary," said Fred.

Jack was serious for a moment or two. "No," he said, "I'm afraid it's a bit open-ended – but we shall have it don't you fear."

He little realised how long a time that would be and the things they would all experience in the meantime.

Travelling back in the train the next evening the two pals bumped into Sergeant Harris. "Have a good weekend Sergeant?" said David.

"Very good my son, yes, very good."

David and Jeremy both noted the 'my son' and the fact that the sergeant was obviously stone cold sober. At the end of a forty-eight hour pass there were a good many squaddies on the train who would be unable to claim that condition and it would have been not unreasonable to expect Sergeant Harris to be in that number. They remained silent, and after a pause he continued, "My wife's come back you see."

The two corporals not knowing why the wife had gone in the first place nodded as if they understood, but still kept their mouths shut.

"We had a bust up before I came up here and she took herself off with the kids to Wales when they got evacuated. Now she's left them there with some nice people on a farm and come back home. She was home when I got there – I never expected her to be there but she was."

"Where do you live Sergeant?"

"It's her parents' old home – they're both dead now – at Canning Town, her dad was a docker in the George V docks."

"How many children have you got?"

In the dimly lit carriage the sergeant did what every soldier all over the world does when he gets into a conversation, he reached inside his battledress blouse and pulled out a photograph of his family. His wife was a very pleasant looking woman and the three kids were, they were now eleven, seven and five. David examined the photograph intently and looked at the sergeant and said, "You know sergeant, she looks far to good for you."

"Cheeky bugger," said the sergeant, but grinning all the same.

The day after they got back David went to the CSM and asked if he could have an interview with the company commander. "Major Grant's away for a few days," said the CSM, Major Scott-Calder will be sitting in for him on Company orders in the morning so smarten yourself up a bit special."

"Yes sir" said David.

The next morning Major Scott-Calder, having dealt with the defaulters, was then told by the CSM, "Corporal Chandler for interview sir."

"Bring him in."

Marched into the Company Office the CSM bellowed, "Halt. Salute the officer. Corporal Chandler sir."

"Well Corporal Chandler, what can I do for you?"

"I would like to apply for a seventy-two hour pass for the weekend of 15th December sir."

"I see, and what grand occasion is taking place then?"

"I've been invited to a wedding sir."

"Oh, anybody I know?"

"Yes sir, it's Miss Parnell." Miss Parnell had often given recitals at Cantlebury's chapel and was well known and liked by all the staff there. However, this reply immediately made the CSM twig that the major knew more about Corporal Chandler than he had suspected.

"Who is the very lucky man?" said the major.

"General Sir Frederick Earnshaw, sir."

"So you want to go to a General's wedding is that it?" with emphasis on the 'general'.

"Well sir, Miss Parnell is my friend, but yes sir, I suppose so sir."

"We do move in exalted circles Sergeant Major don't we?"

"We do that sir."

"But if he wants a pass to a General's wedding we can hardly say no can we Sergeant Major?"

"No sir" said the sergeant major, "not to a Generals wedding, definitely not sir. Don't often get Generals getting married sir."

"Seems to me Sergeant Major that solves that other problem we were talking about earlier."

"Which one would that be sir?"

"If he's going on a seventy-two hour pass on December 15th, it's only fair he should be Guard Commander on Christmas Day and Boxing Day, and have his leave over the New Year, don't you think?"

"I think that would be a very fair arrangement sir."

"That's settled then. March him out Sergeant Major."

"Salute the officer. Right turn. Quick march, left, right, left, right…"

When they got outside the CSM winked at David and said, "You never win them all with that one my lad."

When the CSM went back in the major said, "What do you think of that one Sergeant Major, and young Cartwright?"

The sergeant major thought for a minute. "They are both very intelligent hard working NCOs," he said, "and I can tell you this off the record sir, they were very loyal to their sergeant at a time when they needn't have been, I'll say no more than that. What my grapevine tells me too, is they're very patient with the awkward squad and we've got our fair share of them, particularly some of the ex-borstal boys we got saddled with. They're making good soldiers out of them. I think they're good officer material a damned sight better than…"and then he tailed off, he was going to say, 'than some of the rubbish we've got here', but stopped in mid air.

"Don't be shy Sergeant major; I know what you're driving at. Well, give them another two or three months and see how they get on and I'll have another talk with Major Grant and yourself. Now, is that all you've got for me?"

"Yes, that's all today sir," and he saluted as the major got up and went back to battalion headquarters.

At the end of November the Russians invaded Finland so as to obtain the use of certain territory in the Baltic which would be vital to them in the event of conflict with Germany. They expected a walkover, but the Mannerheim Line held, the Finns counter-attacked and within a fortnight had annihilated two Russian divisions. They found a quick, inexpensive and readily available weapon was a bottle filled with some tar and petrol with a rag stuck into the neck. When a tank approached they lit the wick in the neck and hurled it against the back end of the tank where it exploded and caught fire. The burning tar seeped into the air intake system to the engine which then promptly exploded. They named this device 'The Molotov Cocktail' in honour of the Soviet Foreign Minister and Stalin's right hand man, it was most effective and has been copied in other conflicts all over the world ever since.

Pat had been very busy in the shop during the week that David arrived. They were still able to get supplies of good quality goods, people on war work in particular were earning good money and not knowing if or when clothes rationing would start, were eager to spend it. Most nights therefore she went to bed tired and dropped off to sleep without difficulty. On the Wednesday night before David came home on the Thursday she couldn't get off, she lay there missing his firm strong body beside her more than she had ever known. Well after midnight she said aloud to herself, "Get yourself to sleep or you'll look like an old hag when he arrives tomorrow."

At last she said, "Oh blast," and got up and made a cup of Horlicks to take back to bed with her along with David's most recent letter. As she left the kitchen she heard a 'meow', and there was Susie coming out of the conservatory. "Can't you sleep either?" she asked and bent down to stroke her, but Susie anticipating this arched her back up to receive the caress and rubbed herself against Pat's legs. She ran ahead of Pat along to the bedroom and when Pat entered she was already stretched out on the bed. "Now you know you're not allowed here, don't you?" said Pat and was answered by a long boiler bursting purr. "Alright then – just for tonight," and after her Horlicks had been consumed they both settled into a deep sleep. But it wasn't 'just for tonight', after that, except when David was there, Susie automatically kept Pat company as if it were her duty.

The wedding was a quiet affair except that it attracted a considerable press coverage, Sir Freddie being a well-known name. David had hired his morning suit, the general of course being in uniform. Miss Parnell was so well liked and respected in the village that half the population turned out for the service, filling the church. David met Dr Carew and his wife again and got the news of how his classroom contemporaries who had so far joined the services were getting on, and in addition telling Dr Carew that it was Mr Scott-Calder who had given him his pass to attend the wedding. They both wondered how Dieter was faring, where he was and what he was doing, and how the von Hassellbeks must be in turmoil at the conflict they were suffering in loyalty to their country and hatred of the Nazis.

David had been talking to Pat during the reception about how to address the new Lady Earnshaw, and during the course of the evening broached the subject to Moira and Jack. They were of the opinion that there was no option but to use the full method of address, even though it was a bit of a mouthful in normal conversation after 'Miss Parnell'.

Moira and Jack of course were on christian name terms but that would be out of the question for the younger couple. There were no problems with Sir Frederick; he was addressed as general by everybody, again with the exception of old friends like Jack. The problem was solved by her ladyship herself. During her talk to the young people she said, "Pat, I do hope you'll come and visit me from time to time. The General will be away a good deal from now on, and with David away it gives us something in common that we can console each other about. Oh and by the way, please do call me Kate, both of you, after all if it wasn't for you I would probably never have found Freddie again, you've given me the greatest gift I've ever had."

"What's all this they have given you my dear?" asked the general suddenly appearing at her side.

She held his arm and looked up at him and said, "Just you, that's all." The general laughed.

"Pat is coming to visit me when she can while you're away," said Kate, "and I shall come into Sandbury and have coffee with her from time to time. We're going to cheer each other up."

"I know everybody asks you this as soon as they meet you David, but when do you go back?" said the general.

"On Monday sir, I have to be in by midnight."

"Are you thinking of going for a commission at all?"

David thought, "He seems to know a bit more about me than I would have expected."

"Well sir, I thought I would get some service in first, but yes, I did think I'd apply some time in the New Year."

"Would you stay in the Rifles?"

"As you know sir, it's not an easy regiment to get into. If not the Rifles I would go for my father's old regiment the Hampshires."

"Well you couldn't do better than that, they're a first class lot. Anyway I wish you luck, we can certainly do with people like you with a bit of experience."

"Thank you sir," and they moved off.

The weekend sped past. David had given Pat and the family the news that he would not get Christmas leave, but would be coming on his first seven-day leave on 29th December. Rose was delighted to hear that Jeremy would have Christmas leave, but on the Sunday morning the telephone rang and it was Rita Cartwright. She said that Jeremy had called them and since he wanted to be home for Christmas and he also wanted to be with Rose, could Rose, Ruth and Fred all go down to Romsey and spend Christmas with them. She'd leave it with them to talk it over.

"What about Megan and the twins?" Ruth said. "We can't leave them on their own even though they have Moira and Jack here."

"Not only that," said Fred, "we have been having Christmas with Pat and Jack for years."

There must be more problems about where to go for Christmas, which relatives to be with and when, than any other that raises itself in family life. How do you split yourself in two and keep everybody happy, knowing that somewhere along the line someone has got to be disappointed? In the end Fred said, "I suppose they wouldn't consider coming to us? I know it would be a houseful, but I'm going to close the factory for an extra day after Boxing Day, so I'll have a bit of time to give a hand indoors."

There was a total silence from Ruth, Rose, Pat and David as they stared at Fred. Ruth put her hand to her head. David pulled a chair out and said, "Sit down Mum, you'll be alright in a minute." Rose picked up a tea towel and started fanning her mother while Pat looked on in mock consternation.

"What's the matter?" said Fred.

David turned solemnly towards him. "You should know better than to give Mum shocks like that, and us too for that matter."

And they all burst into peals of laughter resulting in Fred saying, "I don't know what's so bloody funny about me offering to give a hand."

"You know you'd be drummed out of the regiment if you did any housework, Dad."

Fred grinned, "Well normally I'm working too hard to have time but if it's all hands to the pumps, then I'll start pumping."

They decided to delay making a decision until Monday morning, but in fact the decision was made for them by two things that happened. Firstly at seven thirty in the morning Megan burst in having left the twins as usual with Moira's nanny before going on duty. She was so excited she could hardly get the words out, "Harry's got Christmas leave from France. I've had a telegram this morning, he'll be here on Thursday and going back on the 28th."

"I shall miss him by one day," said David. "Oh I am fed up about that."

"You'll have to telephone him here over the holiday dear," said Ruth. "Anyway that's made my mind up about Rita and Buffy, I'll phone her at lunchtime and get it sorted out."

The second thing that happened took place at midday just before Ruth had intended to make her call. Answering a knock at the door she found herself confronted by a stout middle-aged man in army officer's uniform complete with a red armlet, who smartly saluted her, "Good morning – Mrs Chandler?"

"Yes, that's right."

"I'm Major Reilly – district billeting officer. You're on my list of those people who said they would be prepared to billet troops."

"Oh yes, that's right, do please come in."

"Well madam, you won't know because of the security blackout up until now, but today Canadian troops started to arrive in the UK. We have a battalion of infantry being stationed at Hill Camp three miles out on the Maidstone Road. I would very much like to billet two officers on you if I may. They will provide you with their rations of course and we will pay you the set lodging fee."

"In the first place they are more than welcome and in the second place we certainly don't want any payment."

"Ah well you see madam, we can't not pay you because our system doesn't cater for that sort of exigency. Needless to say the payment would not be enough to keep you in comfort in your old age anyway so I wouldn't worry about it if I were you. Now the officers will be…" looking down his list, "Captain Fraser and Captain Napier. I can't tell you what time they will arrive. They leave Liverpool today so they'll be with you some time tomorrow, I should think, once they've settled their men in," and having politely refused a cup of tea he bustled out to his car and was driven off.

"Everything's happening at once," Ruth said to the hall clock as she came back in from seeing the major off. She got on the telephone at once to Rita, but was told there was a delay of approximately three-quarters of an hour, so she booked the call and got herself a light lunch. When the telephone bell rang she explained to Rita all that had happened since they had spoken the previous day and asked if they would come to them. Rita said she would telephone Buffy in London and ring her back, but she felt sure all would be fine, ending by saying how exciting it would be to have such a merry crowd.

"But where on earth will you put us all with the Canadians there as well?"

"You just leave that to us – we'll get it organised," said Ruth, afterwards saying to herself, "Yes, but where the devil will I put them all?" The problem was solved by Jack when he called in that evening. "The Cartwrights can sleep with us," he said. "We'll be together in one place or the other all over the holiday so where they sleep doesn't matter a toss."

"Poor David will feel so left out of it all," said Ruth, "Oh, isn't it a terrible shame."

"How many of us will there be, counting the Canadians?" said Jack.

"Well with all the children there will be sixteen," replied Ruth, "so I shall have to put the kitchen table in with the dining room table to sit down to, and get Fred to bring up a couple of tables from the factory to use in the kitchen. I know they've got some in the canteen. I think we'll be alright for chairs and cutlery and so on though it won't all match."

"Well if necessary we'll bring anything over you're short of, and then borrow from you on Boxing Day! I've not booked a show this year because of the travelling difficulties so we'll have fun at home in the evening."

As they were talking Megan called in having collected the twins, "I've got a problem," she said.

"Only one?" said Jack, "I would have thought with those two you'd have a bucketful."

"What is it dear?" said Ruth.

"I had a telephone call at the hospital today and Mum and Dad have asked if they can come up for Christmas. They dearly want to see Harry and of course the twins as well."

"Well that's two more," said Ruth.

"As long as they all bring their rations," said Jack with a laugh. But there really was no cause for laughter, since from Christmas Day sugar and meat were rationed and would stay rationed for many years to come until well after the war was won.

Chapter Thirty-three

The two Canadians arrived on Tuesday evening and having introduced themselves to Ruth and Fred and dumped enough luggage and equipment in the hall to equip half a battalion, as Fred subsequently commented to Jack, dismissed their driver with instructions to come back at eight o'clock the next morning. Alec Fraser was a sandy-haired fresh complexioned young man of about twenty-five, stockily built, possessing an engaging smile and an outgoing manner. Jim Napier was a little taller and slimmer, with dark hair and complexion, of about the same age but obviously much more reserved than his friend. When Ruth asked them whether they would like a cup of tea Fred said, "If they're anything like those I knew in the past, they'd prefer a beer.

So Whitbread's Light Ale it was, as they took they first mouthfuls, Fred asked, "This your first English beer?" And when he was told it was and in turn was asked what they thought of it they both took another swallow and pronounced it was well worth while crossing the Atlantic for.

On her way home Rose had called in to see Pat and waited for her until she had shut the shop and cashed up before they went on to Chandlers Lodge. As they walked in Ruth said, "Oh, here are the girls."

The two Canadians turned and there was a moment of silence until Alec said, "First we find we are billeted at what must be the most comfortable house in England and then we find it's home to the two most beautiful girls in England!"

There was general laughter as they were introduced, Ruth saying, "Well I'm afraid that's where your luck ends, this is my daughter Rose and this is Pat, my daughter-in-law, both of whose men folk are serving together. David, Pat's husband will not be on Christmas leave but Jeremy will be here on Thursday, and I have to tell you we have a real house full over the holiday so I do hope the noise doesn't disturb you." This prompted Jim to make his first contribution to the conversation by saying that if past experience was anything to go by a great deal of noise would be made by Captain Fraser.

They were an easy couple of chaps to get on with. Jim was married with two children and soon had the photographs out to illustrate the fact. Alec was still a bachelor 'though working hard on it' being his cheerful assurance to the remark that a good-looking bloke like him should have been snaffled up long ago. He was a junior partner in a law firm in Calgary whilst Jim worked in his father's wholesale hardware business in Toronto and was a qualified accountant. Jeremy arrived earlier on Thursday than expected so telephoned Rose from the station and then went on to Chandlers Lodge. Having put his belongings into his room he came downstairs confronting the two captains and said to Alec, who was in the lead, "Good afternoon sir, I'm Cartwright, friend of the family."

"From what we've heard a particularly good friend of one of the family, isn't that so Jim?"

"Unfortunately for you, yes," said Jim.

"Well Jeremy, it is Jeremy isn't it? When we're here as guests, as we are, don't worry about the word sir, OK? I'm Alec and this is Jim and we're very pleased to make your acquaintance."

"Thank you very much sir, I mean Alec," as he shook hands with them both.

At this Ruth appeared, "Oh Jeremy you've met our new friends?"

"Yes Mrs Chandler, and that sounds like Mum and Dad arriving." And he ran out to greet them, returning with a huge cardboard box he could hardly carry. "Hey, let me give you a hand Jeremy," called Alec, "God, what have you got in here, a dead body?"

"Knowing Dad quite a few I should think," said Jeremy. They carried the box into the kitchen and when they reappeared Rita and Buffy were being introduced to Jim and subsequently to Alec. As always they gravitated to the kitchen.

"Now," said Buffy, "there's twelve brace of birds in there, along with half a dozen hares. They'll all need hanging for another couple of days but will be ready by Boxing Day onwards. Our butcher killed one of his pigs yesterday so we've brought a leg and some chops. That'll be the last we get as they start rationing next week."

"What things are rationed?" enquired Jim in his quiet voice, and was told not too much at the moment, butter being the worst problem and a source of total despondency to Fred.

Rose and Pat and Harry and Megan and the twins all arrived at the same time. There was pandemonium, above which Alec's voice was heard to exclaim to Ruth on being introduced to Megan, "Mrs Chandler, is there an end to your collection of beautiful daughters and daughters-in-law?" Everyone, particularly the Canadians wanted to talk to Harry to find out what it was like 'over there', and in the middle of the hubbub, Jack and Fred arrived, Moira would be late that evening but then would be free until the New Year unless an emergency arose.

Christmas Day was on the Monday. The Lloyds arrived on the Friday before, Trefor bringing a whole sheep cut up and packaged to store between Megan, Moira and Ruth, with the largest part going to Ruth of course, 'to help her feed this lot over the holiday'. Pat would be working up until Saturday evening, but Rose finished on Friday lunchtime and Megan had leave so as to be with Harry but in fact came to Ruth on Saturday and Sunday to help out. They saw little of the Canadians on Friday and Saturday as they were hard at work getting the men settled in ready to celebrate Christmas. They had been told firmly by Ruth they were not to think of buying Christmas presents for everybody, particularly since most of the guests wouldn't have known in advance they would be there anyway. On Sunday their battalion had two church parades in the town, one to the ancient Protestant church and one to the small Catholic Church off the High Street. Alec and Jim looked extremely smart in their best service dress and Sam Brownes. At both services the preachers welcomed these men from the Dominion and hoped that the people of Sandbury would take them into their homes to help ease the pain of separation from their loved ones back in Canada. "In some cases if they do that they should be warned to lock up their wives and daughters as well as the family silver," Alec whispered to Jim.

At the time the church parades were being held in Sandbury the orderly officer was mounting the quarter guard at Rainsford Camp Colchester. Corporal Chandler was sergeant of the guard. It was the only time in the year that the guard stayed on for forty-eight hours, an extra day's leave being given to the men on guard for having to perform the double duty. Having relieved the old guard, Corporal Chandler signed for all the equipment, ammunition and other items in the guardroom left in his charge. One item was a certain Rifleman Barclay, a prisoner in the cells. The sergeant handing over to David warned him about Barclay. He was an incorrigible deserter. He was in the first call up in June and in nearly seven months of soldiering had spent only four weeks with the colours, the remainder of the time he had been either on the run or in the military prison at Aldershot, generally known as the glasshouse. He had been caught by the military police only the day before and returned the previous evening, and was now waiting to go before the commanding officer after the holiday to receive most likely another fifty-six days in the glasshouse. The final information from the sergeant handing over was, "Watch yourself – the RSM is in camp over Christmas."

At four o'clock in the afternoon a lance corporal marched six more men to the guardroom where they were inspected by Corporal Chandler and each issued with five rounds of ammunition. They were the prowler piquet, housed at the south end of the camp their duties to patrol the section of the perimeter there in pairs until daybreak, when the lance corporal would march them back to the guardroom and they would hand in their ammunition and be dismounted by Corporal Chandler. At least once during the night the guard commander at the quarter guard would visit the prowler guard hut to see all was well, and in addition the orderly officer would at some time during the night visit both the quarter guard and the prowler guard.

It was very quiet in the camp this Christmas eve, with well over half the men on leave. Later in the evening a few revellers came singing up the road from the village, having imbibed a fair amount of Christmas cheer in one or another of the three pubs there. One or two were so far gone they were being almost carried by their team mates, but David turned a blind eye and told them to get to their huts quickly and not make a noise. Three came in twenty minutes after the official booking in time, but again David said, "As it's Christmas I'll let you off," – if he'd booked them, they would probably have got seven days confined to barracks and that would mean losing their leave, or part of it, at the New Year.

At midnight he decided to visit the prowler guard, leaving his lance corporal in charge for the twenty minutes he would be away. Having checked that the prowler guard NCO had no problems he started to make his way back. It was a bitterly cold clear frosty night and he was moving at rifleman pace to keep warm when he heard shouting obviously coming from the direction of the guardroom. He broke into a run and in a short while burst in to find everybody talking at the same time.

"Quiet – what the hell's going on?" he shouted.

The lance corporal turned to face him and said, "We've lost the prisoner."

As he uttered these horrifying words the door opened and in walked the RSM. They all sprang to attention. "What the devil's happening here?" he bellowed.

David said, "We've lost the prisoner sir."

"WHAAAT?" you could have heard him in Colchester. The RSM was a man with over twenty-two years service who was feared by everyone in the battalion up to, and sometimes including, the rank of captain. He considered the unit to be his own private property and if anybody did anything to it that would in any way harm it, denigrate it, reduce it's efficiency or lower it's swank factor, by God they suffered for it. He'd won the Military Medal when he was seventeen and the Distinguished Conduct Medal when he was eighteen, both in the hell of Paschendale. He'd never married, he was married to the regiment, he lived and breathed the Rifles.

"What happened?" he yelled.

"What happened Corporal?" David said to the lance corporal.

"Why don't you know – why weren't you here?"

"I'd gone to make my first inspection of the prowler guard sir."

"So what happened?"

The lance corporal continued, "It was very cold in the cells sir, there's no heating there. Rifleman Barclay was brought out to sit by the guardroom stove for a while to warm up."

"Who the bloody hell thought of that? He should have been left to freeze solid."

No one answered.

"Come on – who the hell brought him out to the stove?" The RSM was getting more and more furious by the minute.

"Rifleman Beasley," one of the guards piped up.

"The Orderly Officer visited us sir, while the Guard Commander was away. Barclay told him he was cold so he told us to sit him by the stove. After the Orderly Officer had gone he jumped up and was out of the door and gone, he'd got his PT shoes on sir, we didn't stand a chance of catching him."

"And you say the Orderly Officer told you to bring him out of the cells?"

"Yes sir" said the lance corporal.

"I'll have his bloody guts for garters," he roared, and turned and walked out.

There was a total silence in the guardroom. Suddenly the door opened and the men all sprang to attention again as the RSM reappeared. With what passed for a very rarely seen smile stretched the skin on his face he said to David, "Merry Christmas Corporal."

There was again a stunned silence. Here was David at the most miserable moment of his life. He was away from his wife, it was Christmas and he was on guard duty for forty-eight hours, and he had lost a prisoner, yet an RSM, a martinet who had never been known to say a kind word to another human being in all his life, and particularly not to another soldier, had taken the trouble to come back into the guardroom and wish him a merry Christmas.

Rifleman Beasley had the last word.

"I think he fancies you Corporal!"

The Christmas was hectic at Chandlers Lodge and on Boxing Day at The Hollies, but all the ladies were quietly and efficiently organised by Ruth in the kitchen so that they all sat to a beautiful Christmas dinner after the King's speech. He had recently returned from visiting our troops dug in on the Belgium border and in the Maginot Line. There was a big burst of applause from the assembled company when he thanked the Dominions and the Empire for it's sacrifices in coming to the aid of the mother country, along with embarrassed smiles from the Canadian soldiers. They had been into camp earlier to serve Christmas dinner to their troops, an age-old custom inherited from the British Army.

At the end of the meal, which lasted over two hours, Jim asked Fred if he could say a few words. Fred whacked the table with a spoon and called out, "Ladies and gentlemen, pray silence for Captain Jim Napier, Canadian Army."

There were cheers and clapping as he stood up.

"Ruth and Fred, and all you lovely people. I apologise for not having the gift of the gab possessed by my colleague here," pointing to Alec, "but I will try my best to tell you how deeply grateful we are for the wonderful welcome we have been given in the few days we have been here. We had visions of being stuck in some camp miles from anywhere and of spending our first Christmas away from home as dejected as Alec first was when he found out Rose and Pat were spoken for," (much laughter). "Instead we find ourselves as part of a family, and not an ordinary family, an extraordinary family of the nicest people you'd ever meet in a day's march, because we think of you all as one big family. We feel a little guilty too. Our families back home will be thinking we'll be having a miserable time whilst they're enjoying themselves and here we are with all of you. We don't know – any of us – where we'll be next Christmas or the one after that for that matter, but what I do know is the memory of this Christmas will stay with Alec and me for the rest of our lives. So I give you a toast – Ruth and Fred and absent company."

There was prolonged applause as they all stood up and toasted Ruth, Fred and David, and when it died down there was a momentary hush during which Alec was heard to say, "for someone who hasn't got the gift of the gab you did alright."

On Boxing morning, Rose and Jeremy went for a walk in the woods before going to the Hollies. They were strolling along slowly with their arms around each other when Jeremy said, "I don't want to spoil the day, but there's a rumour, and it's only a rumour, and rumours are ten a penny in the army."

"Jeremy Cartwright, what are you trying to tell me?"

"There's a rumour that when we're fully equipped – there now I've done it. Careless talk costs lives – you're not supposed to know we're not fully equipped so don't for goodness sake repeat that to anyone."

"Actually I've already sent the message to the Fuhrer from my built-in high-powered transmitter. You'll probably be attacked within a few hours."

"God, don't be joking about it. Anyway the rumour is that we're being sent to the Middle East to join an armoured division there."

"Where on earth do these rumours come from?"

"Goodness knows – probably someone puts out a rumour we're going to the Middle East when all the time they're going to send us to

Norway or Finland or somewhere. But the point is, it could happen. So what I'm trying to say is, if I spoke to your parents, can we get married, say at Easter. Will you marry me my darling Rose?"

"Yes my love, but need we wait until Easter? I am eighteen at the end of January, couldn't we make it February?"

"We could but I would only get a three days pass, my seven day leave isn't until Easter."

"Then we have a three day honeymoon to start with and then a full leave together a month or so later."

"Always assuming your Dad gives the thumbs up."

"He will, he'll be glad to get rid of me."

"No he won't, and your mother won't either, that's for sure. I'll talk to them when I get an opportunity today, although I still have to warn my parents first."

Rose clung to him even tighter as they walked along, she was so happy and excited she couldn't find any words to express her feelings. Eventually she said, "Do you remember when you first came to the farm with David and he called you Cartwright? And Mum said 'when he's here you call him by his christian name, I don't care what you do at school'."

"Yes, I remember vaguely – your mother has always been so kind to me."

"I was only eight, I've been in love with you for ten years, that's longer even than Pat and David."

He stopped and kissed her. "Here's to the next ten and the ten after," he said, "and who knows how many tens after that?"

When they got back to The Hollies, people had started to arrive although Ruth and Fred and the Canadians were still not there. Spotting his parents talking to Moira, Jeremy waited until Moira went off to greet some visitors and then went up to them, slipped his arms through theirs and said, "Please don't tell anyone yet, but Rose and I want to marry in February if her parents will allow it."

Rita immediately hugged him and said how delighted she was, Buffy put his arm round his shoulders and said he was, "a damned lucky fella."

When Ruth and Fred arrived with the Canadians they told Moira and Jack that Anni and Ernie along with Karl were going to call in for a drink before they went on to the Boltons for Boxing Day. As she was telling them this so they arrived. To the Canadians she said, "Come and meet the rest of my family – this is our daughter Anni and her husband Ernie, and Anni's father Karl, oh and Rebecca, Ernie's sister," she added as she saw Rebecca appearing through the crowded room.

"Now look Mrs Chandler," said Alec, "you've got Jim and I

completely confused. First you produce another beautiful daughter that we hadn't heard about. Second you also produce her father, which sounds odd. Last but no means least, you produce yet another beautiful young lady, and may I ask who you are married to madam," addressing Rebecca.

"Well," said Ruth, "Anni came as a refugee from Germany four and a half years ago and became part of our family. Subsequently Karl escaped and came to us just over two years ago. Anni married Ernie who is one of David's oldest friends and helps run the factory for Fred and Jack and Rebecca is not married."

"Are you telling me that at long last I have met a beautiful English girl who is not spoken for?" exclaimed Alec.

"Well I can't answer that. I imagine Rebecca has a queue of admirers a mile long – isn't that so Rebecca?"

"Let's not exaggerate," Rebecca replied, swiftly joining in the leg pulling, "Let's say half a mile."

"Then I shall definitely join the queue," said Alec. They all started talking together and Karl's heavy accent was quite noticeable to the two Canadians. When he had the opportunity Jim said to Fred, "How is it, as a German, he is allowed complete freedom?"

Fred explained the system of tribunals, which allowed this, ending by saying, "His wife, Anni's mother, was killed in Dachau." This piece of information shocked Jim and Alec too when he retold it to him. They had heard vaguely of concentration camps, but here they were face-to-face with the tragedy those evil places produced. Here was a young woman driven from her home and her father who had been uprooted from his way of life, and losing a mother or wife in the most appalling circumstances.

As they said to Ruth and Fred later, "We're beginning to get a clearer idea of why we're here."

As the lunch was being prepared Jeremy at last managed to get Fred and Ruth on one side. He came straight to the point.

"Rose and I have been talking this morning. As I don't know when I may be posted abroad, we'd like to get married in February if you will give us your blessing. I know it's short notice and we would not expect a reception. We just don't want for me to go overseas without our being married."

Fred looked at Ruth, "It's all blooming weddings this last twelve months mother isn't it?"

Ruth thought, 'he hasn't called me mother for years', but she looked at Fred and said, "This one is very special."

"Then it's alright by you?" Ruth nodded in reply.

"Then it's certainly alright by me," said Fred, "and I couldn't wish for a better son-in-law than you, and that's the truth."

Rose was watching from the other side of the room to try and gauge the result of the discussions Jeremy was having with her parents, and when he turned and smiled broadly at her she ran across and hugged him and then her mother and lastly her father, which combined activities indicated to some of the others present that something unusual was afoot including Jack who, when told the great news, immediately bellowed, "Silence everybody, Fred has something to say."

"Ruth and I have to announce the marriage of our daughter Rose to…" and turning to Jeremy in mock indecision, "What did you say your name was?" there was a burst of laughter. "Seriously ladies and gentlemen," continued Fred, "we've known liked and enjoyed Jeremy's company for the past ten years. You all know what a lovely family he comes from, and Ruth and I will be delighted to have him as our son-in-law. The wedding will be in February and you're all invited."

David phoned on the evening of Boxing Day and having told Pat how much he was longing to see her again in three days time – it would seem like an age – and all the things young lovers say to one and other, spent another ten minutes and two shillings in the box talking to Harry and then Christmas was over. Jeremy had particularly asked that no one should mention the wedding to David – he wanted to spring that on him himself.

David heard no more about the episode of Rifleman Barclay and could only assume that the orderly officer had got stripped off by the adjutant and that would be that. Jeremy came back on the evening of the 28th and filled David in with most of the happenings over Christmas, and ended up by saying, "What's all this about you losing a prisoner and the RSM being in love with you?"

"How the hell did you hear about that?"

"I bumped into Beasley as I came through the guardroom and he told me."

"I tell you this much, if I ever get my hands on our Mr Barclay he'll wish he hadn't been born."

"Now, now Corporal Chandler, you know high ranking NCO's like yourself are not allowed to duff up the rank and file."

"No I suppose not. Do you think if I paid Beasley he'd do it?"

After a pause in the conversation Jeremy went on, "Oh by the way, your sister's getting married in February."

"What do you mean you lunatic, she's engaged to you." And then he fell in, "you rotten sod, you've been here half an hour and this is the first you've mentioned it. I don't know whether to thump you first and congratulate you afterwards, or vice versa."

"Now I'm family if you lay your hands on me I'll tell my wife. Not only that, the Best man is not allowed to thump the groom."

"Well, it's wonderful news. Who'd have thought though all those years back in form 1A you'd end up being my brother-in-law? If I'd drowned you then I would have saved poor old Rose from a fate worse than death. Anyway, what date is it? And have you realised we've got to play our cards very carefully to get a weekend off at the same time."

"I've thought of that. I reckon it would be in order for your father and mother to invite Scott-Calder, that should pave the way. I don't know if he'd sink so low as to go to a Corporal's wedding, but if we invite Dr Carew as well, that might just do the trick."

"You're a cunning blighter. I can see you going into politics after the war. But I think you've got an idea. I'll phone home tomorrow and start getting it organised. Anyway, you haven't answered me, when's the great day?"

"February 17th. I shall only get a three day pass, four if I'm lucky, you'll get your normal forty-eight hours I should have thought."

"Always provided we don't suddenly get whipped away to France or Africa or somewhere in the meantime."

"Yes, that is the worry, though how we could fight with only half our vehicles and equipment I don't know."

David went off the next morning, Pat meeting him at Sandbury Station just after lunch. They spent the afternoon at the bungalow before they went on to Chandlers Lodge in the evening. Before they left and were getting ready to go Pat came and sat on David's lap and said, "It's only twelve days since we were last together, I don't know what you'll be like if we we're ever apart for twelve months."

"You won't get past Sandbury Station waiting room," said David, "so you'd better send Ernie to meet me."

With a laugh she slipped out of his clutching hands saying, "I must get dressed or we'll never get there."

When David was introduced to the Canadians he, like Jeremy before him, stood smartly to attention and said, "How do you do sir," in turn to Alec and Jim.

"David," said Alec, "as I said to Jeremy, we're in your house, being cared for by your family, so I'm Alec and my friend here is Jim – that OK by you?"

"Yes of course, thank you very much."

"Furthermore," continued Alec, "your family and friends gave us the most wonderful Christmas, which we'll never forget, in fact both Jim and I must have put on a stone in weight over the holiday. Another thing that will interest you too is that we have developed a very firm liking for Whitbread's Light Ale introduced to us by your father from his seemingly inexhaustible supply from under the stairs."

"Yet another thing that may interest you," Jim interjected, "is that a certain Canadian captain, as yet fancy free, has developed an instant liking to a young lady named Rebecca, who I understand is a friend of yours."

"Oh – you've met Rebecca? When we were boys at Mountfield, that's a village about five miles from here, all the lads had a crush on Rebecca – except me of course as I was saving myself for Pat."

"He's a quick thinker isn't he," said Pat "and a good job he is or he would have had a clipped ear then."

"To go back to Rebecca," said David, "she's never really had a steady as far as I know. She is an extremely intelligent person and very kind and sweet. She was always a tower of strength to Ernie when he couldn't walk."

"We noticed Ernie was a bit wobbly," said Jim, "are you telling me that it's only recently he's started walking?"

They told them Ernie's story and how Anni had devoted the best part of three years to helping Ernie walk again, and going back to Ernie's boyhood the story of the pancakes, which had everyone in stitches of laughter all over again, though all but the Canadians knew it by heart.

"Anyway," said Ruth, "you'll be seeing her again on New Year's Eve if you can be here, we're having a bit of a party to see the New Year in and they'll be here."

"When you say 'bit of a party' how many will there be exactly?" said Jim.

"Well, there will be Megan and her mother and father, we must try to keep her cheered up now Harry's gone back, and Moira and Jack and the Cartwrights have stayed on. I believe the General and Lady Earnshaw will be coming, she said she'd very much like to see David again, so I suppose there will be eighteen or twenty."

"And that's a bit of a party?" said Jim. "I've heard of this British understatement – I would have thought that was a full blown party not a bit of one."

Alec butted in, "And the General who's coming, is he a proper serving General, and the lady is she a real English Lady?"

"Yes on both counts," said Ruth, "and nicer people you could never meet."

"How do we address them?" said Alec. "I'm sorry to be so ignorant but we've never met a real life Lord and Lady before."

"He's not a Lord," said Pat. "He's a sir, which means that his wife is still called Lady. So you just call him General, or sir as he's a senior officer, and strictly speaking you call Lady Earnshaw 'Your Ladyship', however most people find Lady Earnshaw easier to say. Some people, personal friends of hers, call her Kate, but of course no one would do that unless they were specifically invited to do so. Anyway you'll soon get the hang of things."

The New Year's Eve party was a great success. As was expected Alec made a beeline for Rebecca who obviously enjoyed his company. When the general arrived he was introduced to the Canadians, and told them that he knew several of their senior officers in the division from 'the last lot'. "As a matter of fact," he continued, "you may see something of me in the not too distant future as I'm taking over a corps in southern command of which I understand you will be a part."

Cheekily Alec replied, "Well sir, we may see you in the distance as you drive past, but at least we'll know who you are. I don't suppose at out lowly station in life we shall come much closer than that!"

The general took that jocular remark with some seriousness.

"Now that's what we used to say in the last war – isn't that so Jack? You know we never knew who our commanders were. We probably met our brigadier on odd occasions. We probably knew our division commander's name, but as far as actually knowing him, unless you got a cushy job on the staff you had no idea of what he was like. As for corps commanders, they lived in such a rarefied atmosphere that getting their boots dirty constituted a feat of arms worthy of a further decoration. Generals have got to be known and trusted by the men at the sharp end prodding their bayonets into some Jerry's guts, they've got to be trusted by their junior field officers, and they've got to be seen, not live in some chateau miles behind the lines as they did in our day. Do you know one day we had a visit up on the Somme in the front line by Staff Colonel, something that was absolutely unheard of. We all thought, 'what a jolly good chap coming to see us like this', and at four o'clock he looked at his watch, and in full hearing of the men around him manning the trench said in a loud voice, 'Well I must be getting back, we've got pork for dinner and the General doesn't like anyone being late'. No, this war's going to be mobile and Generals have got to think mobility, and so too have Captains if it comes to that," he laughed, "and here endeth the first lesson," he added as Kate joined the little crowd of men.

"Has he been telling you how to win wars?" she said, holding the general's arm with obvious affection.

"Yes mam," said Jim, completely forgetting how to address her, "and it makes a great deal of sense."

David had been listening to the talk with keen interest. It was so far removed from the rough badinage and obligatory moaning of barrack-room conversation. Although neither he nor Jeremy were prudes or angels the foul language used continuously not only became very boring but irritating as well. The favourite 'F' word of the soldiery was used as a noun, adjective, verb and adverb at every conceivable point in the average conversation. They even found themselves using it from time to time to accentuate a point or when they were angry about something. He thought how marvellous it would be to have a soldierly conversation such as the general had just treated them to without 'effing and blinding' with every word, because strangely enough some of the chaps in the platoon were most interesting people in their own ways and could be most amusing and informative if you got them on their own. He heard the general saying, "What sort of chaps have you got David?"

"Well sir," said David, "we have a few of the old Territorials, like Jeremy and myself."

The general interrupted, "Hear that Fred? He says they've got a few old Territorials like himself – old!! – I ask you."

The little group of men all laughed.

"Well sir, what I meant was that of the original platoon in the City Rifles there are now only half a dozen of us left. We have a few regulars sent from the depot. We have a dozen or so ex-Borstal boys, they were in juvenile prisons and given the option to join the army, and some of them are making good soldiers. The remainder are conscripts."

"Any interesting ones?"

David smiled, looking around to make sure there were no ladies nearby, and continued in a lower voice, "I have one chap whose sole job was riding around Suffolk and Norfolk on a huge stallion that his father gave him for his eighteenth birthday. He would go from farm to farm wherever a mare needed servicing and then stay overnight on the farm or in the local pub, or even occasionally in a barn if he couldn't get lodgings. The money was all cash in hand and he'd got more stashed away than all the rest of the platoon put together. He said in all seriousness that it was a happy life. The horse was happy and a lot of farmers' daughters and a number of farmers' wives all over Suffolk and Norfolk were happier when he'd gone than before he'd arrived." The men roared with laughter at this, which brought them to the notice of the ladies on the other side of the room.

"That sounded like a good one," said Megan.

"And it looks as though it was our David telling it," said Rose.

Jack continued the conversation with a recollection of his days in the Royal Artillery in the Middle East.

"We were on a general inspection," he said, "and one of the teams in the battery behind me had got a stallion on the left-hand side at the rear with a gunner riding it. The next horse forward on the right-hand side was a mare and while we were waiting for the inspection to begin the stallion started having designs on this mare. The gunner riding it gave it one or two surreptitious whacks round the ears to quieten it down. Just as the General, followed by all his entourage, came in front, the horse decided to make its play, and suddenly reared up throwing the gunner flat on his back in front of the General, got all caught up in the traces as it got one leg over the shaft and up on the backside of the mare, and cause absolute pandemonium in both it's own team and the adjacent ones.

"The General stopped and called out to the Colonel. 'Clive – you'd better put some of that stuff you put in the men's tea into your horse fodder' and rode on."

There was a roar of laughter greeting this story, which prompted Ruth to come over and say, "Now come on you men, break it up, you're getting the place a bad name."

When midnight came and they heard the chimes from Big Ben ushering in 1940, they all made the rounds kissing and shaking hands and wishing each and everyone a happy New Year. Alec took full advantage of the situation with regard to Rebecca, bumping in to her quite accidentally of course, on no less than three separate occasions, to which she didn't appear to object and of course having to kiss her a happy New Year. When the noise subsided Jack called out, "Speech Fred," they all turned to where Fred was standing with his arms around Ruth and Rose.

He stepped forward and picked up his glass and said, "First of all, here's to absent loved ones, Harry, Jeremy and our Canadian friends' families." They raised their glasses and drank the toast.

"Ladies and gentlemen. None of us know what 1940 is going to bring, nor where a good many of you will be on next New Year's Eve. I wish you all, particularly our soldiers present and absent, the very best of good luck and the fervent wish that you all remain safe and well."

They all had their separate thoughts about 1940.

Rose was thinking no further ahead than her wedding. Ruth was her quiet efficient self on the surface but deeply troubled within at the thought of her two sons and future son-in-law having to face all sorts of unknown dangers. Megan knew how Ruth felt but neither spoke of it as she felt the same. Pat had not yet developed such a feeling wrapped up as she was with the excitement and passion of her hours alone with David that in her wildest dreams she had never considered could raise such ecstasy in her. Then there was Kate who knew how the responsibility of deciding men's lives weighed so heavily on the general. Rita like Ruth, worried about her only son, and Moira who knew so much more than any of them, including the general, of the true position the allies were in and the tragedy that could unfold, and yet was unable to find solace by confiding in anyone, not even her own dear Jack. Next there were the mothers and wives of the Canadians back home not knowing when their sons or husbands would be committed to action, and with the memories among them of the Great War, when so many Canadians never came back. Lastly there were Anni and Karl still grieving the loss of Anni's mother, not knowing how she died and above all having no place at which to mourn.

Fred, sensing everyone was getting introspective, turned up the wireless which was now playing Jack Hylton dance music and yelled, "Help me roll up the carpet David," which having been speedily accomplished they moved the chairs back and started dancing, the first on the floor to no one's surprise being Alec and Rebecca. Jim and Ruth followed while Fred and David went round filling up the glasses. It was a whale of a party, which went on until nearly four o'clock before the first few drifted away, and when that happened the remainder soon broke up. After they'd gone Rose said goodnight and went to bed leaving Fred and Ruth drinking the inevitable cup of cocoa before themselves retiring, with the observation that 'that lot can wait till the morning', looking at the chaos of glasses, crockery and bottles strewn everywhere.

"I think it will be a long time before we have another party like that," said Fred. And so it was.

Chapter Thirty-four

January 1940 ushered in a year with the worst winter Britain had experienced for nearly fifty years. David returned to camp to find the parade ground thick with ice, so bad in fact it was impossible to drill on it particularly at rifleman's pace. Regimental police had got defaulters chipping the ice away on an area in front of the guardroom so that there was a space to mount the quarter guard, but a combination of slippery paths and hobnailed boots, caused many a rifleman to be upended and to join the ever-lengthening queue for sick parade in the morning

A few days after his return he and Jeremy decided it was time to make the move to get leave for the wedding in February. They went to see the CSM, Jeremy going in first. The first the CSM said was, "Leave? You want a four-day pass? You've only just come back off leave."

"I know sir, but I would like to get married on the 17th February. Oh, and sir, I'm marrying Corporal Chandler's sister so I would like him to be my Best man."

"Is he outside?"

"Yes sir."

"Get him in."

David marched in smartly and stood to attention.

"I understand you're allowing this NCO to marry your sister?" said the CSM.

"Well sir, I don't have any say in the matter. I would have preferred someone more suitable as you can imagine, but there's nothing I can do about it."

The sergeant major grinned, "Well you'll both be due a forty-eight by about then anyway, so I expect we can stretch yours to about four days," looking at Jeremy. "There's no need for you to see the Company Commander, I'll have a word with him today and let you know this afternoon."

They both thanked the CSM, took a pace back and marched smartly out of the office. When they had finished parades that afternoon the company runner came to their hut and shouted, "Corporal Cartwright to the CSM's office." Jeremy presented himself to the CSM who said, "That's all OK Corporal, you can start making your arrangements."

"Thank you very much sir," he paused "sir?"

"Yes, what is it?"

"Sir, please don't think we're trying to suck up to you, because truly we're not, but David, Corporal Chandler that is, and I wondered whether you and Sergeant Harris would care to bring your wives to the wedding. Without giving out any bullshit we have a great respect for both of you for all you've done to try and make soldiers out of us, we'd like you to be there."

"Have you mentioned this to Sergeant Harris?"

"No sir, not yet, we were going to do so this evening."

"What time is the wedding?"

"Two-thirty sir or three o'clock. I'm not sure. Other people have to travel so it will be in the afternoon."

"Well, Mrs Ward is staying up here in lodgings. I'll talk to her this evening and let you know tomorrow."

"Thank you sir," and with that he marched out.

Before Sergeant Harris went over to the mess for his evening meal, the two corporals knocked on his door and put him in the picture with regard to the passes they had been granted, and the reason for them. Sergeant Harris was genuinely pleased for Jeremy, though he added, "How you could fancy this," pointing to David, "for a brother-in-law I'm blessed if I know."

"Beggars can't be choosers Sergeant, that's the problem. But Sergeant, one thing we would like to ask you is could we have the pleasure of the company of Mrs Harris and yourself at the wedding? I would add that we have also asked CSM Ward and Mrs Ward so there should be people there that you know. It's going to be in the afternoon so you could probably meet Mrs Harris in London and then come on down to Sandbury."

"Well I'm blessed. The answer to that is yes. We'd be delighted. There's nothing my Bessie likes more than a good cry at a wedding, she'll love it."

The next day the sergeant major said he and his wife would be most pleased to come, so David dropped a line to his father and the invitations were sent, including one of course to Major Scott-Calder.

Back in Sandbury there was great excitement in planning 'the dress' and the service and all the other thousand and one things that have to be organised. Fred was determined his daughter would have a good send-off, he could well afford it and rationing was not as yet biting too hard on caterers. They decided to have the reception at the Angel, which restricted the numbers to around a hundred, but Fred knew they would pull out the stops for him as they knew him so well. Rose had decided to have Megan, Pat, Moira and Anni as matrons of honour instead of having young bridesmaids or pages, so all their dresses had to be organised. Jeremy and David would travel down on the Friday evening, David returning on Sunday evening and Jeremy to be back in camp on the Tuesday evening. This ruled out any hope of a stag party, but David said they would organise a belated one when they got their seven-day leave. They half hoped that Harry would be able to get leave, but they knew it was unlikely as only married men with children had got Christmas leave from France, the others taking it in turn in subsequent batches in the New Year. In the event because of an expected invasion of Holland and Belgium by the Germans massed on their borders in mid-January all leave was cancelled for British, Dutch and Belgian troops. When Harry had returned to Le Mans after Christmas he found they were to move immediately to a new park near Lille. A few days after they arrived there they started their new run to and from Cherbourg through Caen, Rouen, Amiens and Arras. The distance was about the same as the Le Mans – Maginot Line had been, but once clear of Normandy the countryside was not as interesting. They also had occasional trips to Calais and Dunkirk. Waiting by the dockside at Calais it was difficult to believe you could almost swim home. Back home the discussions were on the possible invasion of France from the North. Fred said, "It stands to reason that with the Maginot Line only stretching as far as the Belgian border, that's what he is going to do. When they said the King visited the entrenched troops along the Belgian border I thought my God we're back in 1914 again."

"The Belgians are being very naïve," said Jack. "You can understand their not wanting to provoke Hitler or give him an excuse to invade by letting us move troops into Belgium and up to their side of the frontier with Germany. They don't seem to realise that he doesn't need an excuse. As soon as he's ready he'll go and they won't stand a chance on their own if he comes in from both the north and the east to get round the top of the Maginot Line. The fact that he said only a couple of months ago that he only wants friendship with Belgium and Holland doesn't mean a tuppenny cuss."

February came with no let up in the freezing weather. Pat's alteration hand was a superb dressmaker and had completed the dresses for the matrons of honour and was well on the way to finishing the bridal gown. The general view was that all the ladies would have to wear lots of woolly underwear as the church was not exactly famous for its heating system, and there would be the inevitable photography session afterwards. David and Jeremy had long discussions as to whether they should wear uniform or morning suit as for previous occasions. They decided to ask their respective fathers who gave exactly the same answers. "One – what does Rose want? Two – are you proud to be wearing your uniform even if you are only buckshee corporals?"

The answers were then speedily forthcoming. Rose said "I'm marrying a soldier, I'd like him to look like one," and the two friends,

"We're proud to be riflemen"– so that settled the matter.

News also came in February that the Russians attacking Finland were being badly mauled. Wave upon wave, division after division, were thrown against the Mannerheim Line and it had been estimated that two hundred thousand Russian troops had been killed in these futile frontal assaults. The Russians were suffering the results of Stalin's purges of higher-ranking officers over the recent years. There was hardly an officer left over the rank of colonel and certainly very few with any previous combat experience. To aid the Finns the allies, who had been sending them arms since December, now decided to send three or four infantry divisions to help on the ground.

"Where the hell are we to get four divisions from when Jerry has got an estimated one hundred divisions facing us?" roared Jack. He had to express his feelings to Fred and Ruth because he could not of course discuss this subject with Moira, even when she was there, and at this period she was in London for three nights in the week so he didn't see a lot of her anyway. In the event a general named Timoshenko was put in charge of the army facing the Finns, launching a well-planned and sustained attack on one section of the line until it broke and within a month he had subdued the Finnish forces. Two things arose out of this action. Firstly as Jack said, 'Damned good job it happened when it did, that is before we shipped our men there' and secondly the irony of the fact that in 1940 we could have been fighting Timoshenko, whereas in three years time he would be a hero in Britain for the bravery of his army against the German hordes invading Russia.

A few days before the wedding Pat and her dressmaker brought the wedding dress home to Chandlers Lodge and with Ruth helping, had the final fitting. With one or two minor details dealt with on the spot it was pronounced 'perfect' and was carefully covered in a voluminous thin cotton bag and hung up. The dressmaker said her goodbyes and Rose hugged her, thanking her for making such a beautiful gown for her. "I'll come in an hour before you go and make sure that everything is alright," she said, "and then I'll scoot along to the church. You'll look an absolute picture." She was obviously very proud of her handiwork – and rightly so.

Ruth saw her off saying as she went out, "Supper in fifteen minutes," to the two girls.

Whilst Rose was putting her day dress back on and finding her indoor shoes she said, "Pat, can I ask you something?"

"Yes of course, what is it?"

"Well I don't know how to put it."

Pat took her hand, "Come on, spit it out, you know we are best friends."

With a rush Rose said, "Well, I'm afraid I won't know what to do – on my wedding night I mean. I've been worrying about it. Mum told me more or less what happens, but supposing I'm a failure and I spoil everything, supposing he wishes he hadn't married me."

Pat hugged her close and felt she was trembling, she was obviously so upset. Pat sat her down on the edge of the bed and sat with her arm around her.

"Now first of all dear Rose, there is nothing to be anxious about. Jeremy is a dear gentle boy – it will be lovely and exciting for both of you. You may not reach the heights at first but gradually you will experience feelings you didn't know existed – I promise you."

"Yes, but what do I have to do to make it right for him?"

"Well, I think the best thing I can say is that you lovingly respond to the approaches Jeremy will make. You will find it the most natural thing in the world – you will both be in heaven."

Rose seemed to have been reassured and as Ruth called up the stairs that supper was ready she said, "Thank you Pat, I suppose all brides are a bit like me at this stage."

"One of these days you'll be talking to your own daughter like this probably."

They linked arms and walked down to the big kitchen, where Fred and the Canadians were sitting waiting for the girls to arrive. Pulling Alec's leg, Pat said, "And how is Rebecca these days, Captain?"

"Do you know we're getting on like a house on fire," said Alec, "it really started off as you know a bit of a leg pull, but she really is a most charming person. I don't see her all that often as she works long hours travelling to and from London each day, and sometimes I'm tied up at weekends on duty."

Fred butted in, "Have you got your feet under the table yet?"

Seeing the lack of understanding on Alec's face Rose said, "What my nosy father wants to know is, have you been invited to her home yet?"

"Well the fact is I'm going on Sunday week, although I was going to ask you a question about that, and that is, if I go to have Sunday tea with them does that mean in England that you are going steady?"

Jim butted in, "As I understand it, here in England it's tantamount to a proposal of marriage."

They all laughed at this, but Fred soon put him wise. "Now if you go to Sunday tea the object of the exercise is twofold. One, the girl is showing you off, two the parents are sizing you up, but there's no obligation on either side at this stage. You'll be safe for at least a fortnight."

Alec looked at Ruth. "Can you help me," he said. "I can't get any sense out of these people, but then I didn't expect to."

Fred continued with the chaff. "As it happens Alec, I think you'd better stake your claim. They tell me that the Australians and New Zealanders have started arriving, and that the Australian Air Force is having a fighter squadron here on the Sandbury aerodrome. I mean if she sees one of those tall sunburnt Aussies you never know what might happen."

"God, it comes to something when they've got to let gangs of ex-convicts into the country. I don't know what the world is coming to, honestly I don't," he replied.

"In that case," said Jim, "you'd better – what is it? – Oh yes, start getting your feet under the table."

Ruth was listening to this banter with amusement, but inside she felt the sadness of knowing her own three boys, she always thought of Jeremy as being one of her boys, were probably in some miserable barrack-room somewhere whilst these two young men had usurped their place. On the other hand she acknowledged that although the two captains were undoubtedly in good company and in comfortable surroundings it wouldn't always be like that, and again their families back in Canada would be suffering the heartache that she herself was experiencing.

Fred turned his attention to the two girls saying, "I read in the paper that you will both be in the monied classes from next week."

"What do you mean?" asked Rose.

"Well, army wives are now having their allowance increased to three shillings and sixpence a day, so that puts you in luxury."

"I don't know how ordinary soldier's wives manage at that rate," said Ruth. "I know they get another five shillings or thereabouts from their husbands pay, but that only takes them up to around one pound ten shillings a week, and if they have to pay around ten shillings a week rent they've only got a pound a week to live on. I suppose they just have to go out to work to make ends meet."

"Well at least there's plenty of work around now," said Fred, "but I suppose getting babies and young kids looked after is a bit of a problem for a lot of them."

"The factory ought to run crèches," said Ruth, "like they do in Russia."

"When were you last in Russia?" teased Fred and, "on the other hand that's not a bad idea if we get short of operatives."

Rita and Buffy arrived on Thursday, laden again with non-rationed goods for the store cupboard. They were staying at Chandlers Lodge whereas Jeremy would be at the bungalow with David and Pat. As Jeremy said to his prospective host, "that'll cut your capers for one night old son, you'll have to make up for it on Saturday."

"What's wrong with Sunday?" said David, "the train doesn't go until six o'clock."

The two friends arrived at Sandbury at half past seven and were met by Pat. The shop was now closed each day, including Saturdays, at five thirty, in fact the days of late night opening were gone forever, never to reappear. She found therefore she had time to go and see Rose before she went to the station, and found her calm and collected and eagerly awaiting the great day.

The day dawned very cold but bright and sunny. Sergeant Harris travelled down with CSM Ward and Mrs Ward and met Mrs Harris at Liverpool Street, arriving in Sandbury at 12.30 in plenty of time for a snack in the Angel before going on to the church. They both looked extremely smart, and when they slipped their khaki greatcoats off there was considerable interest from others in the bar in the number one service dress they were wearing, green tunic with black belt and buttons, black trousers and their ornamental badges of rank on one arm only. A Canadian sergeant came over and spoke to CSM Ward, who with his Great War ribbons, clipped moustache and iron-grey hair looked every inch the soldier he was. "Excuse me sir," he said, "I apologise for intruding but my men and I would very much like to know the name of your regiment."

"We are the City Rifles," said the sergeant major.

"Is that a very old regiment?" queried the Canadian.

"Not as old as some, but more illustrious than any I would say is the answer to that," replied CSM Ward with a smile. "We've been around for over a hundred and fifty years."

"Well thank you very much for the information sir" said the sergeant. "May we buy you all a drink?"

The sergeant major politely declined saying it was the first time in a long career he had turned down a drink but he and Sergeant Harris were strictly on rations as they were going to a wedding. "Mind you," he continued, "what happens afterwards will be a different matter altogether."

Gradually the guests arrived and started to take their seats in the church. Jeremy and David, both in uniform, took their places leaving Pat in the porch with the other attendants who had arrived before them. The general, wearing plain clothes, had the pleasure of escorting Ruth, and was obviously most proud to do so, in the absence of Kate who again had volunteered to play at the service. Promptly – five minutes late! – the bride arrived having been fussed over to the last minute by Pat's dressmaker who slipped into the church after the entry of the bride and was lost among the throng. Rarely could the ancient church of St

John, Sandbury have seen five such beautiful women gracing the aisle as it did that day. The four attendants dressed in a soft peach colour material with a darker shade of peach for their gloves and sashes contrasted with the magnificent white satin dress and train so lovingly made for Rose. Sergeant Harris had said his wife liked a good cry at a wedding and she certainly didn't let him down at this one – not that she was the only one by any means who was affected by the sight of the slim gracious bride beside her burly husband to be and her equally burly brother. Ruth watching from the front row of pews thought as her slim wiry husband stood there with their daughter, how she hadn't realised how much these two lads, as she still thought of them, had filled out.

With the ceremony over, the pilgrimage to the vestry having taken place and the signal given to Kate, the organ burst forth with the Mendelssohn as the procession made its way through the chancel and into the nave. The double doors at the end of the church were closed, and to Jeremy's surprise a Canadian soldier was standing by each section of the door. As they got closer the doors were swung open and outside they found themselves walking under an archway of glistening bayonets held up by twelve corporals from Alec and Jim's battalion. Rose, who up until now had been most serene, smiling to her friends and family as she walked down the aisle, excitedly pulled on Jeremy's arm and said, "Did you know about this?"

"No I didn't – isn't it marvellous."

As they and the main party walked through the archway photographers from both the local press and the Kent County Press, along with an official photographer from the Canadian Division, who was to send prints back as a news item showing how the Canadians were being welcomed in England and in turn were fitting in the local life, took shot after shot of this handsome couple, their attendants and families. No one had known what the two Canadians were arranging. The corporals were all volunteers from Alec and Jim's respective companies and had arrived outside during the ceremony, it was therefore as great a surprise to the family and guests as it was a delight to Rose and Jeremy. The reception, the speeches, and the going away followed its traditional course. As they stepped into the car to be driven to the station Rose turned and tossed her bouquet to Rebecca, but it was neatly caught by Alec and presented to her to the applause of all nearby, led by Rose. The young couple had elected to honeymoon in London – as Jeremy had said to Rose, "We won't want to waste precious time travelling," with which sentiment she agreed absolutely. Her pre-wedding fears confided to Pat proved to be quite unfounded and on Sunday morning she awoke feeling 'like a cat that ate the cream', when asked by her husband how she was.

Jeremy wore his plain clothes for the stroll in St James' Park on the Sunday morning, and after a light lunch and they had returned to their room he said, "I'm taking you to the Ritz for tea this afternoon."

"How exciting," exclaimed Rose, "What on earth gave you that idea?"

"Well, my father suggested it. Apparently he took my mother there on their honeymoon, half of which they spent in London. You see all kinds of interesting people there and to make sure we get a table he has spoken to Mr Salerno, the manager, who is a friend from his Lodge." Rose had only a faint idea of what a 'Lodge' was, but it must be something important for the manager of the Ritz to belong to it to say nothing of Jeremy's father, who she knew to be a very wealthy and influential man in the city.

Jeremy continued, "But that gives us two hours before we have to leave, what would you like to do?"

Rose turned on her heel without a further word and went across to the window. With a movement as swift and definite as her turn had been she pulled the drapes closely together, came back to Jeremy, took the lapels of his jacket and pushed it off his shoulders onto the floor behind him. In another quick movement she slid his braces off his shoulders and said, "you can do the rest."

"You brazen hussie," he said holding her close, "do you realise you have just committed a common assault against me?"

"I get the impression Mr Cartwright, that you are at the moment committing an indecent assault against me, in fact go so far as to say that the impression is getting stronger all the time."

They surfaced in time to get to the Ritz for four thirty and were shown to their table, a very nice table from which they could see a good proportion of the people taking tea and the renowned cucumber sandwiches. When they had been seated a short while the head waiter came to see them and apologised for the fact that they had to seat two other people at their table who would be joining them shortly saying, "We are so busy Mr Cartwright and we do like to accommodate senior members of the forces if we can."

Jeremy told him they didn't mind at all and then said to Rose, "I do hope they're not RAF or Navy – I'm very particular with whom I take tea."

When the newcomers arrived they were in uniform, one a British brigadier and the second a Canadian colonel. Automatically Jeremy stood up as they were ushered to the table and then sat down when they did. The brigadier addressing Rose opened the conversation by saying, "I do apologise for barging in on your table, it's frightfully kind of you to help us out," and then to Jeremy, "I take it you are in His Majesty's

Forces?"

"Yes sir, but how did you know?"

"Well it's my experience that few civilians stand up when I appear, and when they do they certainly don't have their thumbs down the seams of their trousers like a guardsman – you're not a guardsman I suppose?"

"No sir, something infinitely superior – I'm a rifleman."

At this the colonel roared with laughter.

"Well, we'll let that one go," said the brigadier, "since I used to be a Coldstreamer, many years ago I would add."

"I've noticed in the short time I've been here the rivalry not just between army, navy and air force," said the colonel, "but between all you different regiments. Every unit seems to have something to distinguish it from the next. How different is yours from the remainder Mr...?"

"I'm Corporal Cartwright sir, this is my wife Rose."

"You're a Corporal? It's an awfully rude question but how does a Corporal end up in the Ritz?" continued the colonel looking laughingly at the brigadier and then back to Rose. As Jeremy was trying to assemble an intelligent answer he was saved by the appearance of the headwaiter followed by a gentleman in a black coat and striped trousers. It was obviously a person of importance since waiters speedily stood aside to let pass this immaculately dressed authoritative looking gentleman now bearing down upon them.

"This is Mr Cartwright sir," said the headwaiter, "and Mrs Cartwright." He shook hands with them both and said "Good afternoon gentlemen," to the two officers.

"So Jeremy, the wedding was yesterday – did all go well? And how are your mother and father? We saw your father early last week but I haven't seen your mother now since just after Christmas."

"Yes, they are both well, although I have suspicion father would not have too good a head this morning."

They talked on for a few more minutes to the continued interest of the brigadier and his friend until Mr Salerno said, "We have a small gift for you to collect at the main reception when you leave. Oh, and the next time you're on leave in London come and stay here." He added looking at Rose.

"We couldn't afford it on a Corporal's pay," laughed Rose.

"On a Corporal's pay, oh I say how rich," laughed Mr Salerno.

"Now Mario," to the headwaiter, "You are to present Mr Cartwright's account for him and his guests," indicating the two officers, "direct to me – you understand?"

"Yes sir, yes Mr Salerno."

"But we're not Mr Cartwright's guests," said the brigadier.

"Well lets put it this way brigadier," said Mr Salerno, "if military protocol will allow it, you are now," and with a beaming smile shook hands with all four and marched away, acknowledging a greeting here and there as he left the room. When they sat down again there was a quiet moment until the Canadian started to chuckle. It was so infectious that in no time, to the mystified amusement of people at adjacent tables, all four were in fits of laughter. At last the Canadian looked at the brigadier and said, "You can dine out on this for weeks."

Jeremy looked at them both and said, "It could have been worse, I could have been a Lance Corporal," at which they all started to laugh again as their tea arrived.

During the tea, Rose said to the Canadian, "Do you know any of your people at Sandbury?"

"Yes, we both do, why do you?" replied the Canadian.

"Yes indeed. Two of the officers, Captain Fraser and Captain Napier are billeted at my house. In fact not only were they at our wedding yesterday but to our surprise they provided us with a guard of honour outside the church – it was wonderful."

"Now wait a minute then," said the colonel. "You know Alec and Jim, sir," addressing the brigadier. "We were talking about them yesterday regarding that other matter."

"Oh yes, of course I do," replied the brigadier.

The colonel continued, "You wouldn't then be one of the famous Chandler girls?"

"I don't know about famous, but yes, I am one of the four."

"Well in that battalion famous you definitely are!! To hear Alec hold forth there never was such a bevy of beauties gathered together in one place before, and almost with tears streaming down his cheeks and with tragedy in his voice that would have done credit to Hamlet himself, he says he found in turn that each of the four was either married or spoken for. He didn't stand a chance. He swears that if it was not for the fact that he was in the army and regulations didn't allow it, he would enter a monastery, his life was so shattered!! He tells a good story does our Alec."

There was much laughter at the table at this account of poor Alec's sufferings until Jeremy said, "not telling tales out of school sir, but has he neglected to mention in the meantime the name Rebecca?"

"He has deliberately not mentioned the name Rebecca," said the colonel. "Is this something we can mention in passing I wonder?"

"Let's put it this way sir, we understand he's getting his feet under the table next weekend, and she really is a corker."

"What do you mean – getting his feet under the table?"

"He's going home to have Sunday tea. Rose's father has been pulling his leg by saying it's the custom in these parts to propose within a fortnight, and even that hasn't frightened him off."

"Tell me Jeremy," said the brigadier, "have you thought of going for a commission?"

"Yes sir, David and I – David is Rose's brother, we were at Cantlebury together – David and I thought we'd get some service in first. We've now, with our territorial service, been in the Rifles for three years, so when I go back this week we're both going to apply to go to a cadet unit."

"Good for you. Now we must be off. The very best of luck to both of you in your marriage and in your service life Jeremy, and thank you very much for tea at the Ritz."

They all laughed as Jeremy replied, "Well it's on Mr Salerno really sir," and with that they shook hands all round and the two officers left. As they moved away Jeremy noticed that the brigadier had left his swagger stick behind. He called after him, "sir – your stick."

The brigadier retraced his few steps and with a smile said, "You keep it – it will come in handy when you're commissioned," and turning again walked off smiling.

The young couple resumed their seats for a while enjoying the subdued hubbub, spotting one or two famous faces seeing and being seen, and in general revelling in the luxury of being at least for the moment privileged people in a privileged place.

"I wonder what Harry is doing at this minute," said Rose "it's impossible to believe there is a war going on sitting here."

"He's probably in some estaminet knocking back glasses of plonk," said Jeremy. "I know what I would be doing if we were in camp. It's six o'clock so we would go to the corporal's room at the Naafi for a mug of tea and Welsh rarebit, and then back to the barrack-room and read till lights out – exciting isn't it?"

"I thought your Sergeant Harris and Sergeant Major Ward were very nice. I had quite a little chat with them, and their wives were very nice too. I'm glad we invited them, they certainly provided a great deal of interest with their green jackets."

"Well, I don't know about being nice, that's not the word I would usually employ to describe them. Fair, soldierly, efficient, knowledgeable maybe, I think we could agree on that – but nice – I don't know so much! Anyway I bet you a pound to a penny the CSM has stuck me on quarter guard next weekend to show I don't get away with anything just because he came to the wedding."

They decided it was time to go and were bowed out by Mario, who said that Mr Salerno had told him to remind them to call at the reception. This they did and were handed a box neatly wrapped in purple-striped paper. It was about nine inches square and four inches high and fairly heavy.

"I wonder what it is," said Rose excitedly.

"Well it's too small for a chamber pot," said Jeremy, giving Rose a fit of giggles, "which is rather a pity, it would have been a case of classic one-upmanship to have a Ritz po under one's bed."

"Perhaps if we ever stay here we could steal one."

"Rose Cartwright – how could you be so criminal! Not a bad idea though for all that."

On the Monday it was a fine sunny day but still very cold, they were walking in Hyde Park when Jeremy said, "Rose dear, can I talk to you about a rather humdrum subject, namely money?"

"Of course, although I must say I've never thought of money being humdrum, though again to be truthful I've never had to think about it all very much – I've been very lucky."

"Well darling, you'll be getting your army pay, and I shall be making you an allowance. You see I have a substantial sum of my own which I've never had to use. It was left to me by my Grandmother when she died back in 1930 for me to use from the age of twenty-one. It was originally £150,000, but now is over £200,000. If you need any money apart from the allowance, you contact Mr White, my solicitor at Romsey, and he will arrange it. I've suggested you have £2,000 a year for the time being until we can set up house, so you can easily give up your job if you want to. I have made a will leaving the capital sum to you should anything happen to me – and that's the end of the story."

"Oh Jeremy, everyone will think I married you for your money – I truly didn't ever realise you were so wealthy."

"Well I know and you know, that's all you married me for."

She stopped and held him close, "If it wasn't for the fact that people get locked up for doing certain things in Hyde Park, or at least so I've heard, I would prove to you right now that that wasn't the reason."

They walked in silence, until Rose said, "But I would like to carry on with my work – it's useful and it's interesting and will fill my time while you're away – you don't mind do you darling?"

"No, of course not, it's a good idea – as long as those young doctors keep their distance."

"Oh they will. They're all talk. I prefer an action man and to think how gloriously lucky I've been to find one."

Another pause. "What did you say you could get locked up for doing in Hyde Park?" Jeremy asked.

Rose giggled as they walked on with their arms around each other.

All too soon the honeymoon was over. Jeremy changed back into uniform and took Rose to Victoria for him then to go on to Colchester. It had been arranged that Fred would meet Rose at Sandbury Station as she would have the two suitcases, now further weighed down by the mysterious and as yet unopened parcel from the Ritz. As they kissed goodbye on the platform Rose said, "I shall miss you so much tonight darling – I never realised how wonderful it would be, I just can't wait for your Easter leave," and as the train slowly pulled away, "Take care Jeremy."

Chapter Thirty-five

It was nine thirty on a dark night when Jeremy booked back in at the guardroom. A sergeant from C Company was guard commander and greeted him with, "So you didn't desert then Corporal?"

"Desert Sergeant?"

"Well the story going round the mess is that your bride was more than worth deserting for – we didn't expect to see you back!"

"Don't think I didn't consider it, but then I thought of how could they manage without me, so I returned." They both laughed as Jeremy walked out and across back to his barrack room.

As he walked in, David jumped down off his bunk and hugged him, "Well how did it all go? How is Rose?"

"Hey, give me a chance to get my greatcoat off. To answer your question, Rose is fine, she has gone home wandering what the hell women can see in Clark Gable – does that answer your question, and what's the news here?"

"Good news or bad news first?"

"Good news."

"There is no good news."

"Bad news."

"The bad news is that tomorrow morning at eight thirty you are on a fifteen mile full marching order route march complete with weapons and full ammunition, and if that doesn't kill you straight on top of a honeymoon weekend nothing will. Anyway I've got all your kit ready for you and organised a stretcher party to come up in the rear of the column."

"Is that all of the bad news?"

"Sorry – no. You are also Orderly Corporal on Thursday and Guard Commander on Sunday. I incidentally was Orderly Corporal yesterday and I'm Guard Commander on Saturday."

"I told Rose that Wardie would stick it on us just to show we don't get away with anything because he's been to the wedding."

"Oh well it'll keep us busy and stop you brooding about all the married life you're missing won't it? By the way, I passed the RSM the other day and he said, 'Good morning Corporal'– do you think he's going senile?"

"No, like Beasley said when you lost your prisoner, I think he fancies you."

"Silly sod. Anyway I brought a pie back from the Naafi in case you were hungry – here you are."

They chatted on until lights out and at 6.30 when reveille was blasted outside their hut Jeremy found it very difficult to fall out of bed with any enthusiasm for the thought of fifteen miles at rifleman's pace carrying over sixty pounds of kit plus ammunition which confronted him. However, he survived, they were a very fit unit by now and apart from one or two riflemen with blisters, caused by invariably by wearing badly darned socks, the whole platoon gave a good account of itself.

Rose in the meantime had been met by her father and mother at Sandbury. "Well, this is quite an honour," she said, "both of you here to meet me."

"Well your father's getting a bit forgetful now he's getting on a bit dear. I was afraid he might lose his way to the station so I decided to come as well." They both hugged Rose as if she'd been away for a month instead of only three days. When they got home Fred carried the suitcases up to the landing outside Rose's bedroom and then returned to the kitchen. Ruth and Rose followed up the stairs chattering away, and when Rose saw the suitcases outside the door she was a little puzzled for the moment why he hadn't carried them right into the room. Thinking no more of it she opened the door and walked in to find firstly a large arrangement of flowers on the small table in the centre of the room and secondly, in place of her own single bed a new double bed had been positioned complete with a polished oak headboard and side cabinets with a lamp on each one.

"That's for when he comes on leave and stays here," said Ruth, "although we know that most of the time he will want you to go to Romsey. Now, tell me how you got on."

"What I can tell you Mother dear," said Rose jokingly, "is that I can thoroughly recommend married life."

As she spoke Pat and Megan appeared at the doorway, and after much hugging with everyone chattering at once, Pat said, "Well – come on – tell us about it."

"I'm much too shy to tell you all about it," said Rose. "Like the Victorian ladies in India I just shut my eyes and dreamt of England."

They all laughed and were still laughing when Fred knocked at the door and said, "Can the porter bring the bags in now?"

He brought them in and put them at the end of the bed and in doing so the conversation stopped completely. He turned and said, "Well as I'm obviously not going to get a tip I'll push off," and as he went through the door he said to the world in general, "I wonder what married women talk about when they're left on their own?"

Megan called after him, "Wouldn't you love to know." He went downstairs, grinning to himself.

Rose continued by telling them of the episode at the Ritz, but warned them not to say anything to Alec or Jim until the colonel had

327

been able to pull Alec's leg about Rebecca.

"By the way," said Rose, "where are they this evening?"

"They've got a mess night on," said Ruth, "some big noise is visiting them all day and staying for dinner tonight."

"I wonder if it's the brigadier?" said Rose.

"You didn't have any embarrassing moments like the one we had?" said Megan.

"What was that," they all immediately replied.

"Well, Harry was larking about with absolutely nothing on, and I told him to behave himself and went into the bathroom to get some tissues. The second I went he hid himself in the wardrobe, and at that moment the maid gave a light tap on the door and came in to clear the breakfast things – we'd had breakfast in the room. Harry, hearing the clink of cups, thought it was me tidying up or something and promptly appeared from the wardrobe wearing just my going away hat and nothing else. As I appeared in the bathroom doorway there was Harry holding the hat over his bits and pieces and the maid in the process of dropping the coffee jug – it was chaos."

"Did anything like that happen to you?" said Pat to Rose.

"No," she said, "but something did happen that was funny, but I don't want to tell you and shock my poor mother."

"My dear girl," said Ruth, "I was having shocks before you were born, so spit it out."

"Well we were just going to bed one night and Jeremy was lying on the bed while I took my make-up off etc."

"How was he lying on the bed?" said Megan. "Come on, full details."

"He was quite starkers," Rose replied, and the other three giggled at the story to come.

"I was putting some cream on my face and Jeremy was lying there, watching me. What's that stuff, he said. I told him it was Pond's Vanishing Cream. What's it supposed to do he asked. I said it's supposed to make all your little imperfections disappear. It doesn't seem to have worked with you, the cheeky little blighter said. With that I dug out a blob of it and ran across and smeared it on his you know what, and started rubbing it in. You'll see if it works when it makes this vanish I said. He lay there watching me do it for a few seconds and then said, 'look I told you it doesn't work, it's having the absolute opposite effect'– and I'm very pleased to tell you that it was!"

The laughter could be heard clearly downstairs, causing Fred to say to himself, "Looks as though we've got another happily married woman in the family."

The Canadians were home quite late that night. Rose and Fred had gone to bed and Ruth was wondering whether she should follow. She liked to be there when they came in, in case they would like a cup of cocoa, which by now they were quite used to, or a sandwich before they went up. As she was just making up her mind to move she heard the sound of their pick-up crunching up to the front door so she waited for them to come in. They had both obviously had a drink or two, and seeing Ruth was on her own Jim said, "Shhhh – mustn't wake Fred up," holding his finger to his lips.

"Not a sound," said Alec, beaming myopically at Ruth. "Nor Rose either, though I've got a bone to pick with our Rose when I see her."

Ruth stood grinning at her two lodgers.

"You two look as though you've been celebrating something or other," she said, "can you let me in on it?"

"You are now," Jim said in the too clearly articulated speech of the semi-inebriated. "You are now, my dear Mrs Ruth Chandler, looking at two Majors of the Canadian army."

"Oh, how wonderful. Congratulations to you both. How did this come about?"

"Well, two of our Majors are going to be transferred as seconds in command to two new battalions arriving this week, so we are taking their companies over. The other news is that before they go we are having a mess party for the people who have hosted us so you will be receiving an official invitation in the morning mail," said Alec.

"But that isn't all," continued Jim conspiringly. "In addition to our host and hostess each officer is allowed to invite a guest, so there are no prizes for guessing who Major Fraser will be bringing, and I shall ask Pat to come with me, with David's permission."

"When is the great occasion?" asked Ruth.

"It's a bit short notice I'm afraid," said Jim, "but it's on Saturday – give everybody a chance to get over it on Sunday! So you've got four days to get into training."

After electing not to have cocoa on top of the liberal quantities of Canadian Club they had consumed that evening, they tiptoed to bed like a pair of fairy elephants leaving Ruth laughing to herself, but with it suddenly occurring to her that Rose would be left on her own while they all went to the party, she felt that the poor girl would be like Cinderella. As it happened not one, but two invitations arrived in the post the next morning. One to Ruth and Fred and a second to Mrs Rose Cartwright. When Rose joined the others for breakfast they all looked expectantly at her as she opened the envelope from which she withdrew an official invitation card and a short handwritten letter.

"Well," said Ruth, "what does it say?"

"I can't divulge the contents of the billet-doux from an officer and a gentleman now can I?"

"Old married women don't receive billet-doux," said Ruth.

"Well it's from the Colonel we met at the Ritz," said Rose.

"So it was you," boomed Alec. "I guessed it was. All the mess knows about Rebecca and have put two and two together and made about fifty out of it. You two are the culprits. I'll court martial that husband of yours when I next see him, you see if I don't."

"We only told the truth, they were almost in tears at learning of this great romance between the lonely handsome soldier from far away and the beautiful English girl. That's probably why they've made you a Major so that you get a bigger married man's pay allowance," teased Rose.

Ruth butted in, "So stop your teasing and tell us what is in the note."

"The Colonel says will I ask my husband's permission to be his guest at the party, and adds, give him his kind regards."

"Well you are highly honoured," said Jim. "The Colonel is known as a complete misogynist."

"That's the answer then, isn't it," said Alec. "He knows he's safe, can't get ensnared can he? Rose being married and his having met her husband he wins all hands down. A beautiful young girl for a partner for which all the young subalterns will envy him like mad and no possibility of an attachment afterwards!"

"Of course it could be that my poise, charm and sophistication could have appealed to him," said Rose. "After all when a gentleman like him has only the rough soldiery to talk to most of the time it must be a welcome change for him to be in the company of softer and gentler folk to bring him a touch of the normality of life."

"Well, all I can say is that he'd better hang on to you or you'll be mobbed by some of those young lieutenants, come to that both the quartermaster and the MO have an eye for a pretty girl – I think it's a good job your father's going to be there," said Jim.

Rose looked at the clock. "Golly is that the time," she said, "I must rush, can't be late on my first day back," and she hurried off, laughing as she went.

The week went by and David found himself on quarter guard on Saturday morning. The day proceeded without incident. He was kept fairly busy booking people out on thirty-six hour passes. One advantage of being at Colchester for the people who lived in the London area, is that they would get home at weekends if they had a pass. Even if they hadn't got a pass some of them risked it and got off the train at Stratford so as not to be checked by the redcaps at Liverpool Street. When they came back on Sunday evening there was very little chance of being picked up at Colchester as the last train was invariably packed to the roof and MP's were swept aside as the mob came off the platform, non-pass holders keeping well into the middle of the throng. By mid-afternoon things were quiet until David heard the squeak of brakes and then loud voices outside the guardroom door. As the door opened he stood up, putting his cap on, and stood to attention as a staff sergeant from the military police walked in.

"I've got a naughty boy for you Corporal," he said, "picked up at Lambeth the day before yesterday."

With that a lance corporal appeared, handcuffed to a person in civilian clothes who badly needed a shave and a haircut.

"Rifleman bloody Barclay," said David in a voice that contained a distinct lack of welcome.

"I take it you know our friend," said the staff sergeant.

"Oh I know him very well staff. Mr Barclay and I are going to have a little talk together – he nearly caused me to lose my stripes at Christmas, and now we have him back don't we, you nasty, horrible, scruffy little man."

"Well, sign for him here," said the staff sergeant, "and a word of warning Corporal, I don't know what you have in mind but you're signing for him as being sound in wind and limb if you get my meaning."

"Oh don't worry Staff, we shan't lay a finger on him. He'll get seven shades of you know what knocked out of him when he goes to the glasshouse this time so we'll leave it to them. By the way Staff, if you'd like something to eat before you go back I'll send the stick man over with you to the cookhouse. The duty cook is on and it's time for us to collect our meal now, so he can knock you up something."

"Right, a banger sandwich would be very acceptable. Thank you Corporal."

With that he and the lance corporal, accompanied by the stick man went back to the truck. Every quarter guard had a stick man. When the guard was mounted seven riflemen, along with the guard commander and second in command, would parade and the rifleman with the smartest turn out would be nominated by the orderly officer mounting the guard as 'stick man'. He then was excused actual guards, but remained in the guardroom to act as runner and general dogsbody and in the process got a full night's sleep. The other six riflemen did a twenty-four hour stint in pairs on the basis of two hours on, four hours off, although they remained fully dressed and wearing kit all the time they were not actually on guard, even when resting at night.

With the redcaps having departed David took a long look at Rifleman Barclay and then said, "Right my lad, into the cells with you, and believe me you won't move out of them until you go to CO's orders on Monday morning. Oh, and a word of warning, my mate Corporal Cartwright takes over from me and he doesn't like deserters and he particularly doesn't like you dropping me in it at Christmas, so I'd watch your p's and q's when he's on tomorrow. Now, are you hungry."

"Yes Corporal, the food in that Lambeth nick was terrible, worse than the glasshouse."

"Right, we'll get you a proper meal and then you can have cheese and cocoa tonight with the guard at ten o'clock. That should set you up for the night." He watched Barclay as he arranged the blankets on the hard cell bed. "Tell me something Barclay, why do you keep doing it?"

"Well I never wanted to be a soldier in the first place."

"Lots of people don't, but when there's a war on you have to do your bit. You can't leave it to all the others. If everybody acted like you Hitler would walk straight in, then where would you be?" David was trying to keep his reasoning as basic as he could; Barclay was obviously no giant brain.

"Do you know what I think Barclay?" continued David. "The first time you hopped the wag there was no war on, so you didn't really think you were doing anything terribly wrong. Then you got slung in the glasshouse and that made you resent the army and everybody in it. I'll be straight with you, if for some reason that had happened to me I might have felt the same."

"Yeah, but it wouldn't happen to you would it? You're from a posh school from the way you talk, and with two stripes on your arm you've got it made."

"Alright, let's agree on that and come back to you. First you can't keep on taking a bashing in the glasshouse, your sentences will just get longer and longer and for all I know you could end up with penal servitude, which is stupid. Second, it's not such a bad life we have here – ask the other riflemen. If you were serving here it would be vastly more comfortable than double marching all day long inside, added to which people wouldn't think you're a coward and don't want to fight the war."

"Who say's I'm a coward? I'm no bloody coward. I just don't like the army."

"How do you know, you've not given it a fair chance. See those other riflemen out there," he pointed to the guards sitting around the deal table, "do they look that miserable to you? No of course they don't. I don't say everything's a bed of roses in the City Rifles, but by God there's lots of worse places. If you were a rifleman here you wouldn't have to be looking over your shoulder all the time, and not only that people would respect you as being a serving soldier. You might even become as proud of being one as we are in time. I tell you what; you're going to get fifty-six days this time without a doubt. Do your time and come back here and I'll arrange with the CSM that you come back into our platoon. You'll know then that you'll be treated fairly and squarely, and you never know you may begin to like it, you may even begin to be good at it. At least you'll know that somebody else isn't doing your dirty work for you."

With that David swung round, unlocked the cell door and let himself out back into the guardroom. They had no further trouble with Barclay over the weekend and as David had predicted, on Monday morning he got fifty-six days and the regimental police bundled him off back into the glasshouse.

Chapter Thirty-six

While David and his quarter guard were wishing the time to pass sitting around the stove in the guardroom, Ruth and Fred, along with Rose and Pat were getting themselves ready for the party at the Canadian mess. David and Jeremy had both readily agreed that the girls should go when the news was put to them during their usual Friday night telephone calls home, having repeated warnings similar to those mentioned by Alec and Jim about the predatory habits of young lieutenants in all armies, and especially it would seem, according to them, in the Canadian army.

Dress for male guests was black tie with miniatures, and Fred looked every inch the ex-soldier with his immaculately prepared clothes, iron grey hair and his medal bar holding his six medals expertly pinned on by Ruth so that the bar was absolutely horizontal.

"By Jove Ruth," he said, "you've certainly made a good job of this lot – I look almost respectable for a change."

"You'll be the most attractive man there," said Ruth coming up behind him as he looked in the full-length mirror and putting her arms around him squeezing him hard.

"Now you'll better stop there if you want to get to the do in time," replied Fred. She gave a little laugh and went back to the dressing table to put the finishing touches to her hair.

"Come to that," Fred continued, turning to look at her, "there will be a few if any to match up to you tonight. I don't know about the young lieutenants mobbing the girls, I've an idea I shall have to keep an eye on you as well if what Alec says about the QM and the MO is true."

The colonel had arranged for his Humber staff car to collect Fred Ruth and Rose. Alec had taken the pick-up to collect Rebecca, and Jim had organised a taxi to collect him and go on to pick up Pat at the bungalow. The colonel had asked Rose if they could be picked up a little before 7.30 as he would need to be available from that time onwards to greet all the guests and welcome them to the party, so they were in fact the first to arrive. The colonel met them at the door having been given a signal by one of the mess orderlies that the staff car had arrived, and after thanking her again for being his personal guest for the evening was introduced to Ruth and Fred. To Ruth he was very gallant – "I can see where Rose gets her beauty from," being his opening remark and to Fred, "Please have a wonderful evening Mr Chandler, and thank you both very much indeed for all you've done to make us welcome and at home in Sandbury." As they moved inside the colonel said to Rose, "You wouldn't stay with me to help greet the guests I suppose? I sometimes get a bit tongue-tied with people I don't know."

"Of course I will, but I don't believe that for one minute," she replied laughingly.

The colonel took them across the room and introduced them to Rose's surprise to the brigadier they had met in the Ritz. "There you are my dear," said the brigadier to a lady beside him, presumably his wife, "I told you she was a beauty didn't I?"

The introductions having been made the colonel excused himself and piloting Rose across the room back to the door said, "I really am most grateful to you for coming. I do hope this welcoming business won't be onerous."

"I shall enjoy it immensely," said Rose. "It makes me feel terribly important."

"By the time you've shaken a hundred hands you may have different ideas."

In fact Rose found she knew quite a number of the guests, even if only by sight. The colonel was introduced to the guests by the officers who accompanied them and he in turn introduced Rose as 'My guest Mrs Cartwright', Rose noticing on several occasions the raised eyebrows and sidelong looks at her by the officers, who had never ever heard the colonel talk about a woman, let alone actually be with one, and particularly one as young and lovely as his present companion. This was the first time that Rose had been involved in formalities of this nature, but she soon got the hang of it and found that far from being lost for words she was readily able to complement the welcome from the colonel with friendly greetings of her own.

In the meantime Fred and Ruth were talking to the brigadier and his wife.

"You've heard the story of our meeting your daughter and her husband I suppose Mr Chandler?" said the brigadier.

"Yes, Rose told us all about it – they were both very thrilled. It really was most kind of you to give Jeremy your swagger stick, he's absolutely delighted with it."

"Well, they both struck the Colonel and I as being such a nice natural couple. Agatha and I have never been blessed with children but if we had been that fortunate, your daughter and her husband would have been exactly our ideal."

The brigadier's wife took his arm and squeezed it. "He's a real old softie isn't he?" she said, smiling at him. Agatha Halton was a big-boned woman with a plain but highly intelligent face into which were set strikingly blue eyes, so striking in fact that they eclipsed the plainness of her features and gave an overall picture of a very handsome woman. "Mind you," she continued, "we've had a different home every eighteen months or so since we were married the year the Great War broke out, so life has not been particularly eventless without them."

Fred broke in, "If you were married in 1914 you must have been a child bride," he said, "if you will forgive me for saying so."(That's definitely where Harry gets it from thought Ruth smiling at him).

"Mr Chandler, you may at any time say things like that without let or hindrance," they all laughed together.

"Mrs Chandler do you have other children?" Ruth and Agatha chatted away about David, and Harry and Megan, the twins and Anni, and in the meantime the brigadier said to Fred, "I see you too have the Mons Star."

"Yes, I was in the Hampshires."

"I was a young officer in the Coldstream in that lot," said the brigadier, "do you know there are not many of us left now of the original contemptibles, not of the infantry anyway."

"Jeremy's father was a company commander in my battalion," continued Fred, "but I'm afraid there are very few left other than him."

"I understand from Jeremy that the two boys are applying for a commission now."

"Yes, I think they probably could have got it at the very beginning of the war, but they had this somewhat noble idea that if they had some time in the ranks on a war footing it would make better officers of them."

"Do you know Mr Chandler, I think they're right. This old idea of the officer class is long out of date. Modern war requires more than being able to speak with an Oxford accent and to be able to ride a horse. I think we're going to find that out pretty soon, you mark my words."

Whilst the mess waiters in their short white jackets with highly polished brass buttons were circulating with trays of sherry and bucks fizz, the colonel and Rose were continuing to welcome the guests, most of whom had not been in an officer's mess before and really didn't know what to expect. The Canadian camp, being relatively new, obviously didn't sport the sort of mess you would find in the depot of a British regiment, but nevertheless it was very comfortably furnished, highly polished from floor to ceiling, tastefully carpeted and curtained and provided with snowy white table linen and good quality cutlery and glassware. When the first break came in the inward stream of arrivals Rose said, "You know Colonel, I don't even know your name. Alec and Jim always refer to you as the Colonel, when they're not using other titles of course" – she said with a little laugh – "so as far as I know none of us really knows who you are. Even your invitation said the colonel and officers of etc, etc, and didn't enlighten us."

"I say, that's bad isn't it. I should have thought of that. Just shows you, you need a woman's touch in matters of this nature. Well anyway it's Tim McEwan at your service."

As the colonel turned to greet more guests Rose was able to study him for a few moments until they moved on to her. He was a slimly built, wiry man, very similar in stature to her father. She guessed at his being in his mid-thirties, which she thought was rather young for a colonel. She had always imagined colonels as being florid faced old goats who were hard of hearing and drank port all day. Tim McEwan had a lean strong face, which was not given to smiling, but when it did it gave him a boyish look, which indicated a good sense of humour lying beneath the stern exterior of the professional soldier. He turned quickly to her and noticed her looking at him rather more intently than she had realised. He gave her an embarrassed little smile at finding himself the object of her scrutiny, saying to Mr and Mrs Rogers whom he had just greeted, "This is my guest Mrs Cartwright," and the moment passed but was remembered by both of them long afterwards.

At eight o'clock Colonel Tim rejoined the main party, leaving his second in command to welcome any stragglers arriving late. The mess president called the company to order, asking them if they would kindly take their places according to the table plan. They were mainly in tables of eight, the brigadier and his wife, the colonel and Rose, Fred and Ruth and Pat and Jim on the main table. When all were seated the mess president again asked for silence for Colonel McEwan. Tim arose and said that the evening was for fun and jollity and therefore there would be no speeches. It was being held to thank all the kind people who had taken the rough Canadian soldiery into their homes and made them so welcome since they arrived at Christmas time. He said they were particularly pleased to welcome Brigadier Halton and Lady Halton. The brigadier had been a tower of strength in helping the battalion settle in and he hoped they would soon, with the other two battalions under the brigadier's command, be doing the sort of soldiering they had come here for. "Finally," he said, "I would like to publicly thank Mrs Cartwright for being here as my guest and in helping me to greet you all this evening. I would like you to know that this is with the full permission of her husband who at this present moment is incarcerated in a camp similar to this somewhere in the home forces, and no doubt missing her greatly."

As he concluded the mess waiters brought trays containing small white boxes and proceeded to present one to each lady present. There were gasps of appreciation as they were opened as each one contained a solid silver maple leaf brooch. Colonel Tim, who had remained standing, ended his short speech with, "These brooches were subscribed for by all the officers of the regiment. We hope when you wear them you will remember how very grateful we are to you all." There was loud applause and the colonel sat down whispering to Rose, "Thank God that's over."

The evening went swimmingly. The food and wines were excellent as befits an officers mess, the dancing afterwards enjoyable if a little boisterous as the subalterns began to take over the younger lady guests. Rose had danced the opening dance with the colonel with just them and the brigadier and his wife initially on the floor, and then in turn with her father and the brigadier and Jim. After a while a shy young second lieutenant presented himself and asked her to dance. She looked enquiringly at the colonel who gave a little nod to say it was alright, who followed up the nod by saying, "but if you as much as scrape one of her toes Martin, I'll have you on orderly officer for a month." During the dance the young Martin told Rose that the five second lieutenants in the regiment had drawn lots to who should ask her. "And," he said, "I lost."

"You lost?" exclaimed Rose, "is it such a penance to have to dance with me?"

"No, gosh no, it's marvellous, but we didn't know if the Colonel would blow his top or not."

"He can't really can he, I mean, he's got to be on his best behaviour tonight, hasn't he?"

"Yes, but there's always tomorrow. Anyway I don't care. It's the best thing that's happened to me since I left Montréal," and with the dance then ending and the second lieutenant politely returning her to her table she gave his hand a little squeeze and said, "I enjoyed it enormously."

"You certainly made his day," said Colonel Tim laughingly.

"He's a really nice boy," she said.

Tim smiled to himself. Martin was probably two years older than Rose, and here was Rose saying 'he's a nice boy', I think she's the most charming person I've ever met he was thinking, and then brought himself up sharp. She's not for you; she already belongs to someone else. It was a sobering thought.

At the end of the evening the colonel accompanied them back home in the staff car, and readily agreed 'to come in and have a night cap', when Fred made the suggestion. Alec and Rebecca and Pat and Jim were already there, the men springing up when the colonel walked in. "Oh sit down and stop being so damned regimental," said the colonel, and sat himself between Pat and Rebecca.

"Sandwich anybody?" called Ruth.

"I'd love one," said Colonel Tim. "It's a long time since dinner," and then as an afterthought, "that's if the rations will run to it of course."

It was nearly two o'clock in the morning before they broke up,

Alec having to make the journey to Mountfield, whilst Pat was staying overnight at Chandlers Lodge. When the colonel took Ruth's hand to say his goodbyes she said, "You're always welcome here if you want a break from camp life. Would you care to come to Sunday lunch perhaps one day soon?"

"I would like that very much Mrs Chandler," said Colonel Tim.

"We'll arrange it," said Ruth and kissed him lightly on the cheek.

Rose too then kissed him on the cheek and said, "Yes, we'll arrange it, and thank you for a really memorable evening."

As Alec said to Jim later, "Lord knows what being kissed twice in succession is going to do to his blood pressure. Pity we can't tell anyone. If he found out he'd know straight away it was one of us."

The following Tuesday Ruth had arranged to meet Pat and have lunch together at the Angel. As she approached Country Style she was surprised to bump into the brigadier's wife.

"Hello Mrs Chandler are you out shopping?"

"No, I'm just collecting Pat from her boutique and we're going to lunch at the Angel. You wouldn't care to join us I suppose?"

"Yes, I'd like to very much if I may. The brigadier is picking me up there at four o'clock."

They both went into the boutique and were greeted by Pat.

Lady Agatha looking around said, "I think that I shall have to come back here after lunch, you really do have some lovely clothes here. Clothing rations will be under way soon I'm sure, so it would be a good idea to get a few things to carry me over."

They went off to the Angel where they were warmly welcomed by the owner John Tarrant who met them by chance at the entrance to the restaurant.

"Ruth," he said jokingly, "Fred told me at Rotary yesterday that you were coming and to save the bill for him, so I suggest you have a couple of bottles of champagne, oysters, then boeuf bourguignon, followed by crepes suzettes, and if that doesn't take the smile off his face nothing will!"

"It would be the way to a speedy divorce I fancy," said Ruth as they were shepherded to their table.

"Well, enjoy your meal, whatever you have," was the reply from John as he told the headwaiter to 'take good care of these ladies'.

The menus having been presented, Ruth said to Lady Agatha, "Now Lady Agatha, what can we tempt you to – and it really is on Fred – he told me before he went off to the factory this morning to charge it to him."

"First of all we can forget all this Lady business. I rarely use it. You see, my father was a Duke, so I'm a Lady, bit daft really. He in fact, as is well known after my mother died, drank and womanised all his wealth away and when he died left my poor brother to try and salvage what was left, which wasn't very much. I, of course, was married to Michael while all this was going on and as his family was well-to-do, I was cushioned. Being in the guards I might add you damned well needed to be. Then in the 1930 crash his father lost more or less everything so Michael got transferred to India for five years and we've had to live on his pay ever since. So I may be a Lady my dears, but a blooming plutocrat I am not!"

She said this with such amusing gusto that Ruth and Pat sat enthralled. Her openness and total lack of side so impressed Ruth that she took her hand laying on the table and said, "The brigadier's a lucky man."

The meal passed speedily and pleasantly except for the fact that at times underlying fear surfaced in all their minds that their husbands or sons could soon be involved in a real fighting war. It seemed so impossible that while they were sitting here being pampered and taken care of their menfolk were preparing and planning to kill other men whose womenfolk were doubtless, at the same moment, thinking the same thoughts as these three ladies in the cosy seclusion of the dining room of the Angel. That was the pattern of life at the moment for the families at home. Apart from rationing and the blackout life was almost as normal as it had ever been except that husbands and sons were starting to be called up and many others were volunteering so as to get into the unit of their choice. Those that thought about it guessed it was the calm before the storm it would eventually be to both civilians and serving personnel in countries throughout the world, and that life would never be the same again.

On that same Tuesday David and Jeremy, having asked their platoon commander for an interview with Major Grant their company commander, were paraded by CSM Ward and company orders.

"Left right, left right, halt. Right turn – salute the officer. Corporals Cartwright and Chandler sir."

"Stand at ease. Now, I can guess what this is about," said Major Grant, and looking at David, "You kick off."

"Well sir, Corporal Cartwright and I would like to apply to go to an officer's training unit to get a commission."

"I see. And if you were successful to which regiment would you consider giving the benefit of the talents you obviously consider you have?"

Jeremy answered, "Well sir, we'd like to get back in to the City Rifles if it were possible, but if not we would go into the Hampshires. Both our fathers were in the Hampshires."

"Do you think they'd be any good Sergeant Major," with a smile.

Instead of a jocular reply, to his astonishment Sergeant Major Ward came back immediately, seriously and with some vehemence with, "I think they're exactly the sort we're looking for sir."

"Well no half measures there I must say. Right now, I don't decide these things. You'll have to go on CO's orders tomorrow morning so get yourselves in number one order. I shall be there. As you know the CO is away so Major Scott-Calder will be taking the parade. March them out Sergeant Major."

As they walked back to the barrack-room to get changed David said, "Well, that's the first hurdle over."

"Old Wardie came up trumps didn't he."

"Yes, I think the Major was a little taken aback with his being so definite."

"I reckon we must be better soldiers than we've given ourselves credit for, for him to say that," said Jeremy. "Now if it had been the RSM we might have expected it seeing as how he fancies you so much."

David turned and started pummelling Jeremy, neither of them noticing the approach of Lieutenant Austen, their platoon commander until a well modulated voice said, "And is this how two potential cadets get their morning exercise?"

The two spun around and saluted. "We've got a long way to go yet sir," said David. "We've got to see the CO in the morning and then there'll be the selection board if we get past him."

"I was just explaining to Corporal Chandler sir that if Major Scott-Calder calls for an opinion from the RSM we'll be OK, as it's well known that the RSM fancies him, and he can't make fish off one and fowl off the other can he? So we'll both be home and dry."

Lieutenant Austen grinned amiably. "Are you coming back into the regiment?"

"We're going to try sir, if there's room for us."

"Well, if you want my opinion they'll be bloody mad at the depot if they don't make room for both of you," and with that he walked on, acknowledging their salutes with a wave of his cane to his cap.

After he'd gone out of earshot Jeremy said, "All this praise is going to my head. Do you think we should apply to become at least majors straight away and to hell with being second lieutenants?"

The next morning the RSM marched them into Major Scott-Calder where they again repeated the request they had made to Major Grant. After some questioning Major Scott-Calder told the RSM to march them out and to wait outside. The RSM duly carried out this manoeuvre, telling them to wait until they were recalled.

"What do you think Norman?" said the acting CO to Major Grant.

"No hesitation in recommending them," said the major.

"You've seen a lot of them on regimental duties Mr Harding," said Major Scott-Calder to the RSM. "What do you think?"

"They're the best two prospects we've got in the battalion I'd say," said the RSM. "I've heard a lot about their behind the scenes activities in the barrack-room, helping the awkward squads etc, and do you know they've got three men in their platoon who can't read or write and they write their letters home each week and read the replies for them."

"How do you find out all these things Mr Harding?" said Major Grant. "I didn't know that and they're under my nose you might say."

"Well sir," said the RSM, "you're not doing your job as RSM unless you know everything that's going on in the barrack-rooms. The Gestapo could learn a few things if they sent some people over to an RSM's cadre I can tell you. I reckon Himmler would pay me a fortune if he got the chance." The officers laughed – it wasn't often the RSM resorted to jocularity.

"Then we're unanimous are we?" said Major Scott-Calder. "I wanted your views first. I've known both these lads and their families for ten years now so I have to be extra careful about making a recommendation. However, since we're all of the opinion they'll make good officers we'll send them to the selection board and see what happens. Bring them back in Sergeant Major."

Five minutes later the friends were on the way back to their hut again having been told their names would go forward, but it would be a couple of months before they would go off to Winchester for the selection board. "It's going to seem an age," said David.

March came in and stayed as wintry as February had been. Part of each week was now devoted to building defence positions and putting up barbed wire entanglements on the east coast, and around pillbox emplacements being built inland from the coast. It was hard, cold, difficult work with the barbs from the dannert coils of wire constantly sticking into the hands and sometimes other parts of the body. The ground was frozen making it difficult to drive in the metal stakes that held the wire, and never was the sight of the barrack-room more welcome than when the lorry loads of cold hungry men debussed after a long day in the icy cold and windy sand dunes.

"Makes you wonder what it would be like living out in the trenches in weather like this doesn't it?" said Jeremy.

"Perhaps we'll find out one of these days," replied David. "Although quite frankly it's an experience I could readily forego."

On the first evening of March, Britons received their first introduction to a person who almost became part of their lives for five years. He was christened 'Lord Haw-Haw' and he was a one-man propaganda instrument for Dr Goebbels. Broadcasting every evening his 'Germany calling, Germany calling' nasal tones came over the airwaves bringing visions of defeat for the British people, glorifying the fight of the Aryan peoples over the evil of international Jewry and the communist menace from the east, and encouraging the British to persuade their government to seek a peace with the German people and join with them against their common enemies. There were people gullible enough to believe him, particularly in his vitriolic attacks on the Soviet Union, but in the main for most of the war they listened in order to get a balanced view of exactly what any given situation really was, the general idea being that if you believed half of what he said and half of what our own Ministry of Information put out, you would probably be somewhere near the truth! The problem was, as always, which half from either source to choose!

The month dragged on. On the 21st March the two corporals were told their seven-day leave was to start on the Friday after Easter, which with Easter Sunday being the 24th would be on the 29th. Back at Sandbury there was great excitement at this news. Rose phoned Rita and Buffy and it was arranged they would come up to The Hollies again on the 27th and stay with Moira and Jack and that there would be a party at Chandlers Lodge on Saturday 30th, after which Rose and Jeremy would go back to Romsey with them for the rest of the leave.

Also on the 21st March, as they all went about their various tasks, not in their wildest dreams could they have imagined what was taking place in a heavily guarded room at the Ministry of Supply in London, an event which was to shape the destiny of hundreds of millions of people all over the world for all time. The Chief Government Scientific Officer, Sir Henry Tizzard was chairing a meeting of a very small handful of top people from the War Office, the cabinet and his own colleagues. The cabinet was represented by the Minister for War and an assistant Mrs Moira Hooper, the War Office by the CIGS and senior colleagues from all three services, and in addition there were three scientists from the Ministry of Supply. They had been assembled to hear two scientists Otto Frisch and Rudolf Peierls present a paper to them, a moment in history as significant as 1066, the Russian Revolution or the discovery of America. They commenced by explaining how conventional bombs were made, carried and exploded and then went on to state in calm measured undramatic tones how they had discovered a way to produce an atomic super bomb working through nuclear chain reaction. They explained how one bomb would have the power of thousands of tons of TNT. They talked in terms of astronomical degrees centigrade. They talked in terms of one bomb obliterating a city the size of Glasgow, and all it would need would be a few pounds weight of uranium isotope. In what Moira much later described as the longest morning of her life, they discussed what needed to be done to develop this monstrous weapon, who else would need to be told about it, in fact who else already knew of the possible existence of such a weapon. Following on from that, the dreaded thought, had the Germans yet discovered it and were preparing to use it on the United Kingdom? One of the strangest comments from an RAF air marshall was, 'but you couldn't drop one of those on white people'.

Moira was horrified at all she had heard, but being a true professional maintained her normal outward calm. They broke up for a sandwich lunch taken in the conference room during which her minister, looking very tense, asked her what her views were so far. "All I can say minister is that we have got to get it first."

"Exactly my thoughts," he said. "Imagine Hitler or Stalin with it – God it doesn't bear thinking about."

After an afternoon of further discussion it was agreed that Sir Henry would see the prime pinister that evening with a recommendation to proceed with the development of the bomb. It would then be up to the PM and his advisers to decide where, how and with whom the device would be perfected, and how speedily the final result of a usable weapon could be used to end the war. But, these things do not, cannot, happen in five minutes, and as history shows it was to be five long years before its existence was made known to the world in such an horrific fashion. What history does not show is the strain that the few people who did know of its existence and were closely connected to its development in those five years suffered in knowing that we could be, say, just two weeks behind the development of a similar device by the Nazi or Soviet scientists and facing Armageddon.

When the meeting was closed Moira, who had intended staying in town that evening working on another project through Good Friday, hurriedly phoned Jack who was spending that day at his office. She was lucky to catch him as he was leaving and asked him if he would wait at Victoria for her – she was coming home that night after all. She was very quiet on the journey home and sat holding his arm tightly, which was unusual. Jack said nothing. Although he knew little of her work she was at times more tense than at others and he took it for granted this was caused by the responsibilities she shouldered. They had a light supper, Jack because he had eaten a city lunch and Moira because she 'felt a bit picksome' as she put it. They had an early night, having first crept in to see little John, now over two and a half years old, and when they had been in bed a little while Moira suddenly turned and held Jack with such intensity and sobbed and sobbed.

"Darling, what's the matter, what has happened?" said Jack, seriously concerned. "Is there anything I can do? Can you tell me all about it?"

After a while she calmed sufficiently to be able to say, "I can't tell you about it, that's the problem, but I feel better now, I couldn't have stayed in London on my own."

Normally Jack would have made a joke out of that remark with the rejoinder, "How do I know you'd be on your own?" or something similar, but tonight he just held her tight and said, "Well, whatever it is my love I don't envy you knowing about it for it to upset you like that. But answer me one thing, you're not in any kind of personal trouble of any sort?"

"Oh, no, no it's nothing like that, it's just that I'm involved and will continue to be for a long time."

Jack said no more except, "I think you're very brave." He didn't understand and wouldn't do until several years passed. All sorts of things went through his mind – perhaps they're going to use poison gas again, perhaps they've found a new type of gas, or a means of spreading bubonic plague. On second thoughts that wouldn't be too practical. Still searching his brain for an answer he realised that Moira had gone to sleep in his arms, and although he was far from comfortable he lay still for an hour or more before he gently extricated himself and settled down for the night.

Chapter Thirty-seven

Easter passed quickly at the camp. Half the battalion was on leave, but even so neither David nor Jeremy found themselves on duty. They wandered into Colchester on Saturday, went to a film in the afternoon and then splashed out on dinner at the George in the evening before getting the ten o'clock truck back to the camp. From Good Friday morning until Tuesday morning after Easter they didn't have to make their beds up for inspection as was normally the case, so they were able to lounge around in a certain degree of comfort.

Back at Sandbury, Jack quietly got out of bed at eight o'clock on Good Friday morning and, after washing and shaving, went downstairs in his dressing gown to see Nanny giving little John his breakfast. "I don't want Mrs Hooper disturbed," he said, "She's not had a very good night. So can you take this little monster out to see the ducks or something for an hour so that he doesn't wake her up." He smiled at the sturdy little lad eating up his shredded wheat like his daddy and David had before him.

"Will I see Pat?" he asked his daddy. He loved Pat and delighted in going in to see her at the bungalow, mainly Pat confessed because he adored Susie, who in turn let him carry her around in all sorts of ungainly and uncomfortable looking ways without once seeming to take exception to the indignities he appeared to be inflicting upon her. One day Pat thought he was quiet and went in to the lounge to see what he was up to and found the cat stretched out in a cardboard box that had been used to bring some logs in from outside. To make Susie more comfortable John had raided the settee and armchairs for all the loose chair backs, and there was the silly cat lying in three or four of these and being covered up by the remainder, which John was carefully tucking in all around her.

"Pat is coming for the weekend after work tomorrow," said Jack; "I expect she will take you to see Susie when she goes back home to feed her." John clapped his hands, forgetting he was holding a spoonful of shredded wheat which was promptly splattered all over the AGA, which much to the amusement of Jack quickly followed by laughter from John once he knew he was not going to be told off for doing it.

At nine o'clock Jack prepared some buttered toast, a little pot of marmalade and a pot of tea and took it up to Moira. She had already awakened and was enjoying the rare luxury of being able to lie in bed knowing she didn't have to move until she decided to do so. "You are kind," she said and sat up to drink her first cup of tea, which he poured for her, and then to eat the toast that he uncovered for her. While she was eating the toast he poured another cup of tea and then returned to his side of the bed, slipped off his dressing gown and then got back into the bed again, lying on his side watching her slowly and leisurely eat her breakfast. When he felt his hands had warmed sufficiently he began to stroke her thigh. She stopped nibbling her toast and looked at him "Jack Hooper," she said, "I hope you're not up to what I think you're up to."

"I couldn't begin to imagine what it is you have in your mind as to what I could possibly be up to?" he replied, transferring his caress to the other thigh. She continued with her toast.

"If you were up to what I think you're up to I would remind you that a little monster named John could at any moment burst in here and throw himself on to one or the other of us."

He continued with his caresses. "Like all good generals I have planned a diversion to ensure that the main action succeeds, Nanny has taken John to see the ducks. Secondly I have bolstered my defences by ensuring that the door is locked."

"But you are not a good general nor ever have been."

"True, but now I'm going to prove to you that I could have been and should have been," and he did.

At ten minutes to ten a drowsy, pleasantly fulfilled voice whispered into his ear, "Darling, didn't you have a meeting with Fred and the others at ten o'clock?"

He rolled over and looked at the clock. "Ten to ten – good God," he exclaimed. "If we pretend your husband has just opened the garden gate and I've got to scarper quick, as they say, will you forgive me?"

"He's always very slow putting his bike away and so on," she said, "so give me a nice long kiss and then I'll forgive you."

Jack scrambled into his clothes, went down the stairs two at a time and jumped into the Jaguar. It spluttered a couple of times and then the battery refused to turn the engine. Swearing volubly he jumped out and got the starting handle from the boot, but still it wouldn't start. By now it was 10.15, Nanny's bicycle stood against the garage wall. "Any port in a storm," Jack said out loud and wheeled the machine out on to the driveway. It was an incongruous figure that rode into Sandbury Engineering, this very large man over six feet tall perched on a bicycle designed for a lady not much over five feet in height, his knees sticking out so as not to foul the handlebars, and pedalling in low gear because he couldn't quite see how to change up into a higher one.

Fred, Reg Church and Ernie Bolton roared with laughter at the spectacle and as Jack burst in full of apologies Fred said, "We thought perhaps Moira had laid on your shirt tail."

Jack grinned and said, "In fact dear old sports, that isn't I'm pleased to say, far from the truth."

"Well you might have done your flies up," said Fred. Jack swiftly looked down, but of course they were done up, and through the laughter that his guilty look had engendered he said, "Right Fred Chandler – that's one I owe you." They got on with the meeting.

"Sorry to call you on Good Friday," said Fred, "but we've landed, I should say as a result of the hard work and late hours put in by Ernie here, we've landed another large government contract for modifying vehicles as mobile workshops. In the first instance it's for work which will take eighteen months and, depending on the war situation then, more to follow."

"So the men from the ministry have at least realised the war is going to last more than the six months they first gave it," said Jack.

"It certainly looks like it," replied Fred, "but we obviously have to finance it – any problems Reg? These ministry people are very slow in paying."

"I haven't seen the build up figures," said Reg, "but knowing Ernie as well as we do I think we can take them for granted. As you know, we have to work to set margins with the government, so the only way we can make more is to be more efficient than we calculated for in our original estimates. Any way we can do that Ernie?"

"I've thought of that," said Ernie. "I wondered if we could run a split shift system using largely female labour, and provide a crèche here for the middle shift women with young children. We could run 6-10am and then 10-4pm and then say 4-10pm rotating the early and late shifts each week. I think there might be quite a few people locally and in the surrounding villages who could fit into such an arrangement, and it would leave room for a male night shift at a later date if we found it necessary."

The discussion ran on for an hour and it was finally decided that Ernie should get his scheme organised for starting the first week in May, which would require a certain amount of readjustment in the workshop area to accommodate the new line.

"Thank God we've got good parking space for the vehicles being delivered," said Fred, "they're coming in twenty at a time so we need space for forty at all times."

The meeting having ended Fred said, "Right, lets lock up for the weekend. I don't know about you lot but I could do with a couple of days off. These fourteen hour days are beginning to prove that I'm not twenty-one any more."

"I bet he was a right tearaway when he was twenty-one – don't you Reg?" said Jack.

"Well, I've heard one or two tales in that respect," said Reg. "I spoke to Buffy Cartwright a couple of times – very interesting it was too."

Ernie stood grinning at this repartee. "I think I'd better get off before I hear things I shouldn't hear," he said.

"Yes, you get away," said Fred, "you don't want to listen to their fairy stories – not that I ever had anything to do with fairies I might add."

After Ernie had gone Reg said, "You could do worse than make Ernie a director of the company you know. It would give him a lot of clout when he's dealing with these ministry wallahs, they're so status conscious."

"Put it on the agenda for the next board meeting," said Fred, looking at Jack for agreement, who was nodding vigorously.

"Right then, lets load this velocipede of yours into the Humber and get you back home," said Fred. "See you later Reg."

Fred dropped Jack at the Hollies and as he pulled up at the front door Moira came out, followed by John at a gallop running full tilt at Fred to be picked up and whirled around before being held up in Fred's arms and asked, "What have you been up to today?" There followed an animated account of the visit to the ducks and throwing them bread, and about a big swan that came along and charged in among the ducks and Nanny tried to shoo it away so that the ducks got the bread and it wouldn't go, and Nanny was afraid the swan was going to come and peck them but it didn't and then it went away and they fed the ducks some more until they ran out of bread.

"By Jove," said Fred, "he's got a good pair of lungs – he didn't take one breath during the whole of that story." The others laughed.

"Well I must get home to Auntie Ruth," said Fred. "It wouldn't do for two of us to be late in one morning, no matter what the reason was, would it John?"

John was a bit puzzled by the question, Jack laughed, Moira blushed and Fred put John down and walked round to get into the car. "See you later," he said as he drove away grinning.

They had a quiet Easter, but intended to make up for it the following weekend when the 'boys' were home. The party was to include not only Jack and Moira and Rita and Buffy but in addition Megan and the immediate family, Anni and her father and Ernie would be coming, and Alec was bringing Rebecca. Ruth met Lady Agatha again in the town and asked if she and the brigadier would like to come and suggested they might ask Tim McEwan. "By all means do," she said, " we'd love to come and I'm sure now Tim knows you so well he would too. He's a very reserved sort of chap, but I like him enormously."

The invitation sent and accepted, and Jack asking if Sir Freddie and Kate could be included, it looked to be a goodly crowd. Talking of it over the holiday Fred said to Ruth, "Who would have thought a few years ago that we would be hobnobbing with Germans and colonels and Lady this and Lady that, we're certainly moving in high circles these days."

Ruth had answered in her usual pragmatic down to earth fashion by saying, "Well it's all happened by accident really and they are all such nice genuine people. They wouldn't get past the door if they weren't I can tell you."

"I tell you this my love, not one of them is nicer or more genuine than you are, and that's a fact."

"Oh yes, what do you want to borrow?" she said.

"You'll never guess," he said, making a grab at her.

"Fred Chandler, you're too old for that sort of malarkey."

"When I'm too old you can put me in the box and screw the lid down," he replied.

"I'll remind you of that one day."

The weekend passed and the days dragged on for both the folk at Sandbury and the soldiers at Colchester waiting for Friday to come. Rose and Pat made surreptitious appointments at the hairdressers for Friday morning and arrived together, much to each other's amusement. In the meantime Rita and Buffy arrived laden with all manner of goodies.

"Saved my petrol for this trip," boomed Buffy, "Have to drive myself now. Thompson's got a war job at Chandlers Ford and earning three times what I paid him. Still good luck to him I say."

On the Friday Rose and Pat, after visiting the hairdresser, had a snack together prior to going to the station. Buffy had arranged to wait outside while the young people greeted each other and then run them home, Fred unfortunately being tied up with some ministry people at the factory. The saying hello seemed to take an awful long time to the impatient Buffy waiting outside who was eager to see Jeremy to a far greater degree than he would have let on to anybody, even Rita. Eventually they emerged from the station and made the short journey back to Chandlers Lodge. That evening Jack had proposed that they all go to the Angel for dinner. Ruth was secretly pleased at this arrangement as it meant she could leave her kitchen all laid out with masses of goodies she was getting ready for Saturday night. Jack's point that it would be slavery for her to have two big meals to get in succession she said was most thoughtful, so the Angel it was. Nanny had had the time off Easter Monday until Thursday so she was able to look after John and the twins. Megan was very much looking forward to the evening out, she so rarely got out these days although it has to be said she received frequent invitations from the young, and the not so young, medical staff at the hospital, all of which she politely refused.

Buffy dropped Rose and Jeremy off, and when David had said hello and had a few words with his mother, took him and Pat on to the bungalow. "I'll pick you up at six thirty," he called as he left them on their front doorstep. When the door closed behind them David held Pat close and said "Now I can really tell you how much I miss you," only to be interrupted by a large tortoise shell cat vainly trying to climb up his leg and purring its head off. David bent down and picked her up, claws opening and closing, pushing her nose into the folds of his battle dress and making so much noise that David said, "Heh, people will think the air raid warning's going." They walked on into the sitting room, he still cradling the cat and Pat with her arms still around him so they had difficulty in getting through the door together.

After a short while Pat said, "Is there anything you want?"

He looked at her and said, "That's a dangerous question to ask a soldier newly home from the wars. Do you know the wife of the Duke of Wellington wrote in her diary 'the Duke returned from the wars today and pleasured me twice with his boots on'?"

"You have not returned from the wars."

"Now you don't know that," he replied, gently putting Susie down on an armchair. "For all you know I might have been on a terribly dangerous secret mission over the past few days that I can't tell you about."

"Do you mean like going to the pictures in Colchester?" she said, sliding her arms back around his waist.

"Well that can be dangerous if there's a gang from the Essex Regiment there."

"In that case we'd better not waste the hot water bottles I left in this morning had we? But take your boots off first – please."

"You're a brazen hussy," and then he continued. "You know this business with the Duke of Wellington – he wore spurs – must have made an awful mess of the bedclothes I would have thought."

They had a very pleasant evening at the Angel. John Tarrant had pulled out all the stops within the limits of the rationing situation and, although he was husbanding his wine stocks, he brought out some claret he had set aside which was greatly appreciated, particularly by Buffy and Jack. David and Rose made a particular fuss of Megan, she being seated between them. During the evening Jeremy found himself alone with David for a few moments. "Your mum's a real gem isn't she," he said.

"You only just found that out? Anyway what makes you suddenly

351

realise it?"

"Well after you left with my father she turned to us and said 'well you two, I've got a lot to do in the kitchen, so you'd better have a rest and we'll see you down here at six thirty'. I was so taken aback, I'd been sweating on how I could whisk Rose away without it appearing too obvious and she just organised it for me. I mumbled a few words like I am a bit weary after the journey or something equally stupid and she disappeared. Don't you think that was marvellous?"

"Well you see, my Mum has been married to my Dad for over thirty years, and he's nearly as randy as you are, so she knows the score." For this statement David got a thump in the ribs he hadn't expected.

They were all looking forward to the party the next day. Pat felt she had to go into the shop it being Saturday, the rest of the week Mrs Draper was going to cope on her own. David caught the bus in at lunchtime and they had a quick snack in the bar at the Angel. As they were leaving David was thrilled to bump into George and Bessie Turner who he hadn't seen for eighteen months or more. "My goodness," said Bessie "doesn't he look smart – and look at the way he's grown."

Pat excused herself saying she had to get back to the shop so that her other lady could go to lunch, so David went back into the Angel to catch up on the news from Mountfield. Sir Oliver Routledge, who owned the farm, had had electricity laid on just before the outbreak of war, as a result they not only now had electric light in the cowsheds but also in the cottage, which was a tremendous boon – "saves all the dripping candle grease on the stairs," George said. In addition Sir Oliver had built a milking parlour, all the equipment purchased from Sandbury Engineering, which was now going well. "You'd never believe the work and backache that saves over the old method," said George, "although I must admit we had a lot of trouble in getting the cows to understand what was going on."

"How's the bull?" said David.

"He's still as mean as ever," laughed George. "I might tell you that if this artificial insemination lark really catches on I shall be more than pleased to say goodbye to the nasty brute, though I can't say the cows are going to be so pleased!"

Bessie chimed in, "George, don't be so rude." They all laughed. Bessie continued, "We hear Rebecca is quite taken with one of your Canadian officers David, is he a nice chap?"

"He's one of the best," said David, and then gave a hilarious account of the leg pulling Alec had received after Rose and Jeremy had bumped into his colonel.

The time passed quickly until George looked at the bar clock.

"Look old son, I've got to push off, time and milking cows wait for no man. So you take care of yourself, there aren't many around like you," and with a firm handshake from George and a firm kiss from Bessie, they raced off to catch the two o'clock bus back to Mountfield.

David wandered around Sandbury until four o'clock and then went into the boutique. "Thought I might as well scrounge a cup of tea here as buy one," he said to Mrs Draper, seeing that Pat was serving a customer.

"I'll make one straight away," she said bustling into the spotless little kitchen at the rear of the showroom. David followed her.

"How's trade?" he said.

"Quite good," said Mrs Draper. "We could sell a lot more if we could get what we want. People are earning good money and are spending it – ask any of the publicans in the town."

They sat chatting for a few minutes until Pat came back to them having made her sale and wrapped it for the customer.

"It's nearly half past four," said Mrs Draper. "You push off now, I can finish off and bank up, and I'll see you next Saturday if I don't bump in to you before then in town. Have a lovely leave the pair of you, and the best of luck David if I don't see you before you go back – Pat tells me you're going for your commission – you'll walk it I'm sure."

"I wish I had your confidence," replied David, "but thanks all the same."

He shook hands, Pat got her coat and handbag and they went off arm in arm, with the serious face of Mrs Draper looming after them, saying to herself, "Oh my God, I hope nothing terrible happens to him."

Without his knowing it, the same thought was echoed by his mother later in the evening. The party was going with a swing when she found herself on the edge of the room looking to where David and Jeremy were laughing in a huddle with Pat and Rose. The same thought went through her mind and left her face looking strained and pensive for a few moments. 'Oh my God,' she thought, 'I hope nothing terrible happens to spoil their lives'. She was interrupted in her thoughts by Colonel Tim.

"Anything you can share with me Mrs Chandler?" he said.

She turned to him. "Was it as obvious as that?" she answered. When he did not reply but took her elbow in a firm grip she said, "I was just thinking how terrible it would be if anything happened to the two boys. Now I realise how selfish that was when you and Alec and Jim are all going to have to face similar dangers when the war really does start." Colonel Tim turned and looked at the foursome.

"It's people like you and the girls who have to carry the main burden," he said, "but in all truth I can see no way out of it. This is going to be a long hard fight, but of all the wars that have ever been engaged in I firmly believe this is the most just. The evil of Nazism is so great that even yet the majority of people cannot begin to comprehend it." He was still gripping her arm and his face was deadly serious. He stopped speaking. "I'm sorry Mrs Chandler, I suddenly put my preacher's hat on," and the smile he gave her altered his face completely and gained a similar reaction from Ruth.

"First of all, please call me Ruth. Secondly you so rarely speak about yourself – do you have a family?"

"My mother, father and sister – that's all," said Tim. "I've never married. Too shy when I was young, and now too old for anyone to want me."

"Now that can't be so. You've met the General over there. He and Lady Kate were only married a few months ago and neither had been married before."

"Well, when we get this job over maybe I'll look seriously. I tell you something for your ears alone, if anyone like you was to come along I wouldn't hesitate."

"Now you're getting as bad as Alec – I'm old enough to be your mother, but thanks for the compliment anyway," and then they were both laughing as Fred joined them breaking off from his seemingly endless task of doing the rounds topping up empty glasses.

"The brigadier's having quite a talk with Anni's father," said Fred, "they seem to be getting on famously."

"So does Alec with Anni's sister-in-law," said Ruth with a laugh.

"By the way did you hear how Alec got his feet under the table?" she said turning to Tim.

"Jeremy told us about it originally," said Tim, "but of course since then he's been ribbed mercilessly in the mess. I must say he does seem genuinely keen on her and she is a most charming girl. What do her parents think about it all?"

"Well, Ernie, her brother, tells us that they have really taken to Alec. Rebecca is a very intelligent and sensible girl. She is obviously very fond of him but they both have sufficient sense to know that there is a war on as far as I can tell from the snippets Alec lets drop to me occasionally. They are going to remain 'loving friends' being the best way I can describe it. Anyway, as I see it, they are both well over twenty-one and you only live once."

"Mrs Chandler, what are you suggesting?"

"I'm just saying they are two lovely people who should find what happiness they can while they still have the chance."

"You're a very nice lady Ruth," said Tim. "Now who else can we talk about? What are Jeremy's parents like?" and so these two talked on, as did other couples in other parts of the room as one does at parties. Again David and Fred rolled the carpet back and the gramophone was put into service. At the third dance Tim went over to Rose, who was on her own for a short while as Jeremy danced with Megan. "Shall we show them how to do it?" he said. It was a slow foxtrot, which he performed extremely well.

"You've been leading us on," said Rose.

"What do you mean?" replied Tim.

"You don't learn to foxtrot like this at the school of Canadian Infantry."

"My sister was a keen dancer, so she used to drag me along with her when we were in our teens. I've never forgotten it, but I must confess that I haven't ever enjoyed it as much as I have with you at the mess, and now here."

"Colonel McEwan, you are flirting with me."

"No, not really, just being honest and saying a bit too much because I've had one or two of your father's noxious brews!"

Rose gave a tinkling laugh. The dance ended and he took her back to Jeremy, but he remembered her closeness, her beauty and the warmth of her personality continually for a long time afterwards. He had never been in love before, now he knew he was, and he knew it was hopeless. Nevertheless he was not, strangely enough, terminally depressed about it. He knew he could only love from a distance and yet being able to do that instead of it's being the end of the world, gave him a happiness he had not experienced before. He analysed his feelings over and over again when he was alone and always came to the same conclusion. "It sounds trite," he said to himself, "but the fact that I have met her, known her and know that she likes me as a friend, which she apparently does, is more joy than millions of other people ever experience." The final satisfaction he enjoyed was that no one, not even Rose herself, ever suspected the feelings he held, and as far as he was concerned no one ever would. Over breakfast on Sunday morning those at Chandlers Lodge held an inquest on the party and came to the conclusion it was an unqualified success.

Alec said, "Do you know the General was speaking to me like a long lost brother, I didn't realise Generals were even human until now."

Rose chimed in and said, "Since you were gazing constantly into Rebecca's eyes all the evening I don't see how you had the time to talk to anyone else."

"Will you control your wife please Jeremy," retorted Alec.

"The point is," said Jeremy, "Jim and I were just saying more or less the same thing. Mind you to be fair if we were in your shoes we'd probably have been doing the same. Incidentally, have you set the date yet? David and I would both like to be there of course."

"Now don't you push your luck young Jeremy. I still haven't forgotten the episode at the Ritz, though I suspect the prime mover in that instance was probably that utterly delightful mischief making wife of yours."

Ruth and Fred sat back listening to all the chaff – it was like the old days with Harry and Megan and Jack and David around the table. Jim joined in, "I've told him about the Bolton's twelve bore under the stairs, but even that hasn't put him off. The only thing I can suggest is I see Colonel McEwan and get him posted to Scotland or somewhere, perhaps that will bring him down to earth."

"The battalion would fall to bits without me there," said Alec.

"Talking of the Colonel," said Jeremy, "he strikes me as being quite a nice chap."

Alec and Jim looked at each other. Jim answered the pronouncement with, "The Colonel is a professional. He's as hard as nails, no one in the battalion can ever put one over on him but he's always fair. It's good for all the men to know they've a chap of his calibre at the head of things. He could have gone on to staff college and got some red tabs if he'd wanted to but he wanted to stay with the battalion and when it came overseas he was chosen over the heads of a couple of more senior people to command it. In our opinion they did the right thing."

Ruth continued the conversation with, "I felt that underneath that professional soldier appearance he is in fact quite a sensitive man who is very much aware of the responsibility he holds for the lives of you all." Both Jim and Fred agreed on this point and there was silence for a few moments.

"Well," said Alec, "I'm field officer of the day today so I'd better be off and put in an appearance to let them know I'm still alive. See you lunchtime." And with that he bustled off. Rose and Jeremy went up to finish their packing for the stay of the remainder of their leave to Romsey. Jim and Fred wandered off to the sitting room to read the Sunday papers and Megan said she'd better go and get the twins from Nanny before they drove everyone at the Hollies mad, but she'd help Ruth with the washing up first. As they swiftly dealt with the breakfast cutlery and crockery inevitable the subject came up of "I wonder what Harry is doing now?" It was a fact that very little was going on at the front, but as far as those concerned with the distribution behind the lines there was always plenty to do. Feeding, equipping, arming and moving an expeditionary force the size of the BEF from ports two, three or four hundred miles away required tremendous skill and organisation and continual grinding hard work. It was a job so different to that of infantrymen in the front line suffering boredom and extreme discomfort day after day never knowing when all hell was going to break loose and he would find himself in the thick of it. Harry was on the short run this week, either Calais or Dunkirk, and standing in Calais docks that same Sunday morning he said to himself, "Only sixty miles or so as the crow flies and I could be having breakfast with them."

A very great deal would happen before he breakfasted with them again.

Chapter Thirty-eight

Their leave passed so quickly. With invitations to visit friends and relatives, shows to go to, families to be with, the two young couples each found it was their last night together. They had enjoyed so much the closeness and passion of their young love together and there was an unspoken sadness when the dreaded Friday morning came. Fred and Ruth took Pat and David to Sandbury station whilst Rita and Buffy did the same at Romsey, the two couples to meet at Liverpool Street and then the girls would come home together. On the train each couple sat closely together, arm in arm, not talking very much. Like all wartime trains they were crowded with service personnel, many having said goodbye to loved ones and others, more fortunate, soon to say hello. On David's train there was a crowd of Canadians going on leave to London who made as much noise as all the rest of the train passengers put together.

"They intend to enjoy themselves," said Pat.

"And jolly good luck to them," said David.

They met at Liverpool Street Station as arranged and, as they had over an hour before the Colchester train left, they went over the road to 'Dirty Dicks', the pub every soldier had to visit or he couldn't really say he'd seen London. Its sawdust floors, low beams, cobwebs and dead cat skeletons hanging from the ceilings were certainly a shade different to the Ritz as Rose put it. The atmosphere was noisy and ebullient and it was just the place to spend half an hour experiencing something probably unique in the world at a time when you could easily become sad and introspective.

"We'd better go now," said David to Jeremy.

They spent a few minutes in lingering farewell among dozens of others at the entrance to the platform, and then the girls stood arm in arm watching their two men walk down the train and then turn and wave before they boarded a compartment. The two girls turned towards the underground, neither of them speaking, but holding arms closely as they went down the stairs through the throng to buy their underground tickets. It was Victoria Station before they spoke to each other.

"We never really know when we're going to see them again do we?" said Rose. "Look at poor Megan, and I heard my Dad talking to the brigadier the other evening and asking where he thought the spring offensive would come. Apparently in the last war there was a spring offensive launched by both sides. I thought well, if there's going to be a spring offensive by either side it will be soon. After all it's April already."

"Well," said Pat, "perhaps they'll hear about their commissions when they get back. That will keep them here a few months training to be officers, so David said."

"Oh, I didn't think of that, oh I do hope so," said Rose, her spirits lifting a little.

Fred met them at Sandbury to their surprise. "I guessed you'd be in this one," he said, "so I thought I'd save you a taxi fare." Actually it was nothing of the sort, he had missed Rose during the days she'd been away and wanted to make sure she was alright. Pat stayed for a while and then went on to the Hollies where she was gong to stay over the weekend, with visits to a disconsolate Susie wondering where her David was and continually prowling around looking for him. The boys telephoned that evening to let the family know they had arrived safely and arranged to telephone again the following Friday.

On Saturday 6th April those not on duty after parades finished at twelve o'clock were beginning to get their boots and battle dresses into walking out order when the orderly corporals came round to each hut with the message that everyone was confined to camp. There was immediate vociferous moaning, no one it seemed knowing the cause of this. They went to dinner and as they were eating and moaning the battalion orderly sergeant walked in with Major Scott-Calder, acting commanding officer.

"Silence for the Commanding Officer," he roared.

The men started to get up from their benches at the tables.

"Stay seated men," and then after a pause, "As you have heard we have been confined to barracks. I can't tell you yet what the flap is all about because I don't know. I'm going to brigade headquarters at two o'clock to be briefed and I will tell your officers exactly what is happening when I return. In the meantime, overhaul your kit, and keep a note of deficiencies in case we need to remedy them. That's all. Stay seated." With that he went out. There was a buzz of conversation and all sorts of conjecture about what could be happening. The two main views were that either Jerry had attacked France or he was trying to invade the UK. If the latter then that would explain why they were on stand-to being as they were at one of the most likely invasion points, the beaches of the east coast.

They drifted back to their barrack rooms all talking animatedly. Sergeant Harris came into the room and bellowed, "Kit inspection two o'clock, weapon inspection two thirty – and it had better be perfect or I'll have your guts for garters. See to it you NCO's," this latter directed with a fierce look at David and Jeremy and two of the lance corporals standing together.

They each got checking on their respective sections, knowing the ones they could trust to be up to scratch, and chivvying the odd one or two who, if it were possible to having anything wrong, would undoubtedly have it wrong. The weapons they had few qualms about. It was said that a rifleman slept with his rifle to the exclusion of all others. It was kept to the peak of perfection. Riflemen treated their weapons like precision instruments. Unlike the guardsmen and ordinary infantrymen, the rifleman never banged his butt on the ground just to make a noise, that would be mistreatment of a high order. Banging the rifle about could and would easily misalign the sights only perhaps by a tiny fraction of an inch, but at four hundred yards when a rifleman wanted to make a kill with one shot, that tiny fraction of an inch could make the difference between a hit and a miss, and in the extreme, winning a battle or losing a battle.

At two o'clock sharp Sergeant Harris appeared with Lieutenant Austen. "Stand by your beds," he bellowed. The men stood to attention beside their bunks and were stood at ease by the officer. It was an easy inspection since, with the exception of one very 'holey' pair of socks displayed by one of the riflemen and a worn pull-through unearthed from another rifleman's rifle butt, the kit was in good order – always a good sign of an efficient team of NCO's. Mr Austen then told then to repack everything and he would be back during the afternoon as soon as he had had his briefing. By four o'clock he still hadn't returned so the men drifted off into the dining room again until about ten past.

Rifleman Piercey saw him through the window coming across the parade ground. He nipped into the sergeant's room, "Officer coming Sergeant."

"Right lad, thanks," and he put his belt on, did up his collar and put his cap on ready.

Having been called up to attention by Sergeant Harris and then told to stand at ease by Mr Austen, an expectant hush fell over the thirty odd riflemen.

"I've been told to inform you," he began, "that we are on stand-to at the moment to be ready to move tomorrow to Harwich Docks Transit Camp. The Germans are in the process of invading Norway and a British expeditionary Force is being assembled to be sent to Norway to oppose them immediately the troop carrier is available. I have to tell you all this is top secret. The telephones at the Naafi and officers and sergeants messes have been disconnected. No one will leave their immediate barrack-room area without the authority of the Platoon Sergeant. No one will leave the camp under any circumstances without the written permission of the Adjutant. Any questions?"

There was silence. Then David spoke up, "How will we use our transport and Bren gun carriers in a place like Norway?"

"We shall not be taking our transport. We shall not be operating as motorised infantry. We shall be operating in a normal infantry fashion at least to start with. The carriers however will go with us."

"Anything else? Right, fall them out Sergeant Harris."

There was general hubbub as Mr Austen left. "Norway" said rifleman Beasley, "who the bloody hell wants to go to Norway? It's all bloody hills and mountains isn't it? Who the bloody hell wants to carry sixty pounds of army rubbish up a bloody mountain?"

"The girls are very pretty," said Jeremy, "lovely blondes with long legs – just up your street I should think, and they all believe in free love."

"You kidding corp?"

"No, I'm deadly serious; you ask Corporal Chandler, he's an expert on these matters."

"Quite true, I'd certainly take a couple of French letters in your field dressing pocket, you never know when you might need them."

Rifleman Beasley was beginning to feel the prospect of visiting Norway much more to his liking.

The next day, Sunday, they were paraded at eleven o'clock in full marching order to get on the RASC wagons and debussed at Harwich Docks Transit Camp situated just outside the town. The next day they were still there. On Tuesday they were told the Germans had now marched unopposed into Denmark, but still they just waited around. The company commander got some PT going so as to break the day up a little but when you have over six hundred men cramped into a comparatively small area expressly forbidden to leave camp, it is extremely difficult to keep them occupied. An added problem was that as yet they had no maps and no indication as to exactly where they were heading. As David said, Norway has a very long coastline, with several major ports and dozens of smaller fishing ports, they could end up anywhere.

By Thursday they had been in the camp for four days and many were getting restless. It's bad enough to know you're going into action for the first time, but to have to face a voyage over the North Sea, and then a landing, possibly opposed, was not a pleasant thought, and waiting around in this godforsaken place day after day didn't improve the prospects one little bit. On Friday the moaners were having a field day until noon the bugler blew for the company commanders to go to battalion HQ. They were there only a very short time before they returned and had their respective companies paraded. Major Grant was tight lipped when the men had been drawn up and stood at ease.

"I have to tell you," he began, "that our part in the operation to Norway has been cancelled and that we shall be returning to Colchester to await the call of other duties. That is all. Fall them out Sergeant Major."

As they drifted away back to their huts David said, "He didn't look too pleased with life did he?"

"It is infuriating I suppose when you've got yourself ready to take your company into action and then you have the ignominy of having to crawl back into camp again. What do you think happened?"

"Well, it seems to me that while we've been sitting here on our arses waiting for transport, Jerry has sailed into the port we were suppose to occupy," David said. "It's what they call in staff circles I believe a GMFU, and there are no prizes for guessing what that stands for. To be honest I don't know whether I'm pleased or sorry. He who fights and runs away et cetera, except of course we didn't do any bloody fighting." Jeremy could tell David was angry, he rarely swore unless he was very upset. He continued, "It might prove to be a good thing in the long run, not going I mean. If something starts as a cock-up, it usually ends as a monumental cock-up." Little did David know how prophetic he was being.

Back at Sandbury Pat and Rose didn't get their usual Tuesday morning letter, which they looked forward to so much. The routine was that their respective husbands wrote to them on Sundays and the post corporal collected the mail first thing on Monday mornings. The cooperation between the army post office and the GPO was excellent, as a result the mail dropped on the mat at Sandbury as regular as clockwork on Tuesday mornings. But nothing came. Nor did it Wednesday. On Wednesday afternoon Pat rang Rose to check whether she had heard from Jeremy, and when she found out she hadn't she got a little concerned. "If one of the letters went astray or one of them couldn't write I would understand it," said Pat, "but as we've not heard from either of them I wonder what is going on."

"Well perhaps we'll hear tomorrow," said Rose. "If not they're bound to telephone on Friday evening as usual."

"If they don't I shall be really worried," said Pat.

There was no letter on Thursday or Friday. The men returned to camp on Friday but the restrictions regarding communication with the outside world were to be strictly observed until further notice to cover the security of the force that had been sent. There was therefore no telephone call or letter or either Pat or Rose, and by this time all three families were concerned at the continued silence. Even if she had been able to Moira couldn't help. She told Jack she was on an entirely different project to land forces, so she had no means of knowing what the City Rifles were up to.

On Sunday 14th British troops commenced landing in Norway and on Tuesday the news was made known by the BBC.

"So that's where they are," said Jack. For Pat and Rose, this was the beginning of the reality of what it was like to be married to a front line soldier, not knowing what dangers and hardships their husbands were being called upon to endure, not knowing whether a War Office telegram would arrive at anytime, and if did it would it say dead, wounded or missing. It was the beginning of a succession of nights lying in bed with stomach churning, fingers clenched trying not to cry and waiting for sleep that wouldn't come.

When Rose came down to breakfast on the Wednesday morning she looked so drawn that Ruth instinctively held her close and said, "I know darling, I know what you're going through. I didn't know where your father was for weeks on end in 1914, so I know how you feel. But he'll be alright, you'll see, they both will I'm sure." She had no way of knowing of course but the re-assurance comforted Rose a little.

On the 16th, while they were still under the security blanket, David was called to the company office during the dinner hour. As he marched in to CSM Ward's office he was greeted with, "Man here wants to join your section, Corporal Chandler," and when David looked behind him he saw it was none other than Rifleman Barclay who had been obscured by the open door as David had marched in. Rifleman Barclay was a good deal leaner than when David saw him last. He was standing to attention in full marching order, all his kit in the telltale scrubbed white condition which immediately singled out men who had just come out of the glasshouse.

"Man here wants to join your section Corporal Chandler."

"Very good sir, I'll clear it with Sergeant Harris."

"March him off then, and don't let me see you in here again Barclay."

"No sir."

Barclay's arrival created quite a stir when he came into the hut. There was a feeling of hostility towards a man who the others felt was continually leaving them to do his dirty work. If he had received fifty six days for thumping a sergeant or something equally interesting, that would have been acceptable, he could even had been a hero, but to keep running away and leaving his mates to carry the can was not considered an activity much to be admired.

David told Barclay to wait while he cleared things with Sergeant Harris.

"You going to do some bleeding missionary work do you reckon then Corporal?" was the sergeant's first reaction to David's asking him if he could take Barclay on.

"More like the Salvation Army really Sergeant. If we can't save

363

his soul this time he'll be faced with eternal damnation I reckon."

Sergeant Harris grinned. "I've seen it happen before though. When I was a corporal in India I had a bloke who was always in and out of clink, military and civilian on one occasion. When he came back from the local jail I beat the daylights out of him and told him he could report me if he wanted to. He didn't and he turned out a good soldier in the end."

"You recommend I go and give Barclay a good bashing then Sergeant, do you?" said David with tongue in cheek, "as the first part of his rehabilitation?"

"Well you can try the soft pedal first, you never know, it may work. Now bugger off, I've got more important things than bloody Barclay to think of."

David walked out grinning. He and Jeremy had established a good relationship with Sergeant Harris. There was no longer the resentful antagonism from the sergeant towards them. On his part they were very good NCO's, reliable and loyal, whereas on their part they respected his knowledge and experience and the authority that those two qualities had brought. As a result there had grown a professional camaraderie that allowed just a trace of familiarity between them, which would never be allowed to go beyond good military discipline but nevertheless made their lives a little more pleasant.

"Right then," said David, "that's organised – you had dinner?"

"No Corporal, I was waiting in the battalion orderly room for over half an hour before they sent me over to Mr Ward."

"In that case I'd better come to the cookhouse with you, dinners are finished now and if you go in on your own the cook-sergeant will think you're trying to come the old soldier and get a second meal."

They went to the cookhouse and David explained to the cook-sergeant that Barclay had arrived back late and missed his meal.

"What, did you have to run all the way then?" said the cook-sergeant, looking at Barclay's white gaiters and referring to the fact that wherever you went in the glasshouse you went at the double. Nobody liked the cook-sergeant. It was firmly believed he flogged the rations on the side. More than one rifleman had expressed the view that he'd like to have a peep into the cook-sergeant's kitbag when he went on leave, and the fact he was nearly as round as he was high gave little credence to his living on one man's rations. In the event, as there had been a fair amount left over of stew, potatoes and cabbage with roly-poly and custard for afters, Barclay got a bigger dinner than he could reasonably have expected. "See me as soon as you get back to the hut," said David.

And thus began the rebirth of Rifleman Barclay.

On Saturday 20th the security was lifted, although the telephones in the camp were not as yet connected. As soon as parades finished David and Jeremy made their way into Colchester to the George where they knew there were two public phones tucked away by the dining room. They were second in the queue but eventually, each locked in their own little box, they got through, David to Pat in the shop and Jeremy first to Chandlers Lodge and then to Romsey to which he had to reverse the charges after using all his change up on the call to Sandbury. The girls were laughing and crying at the same time to hear their voices, but both David and Jeremy said to each other afterwards how embarrassed they were to have caused all this worry when they hadn't been anywhere or done anything. That didn't worry the families though, the fact the boys were safe and well was all that mattered to them, though as David said to his father later, they felt that someone else was being left to do their fighting for them. Fred's reply was typical and prophetic "I shouldn't worry, you'll have your fair share before you're finished I'll be bound."

The following week Colonel Tim telephoned Ruth and said he was getting a little party together to go to town to see the new film 'Gone with the Wind', which had just had it's premiere. He had been sent eight tickets from a friend of his, a military attaché at Canada House, the tickets he understood being like gold dust, the film had made such an impact. Along with Fred and Ruth, Rose, Pat, Rebecca, Alec and Jim were included, they would have some supper in the Coventry Street Corner House afterwards and would travel in the colonel's staff car, with Alec and Rebecca following in the pick-up. As Colonel Tim later said, "I know they'll be bitterly disappointed not being with the rest of us there and back, but we all have to make sacrifices in war time." Without it appearing in the slightest bit obvious he managed to get himself seated between Rose and Pat in the cinema and between Rose and Ruth at the restaurant. Travelling each way he sat at the front with his driver, but with the partition down so that he could talk to his guests. He had managed to get Rose sitting on the driver's side on the rear seat with Ruth and Pat where, whenever he turned to make conversation, he was able to look at her without again it being obvious. Altogether he congratulated himself afterwards with an extremely well planned and meticulously executed operation worthy of the great Duke of Marlborough himself, who incidentally he admired enormously.

It was a wonderful evening. The film was an experience the like of which they had never seen before. With Rose crying her eyes out on one side and Pat likewise on the other, at one point in the film Tim leaned forward to Fred and whispered, "I'll run out of handkerchiefs in a minute," getting a dig in the ribs from Rose in the process.

After a very jolly and pleasant supper Fred acting as spokesman thanked Colonel Tim for a superb evening, which was answered by Tim saying, "It's nothing compared to what you have done for us," and then as an afterthought, "I wonder how much longer Jerry will let us roam around London as we have tonight?"

The answer was, not for very long.

Chapter Thirty-nine

During the mid-morning break the following Tuesday 23rd April, Mr Austen appeared at the platoon barrack-room and approached David and Jeremy. "Don't dash off to the Naffi," he said, "you're wanted at the company office – I'll come with you."

They covered the hundred and fifty yards to the small wooden building with its veranda on the front, Mr Austen returning the smart salutes of the passing riflemen with the amiable wave of his stick towards his hat, and as they reached the steps up to the office door he said, "I always expect to see Gunga Dhin sitting out here on the veranda." He knocked on Major Grant's door and walked in, "Got the two budding field marshals here sir."

"Right, come in you two." They marched in and saluted. "We've had a backlog of post which has just caught up with us as a result of the blasted argy-bargy at Harwich," he said, "and it appears you are due at Winchester tomorrow afternoon for the selection board on Thursday and Friday. We're making out your passes and travel warrants. There's a list of kit here which you have to take, not very much as it happens. If you need money see the Colour Sergeant. There will be a PU here for you at eight o'clock tomorrow morning so get an early breakfast. As the board finishes at four o'clock on Friday you can have a pass to be back here Sunday night. Any questions?"

"Sir, would you have any idea how long it takes for the board to make up its mind about us?"

"I would think about a month, though in my opinion for what it's worth, unless you make a monumental cock-up like getting drunk on the dinner night you shouldn't have any great difficulties. We want you to get through and Mr Austen is going to talk to you and give you some tips," and a rare joke in front of corporals, "after all, if he can get through anyone can I should have thought."

Mr Austen grinned his amiable grin and replied, "Actually you two, it's a well-known fact that subalterns are the backbone of the army."

"Right, off you go then," said Major Grant. "Collect all your bumpf and come on company orders Monday to let me know how you get on."

The two took a back pace, saluted and marched out, followed in his usual leisurely fashion by Lieutenant Austen. They went to the platoon office where Sergeant Harris was doing some paper work. "Right sit down you two," said the officer, "and I'll see what I can remember that will help you – they're of to the selection board in the morning Sergeant Harris," he said by way of explanation.

"Do you want me out sir?" said the sergeant.

"Good lord no," said Mr Austen, "You may very well be able to give a hand."

He went through the procedure of what they might expect. "Your main problem is that when you're fell in there will be all sorts and conditions of men from all different regiments and corps, so the silly sods don't do rifle regiment drill they do redcoat square bashing. There won't be much in the way of foot drill and certainly no arms drill otherwise you would be up the creek, sloping arms and all that rubbish. The main thing is they will march more slowly than you're used to."

He then went on to talk about the 'trick cyclist' tests, for which he had profound contempt, and the dinner night the major had referred to. "Provided you don't drink your soup out of the front of your spoon or start scoffing before the officer at the head of the table – almost certainly a Great War Colonel – starts his meal and you don't get pissed in the bar before the meal, you should have no problems. The selection officer will be circulating in the ante-room before the meal; will sit among you during the meal, and talk with you after the meal. The trick is to talk intelligently to them without being a bloody know all, to show a sense of humour without telling strings of barrack-room jokes and never never tell them of your uncle George who is on Sir Edmund Ironside's staff." Sir Edmund was the CIGS.

Mr Austen continued. "One of the main questions, and probably the most difficult one is – and they ask it every time – why do you want to be an officer? I'm not going to guide you here because it's something you should feel inside, and be able to answer even if it sounds a bit trite. Lastly, you'll have an obstacle course to go over. Its common sense really. You'll be in parties of six usually and you carry a heavy thick log round this obstacle course. The idea is to get you thinking as a group how to overcome the various obstacles. What they're looking for is the bloke who stands back and lets everybody else do the work or have the ideas. He won't pass and will wonder why. At the other extreme you'll get the chap that is all talk without having given the problem sufficient thought – he's the sort of chap who would rush his platoon into action without having made a plan and get them all killed – he won't pass either. Well I think that's about out all I have to tell you – can you think of anything Sergeant Harris?"

"I was wondering if they might be asked what they thought made a good platoon officer sir, and if so I'd point them in the direction of getting the confidence of the men and in particular of the NCO's. They could say they're particularly aware of this themselves, being NCOs themselves in a crack regiment. Wouldn't hurt to show them what we thought of the Rifles sir. The other thing is to see if they can get in something about the men's welfare being vitally important, interest in and concern for their families and so on, wouldn't do any harm I shouldn't think."

"You're absolutely right – couple of good points there," said Mr Austen. "Anything else? Right then, you can have the rest of the day to get your kit ready. Get an early night and an early call so that you get away on time, and we'll see you on Monday."

They both stood up. "Thank you very much sir, we'll do our best," said Jeremy.

"We certainly will sir," said David and they went back to the barrack-room.

They spent the rest of the day getting their best battle-dresses pressed up by the regimental tailor, who could be very accommodating at the sight of a silver shilling piece waved in front of him. They visited the regimental barber and told him not to completely scalp them. They blancoed their belts and gaiters and polished their silver cap badges as for CO's inspection only more so. They decided to travel in their second best battle dress in case some lunatic spilt a bottle of beer down them on the train – or worse, and then it was time for the Naafi to open so that they could phone home with the good news. Jeremy arranged that Rose would go to Romsey – she said she would get the half-day Friday to travel down, and then she would meet up with Pat at Liverpool Street on Sunday evening as before. They were lengthy calls with all the family coming on to wish them luck. Ruth said, "It's like going for the scholarship again isn't it dear," to which he replied.

"Do you think you'd better send me sixpence in case I need to buy a cup of tea?"

"Fancy your remembering that," said his mother laughing fondly, "it seems so long ago now, and yet again it seems only yesterday."

David couldn't quite puzzle out this contradiction so he said, "Well I'll tell you all about it at the weekend."

The pick up was waiting for them at company office sharp at eight o'clock ready to catch the 8.40 to London. The lads in the hut, particularly Beasley, Barclay, Piercey and the usual gang, all wished them well and Sergeant Harris came out and shook hands with them. "We chan't be able to show our faces back here if we don't pass," said David.

"You'd better bloody pass or I'll bust you to rifleman," said the sergeant grinning broadly.

They had an uneventful journey. "Why is it when you've got a pass to flaunt no blooming redcap wants to know where you're going?" said David.

"I imagine the War Office has sent information ahead to all stations about us. After all they don't get potential generals passing through every day of the week."

"I thought Austen said field marshals."

"Court martial is about all you'll ever get," said Jeremy.

There was a truck waiting at Winchester Station where they found themselves among a dozen or so candidates who had arrived on the London train. They were taken to the Selection Board building in Winchester barracks and registered by a colour sergeant in the Rifles who, seeing their badges, gave them a friendly grin of recognition and told them that they would be shown to their rooms, and that dinner was casual from 7 – 8.30 that evening. He then added that Sergeant Jarvis would be along in a few minutes to show them the layout of the place. Waiting for Sergeant Jarvis they studied the others being registered, most of whom appeared to be youngsters straight from school who had just completed their basic training at various depots and would therefore be very wet behind the ears in the opinion of the two 'seasoned soldiers'.

At the approach of Sergeant Jarvis, all conversation stopped abruptly. The reason for this was the fact that Sergeant Jarvis was one of the most pulchritudinous pieces of crackling that any of them had ever seen. Even the severe cut of her uniform; lisle stockings, short haircut and flat shoes couldn't disguise the fact that she was something very different to the usual run of ATS sergeants of the day. David nudged Jeremy and nodded towards a young soldier from the DCLI: the lad was standing there literally with his mouth wide open mesmerised by the sight of this vision in khaki, and totally oblivious of the world around him.

"Well gentlemen," she was saying. "You have been given your room numbers by Colour Sergeant Elliott and I will take you to them in a few moments. Batmen will wake you at 7 o'clock with tea; breakfast is at 8 o'clock onwards. At dinner this evening and at breakfast and lunches you may sit anywhere. For the dinner night tomorrow, you will be given specific places, which will be marked up on a chart in the anteroom. While you are here you will be considered to be cadets and the staff will address each of you as sir, if you have any problems please do not hesitate to come to my office over there."

"Ten men killed in the rush," whispered David to Jeremy.

They each had a small room with a washbasin with hot and cold water and, luxury of luxuries, sheets on the bed! They were allocated rooms in alphabetical order, so David found himself next door to Jeremy.

"If this is how officers live, I'm all for being an officer," said Jeremy wandering into David's room. "Hot and cold running batmen –

shouldn't it be batwoman? Well whatever, sheets on the bed, beds made for you, tea in the morning when you wake up, none of your snoring half the night keeping me awake, and all controlled by that super gorgeous Sergeant Jarvis who could knock Jean Harlow for six any day."

"Listen to the man. Married only a couple of months and lusting after another woman already."

"You've got loads of room to talk, you were drooling all down your chin while she was talking. Anyway, she's probably got her card marked by a Colonel at least."

After a sound and comfortable night's sleep they were wakened by a buxom ATS girl with a gorgeous Devonshire accent bringing them a large cup of tea with a saucer and a separate sugar bowl. Very civilised thought David. They had been told that all that day would be spent in denim overalls except for PT and gym session, so they did not have to dress up for breakfast or lunch. In the evening they were aware they were being fed all sorts of leading questions from the selecting officers, sometimes individually sometimes in pairs or groups. There had been no competition between the candidates themselves, if they were all good they would all pass, if none were any good none would pass, they had to be themselves and show they reached the standard the examiners were looking for. They would be judged on ability and the examiner's view of their potential and nothing else. That evening they were eventually released at a quarter past ten and both David and Jeremy fell into their beds as exhausted as when they had completed a fifteen mile run.

The next morning they were faced with the obstacle course. Although they had hoped they would be in the same squad they guessed it would be unlikely, and this it proved to be. It was a very tough demanding course and both David and Jeremy gradually emerged in their respective groups as the one with the initiative and sheer physical strength that was necessary to complete the exercise within the time allowed. Only three of the six groups completed in time and, as Jeremy said to David afterwards, "Thank God that's over – but the Rifles did alright didn't they?"

Neither of them had a clue as to how they fared with the 'trick cyclist', and when they discussed it with some of the others afterwards they were not alone in this. "I reckon," said Jeremy to David, "he'll probably conclude that you're a sex mad licentious pervert totally incapable of knowing right from wrong, and fully capable of violent assaults on old ladies for their money."

"In that case I should pass for an officer with flying colours wouldn't you say?"

The final test was the interview with a panel compromising a colonel, a major and a captain, all with substantial service records if their medal ribbons were anything to go by. As Mr Austen had told them 'Why do you want to be an officer?' was one of the inevitable questions. David answered this by saying he had learnt to accept responsibility as an NCO in a superbly professional regiment (remembering Sergeant Harris) and he felt he would now like the challenge of greater responsibility which he was confident of being able to shoulder. Jeremy was asked the same question but prior to this was asked whether he came from a military family. He was therefore able to tell the board of his father's record in the Hampshires and to the question of why he wanted to become an officer he too was keen to accept the added responsibilities of commissioned rank and to follow in his father's footsteps, difficult though that would be.

When it was all over the colonel commanding addressed all the candidates and wished them well. He added that if some had not passed they were not to be discouraged but to try again when they had more experience of army life. David and Jeremy hustled to their rooms to collect their kit, both talking nineteen to the dozen illustrating the relief they felt that the ordeal was over. They both felt they had done as well as any of the others but hedged their bets with, 'on the other hand you never know what these stupid examiners say to each other when they get round the table and compare notes'.

Their next move was to get the truck to Winchester Station, where Buffy would be waiting, hopefully with Rose, who should have arrived at four o'clock. David was to get the 4.40 back to town and would get into Sandbury at about seven thirty, a meal at Chandlers Lodge, and then the part he was looking forward to most, home to the bungalow. All went according to plan and having been greeted warmly by Buffy and Rose David made discreet conversation with Buffy, whilst Rose was greeted even more warmly, by her husband of in theory over two months but in fact for only less than two weeks. Both Rose and Buffy were eager to know how they got on, to which David replied that since they started a fight with two others from another regiment he thought it not only unlikely they would get commissions but they would also probably be busted to riflemen when they got back to camp. Rose punched him in the ribs and said to Jeremy, "Can we get more sense out of you do you think?"

"As far as we can tell we did quite well, but you never know. I mentioned that Dad was a regular in the Hampshires and the Colonel said, 'Oh yes, we've heard of him' in the tone of voice that intimated that failure was on the cards," with that Rose punched him in the ribs.

"Honestly Father," she always called Buffy father, which gave him a little thrill of pleasure each time she said it.

"Honestly Father, how can we possible expect to win a war with a pair of nincompoops like these two on our side?"

"I must get over to my platform," said David, "If the train's on time it will be here in five minutes."

"If it's on time it will be the first time this year," said Buffy, and aside to Rose. "It's all those blasted troops continually coming on leave that slows them up you know."

She smiled a big happy smile and clutched Jeremy's arm even more closely. David said his goodbyes and wandered across to the London platform, asking a porter on the way which end of the train the third class section would be – other ranks travelled third, only officers travelled first class. Having been told the rear half of the train he wandered down towards that section of the platform. Being Friday afternoon it was more crowded than usual, many going home or to London on weekend leave, and as he skirted a crowd of RAF wallahs he found himself face to face with none other than Sergeant Jarvis. "Hello Sergeant," he said, "fancy bumping in to you again," which afterwards he thought must have sounded somewhat inane, "going on one of your innumerable weekend leaves?" she smiled at his pleasantry and in doing so totally illuminated platform three.

"We have to work through one weekend, so we get forty eight on the other," she said, "although I too have applied for a commission so it could be that I shall not be here much longer."

They chatted away until the train arrived. They managed to squeeze into a small space on one of the seats and David could not help noticing the looks of admiration on some of the faces of the sqaddies in the carriage and others standing in the corridor of this very attractive girl he was with. He could imagine what they were saying to themselves, just as he would be if he were looking on – 'Jammy bastard, what's he got that I haven't got more of?'

David judged she was a year or so older than he was, and sitting all squashed up, although he made as much room as he could, he noticed further how flawless her skin was, how white and even her teeth and how her eyes sparkled as she laughed. She asked how long he had been in his regiment, and they engaged in all the small talk that two people do who have a journey to make together. He asked if she was going home for her weekend or staying in London. She said she was going home to Bromley in Kent where her father was a doctor. She had taken languages at university, had worked for a year with BP afterwards and then joined up when war broke out. Promotion had been rapid as a result of her being a graduate and now she was hoping to get a commission and move into intelligence where she could use her knowledge of German. "So that's my story, what about yours?" she said.

David started by saying, "Well, I'm married to a lovely girl called Pat."

"I know," said the sergeant, eyes twinkling, "I looked up the records you brought with you."

"Well it was a good job then that I didn't make a pass at you, wasn't it? Although I imagine that would not be exactly a unique experience as far as you're concerned." Again that twinkling laugh. David went on to say she probably also knew then that he lived at Sandbury and, as Bromley South was on the Sandbury line from Victoria, they could cross London together from Waterloo. "It will at least prevent your being accosted by people from other and inferior regiments," he explained to her amusement. He went on to tell her there were two women in his life and at her eyebrows being raised, swiftly told her the other was a tortoise-shell cat called Susie who rarely moved a yard from him all the time he was home. They had a most congenial journey together that swiftly passed the time until at last he stood and shook hands with her as she alighted at Bromley South. Ruminating on this chance meeting he thought that, as so often happens in wartime, you meet someone nice who could become a very good friend, male or female, and after a few hours or a day or so you separate never to see each other again, only the memory lingers. In the case of David and Sergeant Hilary Jarvis this was not, strangely enough, to be the case.

Thoughts of Sergeant Jarvis quickly disappeared as David arrived at Sandbury into the welcoming arms of Pat, very impatient at the train being fifteen minutes late. They went to Chandlers Lodge where David was quizzed mercilessly by Pat and his mother as to, 'How he got on – was it very difficult – did Rose get there alright? – Did Jeremy do well? How was Buffy?' and a thousand other questions that only wives and mothers have the ability to dream up. When eventually the flow stemmed a little Fred was at last able to ask the question he'd been waiting to put, namely "What happened over this Norway lark? We've heard that British and French troops are at Korsor, Trondheim and as far north as Narvik. They tell us that there have been big naval battles and ten Jerry destroyers sunk and they've lost troop ships as well. I just hope this isn't another instance where they split our available troops up and then hit us in the solar plexus when we've got no reserves to use." He had no way of knowing how near he was to the truth.

The weekend flashed past and in no time at all David and Pat were on their way to Liverpool Street to meet Rose and Jeremy. It was Sunday so there was no opportunity to visit Dirty Dicks. They luckily found an empty bench seat on the forecourt and passed the time talking together until the men had to join the train, waved down the platform until they disappeared into the throng, by then the two girls standing arm in arm, already the subject of cheeky remarks from passing servicemen.

"These chaps seem to lose all their inhibitions once they get a uniform on don't they?" said Rose. "Can you imagine a perfectly strange young man coming up to you at this time last year and asking the things they ask?"

"Have you been asked something interesting then?" replied Pat, "come on tell me more."

They continued talking in this light-hearted vein as they crossed to the underground. It certainly helped to take away the sick feeling each felt at the pit of her stomach at having to part again from someone with whom she was so deeply in love, and as the recent months had shown, not knowing when or even if she would ever see him again. The old adage of men must fight, women must wait, though not entirely true in these modern times was still true enough. The question was, which was the worse of the two?

Back at camp there was a renewed emphasis on building east coast defences. Poland, Denmark, Norway – who would be next? Would Hitler outflank the armies in France by invading England? Most people thought this was unlikely as the Royal Navy would prevent it. But the Royal Navy couldn't prevent the landing in Norway although they had sunk quite a number of German troop carriers and war vessels, in the process receiving heavy casualties themselves. David and Jeremy, first having attended company orders and told Major Grant how they thought they had fared, found themselves working long hours in building barbed wire entanglements, not only along the coast but also around a number of airfields within travelling distance of Colchester. On Friday evening May 9th the weary riflemen jumped down from their trucks and, having had an evening meal, they only had haversack rations during the day, two thick rounds of margarine sandwiches, one cheese, one ham and a piece of fruit cake, they washed and the majority of them rolled into bed. They had been told that apart from weapon inspection the next morning they would have Saturday off. David and Jeremy went over to the Naafi, made their usual Friday evening phone calls and then too got into their blankets and were soon fast asleep It was a body blow therefore that at 6 am 'stand-to' was blown, and they piled out of their bunks warming the cool morning air with the heat of the expletives being used to describe whatever it was that had got them out of bed at that time in the morning. They manned their posts until eight o'clock when they were told, without explanation, to stand down. They drifted off to breakfast without shaving first, and then came back to get ready for parade for weapon inspection. When Mr Austen arrived

Sergeant Harris said, "What was all the flap for sir?"

Mr Austen said, "I'm going to address all the men now Sergeant, but I can tell you it's my guess we won't be in these comfortable billets for very much longer. Can you call the men on parade now please."

With the usual bark from Sergeant Harris of, "get fell in," the platoon lined up in its three ranks ready to hear from their platoon commander.

"I have to tell you that the 'phoney war' would appear to be over. At three o'clock this morning Germany invaded Holland and Belgium without warning. We are now in a state of readiness to move at twelve hours notice. All weekend passes are cancelled and all people on long leave are being recalled. All mail from now on will be censored by the platoon officers, so if any of you are in the habit of writing rude remarks about me to your nearest and dearest I advise you to think twice. The QM is getting all laundry back, from now on you do your own until further notice. I shall have a final kit inspection this afternoon. Any questions?"

David spoke up. "Do you know the sort of resistance they are meeting sir?"

"No, all I know is that if the blasted Belgians had let us in up to their border with Germany instead of playing the game of staying neutral, we would be in a much better position. However, that's politics and we're not supposed to talk about politics."

On the Thursday before that Saturday however, May 8th, occurred one of the greatest and most far reaching events ever on the British political scene. Neville Chamberlain, the arch appeaser, was told in the House of Commons, 'In the name of God – go!' and, as a result of his resignation he was replaced by Winston Churchill, who for the next five years was to lead a coalition government to ultimately bring us victory. On that day also the King formally cancelled the Whit Monday bank holiday on the 13th, we were now totally at war, we could not afford the luxury of a bank holiday. The public were warned that they must carry their gas masks at all times and that air raid precautions would be strictly enforced. All in all the British people were now being rudely jolted out of the lethargy of the last eight months, a period when only the navy and the air force were carrying the attack to the enemy. Now without a doubt it would be the army's turn, and not long after the civilians would be on the receiving end to an extent that they had never dreamt possible.

On the same Saturday, May 10th, Harry was at Calais having arrived the night before with his section of around thirty three-ton lorries. They were standing by a ship, flying the explosive's flag on a dock some way away from the main dock, and were waiting to each take a load of ammunition up to the main park near Lille. At 6 am the air raid warnings started in the town to be closely followed by the ships in the harbour. Within minutes flights of Stuka dive bombers appeared, furiously attacked by anti-aircraft fire from land batteries and from the armed merchant and Royal Navy vessels lying in the harbour and its approaches. The only shelter Harry and his men could get was under a concrete flyover running parallel to the dock, which could provide little protection from the bombs but at least would prevent their being hit by shrapnel. From this shelter they watched one Stuka which had obviously picked their ship as its target. It banked out to sea at probably Harry guessed five to six thousand feet and then heading towards the dockside, tilted its nose downwards until it was almost vertical. The Stuka carried five bombs, four of them weighing around one hundred pounds and the fifth weighing over five hundred pounds. They were dropped as a cluster. To add to the terrifying effect of having an airplane hurtling straight down at its target, it had a pair of what were known as Jericho Syrens on its fixed landing legs which produced a high pitched scream as the aircraft descended, designed to shatter the morale of the defenders below.

Harry saw the Stuka release its bombs and begin to pull out of the dive. They seemed to splay out from the centre instead of, as he would have expected, all falling together in a group. Three of them went harmlessly into the dock around the ship, the big one veered of to Harry's left and exploded three or four hundred yards away on the dockside, blowing up a warehouse and in the process wrecking several of the three-tonners. The last one landed on the other side of the flyover to where Harry and the men were now lying flat on their faces, and failed to explode.

Almost immediately other aircraft noise was heard and at higher level two squadrons of Dorniers appeared and commenced dropping sticks of bombs across the city towards the harbour. The noise was deafening. Plumes of smoke were beginning to rise from within the town, from an oil storage installation on the road south to Bouloogne, and a series of explosions were seen from what was probably a chemical factory on the marshes half a mile from the harbour. To all this noise they now heard the rat-tat tat of machine gun fire and, looking up through the thin clouds, they saw a number of Hurricane fighters engaging the bombers and as suddenly as it had started it was quiet again with the exception of some heavy anti-aircraft fire in the distance.

"I can do without this on a Saturday morning," said Harry to no one in particular, to which Yorkie Trent, one of his drivers, replied in the lugubrious manner of the true tyke.

"I can manage without it any bloody time."

They looked at the wrecked vehicles. Four were complete write-offs and the fifth had its superstructure ripped away. Captain Henry, Harry's boss, said, "I'm sure if the Germans knew the amount of paperwork involved in writing off five lorries they wouldn't be so unkind as to do this to me. I think the best thing we can do is to get loaded as quickly as possible and bugger off before I get snowed under with some more."

The news of the invasion of the Low Countries was greeted in two different ways back at Sandbury. Ruth had fallen into a sense of false security regarding Harry. Little was happening, therefore little would happen. Now the balloon had gone up she and Megan were back on tenterhooks, particularly since they had no clear idea of exactly where he was. Moira was working through the weekend and Nanny was away at a family wedding on Saturday so Jack brought young John round for the day and would go on to the bungalow with Pat on Sunday. Fred came back from the factory at lunchtime and was greeted by Jack with, "What did we say? We said that while we were stuck in our impenetrable Maginot Line the crafty bugger would outflank us. The fact he was professing eternal friendship with the Dutch and Belgians was absolute eyewash. I bet he's got cardboard soldiers stuck in his Siegfried Line while the French and ourselves have got the bulk of our army facing them there. I ask you, the general Staff couldn't run the bloody Boys Brigade. He'll walk through Holland and Belgium, you mark my words and the BEF will face forty or fifty divisions." All this was said with barely a breath and with a fury that was so unlike the usual jovial and benign Jack, that little John instinctively clutched Ruth's hand and huddled against her. Fred replied that he couldn't agree with him more, and they'd better put the one o'clock news on to hear if there was any more information.

"At least," Fred continued, "Winnie seems to be getting a decent cabinet together. Atlee will make a damned good Deputy Prime Minister; he knows at first hand what war is all about. With Beaverbrook in charge of production, sparks will fly and I think putting Ernie Bevin in as Minister for Labour is an absolute masterstroke. Talk about poacher turning gamekeeper, if anyone can get the labour force a hundred percent behind the war effort he can. He ruled the General Workers Union with a rod of iron and what's more he'll stand no nonsense from employers, civil servants or anybody – even Churchill himself."

During the day news came in that German paratroopers were dropping at Rotterdam which had been heavily bombed and that other thrusts were being made towards Brussels and from the Ardennes around the tip of the Maginot Line. On Sunday 11th the British moved forward into Belgium taking up positions in a line from the mouth of the Scheld to Louvain. In all, nine British divisions were involved, which even when combined with a demoralised Belgian army in full retreat, was hopelessly outnumbered by some thirty German divisions and three thousand tanks supported by fighters and bombers from the Luftwaffe. It was obvious to everybody that a lot more ground would have to be given up before this advance could be halted, but very few indeed ever imagined that the BEF would end up in the sea.

Chapter Forty

Monday 12th May started off as a beautiful morning. Ernie Bolton and Anni were having a last cuddle together in bed before Ernie said, "Look at the time, it's ten minutes to seven, I'll get the sack," but the thought didn't stop him from continuing to stroke and caress Anni until she said.

"If you carry on like this it will be me who will stop you going to work. In fact you'll be too tired to work."

He gave her a big kiss and rolled out of bed. Having washed and shaved quickly he went on downstairs to put the kettle on to make tea, then to take a cup up to Anni. He was thinking as he descended how marvellous it was to be able to go up and down stairs like this, even if he couldn't take them two at a time he was able to negotiate them comfortably provided he had one hand to steady himself on the banister. As he reached the kitchen there was a ring on the front door bell. 'Postman's early', he thought as he walked to the door. When he opened the door he was confronted with the burly frame of Superintendent Watts, head of the local police, who he had met on several occasions, particularly when he and Anni had been to Rotary functions with Anni's father.

"Hello superintendent, what brings you here at this time in the morning. Would you like some tea?"

"No I won't stop Ernie," said the superintendent. "I called in to see Karl, if you could get him for me."

"Of course, come in, come into the sitting room."

As this conversation was taking place both Anni and Karl appeared in their dressing gowns, both wondering what was going on at this time in the morning.

"I'll come straight to the point Karl," said the superintendent. "We've had instructions to assemble all German and Austrian aliens in our area. I'm afraid they're interning you and I thought I would come and see you rather than someone you don't know breaking it to you. You don't know how sorry I am for both you and your family, and we shall miss you both at Rotary and in the town. I understand from the Assistant Chief Constable who I talked to on the telephone this morning that you're category, category B, will only face temporary internment, as soon as the present emergency is over the order will be rescinded."

"But why are they doing this to my poor father who so hates the Nazis and so loves this country," cried Anni, standing with her arms around Karl.

"I understand," said the superintendent, "this is to do with the fact that in Norway and Holland in particular there were so many, what are they called, fifth columnists living in the country who gave enormous help to the Nazis. If Germany attempted to invade this country the government are seeking to prevent it happening here. I know and you know that my dear friend Karl is not one of these people, but in war you have to take extraordinary measures, and this is one of them."

"Now look," said Karl, "England has treated my daughter and me wonderfully well, and if it means that it will help the war effort against these foul Nazis for me to be locked away for a while I am more than happy that that should happen. If by locking away all the Germans and Austrians the handful of fifth columnists is locked away with them, so it must be. It will not last forever. Millions of men are being taken away from their families to fight for us, a small sacrifice like this is nothing compared to theirs. Now Charles, what time am I to be ready and what shall I take?"

"We'll collect you at 10.30 and you can take one large suitcase. Bring with you any medication you have to take, and don't forget all your papers, spectacles and other necessities."

"Do you know where we will be going?"

"I'm not sure, but I think it's either North Wales or the Isle of Man. What the regulations will be regarding visits from your families, writing letters, receiving parcels and so on I don't know, you'll be told all that when you get there. We shall all keep in touch, and I'm sure you will be back again soon. Well now, I must be off, I'll see you at the Police Station later. Goodbye all."

"Goodbye my dear friend," said Karl, "and thank you so much for taking the time to come and see me." The superintendent departed and Karl continued, "Now you two, no tears or sadness. I am just going on a holiday, a bit longer than the usual holiday probably, but it's all in a good cause. So you Ernie get to work and you Anni help me pack." Ernie hastily swallowed a cup of tea and a slice of toast and rushed to the factory to tell Fred the sad news. Fred immediately said he would collect Ruth straight away to go round and say goodbye. Rose too was still there when he arrived at Chandlers Lodge so all three went to town to let Karl know how much they would miss him. Karl was completely overcome, not only by the visit of the Chandlers, but a host of other people, Megan, Pat and Jack and a dozen or more of his Rotary friends who were in business in the town and who Charles Watts had contacted with the news, all crowded in to let him know he would be missed. When the police van came at 10.30 Karl said to Anni, "Now remember, no tears. And while I'm away why don't you find a little grandson for me – heh?"

But there were tears, buckets of them once he had gone. Ruth knowing how lonely she would be until Ernie came home came round at eleven o'clock and said, "I've got to go to Maidstone – will you come with me to keep me company, we can have a bite to eat in the 'Kardoma' when we get there." Anni knew she was probably manufacturing a reason for going to Maidstone, but she readily fell in with the suggestion. When they came back later that afternoon she had reconciled herself to the fact she would not see her beloved father for some time to come, and in the process had gained a deeper appreciation of the heartache that Megan, Pat and Rose were feeling, to say nothing of Ruth who carried the burdens of all of them. Thinking along these avenues, as she left Ruth she hugged her tight and said, "You know I do love you all so much, I am so fortunate to belong to this loving family." Ruth said nothing, nothing needed to be said, she just hugged her back.

That night Anni told Ernie what her father had said. "I think it would be cruel to deny your father his last wish before he was led off to captivity," said Ernie, "so from now on, as a matter of duty of course, I shall take every opportunity to ensure his wishes are carried out. I think that will have to mean we come home for lunch tomorrow, purely in the course of duty you understand, as well as waking up half an hour earlier every morning and going to bed half an hour earlier each evening."

"Ernie Bolton, you'll be dead in a week at that rate."

"Yes, but what a lovely way to die!!"

But they carried out Karl's wishes all the same even if they didn't quite go to the extremes Ernie had suggested.

Tuesday 13th May saw General Guderian cross the Meuse at Sedan and commence his headlong advance towards Arras and Lille, slicing through the French almost as if they weren't there. The armchair strategists said he was exposing his flanks so dangerously that he could run in to serious trouble, but Guderian was taking the sorts of calculated risks that would have failed any prospective commander at staff college courses or on war games. But then Guderian was probably the greatest tank general ever. On the 14th the Dutch ceased fighting and surrendered on the 15th. In the meantime Queen Wilhelmina departed for England, and in doing so had all the gold and diamond reserves in the country loaded on to British warships and sent to the UK to help prosecute the war. In addition she ordered the complete Dutch merchant navy at home and all around the world to be put at the disposal of the British Government. Holland could no longer fight, but their commercial power was still great and of immense value.

David and Jeremy in the meantime, along with the other six hundred odd who made up the City Rifles, had at long last got their full complement of equipment and vehicles. On the 14th and 15th they were taken to the ranges to zero their rifles, the name given to setting the sights correctly so that they fire accurately, and then to fire ten rounds.

So far ammunition had been so short they had only fired five rounds and that was at the beginning of the year, which meant that many of the newer recruits had had no firing practice at all until now. The Bren gunners too had an opportunity to fire their new weapons, which they immediately fell in love with, they were such an improvement on the old Lewis guns, most of which dated back to the Great War.

While they were eating their haversack rations at midday on the second day in the butts, David and Jeremy were joined by Sergeant Harris.

"Not heard anything yet then?" he asked, obviously referring to the selection board visit.

"No sergeant," said David, "but then we thought it would probably be a couple of weeks yet."

Jeremy said to the sergeant, "All this security and kitting out and range work, does that mean we'll be sent over soon?"

"I don't think it necessarily means that," said the sergeant. "The RSM was saying last night in the mess that all the full strength battalions have been put on a state of readiness. Doesn't mean they would all have to go, particularly with the invasion scare on. After all, if the French can't hold Jerry with all their divisions, we certainly wouldn't be able to get enough men there in time to do it. No, the French have got much more armour and heavier too than the Jerry, and they'll hit them with it when they are ready."

Little did the RSM know that the French general staff were so badly served by the communications with their army and corps commanders that they just didn't know what the situation was day by day and as a result when the German flanks were vulnerable nothing was done to hit them. They still had the trench warfare mentality, mobility wasn't in their vocabulary, and they and the whole of Europe were to suffer terribly as a result.

Prime Minister Churchill in the meantime flew to Paris to try and galvanise the French into action. He had already told the British nation that he could offer them only, 'Blood, toil, tears and sweat', and the nation rallied behind him as they would never have done had Chamberlain still been in power. On paper the French were as strong as the Germans, had more and larger tanks, had the benefit of being in defence, and the very substantial backing of the RAF fighters and bombers. As the Germans attacked towards Tournai, British Whitley and Wellington bombers, covered by fighter screens, wreaked havoc among the panzers, and it was claimed that in the week from May 10th nearly a thousand Luftwaffe planes were destroyed. Despite this the panzer thrusts continued. On the 17th the German army occupied Brussels. On the 18th they took Antwerp and St Quentin, and Cambrai further south. The BEF fell back towards Dunkirk, the retreat being orderly and well executed. At Arras they turned on the Germans, attacking with two divisions, a handful of tanks and some French cavalry and succeeded in driving the Germans back and taking several hundred prisoners, but this was not sustainable and they had to continue to fall back.

On the 17th back at Sandbury the Chandler family were all desperately concerned about Harry. As Megan said to Ruth, "I have this sick feeling in my stomach every night when I get to bed, and I jump out of my skin if there is a knock on the door in case it's the telegraph boy."

Ruth held her close and said, "I know how it is my love, I know how it is." There was little else she could say.

As they were talking Fred arrived. "They've asked Jack and me to join the LDV mob they're forming," he said. "The idea is they issue you with a rifle and organise patrols at dawn and dusk to watch out for parachutists, or so I'm given to understand."

"What does LDV mean for goodness sake," said Ruth, "and what good would an old chap like you be, I don't suppose you know one end of a rifle from the other after all this time."

"Well I agree with you in one respect. I don't think I could do a ten mile route march in full kit these days, but I can still shoot straight I reckon, and if it means we release front line troops it will be a good thing. LDV incidentally means Local Defence Volunteers – they'll be mainly old soldiers like me and young fellows that are in reserved occupations. Anyway there's a meeting tonight at the drill hall so I'll go up and find out all about it. By the way, any news from the lads?"

"I had a letter from Harry this morning," said Megan. "He was his usual cheerful self but apart from that didn't mention the situation over there. It took six days to get here which is unusual; they're usually here in three."

"Pat and Rose had letters today," said Ruth. "They are being censored, but reading between the lines they're still at Rainsford Camp."

"This is always the worst part – waiting," said Fred. "By the way, the Canadians have cancelled that dance they were giving at the weekend. Jim told me they thought it wasn't right they should be having a knees up while our lads were taking a pasting over there."

"Well, it's very considerate of them," said Ruth, "but it's a sad fact that some people have got to do the fighting and I'm sure they wouldn't object to others enjoying themselves. After all, it could be the Canadians' turn next; they haven't come all this way just to sit in their barracks. I don't suppose for one minute you didn't enjoy yourself when you came out of the line just because your mates weren't there."

"Oh you're quite wrong there," Fred replied. "I used to go to church and write letters to you all the time."

"Look Megan he said that without a blush."

Their banter eased the tension for a while as they had tea together, then Fred went off to the drill hall and Megan went to collect the twins from Nanny. Having got them home and bathed and bedded down the sick feeling soon returned, until she found herself saying, "Now pull yourself together Megan Chandler and put the dance music programme on," which she did, and felt much better as a result.

Pat rode her bicycle home thinking what a lovely day it was and wishing so much that David would be at the bungalow to greet her. Instead she was welcomed as usual by Susie who, although sitting in the front porch when Pat came through the gate, was halfway down the drive in a flash and rolling on her back for Pat to stop and rub her tummy before she took off through the bushes to race Pat to the house. Pat put her bicycle in the shed and bent down and picked her up. "As your Dad would say, you'll bust your boiler in a minute," she said, and continued, "You know Susie Chandler, I don't know how I'd manage without you," and Susie purred back a perfectly intelligible reply even if it could only be completely understood by another cat.

Jack had said on several occasions, 'Why don't you move in with us?' to which her reply was always, 'Really Daddy, I'm alright, I have Susie to keep me company', and in this was a very real thing. Susie never moved out of her sight when she was at home and the nightly ritual of being fed and then trotting along to the bedroom and up on her place at the foot of the bed was a routine that made life seem normal even if it wasn't. As Pat lay in bed, the movement of Susie washing herself, teasing at her fur and chewing her paws was a comfort to her, and when Susie had finished her ablutions and turned around two or three times before making the all important decision on which way to lie, the resulting plonk as she settled down was a signal to both of them to go to sleep, which mostly they both did.

Rose had worked a little later than usual and at around six thirty was waiting at the bus stop to go home. She normally rode her bicycle to and from the hospital but it had let her down that morning. When she went to the garage at the side of the house where it was kept she found the front tyre as flat as a pancake, and there was not time to mend it so she caught the bus. Standing at the bus stop presented a minor, but sometimes enjoyable hazard, in that the Canadian soldiers passing in their trucks from time to time would naturally call out an assortment of compliments, invitations, witty remarks and make the inevitable wolf-whistles which are the stock in trade of soldiers in all armies around the world. Rose being extra pretty attracted more than her fair share, and normally just waved and smiled. She was looking at the rear of a three-tonner with half a dozen young men in it who had whistled her as they passed, and giving them a little wave, when to her surprise an army staff car pulled up beside her, the door at the rear opening as it stopped.

"Now what's a nice girl like you doing standing in a place like this," said the voice of Colonel Tim as he leaned forward. "Are you going home? – We could give you a lift."

"Tim, how lovely to see you. Yes I'd love a lift if you're going my way. I think this bus must have run into a ditch, it's terribly late."

Rose jumped in beside him, and Tim gave directions to the driver.

"Where are you off to?" said Rose.

"I'm going back to camp. I've been up at Div HQ this afternoon on a meeting."

They chatted for the few minutes it took to get to Chandlers Lodge and when they arrived Rose said, "You will come in for a drink won't you? Dad should be back from the factory by now and will be so pleased to see you," and then she added, she didn't know why, "As we all are at any time." These latter words really made his day.

In fact Fred wasn't there, having gone with Jack to the Drill Hall, he expected to be back at about seven thirty in time for dinner. Ruth was very pleased to see him and said, "Can you stay to dinner; Jim and Alec are not in this evening, they're running some course or other so you can eat their rations."

Laughingly Tim said, "It would give me the greatest pleasure to know I'm eating their rations, I'd love to stay, I'll send the driver off and telephone when I want to be picked up if I may."

He sent the driver back to camp telling him to instruct the duty transport NCO to have a duty driver ready to collect him later that evening when he telephoned, and then came back to be welcomed with a pint of Whitbread's Light Ale, a half of which he disposed of without a breath, then saying "By Jove, I needed that. If these Div people could fight as well as they can talk we'd win the war in a week." He asked the news of the three lads, and was told all they knew, which was precious little.

"Well," said Ruth, "I must put the finishing touches to the dinner so I'll leave you to talk to Rose, Fred shouldn't be very long now." Fred can be as long as he likes thought Tim, and then felt guilty about thinking it. Although he was older than Rose they seemed never to be at a loss for things to talk about. He asked about her work and showed a keen interest in it. She asked about his life in Canada, what his part of Canada was like from a scenic point of view, what he liked about being a soldier, and what it was like to command several hundred men. The time flew past and to Tim it was like being in heaven, although as he ruefully had to admit to himself, only a very temporary heaven. Fred arrived and told them all the news about the LDV. He had been put in charge of a section of twelve volunteers, and had to work out a rota to patrol the high ground overlooking Sandbury and the airfield just outside the town.

"We'll be on bicycles," he said, "and will keep our rifles and ten rounds at home. It wouldn't be practical to have to go to the Drill Hall to collect a weapon every time you're going on duty. I can see lots of snags cropping up, but we'll get it properly organised in time. Jack is in charge of another squad on the south side of the airfield."

"Do you get a uniform?" asked Tim.

"No, just an armband with LDV on it," said Fred, "although I can see what you're driving at. Civilians with rifles aren't treated as soldiers by the enemy are they?"

"No, I guess they'll give you uniforms sooner or later," said Tim. "I think the whole idea of having ultimately a trained force to operate in it's own locality, where it knows every tree, bush and house is an excellent one, but for the time being all these hundreds of thousands of pairs of eyes on the watch will surely mean that we won't be caught napping if they do drop saboteurs and fifth columnists as they have done in Norway and Holland, and probably France as well as we'll no doubt find out in due course."

They spent a pleasant evening together. Tim was always careful to address the bulk of his conversation to Fred and Ruth, but the mere fact of being with Rose gave him greater pleasure than he would have dreamt possible. When he left that evening Fred shook hands, Ruth gave him a little kiss on one cheek and then to his enormous pleasure Rose followed suit, thanking him for giving her the lift home. She smelt so sweet and fresh that he was unable to answer for a second or two, and then jocularly replied, "All my pleasure ma'am," in an exaggerated trans-Atlantic accent which left them all smiling as they watched him jump into the staff car.

"What a lovely man," said Ruth, "I could really fancy him if I were a bit younger."

"I will not make the obvious remark," said Fred, "but I agree, he's a jolly good chap." The weekend passed without incident except that they heard the news that Sir Oswald Mosley and many of his fascist friends had been arrested. "About bloody time too," was Jack's comment, "although I can tell you that there are still fascist sympathisers in the city and elsewhere I've no doubt, who would be licking Hitler's boots if he ever did get here. I'm told by knowledgeable people that this extends even into the aristocracy. I think the problem is that they're so blinded by their hate of communism that they can't see that fascism is even worse – if that's possible."

The war seemed so far away as they sat out in the garden on that beautiful warm Sunday morning. Heavy fighting was reported around Lille on the Belgian border and further south around Arras and Amiens.

"Why the hell don't they send us out to help," said Alec, "here we are sitting on our backsides when we could be there lending a hand. After all, that's what we came here for in the first place."

"I think until we can contain them and establish a reasonable line; the powers that be will be reluctant to do anything," said Jack, "particularly as the French seem to be totally paralysed."

These amateur strategists, sipping their beers in the sun felt so helpless thinking of what their countrymen, and the French and Belgians, were going through over there. Fred knew at first hand from his own experience on the Mons retreat what it was like to keep giving ground, even if it was done in an orderly and professional manner as it was from Mons. Thinking of this he suddenly said, "But then they didn't have tanks."

"What do you mean Fred?"

"Oh sorry, I was thinking aloud about the retreat from Mons. Fight and move back, day after day, it knocks the bottom out of your morale, but at least there the enemy didn't have tanks."

"They had cavalry though," said Jack.

"Yes and they used them constantly to hit our flanks," said Fred. "You know, one day we had moved back through a guards' battalion covering us, and we were marching in fours in column of route, there were only about three hundred of us left by then, when to our right at the edge of a long wood about four to five hundred yards away appeared hundreds of what turned out to be Uhlans – German cavalry. We were on an elevated road and the colonel halted us as if we were on the parade ground. Right turn he shouted. 'Open order march'. On the command 'move front rank prone, second rank kneel, third rank stand, fourth rank about turn to guard the rear'. While he's shouting all this, the Uhlans had wheeled in to a line about three hundred abreast and had drawn their sabres. 'No one is to give fire until I give the command', he yells. 'Now move'. We carried out the movement. The Uhlans started towards us at a canter and at two hundred yards the Colonel gave the order, 'Fire'. They started going down like ninepins, and at a hundred yards their commander who was way out in front gave the signal to retreat. The Colonel gave the order to cease firing, although they were still within range, shouting to the men, 'The Hampshires don't shoot brave men in the back'. There were twenty or thirty horses down, unable to get to their feet and from the wood cantered three farriers with large pointed axe heads over their shoulders. 'Hold your fire', shouted the

Colonel and the farriers were allowed to go among the fallen animals putting them out of their misery. When they had finished they were only a hundred yards or less from us. They remounted and wheeled to face us, the Colonel called us to attention, they saluted the colonel and he saluted back and they rode back and disappeared into the woods. It was all over in less than half an hour."

Silence followed Fred's story. It was probably the longest continuous speech they had ever known him to make. Alec broke the silence. "I think that's the most amazing story I've ever heard," he said.

"What an honourable man your CO was," said Jim, "were there many instances of this mutual esteem once the war got under way?"

"Oh, I think so, from time to time," said Fred, "at least on the Western Front, I don't know about Jack's lot."

"I would say it was non-existent with the Turks," said Jack. "In fact at Gallipoli a complete battalion of the Norfolks were taken prisoner and murdered out of hand, so lord knows what they did to individuals they captured."

"Do you know," said Alec, "we've known you both now since Christmas time and neither of you ever talk about what you did or what happened to you during the war. You could write a book between you."

"So could a million others," replied Jack seriously, looking at Fred, "but all the time you'd be thinking of the wonderful chaps you knew who you'd left behind and it wouldn't seem right somehow."

Fred nodded in agreement, and then added so as to lighten the mood, "Anyway neither of us can spell very well to start with."

As they laughed they heard the melodious voice of Ruth calling, "Dinner's ready," and walking to the house Jack said, "I bet we'll do better than poor old Moira today with her canteen meal. I do wish she didn't have to work so hard."

After Sunday dinner Alec went off to Mountfield to see Rebecca, mounted on a second-hand Raleigh he'd bought in the town. Restrictions on the use of motor vehicles by the military were beginning to bite, except for the usual recreational transport from the camp to Sandbury, and occasionally to Maidstone, so he now had to rely on pedal power! "It seems a bit infra dig as you would say Jack to arrive at one's lady love's house on a bike, but needs must when the devil drives," Alec had said.

"And what sort of devil is driving you I wonder," was the reply, to the general amusement of the others.

"Tell me Alec, what happens if someone salutes you as you ride along?" asked Ruth.

"Well, I take one hand off the handlebars and salute back," replied Alec.

"And then fall arse over tip into the ditch I suppose," said Fred.

Alec grinned his cheery grin, "It nearly ended up like that once or twice when I first started again," he said, "but they say once you've learnt to ride a bike you never forget how."

"I understand you enjoy one or two other activities that fall into that category," said Jim.

"Major Napier, what do you mean!" said Ruth.

After tea Jack went off to meet Moira at the station leaving Ruth and Fred, Rose and Jim to spend a quiet evening listening to the radio and reading. The nine o'clock news repeated the constant communiqué about our troops retreating in good order and inflicting heavy casualties on the enemy. Fred always got irritated at the bland announcements in the Oxford accents of the newsreaders. "God to hear them talk you'd think we're winning," he exclaimed, "instead of having to give ground everyday." They all went to bed depressed at the general situation and their specific anxiety over Harry being somewhere in the middle of it all.

Monday 20th May was to be a day that none of the Chandlers would forget. When Ruth awoke that morning she had a terrible premonition that David was in trouble. She tried to shake it off by laughing at herself, "You're not a witch, you haven't got second sight," she said aloud to herself, and looking into the kitchen mirror, "even if sometimes you look like one."

"What's this – talking to yourself Mum?" said Rose walking in wearing her soft slippers.

"Well when you approach senility like me you do that sometimes," said Ruth.

"Senility? Why you're in the prime of your life," said Rose putting her arm around her. "Mum, I've got something to tell you, but I don't want anyone else to know until it's confirmed this morning." Her shining eyes told Ruth all she wanted to know.

"Oh how lovely" said Ruth, "You will telephone me once you know for certain won't you? I can't possibly wait until you come home tonight."

"I will, I promise."

At ten o'clock Rose saw her doctor and was given the good news. The doctor was a Rotarian and a good friend of Fred and the family and he was delighted for them all. As she went out through the waiting room she saw Anni sitting with her back towards her, reading Country Life, February 1938 vintage. She tapped her on the shoulder.

"Rose, what are you doing here, are you alright?" she enquired.

"I've just heard you're going to be an Auntie," said Rose, and when the penny dropped Anni hugged her so tight Rose said, "Don't damage the little one for goodness sake! Oh, and not a word to anyone until I've confirmed it with Mum."

"Of course – my lips are sealed. Now I can tell you a secret. When they took my father away he asked if he could have a little grandson to greet him when he came home again." Their heads got closer together as she continued in a low voice punctuated with considerable giggling from both of them. "Ernie said that my father's wish was his command or something daft like that and that we'd better start that moment. I even think he considered taking a week off, drawing the curtains and pausing only for food and occasional sleep, but I persuaded him against that. Anyway I seem to have clicked already, so if it's not a false alarm we shall be in Sandbury Hospital together perhaps!!"

"Well like you I won't say a word. When you know you must come and break it to Mum and Dad – I know what Dad will say, 'Another couple of Christmas presents to find' – but they will both be absolutely thrilled."

Anni was called by the receptionist, so Rose made her way to Pat's shop and asked if she could use the telephone. "Of course," said Pat looking at her curiously, "but why aren't you at work?"

"I'll tell you in a minute," said Rose, and closing the door to Pat's little office dialled the Sandbury number.

Ruth answered immediately. "Is that you Rose?"

Rose put on a deep voice and replied, "No, this is Winston Churchill."

"Oh Rose, don't play the fool, tell me the result."

"The result dearest Mother is that you should be a granny again round about the end of January next year."

"Hooray – now I can spend your father's money telephoning everyone with the news."

"Except Pat and Anni," said Rose. "I bumped into Anni at the doctors and I'm with Pat now."

As quick as a flash concern immediately showed in Ruth's voice. "What was Anni doing at the doctors?"

"Oh it was nothing serious, just a touch of cramp or something."

"Well, I'll ring her this evening to make sure she's alright," said Ruth accepting the explanation without question, but too old in the tooth to believe everything she was told.

When Fred arrived at the works at eight o'clock on that Monday he found two men from the Air Ministry already waiting for him. They had been driven from London in a Humber saloon.

"Have you had breakfast?" asked Fred, and when they said they hadn't he called Ernie in and asked him if he would be so kind as to get the canteen to rustle up sausage sandwiches and tea. "That's if Ministry people eat anything as common as sausage sandwiches," he added.

"You just watch us," said the senior one laughingly, and when Ernie had disappeared continued. "I'll come straight to the point Mr Chandler, I've had a personal recommendation from a certain very highly placed individual in the Ministry of Supply that you are one of the few firms in the field I'm interested in that do a good job at a fair price, but most importantly have never been late on a contract."

"I have to advise you here Mr Tennant," Fred replied, "one of the reasons we've never been late is that we've never ever given a stupid delivery time just to get the order."

"That too I've been told. I've also investigated your financial status carefully and find you're very well placed in that respect." Fred listened on, wondering what exactly he was driving at.

"We therefore wish to place an order with you, provided the price is not unrealistic, for some special fuel tanks and release gear which we intend slinging under certain of our aircraft for obvious purposes, but delivery must start in two months time and must continue on a set pattern in accordance with this programme sheet." He handed over a chart, the numbers ran into thousands.

"I shall have to get Ernie in to look at the drawings and then give you a price," said Fred, his mind already racing as to how they could set up a line to manufacture these products.

"What about materials?" said Fred.

"All fairly standard and we'll arrange for you to have priority licences to get them," said Mr Tennant.

"Right, here's the sausage sandwiches. If you'd like to take half an hour over your breakfast, Ernie and I will look at the drawings and give you a price."

Which they did. The price was right. The contract was verbally given and subsequently confirmed and the firm not only made these tanks for the rest of the war, but later made thousands more for the United States Air Force. It was the biggest single order they had ever received and it was one of the major factors in establishing their fortunes. At the end of it Sandbury Engineering was proud to say, 'We were never late'.

When Megan arrived at Sandbury Hospital on that Monday the 20th she was asked to see the Matron. "You have to clear your ward immediately," she was told. "Send those home who can go home and split the remainder up into the other wards, I don't care if men have to go in with women or children, curtain them off if you have to. We are receiving a convoy of wounded from Dover at around noon, and your ward will receive them."

"How many will there be?" asked Megan.

"Between twenty and thirty. I don't know what sort of state they are in. I imagine they've been patched up in the field hospitals, but we'll just have to take things as they come. Now I want you to give your juniors a good talking to so that they know what to expect. I know they are used to traffic accident casualties, but having thirty all at once, possibly badly shot up, could be very upsetting for them. At least they won't have the ghastly sights that we had in France of the men who had been gassed and blinded – that experience has never left me. Oh, and Megan" (this was so unusual. She was a stickler for discipline, it was always sister, never a christian name.) "I know you'll be thinking about Harry, and we all do as well," she paused, "well I'll be over during the morning to see all's well, but it looks as though the war has really started as far as Sandbury Hospital is concerned."

After the men arrived just before twelve o'clock Megan worked straight through along with all her staff and the night relief until midnight. She arranged with Nanny to keep the twins, Nanny being more than pleased to help in anyway she could and it was not the last time Sister Megan Chandler would be called upon to do a sixteen hour shift, and not the last time Nanny would do her bit for the war effort.

On the morning of the 20th, Harry found himself with part of his section again on the docks at Calais loading ammunition to take back to Lille. The day before they had heard heavy gunfire from the east of Lille towards which the BEF was falling back from Tournai. By ten o'clock they were loaded and on their way up the coast to Dunkirk and then inland towards their destination. The roads were heavily congested not only with military traffic but also with large numbers of civilians in motor vehicles and on foot. As the approached Armentieres the convoy was stopped by a military police roadblock. Harry rode up to the front of his vehicles, parked his motorcycle, and walked up to the sergeant on the roadblock.

"What's up?" he asked.

"Which company are you?" said the sergeant looking at a clipboard in his hand, and when Harry told him he said, "Your Park has been relocated at Bergue, about ten miles out of Dunkirk. You'll have to turn about. Come through the barrier and turn on that hard standing over there, and for Christ's sake try not to run over any civilians or their animals – we've got enough problems."

Harry thanked him and said, "Good luck," to which the MP sergeant said, "I've got a faint idea we're all going to bleeding well need it before very long."

It took Harry nearly half an hour to get his vehicles turned and on the way back to Bergue. By the time they reached the town outskirts it was seven in the evening, but here they had a piece of luck in that they spotted one of their company vehicles turning into a side road ahead of them so Harry raced after him, flagged him down and got the directions to the new park. The men were all desperately tired, they had been in their vehicles for twenty-four hours with only haversack rations and their water bottles. Gone were the days when they could pull into an estaminet and get a good meal for fewer than fifteen francs with as much wine as they wanted. When they were lined up in the new park Harry's section lieutenant came out from the makeshift office. "You've got to move this lot out to the RAOC depot at Oost Capel at first light Sergeant Chandler, and then take them back to Calais, collect rations from the docks and then come back here. By then things should have sorted themselves out."

That was the understatement of the century.

Monday the 20th started as just another in the continuing saga of waiting and training for David and Jeremy. At 8.30 the company runner came in the barrack-room and said Corporals Cartwright and Chandler company orders ten o'clock, fatigue dress. This latter indicated that they weren't in any trouble otherwise they would have to be ordered to parade in best battledress. They told Sergeant Harris, his rejoinder was, "They've bloody well caught up with you at last, and don't let the fatigue dress fool you, that means they're going to bust you and send you to work straight away in the cookhouse." He then paused. "Seriously, good luck to the pair of you – I'll keep my fingers crossed."

"For God's sake don't do that Sergeant, it'll put the mockers on us straight away," said Jeremy. They all laughed as the two friends made their way back to the barrack-room. At ten to ten they reported to the sergeant major at company office. He had the usual cluster of defaulters; NCO's who had charged them and others seeking interviews for one reason or another. The defaulters were swiftly dealt with, the requests for interview took a little longer and at twenty past ten David and Jeremy were marched into Major Grant.

"Sorry to keep you waiting," said the major. (Blimey thought David, I've never been apologised to by a major before, the news must be good.) The major continued, "I'm pleased to tell you that you have been selected for cadet training and have to report to the new cadet unit at Worcester on Tuesday 6th June."

At that moment the CSM came in, "You're wanted straight away at CO's office sir."

"Oh very well. Look you two, you wait here till I get back, there are several other things I have to tell you."

They stood to attention as he picked up his hat and stick and went quickly out. "Come into my office and wait," said CSM Ward. "Blinder, get some tea for the Corporals," yelling at the orderly.

"Well, congratulations to you both," said Mr Ward, "you coming back into the Rifles?"

"Well if we can get in sir, we'd like to" said David, "but as you know people who have had fathers in the regiment get preference so it depends what the score is when we apply and, of course, if our faces fit with the Depot Colonel."

"We've got to get through the blooming cadet's course first," said Jeremy.

"I don't think you'll have trouble there provided you stick at it, and I know you will, otherwise where will you go?"

"In the Hampshires" they both replied together.

"Of course, that's your father's mob isn't it? I remember talking to them at the wedding."

They talked on, but it was over an hour before Major Grant returned. He called the CSM in and was with him for several minutes. Mr Ward reappeared and said, "In you come." They marched in, "Halt, right turn, salute the officer," and Major Grant continued exactly where he had left off.

"You have to report to the new officer cadet unit at Worcester on June 6th. However there is a little hiccup. I have just been told, and the officers are telling the platoons at this moment that we move out at four o'clock this afternoon to Harwich and will be in France first thing tomorrow morning. This means that as a new battalion will be moving in here in a few days I shall have to post you to Winchester depot from which you can then move to Worcester in a fortnight's time."

David and Jeremy looked at each other. They both knew instantly what the other was thinking and without hesitation both said, "We'd rather stay with the battalion sir."

"Now there's no need to be heroic," said Major Grant. "I don't know if you'll get the opportunity again."

"If that piece of paper wasn't delivered until tomorrow no one would be any the wiser sir, would they?" said Jeremy.

"And our platoon really couldn't manage without us could they sir," said David looking at Mr Ward and then to the major.

"Seriously sir, we've worked and trained for this for over three years, please let us go."

Major Grant thought long and hard and at last said, "We can do with people like you. Alright, I'll lose this for twenty four hours and then get a postponement so that you can go when things settle down," but in the back of his mind was the sickening thought, 'If you survive'.

They embarked that evening at Harwich Docks, their vehicles being expertly stowed by the stevedores so that they would be unloaded to coincide with the disembarkation of the platoons to whom they belonged. At eleven o'clock they felt the ship under way and were all somewhat subdued not knowing what the morrow would bring, and the day after, and the day after, if there was one.

Rifleman Beasley broke the silence, addressing David. "Corporal, you've been abroad. What does a knocking shop look like?"

Rifleman Piercey chipped in, "I don't know why he wants to know he still thinks it's to pee with."

Jeremy looked at David. "Subject normal," he said, and the two friends looked at each other and smiled the smile of true comradeship.

The 'phoney war' had ended for all the Chandlers.